PRAISE F

"The latest queen of erotic literature."

—*The Sunday Times*

"Malpas's writing is spot-on with emotions."

—*RT Book Reviews*

"A brave, cutting-edge romance."

—*Library Journal* on *The Forbidden*

"Unpredictable and addictive."

—*Booklist* on *The Forbidden*

"Super steamy and emotionally intense."

—*Library Journal* on *With This Man*

"Jodi Ellen Malpas delivers a new heart-wrenching, addicting read."

—*RT Book Reviews* on *With This Man*

"Malpas's sexy love scenes scorch the page, and her sensitive, multilayered hero and heroine will easily capture readers' hearts. A taut plot and a first-rate lineup of supporting characters make this a keeper."

—*Publishers Weekly* on *Gentleman Sinner*

"A magnetic mutual attraction, a superalpha, and long-buried scars that are healed by love. Theo is irresistible."

—*Booklist* on *Gentleman Sinner*

"The characters are realistic and relatable, and the tension ratchets up to an explosive conclusion. For anyone who enjoys *Sleeping with the Enemy*–style stories, this is a perfect choice."

—*Library Journal* on *Leave Me Breathless*

"*The Controversial Princess* is an all-consuming, scorching-hot, modern royal romance with twists, turns, and a jaw-dropping cliff-hanger that will leave you begging for more."

—Mary Dube, *USA Today HEA*

"*The Controversial Princess* provided us with the romance our hearts needed, the passion our hearts craved, with jaw-dropping twists and turns that kept us guessing and eagerly flipping the pages."

—TotallyBooked Blog

The *Invitation*

OTHER TITLES BY JODI ELLEN MALPAS

The This Man Series

This Man
Beneath This Man
This Man Confessed
All I Am—Drew's Story (A This Man Novella)
With This Man

The One Night Series

One Night—Promised
One Night—Denied
One Night—Unveiled

Stand-Alone Novels

The Protector
The Forbidden
Gentleman Sinner
Perfect Chaos
Leave Me Breathless
For You

The Smoke & Mirrors Duology

The Controversial Princess
His True Queen

The Hunt Legacy Duology

Artful Lies
Wicked Truths

The Unlawful Men Series

The Brit
The Enigma
The Resurrection
The Rising
The American

The Belmore Square Series

One Night with the Duke
A Gentleman Never Tells

This Woman Series

(The This Man Series from Jesse's POV)
This Woman
With This Woman
This Woman Forever

The Invitation

JODI ELLEN MALPAS

This is a work of fiction. Names, characters, organizations, places, events, and incidents are either products of the author's imagination or are used fictitiously. Otherwise, any resemblance to actual persons, living or dead, is purely coincidental.

Text copyright © 2025 by Jodi Ellen Malpas Ltd
All rights reserved.

No part of this book may be reproduced, or stored in a retrieval system, or transmitted in any form or by any means, electronic, mechanical, photocopying, recording, or otherwise, without express written permission of the publisher.

Published by Montlake, Seattle

www.apub.com

Amazon, the Amazon logo, and Montlake are trademarks of Amazon.com, Inc., or its affiliates.

EU product safety contact:
Amazon Media EU S. à r.l.
38, avenue John F. Kennedy, L-1855 Luxembourg
amazonpublishing-gpsr@amazon.com

ISBN-13: 9781662530029 (paperback)
ISBN-13: 9781662530036 (digital)

Cover design by Hang Le
Cover image: © Lena Granefelt / plainpicture; © janniwet / Shutterstock

Printed in the United States of America

To every woman who has felt like she's had to choose between a career and love

Chapter 1

I'm at my desk, five floors up and five rooms back, and I can *still* hear the blare of the car horn from the road outside. I take a deep breath and ignore the beeps of my phone, all messages from her. "Absolutely, Mr. Jarvis," I say, checking the time. I'm late. "Let me look into that and get back to you." I cringe, hearing the horn blaring again.

Gary appears at the door and tilts his head, making his grey quiff wobble, his lips pressed into a straight line. I hold up my hand, my expression full of apology, and get back to my call. "It's a small shift, Mr. Jarvis. I honestly don't think it's cause for panic stations just yet."

"When you're playing with your own money, Amelia, you can be the judge of that." Mr. Jarvis hangs up, and I exhale, slumping back in my chair.

"Aren't you supposed to be off today?" Gary says with scorn, looking at the mini suitcase by my desk.

"You tell that to the FTSE 100," I mumble, gathering up Mr. Jarvis's file and popping it into my handbag. "He's having a complete meltdown." And I can't really blame him, considering Mr. Jarvis is a heartbeat away from retirement and all his investments are due to mature in a matter of months.

I grab my bag and case, leaving the office before Abbie brings the buildings of Kensington down with her persistent honking horn. "I'm off." I have no idea when I'm going to get back to Mr. Jarvis. Maybe while the girls are distracted during one of their treatments, I can whip out my laptop and snatch a few moments to reassure him his retirement pot is safe. No need for any drastic action just yet.

"Have a wonderful day," Gary calls as I head to the elevator. "And, Amelia?"

I press the call button and turn.

He smiles, slipping off his glasses. "Happy birthday."

Oh yes. Thirty today. "Thanks," I say on an exhale, stepping into the cart. I escape the sound of Abbie's horn in the time it takes me to ride down to the foyer, but the racket starts again the moment the doors slide apart.

Rushing outside, I fling open the passenger door, shoving my head inside her car. "Really?" I say as she grins at me. "The whole of Kensington knows you're here." I throw my case on the back seat and slide in, and Abbie pulls off fast, her Audi TT quite nippy.

"We're late picking up Charley," she says, her attention split between the traffic and my lap. "Nice dress."

"Thanks."

"I'm sure a cream pencil dress will fit right in at a spa."

"I had to be prepared in case a Zoom call was needed."

"And was it?"

"No."

"So now you look like you're going for a meeting instead of a cheeky spa day."

I point to my case on the back seat. "I'll change when I get there."

Abbie looks at the dashboard when her mobile starts ringing. It's Charley. "She's called eight times since I've been waiting for you." She rejects the call.

"Sorry." I check my mobile, wincing at the icon telling me how many emails are in my inbox.

"Oh, please turn it off, just for today," Abbie pleads, turning her beseeching blue eyes my way. Her chestnut hair is plaited messily over her shoulder, as opposed to my perfect, businesslike bun.

"I will," I assure her, feeling a loose wisp of my ashy blond hair tickling my neck. I reach back and tuck it in.

"Do it now."

"What?"

"Now. Turn it off now."

"Silent?" I try.

"No, turn it off. We're going off-grid. I have your mother helping Corey run the shop for me today, and Lloyd's taken the day off work to look after the kids so Charley can come. The least you can do is turn off your phone." She raises her brows. "Since it's *your* birthday we're celebrating. Just the three of us. Not the three of us and all your clients."

"Okay," I relent, taking the plunge and turning it off. I take a deep breath as I do.

"Happy birthday." Abbie smiles across at me, taking my hand and squeezing. She doesn't say any more. I'm thirty, recently single, and homeless. Life could be better. Could also be worse.

"Thanks."

Her mobile rings again—Charley *again*. Abbie answers this time. "Ten minutes."

"See you in twenty." Charley sighs, then hangs up. It's one of many things Charley and I have learned about Abbie over the years. If she says she's going to be half an hour, she'll be an hour. If she says she's five minutes away, she means ten.

Abbie glances across to me as she turns at the lights. "We should go out this weekend."

I snort. "I'm still not over last weekend." A bit of vomit rises, reminding me of the hangover that lingered for days. "I only started feeling normal yesterday."

Abbie laughs. "Oh, but what a fun night."

"I've still got memories coming back to me," I say, looking down at my phone again. We had gone out for dinner at Amazonico, our favourite restaurant—a little pick-me-up, an obligatory breakup dinner with my girls. It was all very civilised until we moved to the bar area and the Porn Star martinis came out. My white COS dress was absolutely ruined, covered in black marks, and I have no idea how. I frown, looking at Abbie. "You pushed Charley home in a shopping trolley," I say, another flashback coming to me.

Abbie gasps. "Yes! So *that's* where it came from." We chuckle together, the mystery of the Tesco shopping trolley that appeared in Charley and Lloyd's front garden solved. "And we got a rickshaw back to mine."

"Oh God," I murmur, now recalling Bonnie Tyler blaring from the speakers as the driver pedalled like a maniac to get us home. "Hey, has a transaction come through yet from Amazonico?"

"No." Abbie frowns around the word. "So weird."

It is. The morning after, all of us with fuzzy heads, we tried to remember who got the bill. And couldn't. None of us had a payment on any of our cards, and it was then we realised none of us recalled paying. Horrified, I called the restaurant with my tail between my legs. Apologised. I was told there was no need, the bill was paid. But none of our cards had been charged. Still haven't. *So* weird. "How far away is this spa, anyway?" I ask.

"About forty minutes from Charley's, maybe."

"And where is it?"

"Arlington Hall. South Oxfordshire."

"Sounds posh."

"Doesn't it?" she sings happily, reaching for the screen on her dashboard and flicking through the radio stations as I look across at her fresh, makeup-free face.

"Thanks for this," I say quietly, and Abbie glances at me briefly, before taking her attention back to the road.

"Any more flowers?"

"Some last Friday and some yesterday. Mum's house is starting to look like your florist."

"He should buy them from me. I'd give him a discount. Has he called again?"

"A few times," I reply. "It's easier not to answer."

She nods, thoughtful, knowing why I'm taking that stance. Guilt. It's lingering like a bad smell. Speaking to Nick will only enhance it. Cowardly? I don't even know anymore.

I gaze out the window, falling into a daydream. Truth is, he didn't really do anything terribly wrong, except declare out of the blue that he wanted marriage and kids. Like . . . immediately. Things changed from that moment. I felt myself withdrawing, and Nick pushed on the matter more. Suddenly, the small things we had in common felt . . . irrelevant. He liked numbers, I liked numbers. We shared the same network of work friends, and the conversation was always the same. Work. Finance. Financial planning.

Until he made the conversation about babies and marriage. *Constantly.* I couldn't breathe. I told him I wasn't ready. And he told me I wasn't getting any younger.

He told me I was selfish. That I owed him some kind of commitment.

That was the end of me and Nick.

As we turn onto Charley and Lloyd's street, I laugh, seeing our friend standing on the pavement outside their London semi with her rucksack. "She's been there the whole time," I say, glancing down at my phone. Which is off. So I find the clock on the car display. Exactly twenty-one minutes since she last called Abbie. Charley starts hopping on the spot, waving her arms madly, like we could miss her waiting on the kerbside, jumping like a demented jack-in-the-box.

Abbie starts smashing the ball of her palm on the horn, and I look at her, exasperated. "Why all the noise today?" I ask. "This is supposed to be a peaceful, Zen day."

"Are you kidding?" she says, swerving into a space before looking up and down my cream pencil dress.

I open the door and get out on a grimace, pulling the lever of the seat to release it before climbing into the back, leaving the front seat for Charley. I smile at the Tesco shopping trolley that's still in their front garden.

Abbie starts hitting her horn again as Charley dances around the car and chucks her bag into the footwell. She falls into the seat and brushes her curly strawberry-blond hair back while blowing out the side of her mouth. "Finally."

Abbie ignores her light dig. "We remembered where the trolley came from."

"Oh, where?"

"I pushed you home in it."

Charley stills in her seat, thinking, as more flashbacks come to me, the three of us cackling like witches as we bumped Charley across the pavement. "That explains my bruised coccyx. I thought I'd slipped down the stairs." She starts hitting the dash. "Go, go, go."

We laugh as Abbie zips out of the space and zooms off down the road, Charley turning in her seat to look past me out the back window.

"What are you doing?" I ask.

"Feeling needy."

"Do you want to stay?"

She snorts. "No, not a chance in hell. I just hate how he gets on with it. No signs of a fried brain or a knackered body. Nothing." She throws herself back around in her seat. "Looking as perfect as he always does, and here's me with slobber on my boobs and baby puke in my hair."

"Ewww," Abbie grumbles, moving away.

"Hey." Charley turns again, looking me up and down. "Why the hell are you dressed for work?"

Abbie finds me in the mirror. "Because she's *been* to work," she muses.

"Snitch."

"Amelia!" Charley reaches back and smacks my bare knee. "I mean, I know you're on the breakup diet of wine and work, but this is your thirtieth, for Christ's sake. Even Lloyd's taken the day off for it."

"To look after *your* kids," I point out. "So you can come and enjoy this spa day with your two oldest friends." How have we known each other for twenty-three years? It's crazy.

"A spa day!" Charley cries, clapping her hands. "I want all the fizz, fuss, and fantasies."

"Fantasies?" Abbie asks. "We're going to a spa retreat, not a sex club."

"You know what I mean," she mutters. "Fizz and fuss don't feature in my life, therefore it's fantastical."

"Lloyd fusses over you all the time," I reply tiredly. "Don't pretend you're not treated like a princess." The man adores her. Even more so since she birthed his two offspring and now constantly sports puke in her hair. They were married in 2020, fell pregnant soon after, had Elijah in 2021, and fell with Ena when Elijah was one. It's been full-on for the newlyweds, and we all know they're loving their young family.

"You're a fraud, Charley Chaytor," I say on a smile.

"Maybe, but a little pamper day never hurt anyone." She gives me her wide, toothy smile. "Happy birthday, chick."

"Thank you," I say quietly, smiling, my eyes falling to my silent phone. Because it's off.

"Hey, anyone been charged yet for our night out last weekend?" Charley asks, looking between us.

"No, we were just talking about that," Abbie says.

"But they said we paid, right? Because I'll die if I can never go to my favourite restaurant again."

"They said we paid," I confirm.

She nods, frowning, returning her body forward. "So weird."

Chapter 2

We pull off a windy country road and through some gold gates, and I raise my brows, starting to pay more attention to my surroundings after fighting the compulsion this past hour to sneakily turn on my phone and check for emails and calls, or even check the stocks. Jesus Christ, Mr. Jarvis has activated panic mode, and here I am, his trusty adviser, travelling nearly an hour out of town for a pamper day.

Abbie lets her window down as she pulls up to a barrier, where an old, brick-built gatehouse sits, and a green-suited man steps out with a clipboard, checking the registration of the Audi. "Miss Pearson," he says, writing something down. "Welcome."

"Thanks," Abbie replies, her voice quiet as she peeks at me in the rearview mirror.

"Are we at the right place?" Charley asks, leaning over Abbie to see the suited man. "Is this the spa?"

"This is the spa," he replies, not looking up. "Follow the driveway down the stream. An attendant will meet you at the car park and assist with parking." He walks back to the gatehouse and reaches in, and a moment later the barrier lifts.

I rest back in my seat, as does Charley, as Abbie pulls through, slowly and respectfully. We follow the beautifully clear stream on the left that has a few waterfalls dotted along the way and a brick bridge creeping from one side to the other, and on the right is an orchard with endless huge, bushy apple trees.

I recoil when I see a helicopter pad in the field just past it and golf carts trundling across the uneven lawns. "What did you say this place is called?" I ask, a little awed.

"Arlington Hall," Abbie replies, sounding distracted.

"The fuck?" Charley whispers, leaning forward in her seat. "This is it?"

I stare out of the windscreen, taking in the wide, perfectly symmetrical structure, the double wooden doors in the centre framed with climbing plants bursting with white, delicate flowers. Endless traditional sash windows stretch on either side of the main door, all flanked by white stone troughs bursting with perfectly pruned topiary trees. It's almost too perfect to be real, and as I gaze up the front above the door to the second floor, I see a tower with a huge clockface telling us the time. It's nine thirty. I relax back, scanning the driveway, noting the prestigious cars—Rolls-Royces, Bentleys, Porsches, Ferraris. A line of green-suited men wait to park those cars. There's an attendant with a gold luggage cart. A pristine young woman with a clipboard waits to welcome guests. A bloody golf cart stands ready to drive them to somewhere on the grounds.

"Abbie," I say quietly as she circles a fountain that would give the Bellagio a run for its money. "Are you sure this is it?"

"I've checked five times," she says, rolling to a stop and turning off the engine. "This is it."

"Show me," I demand, needing to see for myself.

"Yes, show her," Charley orders, unmoving from her seat, almost frozen. "I didn't wash my hair this morning, and I'm seriously regretting it."

Abbie flicks through her phone and hands it back to me, and I scroll through the confirmation. "They sent me a deal for a spa day," she says. "It was a total steal, and I thought it would be a lovely way to spend your thirtieth."

"It is, and I'm grateful, but this place does *not* look like the kind of establishment that offers deals on spa days."

"Agree," Charley says.

"Agree," Abbie adds as I search for a link in the email. I don't see one, so I go to Google to find Arlington Hall, navigating the menu.

"How much did you pay?" I ask, cringing at the question.

"Sixty quid each."

I laugh out loud, and both the girls turn in their seats to face me. "This can't be it. It's over seven hundred pounds to have a spa day at Arlington Hall."

"Oh God," Abbie groans, putting her head in her hands.

"There must be another Arlington Hall somewhere," Charley pipes in. "And I bet it doesn't look like this for sixty quid."

"Wait." Abbie faces me again. "The man on the gate was expecting us."

She's right. He was. This is all very bizarre.

A glass door just past the big wooden ones slides open, and a beautiful, leggy Black lady appears. She dips, smiling at us through Abbie's open window. "Miss Pearson, welcome to Arlington Hall."

Abbie withdraws. "You're expecting us, right?"

"Of course," she says. Silky, black, poker-straight hair brushes the clipboard when she looks down at it. "You're right here on the list. I'm Anouska. Please, let me get you checked in. I'll have Stan get your bags."

I immediately go to my purse and pray I find some cash to tip, breathing out when I find a tenner. I pass it over to Abbie. "Here," I say, and she takes it gratefully.

"Well, let's go," Charley sings, hopping out, looking up at the building, taking a picture.

"Charley," I hiss.

"What? Lloyd's *got* to see this."

I smile awkwardly to the tall, slim lad taking our bags. "She doesn't get out much."

"Happens all the time," he says, going on his way after Abbie slips him the tenner and he nods his thanks. Oh God, something tells me tips around here stretch further than a tenner.

"Fuck me." Abbie bumps into my side as we wander up the brick path to the door.

The first thing that hits me is the staircase that sweeps round to the left, the wood white, crisp, and spotless, the taupe carpet runner plush, despite the endless feet treading it. The clash of traditional and modern is quite breathtaking. We approach a huge double pedestal desk, where a perfectly turned-out lady waits to check guests in. And today, unbelievably, we're guests. I leave Abbie to do the honours, still a little worried that we will be told at any moment there's been a mistake.

Wandering to the left, I get drawn to an imposing, enormous portrait hanging on the wall halfway up the stairs, the white wooden frame carved beautifully. But the woman in the portrait? She's truly something. Majestic. Classy and elegant. I gaze up at her, seeing her hardly visible smile perfectly. She could be French. She oozes that kind of sophistication. I drag my eyes from her precise French pleat down her cream pencil dress that falls just below her knee, to her slender legs and the beautiful sapphire-blue kitten heels gracing her small feet. I back up a little to get the whole of her in my sights.

Stunning, I think, also wondering who she is as I stroll on, taking in the luxury surrounding me, until I reach a doorway where a gold plaque tells me I'm entering the Library Bar. A rich, polished oak bar runs the length of one side with old beaten brown leather barstools lining it, built-in bookcases frame the brick-built fireplace, and high-backed blue velvet wing chairs are scattered around but seem precisely placed. Endless glass shelves loaded with various bottles line the raw brick wall behind the bar, and smoky-blue, ribbed glass pendant shades hang on gold chains spaced intermittently over the bar.

I pull a cocktail menu toward me, admiring an embossed crest in the corner. The letters *AH* are framed with delicate wisps of golden ivy and apples. I browse the list, seeing modern takes on classics, and the Arlington Hall specials.

"Can I get you something?"

I look up to a waiter in a green waistcoat. "Maybe later," I say on a smile, returning the menu. "I have a spa day to get through first."

"Sounds awful," he says, and I laugh.

"You've no idea."

"You don't look like you're dressed for the spa." He nods down at my cream dress as he polishes a glass, and I find myself smoothing back my already smooth hair.

I hold up my bag. "I'll soon fix that."

"Enjoy."

"Thanks." I back up but pause when I hear someone clear their throat, and I catch sight of a man sitting at the very end of the bar on the return section that meets the brick wall. His head is down, on his phone, and a stray lock of his thick, mousy hair falls onto his forehead. He moves it with a sweep of his hand, sitting up straight on his stool as he does. His shirt-covered chest expands. The material over his biceps pulls taut.

I swallow and step back as he looks up, catching me studying him.

My breath is shaky when I inhale, and his head tilts, his eyes lazy and intense, illuminated by the glow of the lamp nearby.

Jesus Lord above.

He's flawless, despite his face being rugged and rough with stubble. He's solid, despite not being overbuilt. He's loud despite being silent. His thick hair is long enough to sweep behind his ears, and he does exactly that, leaning back on his stool, interested in the woman obviously ogling him. I bet he gets it all the time. My God, I can hand on heart say I've never seen such a stunning man.

I blink.

He latches on to the corner of his lip.

Something explodes in my tummy. Butterflies?

He folds one arm across his chest, relaxed, and brings his other hand to his face, tapping the side of his cheek with the tip of a finger. Thoughtful. My lips part.

Air.

Give me air.

Fucking hell.

I jerk and look away quickly, searching for that air, my body temperature on the uncomfortable side of really fucking hot. What the hell was that? There's some strange energy bouncing around the bar.

Sparks?

I swallow, head down, perplexed.

Breathless.

Intrigued.

The pull becomes too much, and I lift my eyes, both greedy and wary of taking in more.

I'm staring again.

And he's quite amused.

But can I stop myself?

His phone rings, and he reaches for it on the bar, never taking his eyes off me. I feel like this has turned into a challenge. Who looks away first. He answers the call, his blazing gaze still on me, and then he talks. I very nearly puddle to the damn floor, his deep, even tone slicing through my remaining sensibility and taking my dignity with it. Because I'm still bloody staring at him while he listens to whoever's on the other end of the line. Eyes *still* on me.

"Sure," he says. "I'm free in half an hour. Meet me in the Library Bar." He hangs up. Almost smiles, but not quite.

I'm done.

I quit.

I lose.

I look away *and* back away.

"Do I know you?" he calls, stopping me.

No, I'm just staring at you because you're fucking beautiful. "No, I'm sorry, I didn't mean to disturb you."

"You didn't."

And what do I say to that?

I cock my head, every intellectual piece of me failing.

"Hey, birthday girl," I hear Abbie call, and I look back to see her on the threshold of the bar giving me grabby hands. "Come on, come on, we have an aromatherapy body wrap waiting for us."

"I'm coming," I say, watching her run back to Charley, excited.

I don't look at Mr. Handsome again, worried my eyes will explode in my head if I do. So I wander away, frowning at the tingling sensation all over my skin.

"Enjoy your body wrap, birthday girl," he calls softly, forcing me to a stop.

My eyes dart before me. "Thanks."

"And happy birthday."

I turn, my smile curious and unsure. "Thanks."

He leans his forearms on the bar. What is it with the fucking eye contact?

"I should go."

"I'm not stopping you."

"Yes, you are," I say, laughing. *I'm literally paralysed by your fucking eyes, you good-looking bastard.* I don't think I've ever been under such close scrutiny.

Holding his hands up in surrender, he smirks very mildly. He knows exactly what he's doing. I note that his hands are perfect too. Perfectly big. Perfectly formed. Perfectly capable? *No ring.*

"Happy . . ." I scan the bar in front of him. A laptop. A pen. Of course. He's here on business. A meeting? A conference? What does he do? "Happy working," I say, smiling sweetly and lifting my bag. "I'll be off for my body wrap."

His eyebrows raise, and his eyes, which I can now see are somewhere between blue and green, fall down my body. "Lucky body wrapper."

The Invitation

Oh my God. "Nice talking."

"It really was," he murmurs as I inhale deeply, pivoting and walking out, trying to adopt a shameless sashay but, I fear, achieving only a pathetic, trembling stagger.

I make it to Charley and Abbie in the lobby, a hot fucking mess. "I'm ready," I squeak.

They look me up and down. "What's up?" they say in unison.

"Nothing." I pass them aimlessly, not knowing where the hell I'm going but hoping I can cool my flushed cheeks before they get close enough to see them. "I'm ready to be wrapped." *Lucky body wrapper.* I stop and search for a sign that'll point me in the right direction.

"Maybe a mimosa first," Anouska suggests.

"Oh yes, a mimosa first," Charley chirps.

"Let me show you the Library Bar." Anouska motions toward the bar, and my heart flutters. It bloody flutters. My heart has never fluttered, not even for my ex, and it's in this moment I realise, after weeks of examining our breakup, it wasn't just talk of babies that scared me off. It was this missing feeling. Except I didn't realise it was missing, because I've never felt . . . this. And what is *this*? Insane attraction? Not just attraction, but the crazy, knee-knocking, heart-pounding kind.

I watch Charley disappear into the Library Bar, Abbie and Anouska following, and I stand there staring, a little breathless, a lot wobbly. Abbie looks back at me, an unsure smile on her face. "Are you coming?"

Am I? My legs don't seem to be working. I clear my throat, take in some air—and confidence—and force my feet to move. No sashay in sight.

I breach the entrance and immediately find him still at the bar. "Oh God," I whisper to myself, accepting the glass being handed to me by the waiter. "Thank you"—I read his name badge—"Clinton."

"Drink first, wrap later?" he asks, smiling.

I take a long swig, practically polishing off the whole glass in one glug. "Looks like it."

"I'm around all day, so let me know what cocktail takes your fancy and I'll rustle one up for you." He tops me off and gets back to rearranging the back shelf.

"Oh my," Abbie whispers, her glass at her lips as she watches the barman work. "Someone's sweet on you."

My eyes naturally fall to the end of the bar. He's lost on his mobile. "Behave," I say, absent-minded.

"Clinton is an award-winning mixologist," Anouska informs us, pulling the cocktail menu over. Charley places her glass on the bar and helps herself, filling up, shrugging when I throw her a look. "All of the Arlington Hall specials are his creations, except for this one," she says, pointing to the one at the top. "That one was created by the woman behind Arlington Hall."

I crane my neck to see the menu. "Hey Jude," I muse.

"Yes, she named it after her son." Anouska smiles. "And the Beatles track, of course. It's very popular."

"Is that the woman in the portrait in the lobby?" I ask.

"That's her. Evelyn Harrison. Absolute style icon."

"She's beautiful."

"Was," Anouska says, her voice lowering to a whisper. "She passed away."

"Oh, I'm sorry."

"You should try Hey Jude. You'll love it."

"You won't have to ask me twice." Charley perches on a stool. "So, does Arlington Hall often give away spa days for next to nothing for mere commoners like us?"

"Speak for yourself." Abbie laughs. "This is right up my street."

I smile, looking to the end of the bar again. He's still on his phone.

"It was a promotion for our fifth anniversary." Anouska plucks the bottle out of Charley's hand before she has a chance to fill up again. "Not too much alcohol before spa treatments."

She pouts. "I'm child- and husband-free, Anouska. I have to make the most of my freedom."

Anouska smiles wide, revealing pearly whites past her poppy-red lips. "Shall we make our way to the spa now?"

We all place our glasses down, Anouska leads on, and I pick up my feet, nearly walking into Charley when she doesn't move. Her eyes are wide, her mouth hanging open. I don't need to ask her what's up, especially when Abbie elbows me in the side.

"Lord have mercy on my soul for admiring another man," Charley whispers.

"Mercy granted," Abbie breathes. "Fuck . . . me."

I close my eyes and swallow, turning to face what has their attention. Or . . . *who*. I'm wholly unprepared for the impact of him, despite knowing it's faint-worthy. But this time, he's standing, swinging on his suit jacket. His rough, bristly face has that cheeky sideways smile again. A dimple on his left cheek. His hair is so unperfect yet perfectly perfect. He's irritatingly flawless. And tall. So tall.

"Hi," Charley breathes.

"Hi," Abbie squeaks, and I'm pretty sure they both melt on the spot as he passes.

My senses are further invaded when I catch a waft of something dizzyingly manly. Like sex in a scent. He stops and looks back over his shoulder. Eyes on me. They're the colour of the sea. A beautiful, muted teal.

"You should *definitely* try Hey Jude," he says quietly.

"Okay." I'm breathless.

And he leaves.

My entire body starts trembling, and it's totally out of my control. I'm not sure what the others are doing. Mopping up their drool?

"He was talking to you," Abbie says, linking arms with me on one side and Charley on the other. "Only you."

"You're imagining things."

"Sure." She laughs.

"If you won't, I will." Charley flaps the front of her tent dress. "Vows be damned."

I laugh. "You're ridiculous."

"I know." She shrugs. "Let's go cool down in the spa."

"Yes," I whisper, rolling my shoulders to try and loosen my tight muscles. "Let's."

Chapter 3

This was supposed to be a relaxing day. I expected to find myself slinking away from the others to sneak a peek at my emails and check the financial world hadn't collapsed. But instead of relaxing or sneakily disappearing to check my inbox, I was distracted from real life, bracing myself and holding my breath with every corner I turned and room I entered, wondering if another encounter with the man from the bar was written in the stars. And if I would die of pleasure from the thrill. Because that's what it was. A thrill, despite my not being able to perform basic human functions in his presence.

And it pains me to admit that.

"A few more laps?" Abbie says as we reach the indoor end of the indoor/outdoor pool.

"I'm not ready to go home yet," Charley grumbles, her head firmly above water, not daring to get her hair wet. I appreciate it. I've had to wait while she dries it on the one day of the week she washes it. It's a mammoth task, and all three of us have yet to find a blow-dry spray that actually speeds up the painful process.

"I need to catch my breath." Charley holds on to the edge as I haul myself up and sit on the side. "How is work, anyway?" she asks, breathless. "Any closer to partner?"

"Hey, we agreed no work today." Abbie joins me and scowls down at Charley where she's bobbing in the water.

"No, you made that agreement with yourself." I elbow her. "Humour me for a moment."

"Fine."

"It's good. I'm on target and hoping to win a few more clients to beef up my portfolio." Opportunities for partnership are rare, and this one was quite unexpected *and* came up much sooner than I anticipated after one of the senior partners was taken ill and decided not to return to work after doctors diagnosed a ministroke. I just need to accelerate my momentum and prove I've got what it takes. That means hitting targets. Actually, it means smashing them, and I'm on track. It's a good thing, since the end of the financial year is looming.

"If I was stinking rich, I'd give you all my money," Charley says, and I smile. "But I'm not, so I can't."

"It's the thought that counts."

"Is that slimy prick still ruffling your feathers?" Abbie asks. "What's his name?"

"Leighton Steers." I grimace at the mere mention of him. "He's my only competition to make partner, but he's solid competition." And ruthless. "I just need to stay one step ahead of him."

"You've got this." Abbie slaps my wet knee and slips back into the water. "Another few laps?"

"I'm in." Charley pushes off the side of the pool.

"I might go in a steam room," I say as they swim away, a nice, peaceful, steady breaststroke. I watch them disappear under the glass wall into the outside area. The pre-spring sunshine is strong. Mum always says March was historically dull before I was born. The sun today is backing her up, reflecting off the rippling water, casting arrows of light up every glass wall surrounding me. It's unusually mild for this time of year.

I look up to the vaulted glass roof, where climbing plants twine around the steel beams that support the glass structure. A modern twist on a classic, I think, as I brush my wet hair back. It seems to be a theme around Arlington Hall. I plant my hands on the tile either side of my thighs and glance around. It screams tranquillity. The entire place.

Breathing out, I get to my feet, collecting a white Egyptian cotton towel from the wicker basket by the white glass door that leads into the ladies' changing rooms, wiping my face as I push my way through and wrapping the towel around my waist before retrieving my mobile. Two missed calls from Nick. I wince. *Delete.* One text.

> Amelia, please answer my calls. Nick xxx

Another wince. *Delete.* I load my inbox, chewing the inside of my cheek as I do, scanning down the dozens of emails that have come in while I've been unplugged. My heart hammers a little bit faster. I'm going to be up all night clearing these down. I spot one from my boss, Gary, and the subject line catches my attention. I open it.

> To: Amelia Lazenby
> From: Gary Panter
>
> Re: I wouldn't usually disturb you on your day off, but . . .
>
> I just heard a rumour that Tilda Spector is winding down.

I bite down on my bottom lip, not wanting to get ahead of myself. It's just a rumour, after all. Tilda Spector is a renowned independent adviser, massively respected in the industry. She's a force, and *if* she's thinking of winding down, that might mean she's looking for someone she can trust to take on some of her clients. This could push my portfolio from impressive to *really* impressive. The first time I met Tilda

Spector was about a year ago at the FSA Annual Finance Conference; this year's event is coming up next week. We hit it off immediately, and she's kept in touch ever since, dropping me an email every few months or so to say hi and to see how I'm getting on at LB&B. Gary joked he was worried she was looking to poach me. I just smiled. That would be a massive compliment, if it were true.

My mobile rings in my hand, startling me, my ex's name flashing on the screen. "Damn." I throw it back into the locker and slam the door, the guilt borderline unbearable, then walk away, the ringing getting quieter until it's gone when I'm out of the changing rooms. It's been a few weeks since I walked out. We clearly want different things, and I don't know how else to remind him of that.

So I stopped taking his calls.

A Turkish bath greets me when I push through some double doors, and around the white tiled room are a dozen or so doors leading to various steam rooms and saunas.

I unravel the towel and hang it on a hook outside a steam room, then open the door. Steam billows out, knocking me back a bit as I step in and check the digital dial on the wall, pulling the glass door closed behind me. "Jesus," I whisper, feeling the burn on my face immediately. I quickly knock the gauge down from fifty degrees Celsius to forty-five and move through the cloud of steam, lowering to the built-in bench and propping my feet up on the one opposite, stretching my legs, feeling the tug of my muscles.

Exhaling loudly, I let my body loosen and my breathing fall into a steady, deep pace. My head drops back, my eyes close, and I take a moment in the quiet to just . . . be.

Just ten minutes. Sweat out the impurities, cleanse my skin.

Get rid of the stress.

The guilt.

Quiet.

Breathe.

Relax.

Bliss.

I hum, wondering if I should reach out to Tilda Spector, let it be *me* checking in with her for once. It's got to be two months since I last heard from her. I make a mental note to check. Or would it be too obvious if I contacted her now, given the rumours? I hum again. Only if the rumours are true. Are they?

The door suddenly opens, and I'm engulfed in cool air. It's a brief reprieve from the intense heat, and the door is soon closed again, whoever's joining me not wanting to lose the temperature in this sweatbox. *Fuck, it's hot.* I wait for a *hello* or a *hi* and get nothing. So I follow suit and say nothing too, squinting as a body cuts through the steam, just close enough to see it's a man's body. A big body. A tall, lean, *hard* body. He lowers to the bench opposite me, becoming a hazy silhouette, and my wet, hot skin starts to tingle.

Oh no.

I inhale, inflating my lungs and burning them at the same time. It's suddenly a lot hotter. Something skims my ankle. And hotter. *Fuck.* Electricity charges the steam-filled space, and I quickly pull my legs down from the bench as he moves across a bit more, putting himself directly in front of me. I can't see him clearly, but I can feel him. Then he leans forward, his elbows on his knees, and I see his fingers lace, his hands joining. My eyes remain locked there. Those fucking hands.

Instinctively pushing back against the tile wall, I feel bare and vulnerable, despite knowing he can't possibly see me clearly either. Does he know it's me in here? I glance at the panel on the wall, noting the temperature has dropped to forty-six degrees Celsius. Then why in hell does it feel like it's getting hotter? I breathe in, breathe out, reach for my brow, and wipe away the beads of water. Breathe in, breathe out.

Hotter.

I can't stand it.

I get up and move through the unbearable heat, bursting out of the door and taking in air urgently, shaking like a bloody leaf. "Shit," I whisper, quickly closing the door and staring at the glass. I should get a towel and dry myself. I should go back to the changing rooms. I should jump in an ice bath to snap myself from this fluster.

The door opens, steam billows out.

Oh fuck.

He emerges from the mist like some kind of mythical creature, and I'm useless once again. My lungs have drained. I can't talk. Can't think. He's so bloody good-looking. *Dangerously* good-looking. My eyes drop.

Remember that word, Amelia. Dangerous.

I'm staring at his bare feet. Then his calves.

His thighs. His cut stomach. His chest. His neck.

His face.

Our eyes meet briefly before his lazy gaze falls slowly down my body, his lip lifting at the corner. "Are you okay?" he asks.

No. "Yes." I quickly grab my towel and wrap my exposed body, and he pouts. It's so cheeky, his dimple deepening.

"I didn't mean to disturb you," he says, his voice low.

I shudder. *For fuck's sake.* "You didn't disturb me."

"So you usually only last a few minutes, huh?"

I baulk at him.

"In the steam room," he adds, rubbing his chest with his hand, through the sheen of sweat and over glistening, solid muscles.

Have mercy.

He pulls a towel off a nearby hook, and all the signs suggest my torture is about to extend.

"It was particularly hot today," I murmur. *Because I had company.* My eyes nearly cross when every one of his muscles flexes and rolls as he rubs himself down. This is bloody unbearable.

"Wasn't it?" he muses, his eyes burning into me, making me shift on the spot. What the hell is wrong with me? I feel like every sense I possess, including my sense of reason, has done a runner on me. I can't find my tongue either. "What do you do?"

I withdraw. "Pardon?"

"What do you do?"

"For work?"

His smile is mild. Is he going to cover himself with that towel, because I'm really struggling? "Yes, for work."

"What is this?" I ask.

"This is me asking you what you do for a living."

"Why?"

"Should I save meaningful conversation until our first date?"

I laugh, stretching his smirk. "Very good. I'm a financial adviser."

"So you're gifted with numbers?"

"I guess I am."

"Well, I'm really gifted with my hands."

My eyes drop to those hands on a slight hitch of breath. "And what do you do with your hands?" My wondering is unstoppable. He was wearing a suit. Businessman?

"Come for dinner with me and you might find out."

I laugh again, and it's so fucking obvious I'm doing it because I have no idea what to say. "You want me to go for dinner with you?" *I would love to go for dinner with you.* "No." I shake my head.

"Why?"

"I don't know you."

"Would you like to?"

I'm stumped. Totally. And I find myself looking at his hands again. I'm standing here half-naked, as is he, and he's asking me out on a date?

"I'm not going for dinner with you." No dating. No men. No distractions. I hate myself right now for making that promise to myself. Stick to the plan, and the plan is making partner. "But thanks for the offer," I add, smiling.

He starts rubbing over his tight black swimming shorts. "You know where to find me when you change your mind."

"In a steam room?"

"Or at a bar. Or on the end of a phone." He smiles, and I am done for. Don't tell me that every woman he's ever flashed that smile to hasn't passed out on the spot. I'm dizzy. My knees are knocking. My insides are furling. "You're good with numbers," he goes on. "So you'll remember mine if I give it to you."

He's hoping. I can't even remember my name right now.

Extending the perfect form of his torso by lifting his arms, he dries his hair with the towel. I can't take it.

I look away *and* walk away, hotter now than I ever was in that sweatbox. I also pray for some restraint to keep myself from fantasising about him. I'm stronger than that. I reach for my temple and rub. *Be strong, Amelia. Remember you're in the aftermath of a breakup.*

"My number is zero, seven—"

I hold up a halting hand, working hard to keep walking.

"Good talking, Amelia," he calls.

I stop dead in my tracks, staring forward, knowing I will do myself no favours turning for another look. How does he know my name? Maybe he heard one of the girls talking to me. Or Anouska.

"Good talking." *And disintegrating.*

And as I stand here, still staring forward at nothing, in a total mental meltdown, my towel loosens and drops to my feet. I peek down my body—my bikini-clad body—feeling his eyes on my arse. *Shit.*

Cringing to high heaven, I dip, trying not to jut my backside out too much, then try to walk away as normally as possible, feeling the heat of his stare following me.

And as soon as I'm out of the spa and back in the safety of the female changing rooms, I collapse to the wooden bench and gasp for air. "Pure class, Amelia," I breathe, burying my head in my hands. Pure fucking class.

"Hey, what's up with you?" Charley asks, breezing in as she unravels her hair from the hair tie. Abbie's behind her, and both of my friends look at me questioningly.

"I just went in the steam room," I say, needing to get this off my chest. "And someone joined me."

Abbie's eyes widen, and Charley is sitting beside me in a second. "The barman?"

"No, not the barman." I laugh.

"The God?" Abbie breathes.

I nod. "He asked me out to dinner."

"In a steam room?"

"No, outside the steam room."

"In your bikini?"

"I had a towel on," I mumble, mortified. "Until it fell off. Oh my God, he asked me to dinner while I stood there in front of him sweating my fucking tits off—and only partly because I was cooking in the steam room—red in the face, hair everywhere, while he dried his obscenely perfect, sweaty, hard body with a towel." With a smirk on his face, and that tells me all I need to know. He's a player.

"Hard?" Abbie asks.

"Yes, hard, cut, dazzling." Fucking perfect.

"You can just tell if a man's got a good body under his clothes," Abbie says. "And I looked at him and knew there was something special going on under all those expensive threads."

Charley rolls her eyes, even though I know she agrees. "What's his name?"

I frown. "I don't know." *But he knew mine.*

"And you agreed to dinner, right?" Abbie presses.

"No, I did not agree to dinner."

"Why?"

I stall, thinking. *Yes, why?* Because he shows all the signs of a player? But he also looks exactly like the kind of man who wouldn't want anything serious right now. Like marriage and kids.

That's perfect.

Isn't it?

"Wise move," Charley says, patting my bare knee and standing. "Because hot bod and a face like a god aside, we all know a fuckboy when we see one."

I laugh half-heartedly, taking the towel to my hair and rubbing.

Dangerous. Fuckboy.

Avoid at all costs.

Chapter 4

Abbie and Charley permitted me to check my emails on the way home. Thankfully, there was nothing drastic that needed my attention, and Mr. Jarvis had, surprisingly, blessed me with only one brief note apologising for overreacting this morning. Rest assured, he wouldn't apologise if he hadn't seen for himself the market sitting steady all day and close out looking more positive than when it opened. Panic over.

As Abbie pulls into my parents' street, I exhale, feeling the suffocation looming. I reach over and drop a kiss onto her cheek. "Thank you for today, it's been so lovely."

She smiles softly, sensing the despondency creeping into my bones. Because no thirty-year-old woman wants to be calling their parents' house home. "You know you could come stay with me," she says for the hundredth time since I left Nick. But I know she's just being polite. Her apartment is on the smaller side of tiny, and I'd drive her nuts with the endless files I bring home from work.

"I know," I say, returning her smile.

"Or me," Charley chirps, grinning. "You can bunk with Ena."

I laugh. I love Charley's babies . . . once a week, when I pop in to make myself a cup of tea while she flaps around the kitchen clearing up toys, food, and clothes on repeat.

"This isn't a permanent arrangement. I'm registered with all the agents, so I'll be the first to know if something comes up in my price range." I love my parents, of course, but living with them? Facing my father's silent displeasure every day? I tolerate it, since they're helping me out massively, but as soon as something comes up, I'm out of there. "I'll call you tomorrow." I hop out and wave as Abbie honks her horn, driving off.

Letting myself in, I drop my bag at the bottom of the stairs and kick my shoes off, following the sound of Mum in the kitchen. I walk in and find Dad at the table with the *Financial Times* spread out, and Mum at the stove stirring a pot of something. Soup, by the smell of it. Leek and potato if I'm not mistaken.

"Smells good," I say, as Dad looks up over his glasses, smiling.

"Darling." He ushers me toward him with one hand, taking his glasses off with the other. "How is it the first time I've seen you today when it's your birthday?"

I smile as I bend, letting him kiss my cheek. "You were still snoring when I left this morning."

He snorts his disgust. "The only person who snores around here is your mother."

"Dennis!" Mum gasps, outraged. "I do not snore."

Dad winks and pulls me closer. "It's getting worse," he whispers. "Heavy breathing, she says. How was your spa day?"

Not what I expected. "Lovely."

"Did you stop off at work on your way home?" he asks, looking up and down my dress.

"No, I stopped off on the way. I had a panicked client go into meltdown because the FTSE 100 opened on the wrong side of okay."

His face goes straight back into his paper, and I roll my eyes. God forbid I talk about my career with my father. So I go to Mum, and she holds out her spoon, offering me a taste.

"Hmmm," I hum, wiping the corner of my lip.

"More seasoning?" she asks.

"It's perfect." I pick up the bread knife and start slicing the fresh loaf. "How was your day at Abbie's shop?"

"Oh, wonderful," she chirps. "I never knew working could be so much fun." Looking out the corner of my eye, I see her nose scrunch.

I gasp dramatically. "So not only did you do a day's work, you enjoyed it?" I look over my shoulder to Dad, who still has his face buried in his newspaper. "Did you hear that, Dad? Mum went to work and actually enjoyed it. Outrageous."

"What, darling?" he asks, looking up with high, telling brows, as Mum giggles again.

"Nothing," I muse. He heard me. "What else is cooking?" I ask, piling the bread in the basket and opening the oven.

"Lamb hotpot. Your grandpa's favourite."

I close the oven. "Grandpa and Grandma are coming?"

"They're here. In the lounge in their usual spots." Of course they are. They're always here. I head for the lounge to see them. "And Clark will be here soon with Rachel," Mum calls.

I stop at the door, looking back. "A family dinner?" I ask. No one mentioned a family dinner.

"It's your thirtieth!" Mum reminds me. "Of course we're having a family dinner."

I force a smile. "Wonderful." I wanted to eat and go to my room to clear my inbox. Tomorrow is already going to be long. God damn it.

I carry on to the lounge and find Grandpa in his chair on one side of the fire, Grandma in hers on the other side. As always, he too has his face buried in the *Financial Times*, keeping himself in the know, despite having retired long before Dad supposedly retired as well. Grandma's knitting needles are going like the clappers. "Evening, you two."

"The birthday girl!" Grandpa snaps his paper shut and tries to stand.

"Grandpa, stay," I order, hurrying over.

"I'm not a dog, Amelia Gracie," he grumbles, ignoring me and creaking up. "And I still have use of all bodily functions."

"Except your bladder," Grandma says quietly and sardonically, making me laugh.

"What did she say?" Grandpa asks.

"Nothing. Sit down." I help him back to the chair and go to Grandma. "What are you knitting?"

"A scarf for your father." She beckons me into her ample bosom and squishes me. "Happy birthday, Grand Girl."

"Thanks, Grandma."

"I'm so sorry to hear about you and Nick. Such a lovely boy."

I know she's sorry. She's told me every time I've seen her.

"Such a shame," Grandpa adds before going back to his paper. "Such a lovely boy."

"It was for the best."

"Says who?" Dad asks, entering.

I sigh, not wanting to rehash this again. "Me," I say with certainty. "I say, Dad."

He hums, looking most unconvinced, but thankfully, the front door opens, and I hear Clark calling out his arrival, saving me from my daily reminder of my questionable choices.

"Oh look, Clark and Rachel are here." I give Dad a wide smile and go to the entrance hall to find my younger brother. "Thank you," I breathe, throwing my arms around him.

"For what?" he asks, laughing.

"Dad was about to launch into all the reasons why I've made a terrible mistake."

He huffs, pulling away. "Again?"

"Yeah."

"Happy birthday." Clark grins. "Shit, this means I'm only two years away from the big three zero."

"Thanks." I move on to Rachel, his fiancée, who's another reminder that I'm doing things all wrong. "Good to see you."

"Happy birthday." She hugs me.

"Thanks. How are the plans coming along?"

Rachel breathes out her exasperation. "It's nearly a part-time job." Which is fine because she only works part-time in a chemist after happily slashing her hours when Clark asked her to be his wife, and therefore the mother of his babies, and, therefore, when the time comes—and I don't expect it to be long—a stay-at-home mum. Rachel won't be working for much longer.

"Four weeks," she confirms, letting Clark pull her into the lounge to say hello to our grandparents. I follow and take a seat on the couch.

"Clark, come." Grandpa pats the arm of his chair for him to sit.

"He's not a dog, Grandpa."

"What do you make of this nonsense?" Grandpa points at the paper as Dad joins them, ignoring me. The boys doing boys things. I don't bother finding out what nonsense Grandpa is talking about. I've long learned when my input is welcome. Like, never when it comes to business. I gaze toward the kitchen. That's where I should be, and it's where Rachel just went, and where Grandma would be if Mum would let her.

So I pull my phone out and start working my way through my emails. I also check when I last heard from Tilda Spector. Six weeks. I hum to myself, deciding I can wait until the conference next week to talk to her.

"Hey," Clark says, dropping to the couch beside me.

"Done with boys' talk?" I ask with a hint of a smirk.

"Stop it." He nudges me in the arm. "Why don't you stop being so stubborn and let me talk to him?"

"Let you try to convince our father that I'm capable of running the family financial business with you?" Clark pouts, and I roll my eyes. "It's fine." That's a lie. "I'm happy at LB&B." Truth. "And I couldn't stand Dad breathing down my neck over every decision I made. And, with respect, have you as my boss?"

"I'm a good boss."

"Maybe, but you shouldn't be *my* boss." Because I'm the eldest child. And yet because I'm a girl and our father's a dinosaur, I've been sidestepped for my younger brother. I don't hold it against Clark. He's a good brother.

"So how's business?" he asks.

"Good. Don't let Dad hear you asking me that." I reach over and kiss his cheek. "I better go help Mum in the kitchen before the world ends and men replace women at the stove."

"Ha ha," he drones, kicking me up the backside as I walk away. I don't make it to the kitchen, the front door stopping me.

"Are we expecting someone else?" I call, frowning as I divert.

"What, darling?" Dad calls.

"Who's at the door?" I swing it open and come face-to-face with my ex. "Fuck," I breathe. "Nick, what are you doing here?"

He holds up a small, gift-wrapped box, smiling awkwardly. "Happy birthday," he says, as if that explains his visit. I suppose it should, but it doesn't. I've not been answering his calls, his messages. Not out of spite or malice, but because I don't know what to say to him. Like now, as I keep him on the doorstep of my parents' house. He looks well, his usual clean-cut, suited self, his hair, as always, precisely styled, his face smooth. He's a handsome guy, in an Oxford prep kinda way.

"Who is it, darling?" Dad asks from behind me, muscling his way between me and the door. "Nick," he chimes, happy. Of course he's happy. "What a lovely surprise!"

Nick lets loose a small frown as he offers a hand, and I know, I just fucking know, this is my father's doing. "Hi, Dennis," he murmurs.

"Come in, come in. Jenn, you'll never guess who's stopped by." Dad hauls my ex into the house and shuts the door.

"Bet she can," I grumble, scowling at Dad's back.

"I thought you knew," Nick says quietly, at the mercy of my father's over-the-top hospitality.

I breathe out and shake my head, waving a flippant hand. It's not Nick's fault my father's a deviant dinosaur.

"Mum, Dad, Clark, Rachel!" Dad sings. "Guess who's here?"

"I'm going to fucking kill him," I say to Clark when he comes to see what all the fuss is about.

"Oh," he whispers, holding a hand up in an embarrassed hello to Nick. "Well, this is awkward."

"Why can't he let me live my own life?" I march into the kitchen while Dad directs Nick into the lounge to say hello to Grandpa and Grandma. "Mum," I cry on a hiss, pointing in the general direction of the lounge. "He's interfering again."

"Oh, darling, he just wants what's best for you."

"He has no idea what's best for me." I drop my head back and look at the ceiling as Clark passes and gives my shoulder a sympathetic, pointless rub.

"Now come on," Mum says, falling into peacekeeping mode. "You should be all Zen after your day at the spa."

"I was very Zen until Dad invited my ex to dinner." The conniving arse. "Why can't he keep his nose out?"

"He needs something to do since he retired," Clark quips. I glare at him, and he's quick to apologise.

"Why do we all talk about Dad's retirement when he's not actually retired?" He's in the office now as much as he was when he wasn't retired.

Taking his glass of water, Clark retreats to the lounge.

"Come." Mum grabs the cutlery she reserves for special dinners. "Help me set the table."

Irritated, I snatch one of her endless aprons down off the hook and get it on, grabbing the place mats while Rachel gets the fancy crockery. All the women doing women things. I go to the dining room off the lounge and start laying the table, one ear on Rachel and Mum chatting about the upcoming wedding, my other on the men in the lounge talking about the stock market. It's going to be a long evening.

And it is. Long and painful. I don't say much, as everyone happily ignores the fact that this is so very wrong, except Grandma, who definitely keeps checking on me, smiling softly. Nick apologises every chance he gets, and I tell him not to worry. I give all my attention to Grandma, who wants to hear about my day at the spa.

"We didn't have spas in my day, Grand Girl. The only massage you could get was when you rode the rickety old bus into town going over all the cobbles."

I laugh and watch her hands shake as she tries to cut into a carrot. "Want me to do that for you, Grandma?"

She gives up and sighs, and Grandpa is quick to give her arm a reassuring pat, noticing her trembles. "Knitting is becoming trickier," she says. "I keep dropping my stitches."

"Then you should slow those needles down." I chop up everything on the plate that needs chopping and hand back her knife and fork. "There."

"Thank you, Grand Girl." She leans in. "Now, where was this spa?" she whispers, obviously trying to keep me talking so I'm not uncomfortable. She has no idea.

"Oxfordshire," I whisper back, observing Dad and Nick chatting.

"All that way for a spa?"

"It's called Arlington Hall. Very posh." I scrunch my nose. "There was a helicopter pad too."

"Oh, I say. Fancy."

"Very. I had a hydrating aromatherapy body wrap." *Lucky body wrapper.* I shudder in my seat. Feel the heat as well as I felt it in the steam room. The Adonis. *Have dinner with me.* I look up at my ex. Clean cut. Pruned. Boring. Nothing like the man at Arlington Hall.

Nick smiles and sets down his knife and fork, wiping his mouth with a napkin. "That was delicious, Jenn," he says, holding up his glass of red. "Happy birthday, Amelia."

Everyone raises their glass and chants a happy birthday, and I smile, sinking into my seat. "Thank you."

"Here." Nick pushes the little box toward me. Oh God, why would he? I die a thousand deaths. Is he expecting me to open it in front of everyone? I feel terrible enough, without this added layer to my guilt. "I got it a few months ago," he explains. "Before we . . . well, before you left."

I look up through my lashes from the box to Nick. "You shouldn't have."

He shrugs. "It's nonreturnable, so I thought you may as well have it."

I stare at the box. Just stare.

"Open it then," Dad says, excited. "Kill our curiosity."

I want to kill you, dear Father. Taking the box, I pull the paper off and flip the lid open. And inhale.

"I went back and got it," he says. "You obviously loved it."

I stare down at the gold bracelet I saw in an antique store in Camden a few months ago when Nick and I were walking back to our apartment after dinner with colleagues.

"Nick," I breathe. I can't accept this. I also don't want to humiliate him. Everyone's eyes move between us, and I wish the floor would open and swallow me whole.

"What a thoughtful gift." Dad smiles broadly. I want to wipe it off. "Isn't it, Jenn?"

"Very thoughtful," Mum says quietly, avoiding my eyes.

Take the gift. Just take it and return it after this whole horror movie is finished and I don't have an audience. So I smile and take the bracelet out of the box, putting it on my wrist. I could quite honestly slap the smile off my father's face. "Thank you, Nick." The wretched guilt enflames.

"Well done," Clark whispers from beside me, as if commending me for my restraint.

"Amelia went to a spa today!" Grandma blurts. God love her. She might be nearly ninety, but she's got every sense, including her Tension Sensor. I smile across at her as I fiddle with the bracelet. "What was it called again, Grand Girl? Fancy, it was."

"Arlington Hall," I murmur.

"Arlington?" Nick questions, interested.

"Yes, have you heard of it?"

"Hasn't everyone? Why would you go all the way to Oxfordshire for a spa day?"

"Abbie arranged it," I explain. "It was some kind of special deal. She got it for a steal."

"A special deal at Arlington?" Nick laughs. "It was in *The Times* top hotels in England. I doubt they would need to offer special deals."

I tilt my head at him. Why's he so concerned by where I went for my birthday spa and how much it cost? "It was a fifth-anniversary promotion."

"Very fancy!" Grandma sings.

"And what does one do at a spa day?" Grandpa asks, looking truly intrigued.

"One relaxes and unwinds, Grandpa." I smile across at him, my thoughts invaded by what was really special about Arlington Hall. More special than the phenomenal mansion and grounds. And I definitely didn't relax or unwind. *Come to dinner with me.*

"I might have myself a spa day," Grandma declares.

"Why on earth do you need to relax and unwind?" Dad asks.

"A break from you Lazenby boys." She gives the men each a moment of her old eyes, an undetectable smirk lifting the corner of her lips. Each of them snort their disgust.

"I should be going." Nick stands. Thank God.

I jump up, happy to see him out. "Thank you for coming," I say as he makes his way around the table saying his goodbyes. "I'll see you out."

I leave the dining room, Nick following, and open the door for him. "I didn't mean to make your birthday so awkward. I thought you knew I was coming. If you had answered my calls, we may have figured out what your dad was up to."

I ignore his little dig about the calls. "Yeah, I'm sorry about his underhanded tactics."

"Does that mean there's still no chance?"

I shoot him a surprised look. "Nick . . ." I whisper, so tired of rehashing the same thing over and over. "We . . ." I flap a useless hand between us. "You and I . . ."

"Amelia, I only mentioned the words *marriage* and *baby*, and you were gone like a rocket."

"Well, that's not true, is it?" I laugh lightly. It's a laugh of disbelief. "You mentioned it many times." I frown. "You told me I owed you some kind of commitment, Nick."

"Is that wrong? To want all that with you?"

Probably not, but to say I *owed* him? It gave me the instant ick. "What brought it on?" I ask. "You'd never given any hints you wanted that before, and suddenly it's all you talked about."

He shrugs. "We're not getting any younger."

Ouch. "But you know how much my career means to me. I'm working toward partner, Nick. You know that."

He moves in and crowds me. I'm instantly suffocating again. "Amelia, come on. You could go back to work after a baby if you really wanted to."

If I really wanted to? What I *really* want is to have a career and not be judged. I want to have babies when I want to have babies. *If* I ever want to. I might not. I don't know. And that's the point. *My* pace. I want to do life at *my* pace.

"No." I place my palm on Nick's chest and push him back. "I don't want to have a baby." That's not entirely true. I just don't want to now. Or is it more that I can't see my forever with Nick? I inwardly recoil at the unexpected direction of my thoughts. I also consider for the first time that he hit me with marriage and babies not long after I announced I was shooting for partner. Did my ambitions scare him?

Nick sighs and backs out, but something tells me his withdrawal isn't a submission.

"Take care, Nick." I close the door and walk back into the kitchen. Dad's placing some dishes by the sink. I don't make any snide remarks about him doing a woman's work. "You have to stop this."

His hands pause on the dishes momentarily. "Stop what?"

"Interfering."

"Let's not do this now." Mum hands me a tea towel.

I take it, stopping myself from snatching it, and swipe a plate off the drainer, starting to roughly dry it.

"I'm not interfering," Dad says, going to the fridge and pulling out a pot of cream. "Just trying to help."

"I don't need your help, Dad." I place the plate down and take another. "I'm happy." Or I would be if Dad stopped with his kind of *help*.

"You don't need my help?" he asks, his voice suddenly an angry whisper. "Then tell me, Amelia, who is providing your accommodation right now because you decided to walk out on a perfectly good relationship and leave yourself homeless?"

My jaw rolls. I could hardly end the relationship and ask Nick to leave the apartment, could I? "Dad—"

"Now, now," Mum blurts out, getting herself in a flap, wanting to avoid the conflict.

Once again guilt rages inside. I'm usually so controlled around my father and his prehistoric ways. Have learned to keep my mouth shut to keep the peace and avoid fallout. There's just no point trying to make him see. He's unmovable. But today? I don't know. Maybe it's Nick showing up. *Thanks, Dad.*

"What was the point in letting me go to university?" I ask. "If you had no intention of allowing me the opportunity to progress in the family business, what was the point?"

Dad casts a look Mum's way, and I know in this moment that it was Mum's doing. She talked him round. "I thought it was a phase," he mutters.

"You thought my hopes and dreams were a phase?" I ask, stunned.

"Maybe they still are."

"What, you mean until I realise my true vocation in life is to marry and breed?" How the hell I'm talking so quietly and calmly, I don't know.

"Amelia, come on," Mum implores.

"No, Mum. Enough."

"You're punishing me because I gave the business to Clark, aren't you?" Dad says. "That's what this is all about."

"And you're punishing *me* for wanting to have a career. For not wanting to have babies and be a housewife."

"What's wrong with that? Look at your mother. She's very happy!"

I actually *do* look at my mother. Yes, I know she's happy. So when she glances at Dad with an indignant expression, I'm more than surprised.

"Actually"—Mum's body lifts at the shoulders—"after today, working at Abbie's florist, I realise that I might have missed out on something."

"What?" Dad gasps, looking betrayed. "Haven't I taken care of you? Provided? Loved you?"

"Of course you have, but, you know, I'm just saying a woman can want more than that."

Dad, God love that clueless man, is so injured. "I've been a good husband."

"An amazing husband," Mum rushes to reassure him.

"And a good father." He looks at me now, and damn it, I can't refute that. He's an amazing father. Kind, generous, loving. *And* supportive . . . if you're the right sex doing the *right* thing. "Haven't I?" he asks quietly.

I sigh. "You're a good father, Dad."

"And I'll be an amazing grandfather too."

I drop my head back. "Undoubtedly."

"So make us grandparents, Amelia. We need a new generation of Lazenbys to take over what your grandpa and I worked so hard to build."

Better just make sure we have boys. "I'm not ready to be a mum, Dad. I have other things I want to do."

"For the love of God," he breathes. "I've had enough of this madness." He swipes up his *Financial Times* and escapes, giving Mum an accusing glare as he goes.

"I think I should move out," I say quietly.

Chapter 5

Abbie swings the door open and smiles softly. "Welcome home," she says, taking the piles of client files from where they're balanced on one arm. "I see you brought the essentials."

"They won't be clogging up space for too long; I'll take them into the office tomorrow."

"What happened?"

"Dad invited Nick to my family birthday dinner." Abbie's eyes bug. "I don't know how much more of his interfering I can take." He means well, I know he means well, but I wish he would just listen to me. See me. Understand me. I show her my wrist. "Nick got me this."

She winces. "I've cleared the spare room."

"Your office." I pout. "No, I'll just crash on the couch."

"Don't be ridiculous."

"Where will you do all your paperwork?"

"It's fine, I have space at the florist. Wine?"

I exhale my yes as I follow her to the small kitchen, dropping my bags on the floor before dropping my arse to one of the barstools on the other side of the counter. I remove the bracelet and put it in the fruit bowl with a pile of oranges as Abbie gets glasses and a new bottle, opening and pouring.

"Thank you," I say, accepting a glass. "For this and for putting me up."

"Stop it. I already told you there's a bed for you."

"I didn't want to hurt Mum's feelings. I think she likes having me around. Or liked."

Abbie leans on the counter. "How was she?"

"Upset."

"And your dad?"

I laugh under my breath. "Sulking, I expect." He'll do what Dad does. Go quiet. Mull things over. Conclude he's right. "It didn't help that Mum confessed she felt like she'd missed out after helping at the florist today."

Abbie laughs. "Corey said she's a natural."

I smile. "Don't tell my dad." I take my first sip of wine and hum. "Nice."

"It's a new one." Abbie turns the bottle towards me. "This month's case is all French, and it's not helping my urge to escape to Paris."

"Maybe you can, now you have a new apprentice." I smirk over the rim of my glass. "Shit, this really is good."

Scooting around the counter, Abbie heads for the two-seater in front of the TV and drops down. "Now, let us talk about something more interesting than your father's ancient values."

"Like?" I ask, joining her.

"Like the stinking-hot businessman at Arlington Hall today."

I bite at my lip, restraining my grin. "I didn't think he could look any hotter than in a suit." More wine. "Then I saw him virtually naked."

Abbie throws her head back, laughing. "I've never seen you flustered before. That alone means you *have* to go to dinner with him."

"That may be so, but Mr. Stinking Hot didn't divulge his name, so I have no way to contact him and retract my decline of his invitation. Not that I should. Or would." My stomach flips.

"He's worth breaking your cardinal rule for."

"What rule?"

"No sex on a first date."

"He's seen me virtually naked, and I haven't been on a date with him."

"Outrageous."

I pout, trying to push back my mortification. But not so much the memory of that body glistening with sweat. Lord have mercy. I slowly sip my wine, falling into a daydream. *I'm good with my hands.*

"Amelia!"

I jerk, looking at my friend. "What?"

Abbie grins knowingly. "You were thinking about him."

"I was reliving my embarrassment." *Anyway, enough about me.* "How's life on the dating apps?"

She huffs. "I've given up." Then she falls into her own little daydream, and I know that she's thinking about Mr. Romeo. That's not his name; she doesn't know his name, it's just what he's been known as between the three of us since Abbie came back from France two years ago. One night. It was just one night. The best night of her life.

"Abbie," I snap.

She jumps. Sighs. "I couldn't work out if Paris was a blessing or a curse." She takes more wine. "I'm slowly concluding it was a curse. God damn it, he's a marker for all men, and everyone has fallen short since. I've given up."

"Wish you'd shared your names?"

"Kind of." Tucking her legs under her butt, she gets comfortable. "Fancy watching *Bridget Jones*?"

"Christ, Abbie, are we *that* beyond hope?"

"Maybe. I feel like Charley's taken our quota of luck when it comes to men." She grabs the remote control and flicks on the TV, starting to scroll the channels. "Oh, wait." She hops up and disappears, returning a few moments later. "Look what I found at the back of my wardrobe." She holds up my cream hoodie, and I smile, reaching for it. "You never took it home after I gave it to you for your birthday *three years ago*."

I open it up and look at the embroidery, smiling.

I Need a Hug That Leads to Sex

Why didn't I take it home? Home to where I lived with Nick. I don't want to answer that. I definitely need a hug. But sex?

"Thank you." I slip it over my dress and get comfortable, Abbie settling beside me. "What time are you leaving in the morning?"

"I have to go to the wholesalers, since your pro saleswoman of a mother sold me out of most blooms. So probably six."

"I'll come with you. You can throw me out at the station."

"No problem. Don't forget it's Elijah's birthday a week next Friday."

"I won't."

We both get cosy and watch Bridget Jones grace us in all her single and huge pants glory. But my uncontrollable wandering mind takes me back to the steam room.

Chapter 6

When Gary walks into my office, I peek over the stack of files on my desk and smile. "Morning."

He looks across the mess, alarmed, removing his glasses. "What's happened?"

"Nothing happened," I say, trying to make the piles neater.

"Amelia." He wanders over, combing his grey quiff to one side with his fingers, and drops to one of the chairs opposite. Leaning forward, he pushes a pile aside so he can see me. "What's happened?"

My nose scrunches. I haven't told Gary about my personal crisis. I don't want him to think it's going to affect my job and therefore hamper my chances of making partner. I just have to make sure I convince the senior partners that I'm a better bet than Leighton Steers, the company's self-professed golden boy who's also a shameless flirt.

"I split up with my boyfriend," I say grudgingly. "I moved back home with my parents and moved out again last night. I'm staying with a friend." I shrug. "Her place is on the tiny side of small."

"You split up with Nick?" he asks, surprised as he cleans his glasses. "Shit, I'm sorry to hear that."

"It's for the best."

"Why have you moved out of your parents'?"

"Why'd you think, Gary?" I ask sardonically. I would have *loved* to avoid divulging the circumstances of me seeking a job at a rival financial advisory company, but having the name Lazenby shat all over that wish. Everyone knows of Lazenby Finance.

"Oh," Gary breathes, slipping his glasses back on. "Daddy's been reminding you of your obligations as a woman again, has he?"

"You got it."

"And now I'm up to speed on your new relationship status, I'm guessing Nick—"

"Suggested babies, yes."

"Well, good for you for sticking to your guns." He stands. "Heard anything from Mr. Jarvis?"

"He's calmed down. Thanks for the heads-up yesterday about Tilda Spector, by the way."

"No problem. Don't bank on the rumours being true, though, okay?" Translated, *Don't slack on securing new clients.* "And even if they are, she's got the pick of the bunch to leave her precious clients with."

Nodding, I glance at my clock, seeing I've only got half an hour. "I have an annual review with Mrs. Willer at one."

"Sure, you get on. I've got a meeting with the senior partners."

I try so hard to hide my curiosity. Since Paul Montgomery left after his health scare, everyone is wondering who'll replace him. Gary knows I'm capable, and I know he's got my back. But he's also a fan of Leighton Steers. All the partners are.

"A meeting with all the partners?" That's rare.

Gary smiles. "All of them. We're keeping an eye on Galactia."

"Me too," I chirp. I'm living for the day the rumours are no longer rumours and my investment recommendations to *many* of my clients pay off.

Gary leaves, and I brush a stray strand back and tuck it into my bun, collecting Mrs. Willer's file to recap on my agenda, but my mobile ringing stalls me opening the file. I frown down at the unknown number, letting it ring off to voicemail. A few seconds later, it's ringing again. I answer.

"Amelia Lazenby."

The Invitation

"Good afternoon, Amelia, it's Anouska from Arlington Hall."

I sit up straight in my chair. "Hi."

"I hope you don't mind, I got your number from the medical form you completed yesterday before your treatments."

"No problem, how can I help you?"

"Your wallet was found in the ladies' changing rooms this morning by the cleaners."

"Oh?" I dip down by my desk and pull my handbag up onto my lap. "I hadn't noticed it was missing."

"It has numerous bank cards and your driver's licence inside. I hope you don't mind, I had to open it to see who it belonged to."

"Not at all." A good rummage through my bag reveals no wallet. "I use Apple Pay for everything these days." Hence I hadn't noticed it missing.

"I'll keep it in the safe until you can collect it."

"Thanks."

"When might I expect you, just so I can let staff know in case I'm not on shift?"

Good question. "Can I let you know? I'll have to see if a friend can bring me."

"You don't drive?" she asks in confusion, obviously having seen that I have a driver's licence.

"I drive, I just don't have a car. I live in the city. It's Tubes for me. Much faster."

"Oh, I see. Then just let me know when you can pick it up."

I thank Anouska, hanging up and tapping my desk with my ballpoint, my mind taking me back to the Library Bar. Then the steam room.

And I'm burning up.

Get a grip, Amelia.

I flap the front of my dress as best I can to circulate some cool air, pouting as I check the time. "Shit." Flipping open Mrs. Willer's file, I start marking my notes in order of priority. First up, convince

Mrs. Willer she can't skip contributing to her pension pot this financial year or she'll lose a massive chunk of her allowance. I scribble down a few more notes and hop onto the call, sitting back in my chair, smiling when Mrs. Willer appears. I'm certain her hair gets whiter every time I see her, not through age but through bleach. She's a lovely-looking woman in her forties, successful, with three daughters and a bitter ex-husband. "So good to see you, Mrs. Willer."

"Amelia, you've been looking after my money for nearly two years. You know my children as well as I do. Hate my ex as much as me. I think we're past formalities. Call me Violet, please."

I smile. "Violet."

"Come on, then," she says, settling back in her green velvet chair and accepting a flute off a tray being held out by her personal butler. "How much have I lost this year?"

I laugh, getting my graphs up so I can share the screen with her. "You like high risk, Violet. That comes with its cons, but I'm pleased to report a seven percent increase on your investments."

"Oh, delightful! I'll order that new Bentley I've got my eye on."

"Let's not be hasty," I reply, making her chuckle.

"Spoilsport."

"A luxury car is the worst investment you can make, Violet. We've talked about this." And she has ten other luxury cars, for Christ's sake.

"And the best?"

I smile. "Your pension."

An hour later, I'm thrilled—and surprised—to have secured Mrs. Willer's full commitment to her pension, as well as a nice top-up on her ISAs. Checking my diary for my next call, I see I have half an hour to shoot over to Pret to get some lunch. I grab my bag and leave, texting Abbie and Charley to see if they're up for a workout after work. Abbie is all in. Charley has coffee and a playdate with a mum from the nursery.

I travel down in the elevator, checking myself in the mirror, smoothing back my hair and reapplying my soft pink lippy. I smack my lips and brush down my black pencil dress, which falls to my shins, wriggling my toes in my black stiletto slingbacks. I grimace, wishing I'd put on my trainers to do my lunch run. Stepping out of the elevator, I pull my phone out and scan the market as I blindly swipe my card to let myself out and walk as fast as my heels will carry me across the reception area. As I'm crossing the road, I take a call from Mum. "How's Dad?" I ask.

"Oh, please do make peace with him, Amelia. He's driving me mad sulking around the house. He hates that you've fallen out with him."

"I haven't fallen out with him," I say tiredly. "I just want him to know I'm upset."

"He knows."

"So he'll stop interfering with how I choose to live my life?"

"Probably not," she grumbles. "You know your father."

Yes, he's a stick-in-the-mud. "What can I do?" I ask. "Apart from become a baby machine and a homemaker?"

Mum falls silent, which says it all. There's nothing I can do. I'm not interested in proving myself. I accepted that would never happen when I quit being a glorified receptionist at the family firm and got myself a job that did my qualifications justice.

"I'll come over this weekend," I say on a sigh. I don't want to *not* talk to my dad. I love the old bugger dearly. So I'll make peace like I always do, by *not* acknowledging the problem. Brushing it under the carpet and pretending I'm not deeply wounded that he doesn't think I'm capable of running the family business with Clark. As an equal.

"Oh good," Mum chimes, happy. "Rachel wants to finalise the seating plan, we have a final fitting for the dresses, and her best friend, Josie, wants some help with the final plans for the hen party. I'm doing picky bits and mimosas."

"Sounds lovely."

"How's things at Abbie's?"

Cramped. "I've only been there one night."

"I wish you hadn't left."

I push my way into Pret and grab my usual salad, not acknowledging Mum's comment. There's nothing I can say, and telling her I don't need my parents breathing down my neck won't help. "I'll call you." I hang up, order a tea, and pay.

I'm lost in my inbox while I make my way back across the road, juggling my lunch as I push my back into the glass doors of my building. I glance up.

And freeze.

"What the fuck?" I whisper, a wave of tingles rippling through my body, making me wobble on my heels. He's standing at the reception desk. Suited. Looking fucking glorious. "Shit." I come over all silly and girlie, tottering toward the ladies' restrooms, my hurried steps hampered by the tightness of my dress around my legs and the height of my heels.

Rushing in, I free my hands of my phone and lunch, dropping my bag to the floor. My cheeks are pink. Flushed. I pat at them. Why the hell did I run away? Well, totter. Wobble? This is ridiculous. *Pull yourself together!*

I don't have a chance.

The door opens, and he appears, filling the doorway before checking behind him and stepping in, letting the door close. He slips his hands into his pockets. My temperature goes through the roof. Just by his presence.

"I thought I saw you running away," he says quietly, his voice licking my skin.

Oh my God. "You're in the ladies'," I blurt, straightening my shoulders, blinking back how dazzling he is.

"I am?" He glances around, and the move flexes his neck, making it taut. *Jesus Christ.* Then his eyes drop to my salad and iced tea. "You often eat your lunch in the ladies'?"

"I . . ." I roll my eyes, exasperated by myself. "I'm washing my hands." I flip the tap on and squirt some soap into them, massaging it to a lather. "What are you doing here?" Encountering the most delicious male specimen I've ever seen in my life twice in as many days *cannot* be pure luck.

He rests his arse back against the line of sinks and places his hands on the edge. He's getting comfortable? My God, I could cry he's so fucking hot. His pale-grey suit fits him disgustingly well. I look at the door.

"Nervous someone will interrupt us?"

"Interrupt us doing what, exactly?" I continue massaging soap into my hands. "Me asking you why you're following me?"

He laughs under his breath, and the sound is like warm honey trickling over my skin. It's an effort to conceal my hitch of breath, and judging by the amused glint in his eyes, which are on the greener side of teal today, I've failed spectacularly. "I'm not following you, Amelia."

Don't say my name, I might die of pleasure on the spot. "You often hang around ladies' restrooms bothering women?"

"Am I bothering you?"

My hands are going to disappear in a minute. But will my brain tell me what comes after soaping? No. I ignore his question and soap some more, my eyes on my task.

"Let me help."

"What?"

He's suddenly behind me, his tall, lean hardness close. *Hot.* My eyes shoot to his in the mirror as his arms circle me and his hands rest on my forearms. I still. Breathe in. Get a potent hit of his beautiful cologne. It's musky but fresh. A bit of oud? I don't know, but it's as intoxicating as the man himself.

Frozen, I watch as he slides his hands down my forearms, his fingers slipping through mine as he starts massaging the soap. My heart batters against my chest. A harsh thud smacks me between my legs, forcing me to tense my thighs. *Oh . . . my . . . God.* His breathing deepens. His groin pushes into my arse. His expression is serious. His lips part, his perfect white teeth bite at the edge, and I find myself mimicking his move. Jesus, he feels divine, his hands as expert as I imagined they would be.

I'm incapacitated as he dedicates time to each one of my fingers, rubbing his middle finger in between, my eyes constantly moving from his to our hands. I'm suddenly not in the ladies', but somewhere else. Somewhere wonderful.

"How was your body wrap?" he asks quietly and casually, as if he's not seducing me with his masterful hands on mine.

"Out of this world," I whisper.

"Good." He dips and smells my neck, and my whole body goes up in smoke, my head falling back a little. *What the fuck am I doing?* "You had the Relax and Unwind. I can still smell the lavender on your skin. Are you relaxed?"

I moan, and I absolutely cannot stop it. "Yes."

His erection pushes gently into my backside. "Me too."

"Oh God." I feel the warm sensation of the water rinsing away the suds, stuck in a trance, sky high on pleasure. My nipples are tingling, along with every inch of my skin.

"Oh God," he breathes in reply, nipping at my neck. I'm done for. I'm about to spin around and kiss him, eat him alive, my inhibitions lost, but the sound of a paper towel being snatched from the dispenser stops me. I snap my eyes open and find he's patting the water away. "So wet," he says quietly.

Then he steps back and leaves me to hold myself up alone. I'm struggling. A sheen of sweat coats his brow, his greeny-blue eyes misty. "Now will you come to dinner with me?"

"You came here to ask me to dinner?"

"No, I came here to see my lawyer on the third floor. Finding you here was just a bonus." He raises his brows, and I'm suddenly on planet Earth again. In the ladies'. With a stranger. If hands could have sex, ours just did it.

I inwardly laugh, smoothing my hair back. If my cheeks were flushed when I entered the bathroom, they're on fire now, along with the rest of my body.

"So?"

I still, my hand on my nape fixing my hair, my eyes on his. "I don't think so." *Dangerous*. Look what he just did. I was putty in his hands. I expect many women are.

"Not even after the best foreplay of your life?"

I laugh. "You're quite cocky, aren't you."

"Tell me it wasn't the best foreplay you've ever had."

I grab my lunch and face him, fighting with everything I have to keep my body and voice steady. *It was the best foreplay I've ever had!* "It was good to see you."

"Good?" he asks as I pass him, taking my wrist and pulling me to a stop. "Stop being so stiff."

I tilt my head, dropping my eyes to his groin. "I believe you are the one who's stiff."

My retort delights him, his grin mischievous and fucking stunning. "You *will* be having dinner with me."

"You're not my type."

"And what's your type?"

"Less forward."

His hands come up in surrender, and he takes one step back. "Life's too short to fuck around playing cat-and-mouse games, Amelia."

"I don't play games at all." I leave the bathroom before I get myself into something I'm wholly unprepared for, walking on wobbly legs to the elevator. I call Abbie on my way, my fingers shaky on the screen. She doesn't answer, so I try again. Still no answer. *Come on, Abbie, I need you!*

I text her.

Answer, answer, answer!

I dial again, and this time she answers on a hushed whisper. "What's happened? Are you okay?"

"Oh my God, Abbie," I wail, hitting the call button for the elevator, looking over my shoulder to the ladies' bathroom. "He's here."

"What?"

"The man from Arlington Hall. I just grabbed some lunch and spotted him in the lobby. He was here to see his lawyer."

"Shit, did you speak to him?"

I laugh. "I think our hands just had sex."

"What the fuck are you talking about?"

"I dashed into the bathroom to hide. He followed me in."

"Why did you hide?" she asks but doesn't give me a second to answer. "Oh my God, you like him!"

"I don't know him." But my hands certainly do. I hit the call button again.

"Wait, we need a three-way." Abbie's phone rustles as she dials Charley and lets her join the call. "Amelia's hands just had sex with the disgustingly hot guy's hands from the spa."

"What the fuck are you talking about?" Charley asks, and then immediately apologises to her babies for her bad language.

"I just saw him in the lobby at work," I explain, trying to get Charley up to speed, looking over my shoulder. I freeze, snapping my mouth shut. And there he is, watching me beat the crap out of the call button while talking urgently down the line. He smiles at the phone on my ear, surely knowing I'm putting in an emergency call to my girlfriends. *Great.* "He's looking at me now," I whisper. "I'm fucking melting."

The girls laugh, and the doors open. I rush inside and start breathing easy again.

"Talk to me about hand sex," Charley orders, clattering and bangs happening in the background. "It's a new one to me."

"He followed me into the bathroom. Helped me wash my hands. I think I groaned. I *know* I groaned. His dick was fucking solid and pulsing into my—" I snap my mouth shut when he appears at the elevator doors, stopping them from shutting. "I've got to go," I whisper as he steps inside.

"Amelia, no!" Abbie yells as I pull my mobile away from my ear. "His dick was what?"

The doors close. "I want to hear more about hand sex!" Charley adds.

I slam my thumb down on the red icon to end the call and shut my friends up, dying on the inside as he joins me. He's so close. So I take a step away, suffocating, staring at the mirrored doors, my eyes on his lovely brown dress shoes and perfectly fitted trousers. I can't stop my gaze creeping up his legs. "Still stiff," he murmurs.

"Jesus Christ," I say, laughing. "And now you're following me into the elevator."

He leans past me, his arm brushing my breast. He stills. "I'm not the only one with something stiff around here."

I press my lips together and will my nipples to pipe down as he hits the button for floor three. Frans Franklin & Co Solicitors. Okay, so he's definitely here on business. It's a coincidence. Just a coincidence.

The elevator starts moving, and he steps back into position beside me, his hands joined in front of him. Those fucking hands. My mobile starts ringing. Abbie. I reject the call. Then Charley. I reject her too, peeking out the corner of my eye at him. And quickly looking away when he catches me.

The lift stops, the door opens and he steps out, giving me air. Or some, at least. He gazes at me through hooded eyes. "My hands want to have sex with your hands again."

He tilts his head, and the doors close. "Fucking hell." I fall back against the wall and fan my face with my salad pot, trying to get my body under control before I combust. I laugh to myself. Cringe. "Fucking hell," I murmur.

By the time I've gathered myself, the girls have called me a further five times and I'm back on my floor much later than I hoped. I have a call to prep for. I text them that I'll see them at the gym after work and ignore their disgust but smile to myself when Charley says she'll be there. Obviously my recent encounter with the good-looking bastard from Arlington Hall is good enough reason to cancel the playdate and get her arse to the gym while the kids are in the creche.

Gary's in my office when I get there, still somewhat flustered. "Hey," I say, dumping my lunch on my desk. "How was your meeting with the partners?"

"Uptight Uriel is still uptight, and Sue is as frightening as ever." He drops a file on my desk. "Check out the new short-term plans released by Hello World. You might like them."

"Thanks." I fall into my chair and pull my salad close, but my appetite has run for the hills, my stomach in knots. I scrunch my nose and push it away.

"The conference next week," Gary goes on.

"What about it?"

"The venue's changed."

"Oh. What happened?"

"The Hilton double-booked us. Luckily, they have an alternative option."

"Where?"

"Arlington Hall," he says, easy-breezy, smiling. *What?* "It's in Oxfordshire. Dead posh. Every cloud and all that."

I stare at Gary's back as he leaves, my mouth lax.

Arlington Hall.

What the fucking hell?

Chapter 7

I'm three miles down by the time Abbie and Charley find me in the gym, and their arrival is a thankful distraction from my most recent encounter with the Adonis. I wasn't able to focus for the rest of the day at work, and that's unheard of. My two late-afternoon calls were a mess of gibberish as I tried to recall what advice I was supposed to be giving my clients, both of whom were most unsettled by my uncharacteristically disorderly meetings. Thank you . . .

What the hell is his name?

Abbie hops on the machine on my right, Charley on the left. This isn't our usual pattern for running. I'm always to the far right, Charley to the far left, Abbie in the middle. Age order, oldest down to youngest, which is me. I'm trapped between them, feeling their eyes on me as they find their pace.

"Talk," Charley demands, tying her wild curly hair back as she jogs.

"Now," Abbie adds, adjusting her sports bra to get her huge boobs comfortable.

I blow out my cheeks, my sweat building. "He asked me to dinner again."

"Tell me you said yes this time," Abbie begs. My awkward smile pointed her way gives her the answer she didn't want.

"No, that would be stupid," Charley pipes in, pulling my attention to her. I smile, happy she's on my side.

"She's already had hand sex with him." Abbie laughs. My eyes go back to her. "What's dinner between two people whose hands have made out?"

I roll my eyes.

"Explain this hand sex," Charley says, lifting her hands and looking at them.

"It was more a massage," I reply, my breath a little shorter than the girls'. A very sensual massage. "I was soaping them for something to do."

"Other than ripping off his clothes?" Abbie chuckles.

"Yes," I breathe. "Have you seen how handsome he is?"

"I have indeed, which begs the question: Why you won't just have dinner with him?"

"Because she's smart," Charley says.

"I'm smart," I reiterate. So why did I let him practically seduce me in the restrooms in my work building? I pout. I should be forgiven. *What that man can do with his hands.*

"You're fucking dumb." Abbie sighs. "You're single. Free. Let a man wine and dine you."

"It sounds like he wants more than wining and dining," Charley muses.

My head swings back to her.

"A bit of bodily attention after the wining and dining can't hurt," Abbie says.

Back to her.

"Can't it?"

Back to Charley.

"Definitely not." Abbie smirks. "I can't even begin to imagine how boring sex was with Nick."

I frown, my head turning back to Abbie. "It wasn't *that* bad." Was it?

"But it wasn't that good."

"How do you know? I've never talked about the sex I've had with Nick."

"Exactly. And yet you were straight on the blower to me after just a bit of hand sex with the mystery hot man."

A shudder mixes with the guilt. It's true. Sex with Nick was as predictable—and boring—as my father's misogyny.

"Did he ever make you come through penetration?" she asks.

"Abbie!" I gasp.

"You're so uncouth," Charley grumbles, now getting a little breathless too.

"What about you?" Abbie goes on. "Has Lloyd got the magic moves?"

Charley's nose goes in the air. "A married couple keeps their private encounters private."

"Bollocks." Abbie snorts, laughing. "When you were two bottles deep at my thirtieth, you told me Lloyd likes flicking your bean while you've got your finger up his bum."

I let out a bark of laughter, nearly flying off the end of the treadmill. "Charley," I cry, giving her wide eyes, steadying myself. Her bright-red face—not through running, it should be noted—tells me she absolutely did say that. "How is that even possible?"

"Sixty-nine," she grumbles.

"I'm never sharing a bag of crisps with you ever again."

"I wash my bloody hands."

"Back to hands!" Abbie sings. "Could you have come?"

My head is swinging back and forth so much, I think I've given myself whiplash. "I think I could have," I admit, reliving the whole amazing experience. "I was a puppet on a string for him."

"How delightful," Abbie muses.

"And dangerous," Charley adds. "Don't lose yourself. Remember, that's the whole reason you ended things with Nick."

"I love how sensible you are." I reach across and pat her arm. "Thank you."

"Welcome." Charley looks across to Abbie and sticks her tongue out. "Now, when is our next night out?"

"Still no transaction from Amazonico?" I ask them both, getting a shake of their heads.

"But they said we paid, so we can go back, right?" Charley says.

"I guess so."

"So when?"

"We're easy," I remind our dear friend and mother of two. "So you tell us."

"Not Saturday," Abbie says. "I've got a full-on morning in the shop and a wedding to sort in the afternoon."

"And not Sunday. I've promised my mum I'll go make peace with my father. Maybe Friday?"

"Let me run it past the boss," Charley says.

"We all know who's boss in the Chaytor household." Abbie laughs.

"Do you think Arlington Hall will run their special offer again?" she asks. "It was nice, just the three of us."

"The three of us and the God."

I smile, trying to keep it to myself. "I have a conference there next week."

"At Arlington Hall?" Abbie hits the slow button on her treadmill, stepping onto the sides and grabbing her water.

"Yes," I confirm. "It was supposed to be at the Hilton, but they double-booked."

"So now the company is dragging everyone out to Oxfordshire?"

"Yeah."

"Oohhh, take your bikini. You might steal a chance to dip into a steam room and sweat it out with the God again."

"What are the chances of him being there?" Charley asks.

The thought is annoyingly thrilling. Yes, what *are* the chances? But still, I saw him first in Oxfordshire and second in London. I'd say the chances of bumping into someone in two separate counties in two days were pretty slim.

Chapter 8

Charley couldn't wangle a girls' night on Friday—something about Lloyd being out for a long-planned lads' night that she totally forgot about, so Abbie and I descended on the Chaytor household with wine and nibbles for the adults, and marshmallows for the kids.

"God please, not too many artificial preservatives at this time of day," Charley says as she tips a bag of snacks into a bowl, and I entice Elijah over with a rustle of the bumper bag of the squidgy, sugary treats. "They're hyper enough."

"Look what Aunty Amelia has," I coo, smiling at his chubby bare feet stomping across the wooden kitchen floor. I scoop him up when he makes it to me and pop the marshmallow in my mouth, offering him a bite. He giggles and snatches it from between my lips, leaving me with a small piece to chew through. "Say thank you." He plants a sloppy kiss on my cheek. "Open the wine," I order Abbie as she puts Ena in her high chair and straps her in.

"How long before the sprogs go to bed?" she asks.

"In about six hours, if you give them those marshmallows."

My eyes widen, and I quickly snatch the treat out of Elijah's hand as Abbie takes the bag from me, slams her foot on the pedal of the bin, and drops it in. "Anyone got any sleeping pills?"

I laugh and take a seat at the island with Elijah on my lap, accepting the wine Charley slides across. "Thanks."

"Glad it's the weekend?" she asks.

"Yes."

"Why?" Abbie says, joining me after giving Ena her Tommee Tippee cup. "You work on weekends too."

"This weekend I do," I grumble. "I've got things to catch up on after taking a day off." And falling into too many conflicting daydreams. *You will be having dinner with me.* Only if I agree. And yet I'm certain he could get a yes out of me, despite my adamance. "I—" My mobile rings on the island, buzzing across the marble.

"Don't you dare answer that," Abbie warns, pulling it away from my reach before I have a chance to see who's calling me.

"Come on, it could be a client."

"Exactly, and it's Friday evening." She looks at the screen.

"Who is it?"

"No name," she says, and I settle. I have all my clients saved. "It's probably one of those annoying sales calls." She answers, clicking it to speaker. "Hi, this is Amelia's phone. She can't take your call right now because she's busy fantasising about having hand sex with a perfect stranger in the ladies'. Please leave a message, and she'll call right back when she's *come*."

Charley nearly chokes on a Quaver, while I shake my head in mild despair at my wayward friend.

"She doesn't need to fantasise," a low, deep, sexy voice says, an edge of seriousness lacing the edges. "I'd happily fuck her hands again, or anything else she wants me to fuck."

The Quaver Charley was choking on flies out of her mouth when she coughs, I nearly drop her eldest baby, and Abbie throws my phone on the counter like it's caught fire, looking at me with wide, disbelieving eyes.

"No," I whisper, horrified, frozen, and everything in between, as I stare at my phone, the call still connected.

Elijah bounces on my lap. "Ring, ring!" he cheers. "Hi, hi!"

Charley throws her upper body across the counter, getting her mouth close to my mobile. "There are children present!"

I scramble to reach for my phone, punching at the screen to cut the call. "Oh my God," I breathe, as my friends stare at me with gaping mouths.

"You have to go for dinner with him," Abbie says. "I'm living for this sexual showdown."

"No," Charley snaps. "He's obviously only after one thing."

"And what's wrong with that?" Abbie asks. "She's a free agent. Do you expect her to be celibate until her happily ever after comes along?"

And that's a good point, isn't it? This man isn't happy-ever-after material. And given I'm not interested in a happily ever after *ever* right now, he's a good bet. A safe bet.

Right?

Charley laughs. It's sarcastic. "Don't take relationship advice from the woman who compares every man to a one-night stand she had in France with a man who wouldn't even give her his name."

"He didn't know my name either," Abbie protests. "It was a mutual understanding."

"It's unhealthy."

"Well, I'm sorry, but life doesn't work out perfect for everyone like it has for you." Abbie reaches for the wine and tops up. "Fuck the God, Amelia," she snaps. "That's an order."

"For God's sake." Charley puts her hands over Ena's ears and looks at me to do the same with Elijah. I shrug. One hand is holding my wine, the other holding Elijah on my lap.

"I . . ." I frown when I hear the distant voice of a man. "Can you hear that?" Everyone stills and listens. "There it is again." I follow the sound of the voice.

All the way down to Elijah's hands.

Where my mobile is held between his chubby fingers.

The screen is illuminated.

Oh my God, he's called him back!

I jump up, off-load Elijah onto Abbie, and snatch the phone out of his hand. He immediately screams. "Shit, I'm sorry," I say to Charley as I stare down at the number, cringing.

"Talk to him," Abbie hisses, flapping her hand at me.

On a sigh of resignation and a ton of yet more mortification, I take my wine and leave the kitchen, my phone at my ear. "Hi."

"Who's your friend?"

"Which one?" I ask, looking back to see Abbie following me, her ears pricked. She doesn't make it far. Charley hauls her back to the island and pushes her down onto a stool. I go into the lounge and swipe the toys off a cushion, lowering.

"The loud one," he says.

"That's Elijah."

"Your boyfriend?"

I roll my eyes and try not to smile. "It's Charley's eldest. He's a toddler."

"And Charley is . . . ?"

"One of my best friends."

"From the hotel?"

"Married, kids, house."

"Sounds disgusting."

I lose my fight and smile, and it's so fucking wide. "You're calling me as well as following me now? How did you get my number?"

"From the forms you filled in for your spa day."

"And how did you access those?"

"I know Anouska."

I bet he does. I won't ask how. "That's confidential information."

"I told her it was an emergency."

"What's the emergency?" I ask, sipping my wine.

"My painfully solid cock."

I cough, waiting for him to laugh. He doesn't. "Look—"

"Uh-oh," he breathes. "I have a feeling I'm about to be put in my place."

"I'm flattered, but I'm taking a time-out from men."

"Why?"

"You don't need details."

"No, but I want them."

Take the sex.

This is dangerous ground. "I'm on the breakup diet. It involves wine and work and nothing else."

"Sounds utterly boring. Where's your sense of adventure?"

"You want to take me on an adventure?" I ask, not meaning to sound coy. But I do. I know I do.

"Oh, Amelia, I want to take you to many places."

"Why?"

He's silent for a moment, and I wonder what he's thinking. What he's going to say. "I've never experienced that instant chemistry people bang on about." His voice has lowered, and so has my glass to my knee as I stare at the blank TV screen. "With you, I did."

I bite my lip, intrigued. *Way* too intrigued. He's a man of a certain type. And I'm not talking about his looks, although they're otherworldly. I'm talking about the aura around him. It screams *playboy*, and his behaviour seals my conclusion. I've no doubt sex with him will be an experience I won't forget. I'll probably crave more. I'm already unhealthily addicted to his persistence.

And his hands.

"Have dinner with me," he says quietly.

But I must stick to my guns. Be strong in the face of temptation. I *have* to make partner at the firm, not to prove anything to my dad or the company, but to prove to myself that I can do it. I have to stick to the plan, remain focused. I'd make a mockery of myself if I didn't. He's already blindsided me with a bit of dirty talk and hand sex. I can't even begin to imagine how distracted he could make me if I let him. "I shall politely decline."

"I won't accept your polite decline."

"Then I won't be polite," I say, standing. "Fuck off."

He laughs, and the sound alone forces me to lower back to the couch. "If there's one thing you should know about me, Amelia, it's that I love a challenge."

"I think the one thing I should know is your name."

"Why, if you're refusing to have dinner with me?"

"It feels a bit unfair, since you apparently know so much about me."

"Like the fact you're allergic to nuts?"

"You really did read all the details on that form, didn't you?" I ask, trying to recall everything that was asked and answered.

"I particularly liked the response to the pregnancy question."

I cringe, my nose scrunching. What did I write?

"Not on your fucking Nelly," he says. I can hear the smile in his words. "Does that explain why you're so stiff?"

Stiff. I'm getting drawn in, and I don't want in. I want partnership. "Perhaps go find someone loose," I say, hanging up.

And, weirdly, it doesn't feel good. Not because I'm giving him the cold shoulder, but because I'm denying myself what I know could be a really fucking amazing experience. But I'm wary, and I have a feeling I should be. I stare down at my blank screen, biting at my lip.

It's done.

I stand up, fill my lungs, and go back to the kitchen. The girls both look up. I shake my head.

Abbie sighs.

Charley smiles softly.

Chapter 9

The next morning, after sweating my arse off at the gym, hoping to run off the tension and chase my wandering thoughts away, I walk through the automatic doors of M&S and grab a basket, calling Abbie as I meander down the fresh fruit aisle. "I'm in M&S," I say when she answers, reaching for a pack of sliced mango pieces and popping them in my basket. "What do you fancy for dinner?"

"You choose."

"Busy?"

"Run off my feet. Have we rewound a month back to February? I feel like every man in the land has stopped by to pick up flowers for the woman in their life, and it's not even ten o'clock. Or is it a full moon or something?"

I laugh and pluck a bottle of wine out of the fridge. "What, like it's sending women everywhere crazy, and the men think it's their fault?"

"Maybe."

"I'll get chicken." I pluck a tray of breasts out of the fridge. "Make kievs. Sound good?"

"Oh, and those yummy potato things drenched in cheese. And, come to think of it, get more cheese. I'm in a cheesy mood."

I smile and head for the dairy aisle, loading my basket with various cheeses. "This will make the gym totally pointless this morning."

"Who goes to the gym at eight on a Saturday morning, anyway?"

"Me." I pout. "It sets me up for the day." I pull a baguette from a basket as I pass the bakery section and swing it as I stroll. "So it's a cheese coma and movie tonight?"

"Love it. Don't worry about wine, I have a case full of that delicious French stuff. I've got to go, another two blokes just walked in." Abbie hangs up, and I slip my phone into my gym bag, shifting it farther onto my shoulder, as I roam the rest of the aisles, tossing various sweet treats into my basket to try and even up the ratio with cheese.

Once I've paid, I wander out and cut through the park to Abbie's, enjoying the pre-spring-morning chill on my clammy, post-gym skin. When I get back, I let myself in and toe my trainers off, dumping my shopping on the counter. "Alexa, play my favourite music," I say, pulling out the packs of fruit and natural yoghurt. I pause, smiling to myself, when Blondie's "Heart of Glass" starts playing from all the speakers around Abbie's flat. "Alexa, volume up." I wriggle out of my sweater and throw it on the chair before shimmying over to the cupboard to get a bowl. I load it up, dancing and singing my way around the kitchen as I make my breakfast and unpack my M&S haul before lowering to a chair to eat. I open my laptop and start browsing through the latest news bulletins between spoonfuls, checking for any news on Galactia. Nothing. Still a ton of whispers, people with theories, some conspiracies, but no concrete evidence that the company is onto something big. I pout and take a mouthful of yoghurt, resting back in my chair. "Come on, find the oil," I whisper to my screen, sending my positive thoughts into the universe.

The sound of my phone ringing breaks through Blondie, and I hop up and hurry to where I dropped my gym bag. "Hey," I puff, answering to Abbie. She talks as I wander back to the table, but I can't hear her for the life of me. "Wait a minute," I yell, lowering the volume on the Alexa.

"Having a private party?" she asks.

"Just letting my hair down while I have breakfast." On that, I reach for my ponytail and pull out the hair tie, shaking my hair out.

"I know. Mrs. Hobbs just called me."

"Who's Mrs. Hobbs?"

"The old dear upstairs. She tried knocking on the door, but you obviously couldn't hear her."

I cringe. "Shit, sorry." I hurry to the door and pull it open, finding an empty corridor. "Bring some flowers home for her?"

"Behave while Mummy's at work, will you?" She hangs up, and as the screen clears, I see some missed calls. Five in total. Not Abbie. My heartbeat increases as I stare down at the known unknown number. *His* number. I go back to the table and lower to the chair. And it rings in my hand.

"Shit." I startle and toss it across the table. It's as if my head is telling me to get it as far away as possible to lessen the chances of me folding and answering. And it rings. And rings. And rings.

Shower.

Leaving my mobile on the table, I go take a shower, my hands working roughly through my hair, scrubbing the shampoo in as I mentally chant to myself. Tell myself to resist temptation. Walk away from the danger. Listen to my head.

By the time I'm done, wrapped in a towel, and have made it back to the kitchen, I have four more missed calls. "Jesus, give in, will you?" I murmur, wiping the screen clear.

It rings again. I freeze where I stand. My quivers increase. This is bloody crazy. "Hello," I answer assertively, and yet I can hear the breathiness of my voice as well as I can feel my trembles. I don't know what it is about this guy, but he ruins me.

"Do you always play hard to get?" he says, ruining me further with that rough but silky voice. I can suddenly smell him.

"I'm not playing anything," I assure him.

"Sure. And what have you done on this fine Saturday morning?"

"I've been to the gym." Are we having a chitchat? "And M&S." My frown is massive. "You?"

"I was in the gym too."

I still. "Which gym?"

"Not yours," he confirms, and I deflate. "Because that would be weird, wouldn't it?" I snort to myself. And this isn't? "So tonight," he goes on. "You'll come to dinner with me."

"That wasn't a question."

"It wasn't intended to be."

My forehead bunches as I sit, my mind turning in circles. *It's just dinner.* But his approach, his tenacity, tells me otherwise. He doesn't only want dinner. I growl at myself with frustration. "I don't want to have dinner with you."

"Then we'll skip dinner."

And there it is. My brain just can't compute such bolshiness. "Look," I say, standing. "I have other things going on in my life right now."

"What, so you can't fuck?"

"Are you real?"

"Oh, baby, I'm very real, and you *will* give in."

I scowl at thin air, hating his cockiness. And the fact that he could be right. He looks like an experience no woman should pass up. *Fucking hell.* "I'm going to hang up now," I say, my voice noticeably wobbly.

"Where are you?" he asks.

"What?"

"Where are you?"

I shake my head, my frustration growing. "I'm in my friend's kitchen."

"Your friend's kitchen?"

"I'm staying with her while I find an apartment."

"Right. Because you broke up with someone."

"Right."

"Are you sitting?"

"No."

"You should."

"Why?"

"Sit down, Amelia," he orders. "Now." And like a robot, I slowly lower to the chair. "Put the phone on speaker," he practically whispers. "And place it on the table."

"What the hell are you—"

"Just do it."

"No." I snort, indignant. "Why do you want me to?"

"Don't you trust yourself?"

My jaw rolls, frustration and anticipation getting the better of me. "I trust myself."

"Then do it."

On a sigh I want him to hear, I follow his order.

"Put your hands on your thighs."

I bite at my lip, his voice doing things to me a voice shouldn't do all by itself. I swallow and rest my hands there, my skin heating, my thighs clenching. I know what's happening. Can I stop it?

"Keep them there," he says. "And listen to me. Are you listening?"

My swallow is lumpy. "I'm listening," I whisper. And I'm already shaking.

"Don't move your hands."

I close my eyes and let his voice sink into me.

"Think about my fingers weaving through yours, Amelia. You liked that, didn't you? My big, capable, slippery hands working yours."

Oh fucking hell. But I keep my mouth shut.

"Did. You. Like. It?"

"Yes." I grind the word out, unable to stop myself from admitting it.

"Are your hands still on your thighs?"

"Yes."

"Don't move them."

"I won't move them," I grit out, my body tight, my pussy tight.

"It felt so fucking good, didn't it?" he whispers. I groan quietly, back in the ladies' with his hands all over mine. "I could have bent you over that sink and fucked you into tomorrow, and you would have loved that. Tell me. Tell me you would have loved that."

I inhale, my hand creeping to the inside of my thigh, the pressure building, making me shake. I need to suppress the pulse. Rub myself. Ease the tingles. "I would have loved that."

"Not so stiff now, are you?" he rasps. "In that chair desperate to come to the sound of my voice."

My hand meets my pussy over my workout pants, and my breath hitches.

"You're touching yourself," he whispers. "Fuck, you're touching yourself. Does it feel good?"

I can't talk, can only breathe, my chest pumping, the heat rushing through me. I push my back into the chair, feeling it coming.

"Does it feel good?" he demands harshly. "Tell me, Amelia."

"It feels so good," I cry, throwing my head back. It's coming. *It's coming.*

"Take it, baby. And remember who got you off with his voice alone."

Buzz, buzz, buzz!

I startle, coming into my body on a jarring gasp, my climax fizzling out. "Oh my God." I blink, looking toward the intercom by the door. I'm panting. A little confused. What just happened?

"Amelia?"

I look down at my phone on the table. Then at my hand between my legs. *Fuck.* I scramble to grab my mobile.

"Amelia," he says, sounding urgent.

"I've got to go."

"No, Amelia, do *not* hang up on me."

I cut the call and rush to the telephone by the door, so unstable. "Hello?" I gasp.

"Delivery for Abbie Pearson."

I hit the button to open the main door. "Just leave it in the lobby, thanks." I hang up and fall against the wall, still fucking breathless.

A puppet on his strings.

What that man could do to me.

Abbie plucks a yellow rose from a metal bucket and adds it to the bouquet she's building as I follow her around the florist. "I don't know why you don't just have dinner with him," she says. "Worst case, you get a free dinner. Best case, you get a ride on the stallion."

I roll my eyes. "You're not helping."

"Then why did you come to see me and not Charley?" she asks as she pulls a few sprigs of eucalyptus out and arranges them just so. "Don't answer that, I know why."

I narrow my eyes as she carries on her merry, casual business building a bouquet. "Why?"

"Because, Amelia, you want to have dinner with him, and you know I will encourage you, whereas Charley won't. That's why you're here. Pass me a pussy willow, will you?"

I snatch a twig out.

"And another," she says, placing it precisely as I scowl and pull out another stick. "Thanks." She carries on walking, and I chase her heels. "Have dinner with him. What's the worst that can happen?" She places her built bouquet on a stack of floral paper.

"He nearly made me come just by talking to me, Abbie," I confess, stepping back when she swings around. "He's a master seducer. I'm scared of the power he could have over me."

Abbie blows out her cheeks. "What do you want me to say, Amelia? You're attracted to him. He's obviously attracted to you."

"I just broke up with someone," I grate. "I have to make partner."

"You think sleeping with Mr. Hot as Fuck will change that?"

I laugh under my breath. Yes, actually, he could, because I can't seem to stop thinking about him, and I can't imagine that problem improving if I give in to his persistence and take what he's going to give.

So I won't.

Be sensible.

"Want some help?" I ask. I can't go back to Abbie's, and I have nothing else to do. Except work, and I'm not in the right headspace.

And there's my point. One phone call from the God and I'm a mess.

Abbie smiles, takes my shoulders, and puts me behind the cash register. "You can take the money," she says, throwing me a colourful floral apron with FLORA FLORA emblazoned across the bib. "Corey will show you how to work the card machine. I've got to get the flowers out of the fridge ready for the wedding."

I smile my thanks and shove my bag under the counter, faltering when my phone rings. Abbie raises her brows.

"He's determined, I'll give him that."

"Or his ego's too inflated to lose," I muse, fighting back the mental images of him to the corners of my mind.

He calls a further five times that day.

I answer none.

Chapter 10

My lungs burning, I slow my pace down to a jog and grab the towel off the handles of the treadmill, wiping my forehead and checking the time. Six a.m. The bank of TV screens before me change in perfect sync from *Sky News* to *Good Morning Britain*, and I smile, exhaling. I'm feeling more like myself after spending the rest of the weekend at my parents' helping with all things wedding and then immersing myself in work. He hasn't tried calling again since Saturday night. It's now Wednesday. He's finally given up, and it's a relief. I don't trust myself around him, as proven on numerous occasions. My body just . . . answers him. Sensibility be damned.

A staff member appears in front of me, arms crossed over his inflated chest.

"There's no one else here yet, Chris," I say, retrieving my phone from the band on my arm, now walking briskly. "We agreed six thirty."

"The boss is in early, and no one but you wants to hear about the financial world while they're working out."

I glance around at the empty gym. "But they want to hear the doom and gloom of the real world, do they?"

"The stock market isn't doom and gloom?"

"It wasn't at close of play yesterday." I smile. "And high risk is paying off. Galactia hit gold." I open my screen and smile at the beautiful green numbers that greet me.

"Galactia?"

"There's been whispers for months that they're onto something."

"Gold?"

"Oil, Chris." And now my risky investments have paid off. I'm looking forward to the flurry of calls from my clients singing their joy.

"You said they'd hit gold."

"Never mind." I sigh, slowing to a stop and swiping my screen to check my emails. One's already landed from Mr. Gibbs, who surfs the chat rooms and watches the stocks as keenly as I do. Typically, clients hand over their cash and let me crack on. Not Mr. Gibbs. He's a constant stream of updates, not that I need them. I often ask myself why he lets me play with his money when he's clearly got the time to do it himself. I'm not complaining. He's a chunky percentage of my clients' wealth and a step closer to smashing my numbers. And making partner. I quickly reply to him and hop off the treadmill to go shower. It's a long day ahead.

The finance conference.

A great networking opportunity and a chance to pick Gary's brain discreetly about where the senior partners are at in their search for the new partner. Plus, Tilda Spector will be there. My stomach flutters with anticipation for today and the opportunities ahead. I need to be on my A game, hence my stupidly early visit to the gym.

I go to the changing rooms and lower to the bench, dipping and removing my trainers as I scan the day's schedule. Registration and coffees at nine, keynote speaker at ten—who happens to be the CEO of the event sponsor, Global Finance LLP—a few presentations from financial institutions at eleven, a light lunch at one, a few one-to-one meetings between two and four, and then the closing speech from the FST before the gala dinner. Carriages at nine.

My cheeks balloon. Long indeed. Retrieving my towel and washbag from the locker, I head for the shower, wondering how I'll approach Tilda Spector. I'll let her seek me out. I'm sure she will, and I refuse to be one of what I expect will be many advisers hovering close by like flies around shit. I've always been a medium- to high-risk kind of adviser. I take educated risks and invest my clients' money as if it were my own to be lost. I know Tilda has approached her career with the same mindset, because she told me.

I've got this.

I dry off, then brush my hair and dry it, scooping it up automatically. I pause for thought. Then release it, combing through with my fingers before slipping into my prised Victoria Beckham pencil dress. A total extravagance, but the colour brought me to my knees—a kind of creamy oyster—and I can wear it all day without getting one teeny-tiny crease.

As I'm leaving the gym, Clark calls. "Hey," I say, crossing the road to the station.

"Want a ride?"

"Nope."

"Oh, come on," he drones. "We're going to the same place. Don't be ridiculous."

"I'm not being ridiculous. I can expense it. It's an hour on the train, which gives me time to email some clients and write some reports. If I ride with you, I'll arrive with an earache after you've unsuccessfully tried to convince me I should be working for the family business."

"I promise I won't talk to you."

I smile, hovering outside the Tube station rather than descending into the bowels of London and losing my network. "I don't believe you."

"How was Sunday?" he asks.

"I'm not allowed to talk to you about Sunday." It was lovely. Wine, dresses, table plans. Plus, I was able to wangle Abbie and Charley an invite to the hen party.

"I'm not talking about the wedding. You and Dad."

"We're fine," I assure him. "He did what our dad does, and I accepted his non-apology." Which was a guilty smile, a hug, a pat on the back, and a kiss in my hair. Because we'll do it all over again next week, or perhaps the week after, when he forgets himself and tries to fix my life that doesn't need fixing.

"But you're still living at Abbie's?"

"Yes, until something comes up."

"And Mum's okay with that?"

"When I lived with them, I left before they got up, and I saw them for an hour before bed, if I wasn't working late or out with the girls. She won't miss me." We both know that's not true. I suppose I'm justifying it to myself. But I shouldn't punish Mum because of Dad's loose lips. She likes knowing I'm around, even if I'm not around. But, honestly, it's like running the gauntlet of judgments every time I step foot in their house. And I'm thirty. That's one thing Dad was right about. It's unhealthy living with my parents. Not much healthier living with my best friend. God, I hope something comes up soon. "Listen, I'm hanging around outside the station just so you can make me feel guilty."

"I don't want you to feel guilty. I want you to come work for . . . *with* me."

"You're deluded. How many times was Dad in the office last week?"

"Twice. Maybe three times. Or was it four?"

"Clark," I breathe tiredly.

"Okay, it was five."

I laugh. "So technically, even if Dad's retired and has handed the reins to you, you still work for him."

"Not for long, but it needs a delicate approach."

I can't argue with that. All Dad's known is the family business. He's struggling to find his place in life beyond that. Mum's always been the homemaker, Dad the breadwinner. "It's his birthday soon. How about we sign him up for golf lessons?" I suggest.

"Fuck yes. Brilliant idea. You look into that. Let me know how much I owe you."

"I will."

"Let me at least pick you up from the station at the other end so you don't have to piss around with a cab to the hotel."

"Fine," I relent. "My train gets in at eight fifteen."

"I'll be there."

Halfway down the steps, my phone rings again, and I stop when I see an out-of-town number. "Hello?"

"Morning."

My body instantly tenses, a man catching my shoulder as he dashes past me down the steps. *Hang up. Hang up.* And my current state, hot and bothered, heart racing, is exactly why I need to avoid this guy. I've suddenly forgotten where I'm going, who I am. With just one word. The last time he talked to me, he nearly brought me to orgasm.

"This isn't your mobile number."

"No, it's not. You're not answering calls from my mobile, so I thought I'd try calling you from a different line."

He's crafty. "Now's really not a good time." I turn and walk back up the steps, getting out of the way of the commuters.

"But this coming Saturday works, so you'll come to dinner with me."

My God, I've never come across such an indomitable man. So much for my conclusion that he's backed off. "Aren't you hearing what I'm saying to you?"

"I'm hearing, Amelia. You want me."

At those very words, a powerful throb hits me between my thighs. I look around me, at the chaos on the London street. Silence. Just his words bouncing around in my mind.

"Saturday," he repeats.

"No."

"Fucking hell, Amelia," he breathes, completely exasperated. "It's just dinner."

"Is it?" I ask on a laugh. "Because your approach to this point would suggest otherwise."

Silence. He has no comeback for that.

"Look, I've got to go."

"No, Amelia, wait."

A woman catches my shoulder as she rounds the corner into the Tube station, knocking me into the wall. "Oh, Jesus, I'm sorry," she splutters, taking my arm to steady me. "I didn't see you."

I blink, looking at my mobile in my hand.

"Amelia?" he says. "Amelia, talk to me."

I hang up and catch my breath.

"Are you okay?" the woman asks, prompting me to force a smile and reassure her I'm fine. And grateful. I was a heartbeat away from caving. "So sorry," she says again, before getting on her way.

I take a moment to realign and remind myself of where I'm going. Not just today, but in my career. My life. I hurry down the stairs to the Tube, my throat tight, unexpected and unwanted anger getting the better of me.

Not today.

Today, I need to be focused.

Chapter 11

"It's hardly accessible, is it?" Clark says as he weaves the country roads to Arlington Hall. "Whose idea was it to move the conference here?"

"The Hilton double-booked, apparently. This was a last resort." I lift my shades and look at the clear blue sky, inhaling the countryside air through the slightly open window of Clark's Range Rover Sport. I got absolutely zero work done on the train as intended, only adding to my restlessness. "It just smells so clean, doesn't it?"

"It smells like horseshit to me."

"You couldn't live in the country?"

"Fuck no. Look." Clark points to his dashboard, in particular the bars on his network service. "One bar."

I lower my shades and check my own phone. I don't have *any* bars. I scrunch my nose, but then gasp when one bar appears. And quickly disappears again. I drop it back into my bag.

"So explain the new hairdo," he says, looking across at me, smiling.

Uncomfortable, I reach for my long hair and comb through the ashy blond waves. "It's not new."

"It's down."

"And?"

"And you never wear your hair down for work."

"It gets in my way." *Stiff.* I squirm.

"Jesus, these roads are narrow," Clark grumbles, slowing to a crawl on a corner. "Fuck!" An alarm on the car starts beeping, and Clark slams on the brakes, making my hand shoot out and grab the dashboard.

"Jesus, get me there alive, won't you?" I breathe.

"If I can get you there at all. How the hell am I supposed to get past that monster?"

I spot what he's talking about and frown. A huge yellow tractor, as wide as the road is, the gigantic wheels creeping onto the verge on each side. And it just keeps coming at us. "I think he wants you to back up."

Clark looks in the rearview mirror, assessing what's behind us. "I didn't see any passing bays, did you?"

"I wasn't looking." The tractor keeps coming. "Hasn't he noticed us?"

"Shit." Clark knocks the car into reverse and starts backing up the road, and my neck cranes, looking up into the tractor's cab. The old boy behind the wheel looks straight over the Range Rover, and I question whether he's actually seen us.

"He's chewing a wheat sheaf," I say. "And wearing a bucket hat. How country."

"Wonderful," Clark mutters, eventually making it to a small lay-by and pulling in. The tractor chugs past, the farmer's attention never faltering from the road ahead. "You're welcome," Clark says in disbelief. "Ignorant fuckwit." He pulls back out and puts his foot down, and we're soon pulling through the gold gates of Arlington Hall. "Fucking hell," he murmurs.

"I know." I shift in my seat, admiring the crystal-clear stream stretching into the distance.

"You know?"

"This is where I came for my spa day with the girls."

"Of course," Clark breathes, pulling to a stop at the gatehouse. "I thought I'd heard of it when we got the change-of-venue email." Letting down his window, he smiles at the man on the gate—the same man who let Abbie through last week. I read the name on his badge. Nelson. "Clark Lazenby and Amelia Lazenby. Here for the conference."

"Yes, of course." He gestures down the driveway. "Please, there's staff at the entrance who will direct you to the car park."

"Thanks." The barrier lifts and Clark drives through, continuing to ooh and ahh at the plush grounds of Arlington Hall. "Fuck, there's a helicopter pad. I wonder who owns this place? Now *that* would be a client to bag."

"Her name was Evelyn Harrison," I say. "She died. I don't know who owns it now."

"I'll soon find out." Clark hits me with a cheeky grin, pulling up around the fountain. "My God, that's a Jaguar E-Type Roadster."

"What?"

He points to a silver vintage car, practically drooling. "It's my dream car."

"I thought this was your dream car?"

"It was. Shit, a 1961?" He gets out of his Range Rover and walks the length of the car, admiring the shiny paintwork. "Do you know how rare these are? And, fuck, it's in mint condition. It must be worth a small fortune."

"Since when have you been interested in classic cars?" I ask, getting my workbag out and leaving my gym bag on the back seat.

"Since one of my new clients gave me a private viewing of his collection."

Arlington Hall looms over us as I take in air. It's crazy the apprehension I'm feeling. Crazy. But I can't help feeling it. The last time I was here, just over a week ago, I got something wholly unexpected.

Butterflies.

"This way, please, madam," a green-suited man says, guiding me toward the reception area. I walk in and immediately find Evelyn Harrison's portrait.

"That's her," I say to Clark. "Isn't she something?" Just the way she holds herself. So bloody elegant.

"You know," Clark says wistfully, "some people you just look at and know they're richer than God." He spots some colleagues and wanders off as Anouska comes out of a staff door behind reception. She looks up, sees me, frowns, and then realises who she's looking at, smiling. It must be my hair that momentarily threw her.

"Hi," I say, approaching.

"Miss Lazenby, how lovely to see you." I can tell she's dreading the possibility of me grilling her over the information a perfect stranger got from a confidential file she holds.

"I'm here for the conference, so thought I'd grab my wallet."

"Of course. I'll get it from the safe." She hurries off and returns a moment later, handing it over. "Registration is that way." She points to a glass corridor that leads to another part of the hotel. "In the Kent Suite. Just a heads-up, given the change in venue, we're asking attendees to reselect their dinner choices." She smiles, awkward. "Please do make sure you let them know about your allergy."

"I will."

"Is it severe?" she asks, joining me on the walk through the glass tunnel toward the Kent Suite.

"I don't think so. I didn't drop down dead when I took a bite of my friend's Nutella toast when we were ten, so that's positive." I reach into my handbag. "I've been caught out a few times over the years, so I carry these."

Anouska looks at my EpiPens and winces. "Caught out?"

"I picked up the wrong iced coffee in Pret once." My nose scrunches. "It had almond syrup in it."

"Oh no, what happened?"

"Breathlessness, fast heart. A mad dash for the ladies' to sit down in private and let the EpiPen do its work."

"And that's it? You give yourself a shot and you're okay?"

"Pretty much." I slip my EpiPens back in my handbag. "The first few times it happened, my mum would take me to the hospital so they could monitor me, but I've learned to manage it over the years and listen to my body." I'm dying, just dying, to ask her how she knows the man. Who is he? How old, his name, what he does for a living? I quickly pull my thoughts back into line, getting increasingly frustrated with myself and my inability to keep my mind from straying to him.

"Let me know if you need anything—I'll be happy to help." Anouska's peace offering for giving out information on me?

"Thanks." I smile as she walks off, but it drops when I see someone. He spots me, and I groan as he puffs his chest out. Of course I knew he'd be here. Of course I planned on avoiding him; I make a point of it daily at work. Problem is, Leighton Steers likes to be seen. And heard. And admired.

"Lazenby," he says, smoothing a hand through his hair. He should have been a salesman. *Slick.*

"Steers," I say, my smile tight.

"What's with the hair?" He reaches for my loose blond waves and flaps them a little, and it's all I can do not to kick him in the bollocks. He doesn't intend to be sexist. It's in his bloodline.

"Don't touch my hair, Steers," I warn, a little playful, a lot serious. His hands come up in surrender, his body moving back. I can't believe this is the douchebag I'm up against for partner.

"Nice place, huh? I bet the lucky fucker who owns this is worth a few quid." He jiggles his eyebrows. "They'll be my client by the end of the day, just you watch."

"If they own this place, I expect they have their financial affairs in order."

"Everyone is free game." Leighton swaggers off and gets all guy-like with a few of the men from LB&B.

"God, I hate him."

"Why?" Gary's assistant, Shelley, joins me, holding out a lanyard. "Because he's sexist and narrow-minded? Or because he's a plain dickhead?" I laugh as Shelley gives me a sardonic look, and I accept my name badge. "If it makes you feel any better, I hope you thrash him and make partner."

"Thanks."

"I better go hand out the rest of the name badges. I have a special one for Leighton." She holds up a little white card that says PRICK and slips it behind the card with his name on it. I press my lips together and watch Shelley slope off, slipping my lanyard over my head and frowning when I have to reach back and sweep my hair out from under it. I should have tied it up.

After a coffee and a few hellos, we're directed through another glass tunnel and I'm once again in awe of Arlington Hall. Blades of water pour over smooth stone troughs onto pebbled channels that stretch the length of the walkway, and canopies of huge palm leaves climb the glass. White gloss wooden doors lead into a huge auditorium reminiscent of an old theatre, the chairs deep-red velvet, the fittings gold and intricate. It's very art deco, and absolutely stunning.

"It's the fanciest conference room I've ever seen," Gary muses as I gaze up to the gold cornicing decorating the ceiling. With every inch more of Arlington Hall I see, Evelyn Harrison becomes more of an icon.

An attendant guides me to the third row, and I lower to the soft plush chair, with Shelley on the inside of me and Gary and Leighton on the outer two seats. I see many faces I recognise from the industry, nods and handshakes happening all around.

"I like the hair," Shelley says, forcing my hand back up to brush it over my shoulder.

"Thanks." I never anticipated my hair would cause such a stir. I collect the program from the back of the seat in front of me and flick through the schedule, making sure I'm carving out enough time during the one-to-ones to move in on my intended targets. My phone dings, and I open the message from Tilda Spector, smiling.

Are you here? I've not seen you. TS.

Third row back, near the aisle.

The Invitation

I crane my neck, searching the auditorium for her mop of silver hair and signature thick-framed glasses. I come up blank, returning my attention to my mobile when it dings again.

> Oh, I see you. I'm four rows behind you. I didn't recognise you with your hair down. TS.

I roll my eyes and turn, craning my head and finding her past someone directly behind me. "Hey," I say, holding up a hand. "Would be great to catch up later if you have some time."

"Always time for you, Amelia." Her brown, friendly eyes shine behind her glasses. "How's Nick?"

My lips straighten. "He's good."

Tilda takes her compact mirror out of her designer purse and checks her lips. She's so quirky, famous in the industry for being stylish as well as studious. Her frames always match her outfit, and today she's in a cobalt-blue skirt suit with matching frames. "Find me after lunch."

I nod and return my attention to the stage, feeling Leighton's beady eyes directed at me. I look across Gary to him and smile, all friendly, as a woman in a trouser suit walks onto the stage, approaching the podium and adjusting the microphone. Waiting for the noise to die down, she smooths back her slick hair, and I think to myself how . . . stiff she looks. I cringe and tuck one side of my hair behind my ear, not used to it featuring in my working day. For the first time, I question why. And for the first time, I admit to myself that I need to be taken seriously. How hair affects that, I don't know, but a man once said to me while I was working for my father, "Well done, Amelia. So you're not just a pretty face?" And I wondered if that's how people saw me. Just a pretty face. From that day on six years ago, my hair was tied back. How ridiculous.

Or maybe not.

"Welcome, ladies and gentlemen, to the FSA Annual Finance Conference." She pauses, allowing a light applause. "My name is Kerry

Gallow, and I will be your moderator throughout the event. I very much look forward to making the day as enjoyable and productive as possible." She nods, smiling, her hands holding the sides of the podium. So fucking stiff. "Before I hand over to the legendary Garret Palmer—CEO of the FSA—to officially welcome you, we have a small adjustment to the day's schedule in light of the last-minute change in venue. So please welcome to the stage the owner of the fine Arlington Hall, our venue this year, Mr. Jude Harrison."

Turning her body to the stage entrance, she starts to clap, and everyone rises from their seats and joins her. Leighton leans across Gary, smiling at me. "Fair game," he says, winking.

"Have at him," I murmur, returning my attention to the stage. *Such* a dick.

"Lord have mercy," Shelley whispers, just as my eyes land on the man walking onto the stage.

What the ever-loving fuck? My clapping hands slow, my smile fading, as Jude Harrison makes his entrance. "Oh my fucking God," I whisper, jolting where I stand, instantly burning up.

"Right?" Shelley whispers out the corner of her mouth. "He's *got* to be illegal."

Jude Harrison. The owner of Arlington Hall.

Hey Jude.

You should definitely try Hey Jude.

"Fuck, fuck, fuck." I watch him, his long legs, his grey-suited, *killer* body. He reaches up and tucks a loose piece of his dark-blond hair behind his ear, his lazy eyes taking in the crowd.

Jesus, he's . . .

Shit, he's divine.

Coming to a stop at the podium, he clears his throat, waiting for the applause—and probably the awe—to die down. Everyone eventually takes their seats, and he starts to speak. "Good morning, I'm Jude Harrison," he says, leaning slightly over the mic. His words, just a plain introduction, are like feathers tickling over my skin, making my

The Invitation

shoulder blades pull in, along with my breath. I look down at my bare arm. Goose bumps. "What an honour it is to host this year's conference at Arlington Hall." He smirks, and I push my thighs together to suppress the developing throb. How? How can he do this to me? "Despite being an afterthought," he adds seriously. The crowd laughs lightly, and I gaze around to see every woman in the room enchanted.

Jude Harrison.

Fucking hell.

"I can't believe it," I say to myself.

"What?" Gary asks.

"Nothing."

"Arlington Hall is a special place," Jude Harrison continues when the room quiets down again. "So please explore the grounds in between your hardcore business mingling. Enjoy the food, and when business concludes and you allow yourself some time to *loosen* up, maybe I can tempt you with one of our famous cocktails."

I sit up straight. *Loose?*

Fucking hell. Does he know I'm here? I shift in my seat, getting hotter and more unsettled by the second. Then his eyes fall onto me and my insides explode. He doesn't smile. Just holds me in place with his stare for a few moments. Speaking to me without speaking. *Loosen up.* At a work event? Never, although I'm seriously considering the merits of alcohol right now. My nerves are absolutely shredded.

"Some of the best deals are made over a relaxed drink," he says, a definite suggestive edge to his tone. "I recommend the Hey Jude—inspired by me and created by my wonderful mother, the late Evelyn Harrison." My fluster is momentarily forgotten when I see a wave of sadness pass across his otherworldly, handsome face. His eyes drop to the podium, and he seems to smile mildly to himself. *Jude Harrison, you are less steely than you portray.* Evelyn Harrison. His mum. The elegant, graceful beauty in the portrait. I can see it now. The twinkly eyes that straddle the line between blue and green. Almost like the sea. "She's the lady behind Arlington Hall," he goes on, clearing his throat. "I'm the lucky one who gets to showcase her achievements." Jude Harrison seems to inhale and release slowly, as if merely talking about his mother chokes him up. "So on behalf of my family and I, enjoy your day. I'm sure you'll agree by the end of your time here at Arlington Hall, it's a really special place. I hope you remember it, whether that be for a deal you strike, the food you taste, the cocktails you try, or the acquaintances you make." His eyes fall onto me again. "I'm at your disposal. So, please, make the most of me. I sincerely hope it's not the last time I see you."

As everyone stands and applauds, I remain in my seat, scared to even try to use my legs, my eyes nailed to the back of the guy who's in front of me. When Shelley looks down at me in question, I somehow convince myself to rise.

And am forced to take a breath when Jude Harrison comes back into view.

He watches me in the crowd. My insides burn, my heart pounds. What is this madness?

He eventually nods and steps back from the podium, slipping his hands into his pockets. Out of sight. I sense a silent message. I don't know what. He'll keep them to himself?

I drop my gaze, needing a break from his intense stare. He must have known I'd be here. I told him I'm good with numbers. I told him what I do for a living. He would have seen the list of attendees. And he didn't think to tell me who he is before striding out on that stage and giving me the shock of my life? He wanted to catch me off guard. Trap me? My phone dings, and I swallow as I read the message.

> **You look even more beautiful with your hair loose and wild.**

His mobile is in his hand when I glance up, and he's spinning it. Eyes never wavering from mine as he pushes his hair back with his spare hand.

Make time for me today.

It's a demand. My lungs squeeze, air suddenly impossible to find. I can't breathe. I need to breathe. I need air. "Excuse me," I say to Gary, motioning past him, feeling panic rising fast.

"Everything okay?" he asks as I shuffle past him and Leighton, so fucking wobbly.

Shit, how can I explain my behaviour? I need a moment to gather myself. Regroup. Dig deep for the strength I'm going to need today to maintain my focus. "Yes, just a family emergency." I hold up my phone. "I won't be long." I hurry up the aisle in my heels, catching Clark's eye as I pass him a few rows back. His concern is instant. I hold up a hand, smiling, assuring him I'm fine. I'm not fine. I've been struggling to take my mind off Jude Harrison for over a week. His hands, his hair, his stunning face, his tall, lean physique. His chest. His jaw. His fucking eyes that drip sex. What he can do to me without even fucking touching me. And that's when he's out of sight. Now he's here?

"No," I say to myself as I make it outside the auditorium and rush through the glass tunnel. I realise quickly that I have no idea where the ladies' bathrooms are—the only ones I've used here were in the changing rooms on the other side of the hotel in the spa. "Shit." I spot Anouska.

"Miss Lazenby?" she says in question as I approach.

"I'm looking for the ladies'."

"Just through there on the right." She motions back through the glass tunnel.

"Thank you," I call, hurrying back the way I came, but I come to an abrupt halt when Jude Harrison pushes his way out the double doors from the auditorium, looking a little ruffled.

And worried.

"Amelia," he breathes, checking me up and down. I don't do the same. Reminding myself of the splendour before me won't help. Not that I need a reminder. Everything Jude Harrison is embedded in my mind. "What's wrong?" He moves toward me, and I move back, making him still, the concern on his face maddening.

What's wrong? Where does he want me to start? I could be here all fucking day, and I don't have time. I walk away, heading for the ladies', but stop when I hear his fancy dress shoes join the clicking of my heels on the marble.

I swing around. "Do *not* follow me," I snap, backing up, keeping him in place with my eyes. His are full of uncertainty. I'm sure mine are full of annoyance.

I reach the door and push my way inside, not taking even a brief moment to appreciate the opulence surrounding me. I set my phone by the cream marble, resting my hands on the sink and closing my eyes. Jude Harrison. He owns Arlington Hall? All along? All-a-fucking-long?

My darkness is invaded by visions—all him. In the Library Bar, in his lovely suit, the spa in his black shorts, in the reflection of the mirror when he seduced my hands. "No, no, no." I snap my eyes open and stare at myself in the mirror, silently ordering my brain to recalibrate. Today is important. So fucking important. How dare he steer me off course? How dare he! "Come on, Amelia," I say to myself. "Remember why you're here."

The doors open, and I look past my reflection. Of course he didn't listen to me.

Don't wash your hands.

He finds me in the mirror, slowly releasing the door. "Amelia?"

"Jude," I say, for the first time using his name. Because I know it now. Who he is, what he does.

"You're pissed off," he murmurs.

"I'm sorry, were you expecting something else from me?"

"Well, I didn't expect this," he says, remaining by the door. Wise.

I drop my head, looking down into the sink. What the hell did he expect? I've told him repeatedly to back off. It doesn't matter that it's taking everything out of me. It doesn't matter that I'm incredibly attracted to him. It doesn't matter that I desperately want to explore this mad chemistry. It doesn't fucking matter that I'm obsessing about him. I've told him to leave me alone, and he isn't.

Fuck.

"Your hair is down," he says, as if that means more than I've simply changed the way I wear my hair. I flinch. *Stiff.*

"I'm wearing my hair down," I confirm quietly. I don't have the capacity right now to read into my own reasoning.

"Why can't you look at me?"

"I can look at you. I just don't want to."

"Why?"

I bite down on my back teeth. "Stop it."

"No."

"Jude, please."

"Don't make me say it. Don't make me spell out how attracted I am to you."

I inhale, beginning to shake as he comes to a stop directly behind me. *Close.* I can feel myself falling under his spell. Mesmerised by him. The aura sucking me in. This is a man who could derail me. Not with a baby or marriage, but with plain, overwhelming, uncontrollable lust. He's disarming, smart, successful, and devastatingly handsome. Denying my attraction, my desires, would be so fucking dumb. "I can't do this today." Not any day. I tense when his hand meets the small of my back. His touch burns my skin through my dress. He slides it up to my neck. "Jude, please." I soften under his grip as he massages my nape. His front meets my back, his other hand sliding onto my stomach.

"What are you begging for, Amelia?" he asks, pulling me tighter to his body. He moves my hair away from my neck, breathes across my skin. Wildfire sweeps through my veins, my arse pushing back into his groin. "Tell me."

I honestly don't know what I'm begging for. Him? This? Space? Sense? Air?

Resistance?

But you can't resist the irresistible, and Jude Harrison has proved time and again that he's irresistible.

"Dinner," he whispers, bombarding every sense I have.

I moan, letting the feeling take me. I'm a puppet again. Not in control of my reactions, my head and body bending to his will.

"Yes," he whispers, encouraging me to say it too. My heavy breathing becomes heavier. My breasts ache. My thighs clench. "As soon as this event is done, you can skip the gala dinner and eat with me."

Another moan. My God, he's like magic on my body, drawing feelings that are new and fucking amazing.

More.

His mouth moves to my ear. My body rolls. I turn my face toward him, waiting for his lips to find mine. "You owe me a chance to get to know you more," he says, nuzzling my cheek. "And you owe yourself a chance to explore this."

I owe him.

Amelia, you owe me some kind of commitment.

I jolt, coming back into my body, and Jude looks up at me in the mirror, his hands holding me tighter on my neck and hip, as if he's aware—and worried—I'm about to withdraw.

"I have to go," I say.

His frown is colossal. "What?"

I wriggle free of his fierce grip, pulling at my dress, before moving to my hair, brushing through the ends, trying to make myself presentable. My hair wouldn't be an issue if I had only fucking tied it up.

"Amelia, what the hell are you doing?"

"I'm here on business," I say with grit. "I don't believe you are included in that." I walk to the door. "And I owe you nothing."

"What the fuck?" Jude breathes. "Amelia!"

I haul the door open and quickly get yanked back into the ladies'. "What are you doing?" I yell, losing my shit. He's already pulled me away from the conference during the keynote speaker. I'm distracted, my eye off the ball. I can't allow that.

"You wanted me to kiss you just then. So what happened?"

"I don't want to see you, not today, not tomorrow."

He recoils, looking injured. It infuriates me even more.

"Do not contact me." I pull the door open again and storm out, getting more and more worked up. How dare he. I *owe* him?

I owe him a slap. Nothing more. "Fucking hell," I hiss, tugging at my dress, the material sticking to my clammy skin. Distress isn't an emotion I'm used to. I don't like it. Not at all.

By the time I make it back to my coworkers, I've missed fifteen minutes of the opening welcome speech. I apologise to Gary, assuring him everything is fine, and take my seat. But can I concentrate? No. And that only angers me more.

Chapter 12

I'm on the verge of tears, fighting to hold them back, when everyone is guided from the auditorium. It's pure frustration. Disappointment, but only with myself. I remained caught between my focus and daydreams while highfliers of the financial world talked about their journeys, the changes they've seen over the years, and what's to come. Jude Harrison poked at every corner of my mind constantly, disrupting my concentration. I'm not walking out of this conference feeling nearly enlightened enough. Not about matters of my career, at least. I am, however, enlightened, if I needed to be, that Jude Harrison is a man on a mission. And I want him.

But I shouldn't have him.

After dinner I search for Tilda Spector, hoping to get my day back on track. A lady stands outside the Kent Suite, a tray of cocktails in hand. "No, thank you," I say, smiling as I help myself to a water instead. I spot Tilda across the room and smile when she waves me over, forcing it to remain in place when I see Leighton's already sniffed her out. My nemesis is a fucking leech. "Tilda," I say, accepting her continental kiss.

"Amelia, how have you found today?"

I cringe, not because Leighton has just followed Tilda's lead and kissed my cheeks too, but because I'm not nearly as furnished as I should be. So I simply say, "Excellent, you?" throwing it back at her.

"Tilda was just telling me she's gearing up to retire," Leighton says, his smile at risk of splitting his face as he sips his drink. He's not held back on the temptation of a cocktail. No surprises there. I expect he made the most of the free wine on the tables at dinner too.

"Really?" I say, sounding genuinely staggered. So the rumours *are* true.

"Slowing down," Tilda clarifies, giving Leighton a high brow. "I'm only fifty-two."

"And looking ravishing as always."

She laughs under her breath before taking my elbow and leading me away from him, much to his disappointment. Shame on me, I smirk over my shoulder at him.

"Come take a seat with me." Tilda leads me to a table and pulls a chair out, encouraging me to sit. "Now talk to me." She takes a seat. "What's the future hold for Amelia Lazenby?"

Partnership, I hope. "I can only dream of the respect you hold in the financial world, Tilda."

"It sounds like you're on your way."

My glass pauses at my lips. "It does?"

"Gary speaks very highly of you."

"He does?" Why the hell is my voice squeaky?

She laughs. "Don't be coy. You've raced up the ranks at LB&B. Nick must be feeling quite proud."

I wince. No, actually, he tried to stunt my growth. *You owe me some kind of commitment.*

"Is he here?" she asks, glancing around. "I haven't seen him."

"I think someone else is here representing his company this year." I made sure I kept my eye on the list of attendees. I sigh to myself, taking a breath and biting the bullet. It's not that I don't want people to know, but more I just don't want to talk about it. And Nick's clearly not telling people we've split up. Is he still hoping? "Nick and I aren't together anymore."

"Oh, well, that's a surprise." She withdraws. "What went wrong? No, sorry, that's none of my business."

"It's fine. I guess we grew apart."

Tilda hums, as if she's suspicious of the true circumstances surrounding the demise of Nick and me. "What's your client file looking like these days?"

This isn't something I'd usually discuss with another adviser, but, well, this is Tilda Spector. If she's offering an ear, you talk to it. "Healthy, actually, but more room for growth, obviously."

She nods. "Always. I heard you recently took on a certain Mr. Neilson."

"Oh yes, by pure default, mind you. A senior partner left LB&B, and his clients were disbanded between various advisers at the company while they look to replace him as partner. You know Mr. Neilson?"

"Oh, I know him."

That doesn't sound promising. "And?" I ask, tongue in cheek. "Want to share anything?"

Tilda leans in, laughing. "Between you and me, I heard his wife is taking him to the cleaners. I expect he'll be cashing in, probably to try and hide his stash."

"Shit," I murmur, and quickly apologise for it, as I try to remember the value of his portfolio. "He only plays safe," I muse, as it comes back to me. "A ton of ISAs."

"Instant access," Tilda confirms. "Thought you should be prepared."

Brilliant. Not that there's much I can do about it. I can't stop a client from pulling in resources, no matter what they intend to do with the money. Like, in Mr. Neilson's case, hide it. Which is pretty bloody impossible. If I'm asked for records, I'll provide records. It's then up to his soon-to-be ex-wife to prove he's not blown the cash she *thought* he had. "Thanks for the insight."

Tilda sips her drink, a coy smile stretching her lips. "Christ, have you tried this stuff?" She waves a waitress over and plucks one of the ribbed cocktail glasses off the tray. A whole palm leaf coats the inside, the white liquid cloudy. "Here."

"Oh, I shouldn't." I hold up a hand, smiling.

"Look around, Amelia." She glides a perfectly manicured hand around the room, and I look, seeing most people holding a glass containing a palm leaf. "Plus, this drink is like nothing you'll have tasted before."

"No, really." I need my wits about me, and not just because this is a work function.

"Do you want some advice?" Tilda asks, leaning in.

"Okay," I reply, nervous. If she tells me to loosen up, I'll scream.

"Always stay a few drinks behind the rest." She pushes the glass into my hand. "They're all two deep already, not to mention the wine they've had with dinner. This is my first, as it is yours."

I smile and take a sip. "Oh my fucking Christ," I blurt as the liquid caresses its way down my throat. Tilda chuckles. "Sorry."

"Not at all, this is a very refreshing Amelia."

"It's so good." I'm getting vodka, lychee, a bit of pineapple.

"Tell me about it. He was right."

"Who was?"

"The very impressive male who welcomed us to Arlington Hall. This is the Hey Jude."

I look at the glass. "Oh." And feel eyes on me immediately. Jude's by the doors. And he looks furious. He's definitely not licking his wounds. No. He's preparing for battle. *Fuck.*

I place the glass down—a further rejection—as Jude watches, and get back to Tilda. "So, you're winding down?"

She laughs, relaxing back. "Yes, I've done my time, earnt my stripes. I have other things I want to pursue, and now it would seem the vultures are out to circle the meat on offer."

Oh God, I hope she doesn't see me as one of those vultures. "I'm sure." I smile tightly.

"You're not a vulture, Amelia. That's why I like you. Have you ever considered a mentor?" she asks. "I don't mean someone to tell you how to do business, but more how to develop in your career. You've clearly got what it takes. I guess what I'm saying is personal growth is as important as actually winning business and keeping it. What are your boundaries, your principles, your goals for your clients, your own personal goals? That kind of thing. Give me one of your goals."

I'm struggling to concentrate with Jude's burning gaze on me. "I want to make partner."

"Why?" she fires back. "What are you trying to prove and to who?"

I bite my lip. "I want to prove to myself that I've got what it takes. That my decision to pass on other opportunities was worth it."

She smiles knowingly. Tilda knows my father. Tilda knows everyone. "Don't waste time trying to prove others right. You're the head of your own personal boardroom, Amelia. Choose who you invite into that room carefully." She stands, and my gaze rises with her. "It's been a pleasure chatting with you."

"And you, Tilda."

She walks away, and despite not having achieved what I set out to, I feel like I've taken so much from that conversation. And while it makes me happy, it also saddens me that my father has never encouraged me or offered such valuable advice.

I sigh and look at the cocktail on the table before me. I hate that it was delicious. Delicious like the man it's founded on. And I hate that I desperately want another taste. I chew the edge of my lip, my eyes following the source of heat. He hasn't moved, not his body or his eyes, his stance wide, his hands in his pockets.

"So, what's the lowdown?" Leighton drops into the seat Tilda just vacated and leans in toward me, his elbows resting on his knees, totally invading my personal space.

I lean back and narrow one eye. "You want me to relay the conversation I just had with Tilda Spector?"

"Sure, we're friends, aren't we?" He cocks a smile I'm sure many women would find appealing. Unfortunately for Leighton, I know him.

"Friends?" I ask.

He pouts, coming that little bit closer. "Or more, if that's what you're looking for. I heard you've recently become single."

I laugh under my breath. He would totally fuck his way to the top. Do whatever it takes. Screw people over, tread all over them. Yes, you have to be ruthless, but something Tilda just said has resonated. *You're the head of your own personal boardroom, Amelia. Choose who you invite into that room carefully.*

"More?" I ask, moving in closer to Leighton, making sure my smile is demure. I'm not Leighton's type. I have a brain, for a start, which is why I know not to go anywhere near him, not in my personal life *or* my business life. I just have to endure him at work until I no longer have to endure him.

His eyes fall to my lips. "More," he whispers. "I'm sure there's a room available at this swanky place."

He makes me sick. But I don't have the chance to tell him to fuck off. He's suddenly moving back rapidly, falling to his arse, his drink going everywhere. I gasp, seeing his chair clatter across the floor. And then a body appears in front of me, and my gaze climbs the length of it until I'm staring into a raging pair of dark-teal eyes. His jaw ticks as he holds me in my chair with a lethal glare.

It's another side to Jude Harrison.

"What the fuck?" Leighton yells, rolling around like a beetle on his back.

"My apologies," Jude grates, slowly turning that stare onto him. "My foot caught the leg of your chair." He offers a hand. "Let me help you up." He sounds like he's ready to slaughter Leighton, not help him up.

Leighton accepts, and Jude hauls him to his feet as one side of Leighton's body seems to shrink. He laughs nervously. "No problem," he squeaks. Is he in pain? Then he hisses, looking at Jude's hand wrapped around his.

Jude releases and reveals a limp limb that's had all the life and blood squeezed out of it. What the hell does he think he's doing? I stand, smoothing down the front of my dress, and Jude moves in close, his front to mine, just off centre. My eyes are on his shoulder. His head is held high, his hands restrained in his trouser pockets.

"Don't fucking rub it in my face, Amelia."

"Excuse me?"

"You heard me." He turns to Leighton. "Let me get you another drink."

"Sure. And a room for the night would be great." Leighton grins, and, my God, I could smash it off his face. By the tensing and rising of Jude's shoulders, he feels the same. I'm about to tell Jude it's not what he thinks. But . . . do I owe him that?

"A room," Jude muses, as Leighton moves in and slaps him on the shoulder of his expensive three-piece.

"Tell me about your long-term financial plan," he says.

I shake my head to myself and get out of there, heading outside to get some air. Today has been a disaster. I find myself on a patio full of white iron tables and chairs. Heading for the far table, I lower to the green cushion and dial Abbie. "You better get Charley on the line," I say, resting back, exhausted.

"Oh shit," she breathes. "What's happened?"

"He's here. At Arlington Hall," I say.

"Him?"

"His name's Jude Harrison. He owns this place."

"Oh my God."

"I've achieved nothing at this conference except sweating and trying to breathe so I don't have a fucking heart attack." I go to smooth my hair back and realise it's down. *Damn it.* I hold my phone to my ear and gather it into a ponytail. It's casual, but it's off my face, the strands not sticking to my damp, sticky cheeks. "He gave an opening speech. I read between the lines. Then he found me in the ladies' and—"

"You had hand sex again?"

"No." I roll my eyes, flopping back in my chair. "He got close, I'm sure we were heading for . . . I don't know, but I found my senses and left. Then he got all passive aggressive over a male colleague." Taking a breath, I rub my temple. "Abbie, he's a force I'm not sure I can handle."

"You can handle anything," she says gently. "You are literally the strongest woman I know."

I smile, but it's small and it's an effort. "I don't feel very strong right now." Every second I'm in Jude Harrison's orbit, whether that be physically or just on the phone, a little bit more strength crumbles away.

"That's the power of attraction."

"I've no room in my life for a man. I've literally just kicked one out."

"Nick's expectations were unreasonable."

"And Jude Harrison's aren't?" I look up when a waiter appears beside me. "I'm okay, thank you."

He smiles and picks a glass of Hey Jude up off his tray and lowers it. "Courtesy of Mr. Harrison."

I laugh sardonically.

"What?" Abbie asks.

"He's just sent me a cocktail. The Hey Jude. I think it's a peace offering."

"I can't believe he owns Arlington Hall."

"We didn't get Charley on the call."

"You know what Charley will say. Besides, she's at Lloyd's parents' house for dinner. I'm on my way to Waitrose. Chablis, Cheese, and Bridget?"

Our crisis pack. "Yeah," I breathe, because this definitely feels like a crisis. "I'll be back soon."

I hang up and study the glass before me for a few moments, knowing he'll be watching me. So I get up and head back inside, leaving the drink untouched on the table.

"There you are," Clark says, dancing over. "We're going to Evelyn's. You have to come."

"Evelyn's?"

"It's the nightclub on the grounds. Everyone's heading there for drinks."

I don't want to appreciate the nod to his mother. "Do you have a pass?" I ask, thinking Rachel will not love my brother rocking up late totally bombed. He's a terrible drunk. Slurry, wobbly, clingy, and he feels the need to be virtually licking people's earlobes when he's talking to them.

"I've cleared it with the boss. Come on, sis, live on the edge." He claps his hands and does some obscene dance as he backs away. He's such a goofball. Like an excitable child on Christmas Eve.

"What about your car?" I call.

"Rach said she'd bring me over tomorrow after work to get it."

"I'm going to pass." I wave a hand flippantly. I'm looking forward to a wine and cheese coma with Abbie. And off-loading my woes. "I'll get the bus back."

"Oh, we've put the transport back a few hours," Shelley says, dancing past, joining the crowd heading through the glass tunnel to Evelyn's. "Majority vote, I'm afraid. Soz."

My shoulders drop. "I'll get a train."

"Oh, come on, Amelia," she yells back. "Live on the edge."

Easy for everyone else to say. I sense it's going to be really fucking painful if I fall off that edge.

"A club?" I motion down my body. "Dressed like this?"

"Look around you," Shelley sings, laughing. "You're surrounded by suits and pencil skirts."

"I'm wearing a dress," I grumble. "It's Victoria Beckham," I add, like that sets me apart from the others. Now *they* are stiff. I huff to myself. Jesus Christ, I haven't been to a club since I went to Ibiza after we graduated. That was a great trip. None of us wanted to come home and resume adulting.

Glancing around me, I watch every guest from the conference heading eagerly in the direction of freedom from their day jobs. Relief. Hair-down time. There will undoubtedly be a pile of sore heads and regrets in the morning. Someone will end up in the restrooms with someone they shouldn't. It's never been for me, and it shouldn't be now. Especially since it's Jude Harrison's club.

I check the time, then open my Uber app to see how far away the nearest car is to get me to the train station. "No available cars?" I blurt, baulking at my screen. I look up and around, following my feet to the reception area and finding Anouska passing through to the Library Bar. "Hey, is there a taxi firm I can call to take me to the station? Uber has nothing available in the area." I laugh like, *How crazy is that?*

She grimaces. "Yes, we're in the sticks here, you have to order Ubers well in advance, and the nearest taxi firm is in Oxford. Do you want me to call?"

"Would you mind?"

"Sure." A few clicks on the screen of her mobile and she starts talking, telling them where we are and where I'm going. She frowns. Thinks. Covers the receiver. "Two hours."

"Two?"

She nods, eyes a little wide.

"How on earth do guests come and go if they don't drive?"

"Chauffeur. Either theirs or ours. And we have the helicopter pad too."

"Of course." I exhale, exasperated, and think. "Clark," I breathe. I'll use his car. "Thanks for trying," I call, dialling my brother as I wander away. Of course, he doesn't answer, and I growl my frustration as I come to a stop at the entrance to the Library Bar, seeing people dotted around, drinking, chatting quietly. Soft, relaxing jazz plays in the background. I breathe in and let my eyes drift to the end of the bar, remembering every detail of the moment I first set eyes on Jude Harrison. Except then, he was your not-so-average businessman. How wrong I'd been. How fucked I didn't know I was.

I head for Evelyn's, passing through the glass tunnel and breaking out into the chilly nighttime air, following the illuminated gravel path through the pergolas draped in white clematis until I reach the glass building on the other side of the paddocks. The lights from inside shine out, and when I enter, I just *have* to take a moment to appreciate the space. This isn't a nightclub—not like I know nightclubs. This is a cocktail bar on steroids, with a DJ and velvet club chairs that no man or woman has ever thrown up on. The bar is oval-shaped, set dead centre, stools lining the entire circumference, and tubes suspended from the high ceiling cast a hazy light on the white stone surface of the bar.

I search the clusters of people, scan the bar, the seating areas. No Clark. "Where are you?" I say to myself as "Silence" by Delerium starts playing, and a swarm of mid-forties people flock to the dance floor. I smile, seeing them transform one by one into their lost clubbing selves.

Stepping out on the terrace, I spy my brother smoking. "You haven't smoked for two years," I say, approaching with a scornful look.

"Shhh," he slurs, holding the B&H upright to his lips. "Don't tell Rachel."

My God, he's already slurring. "Can I take your car?"

"Huh?"

"Your car. Can I drive myself home in it? Apparently, taxis don't exist around here, and you have to prebook an Uber."

"Amelia, dear older sister, do you have a car?"

"You know I don't have a car."

Clark takes a hit of nicotine and inhales it deeply, dropping his head back and blowing the smoke into the air, sparing me. "I *do* know, which is how I know you don't have any insurance."

"I can't drive on your insurance?"

"No. And I still wouldn't let you, even if you had your own insurance, because you'd only be covered for fire and theft, so if some idiot drove into my shiny new Range Rover, I'd be rather fucked off."

I pout. "You don't trust me."

He laughs. "I trust you with my life. You're the most reliable, sensible woman I know. It's the other road users I don't trust."

"Please?" I beg.

"The answer is no."

Damn it, he's obviously not *that* drunk. "Then what am I supposed to do?"

"Have some bloody fun, Amelia." He takes one last puff and stubs out his cigarette, hooking an arm around my neck. "Why'd you want to leave so bad?"

"I don't."

"Come on, let your little brother buy you a drink." Pushing his lips to my cheek, he smothers me.

"Fine." It's not like I have a choice. I quickly text Abbie to let her know I'm stranded. "I'll have a Chablis."

Clark leads me back inside, where the frenzy on the dance floor continues, the track still pumping. I find myself scanning constantly, every muscle tense. Clark says something. I can't hear him, but when he pats one of the stools at the bar, I get it. I slip onto the green cushioned seat, the backrest shaped like a shell, the legs gold. Beautiful bottles of expensive liquor and fancy glasses decorate the middle of the oval.

"I saw you talking to Spector earlier." Clark's half yelling, half slurring, waggling his eyebrows. "Want to share?"

"There's nothing to share," I reply, frowning. Is the music getting louder? "Everyone suspected she's retiring, and now it's confirmed she's slowing down."

"So what did she say?" he shouts back.

"She told me to consider a mentor."

"I'll mentor you."

I try not to appear offended. "Why, thank you," I say on a smile he won't misread. "But fuck off."

Clark laughs and pushes my wine toward me, leaning on the bar. I see his mouth move but can't hear him.

"What?" I ask, moving closer.

"I said, I'm only saying this to you because I'm half-drunk!"

"Only half?"

"Nick's the most boring bloke I've ever met."

I laugh into my glass. "You're telling me now?"

"What?" he yells.

"I said"—Jesus, I can't hear myself think. That might be a good thing—"you're telling me now?"

"You're better than that. He made you . . . I don't know. Boring too."

"Jesus, Clark."

"Listen to me a minute," he shouts, coming even closer to my ear. "He made you think you weren't good enough at what you do. So you became better than you already were, and his plan backfired."

"Are you saying he only ever wanted me for my baby-making abilities?"

"'Course not. You're a beautiful woman, Amelia. I'm still fighting off all my mates, which, by the way, I'd hap-hap-happily set you up with." He gives me a serious look, and I smile at his eyes wandering slightly.

"All of them?"

Clark snorts, disgusted. "I'm sure you've noticed . . . that Nick only decided . . . he wanted marriage and babies when you told him you wanted . . . to go for partner at LB&B."

I still for a moment. Yes, actually, I did notice that. Perhaps too late, but I've definitely considered it.

"What I'm saying is," Clark slurs on, his volume just high enough for me to hear. "Nick got more than he bargained for, and he's not confident or strong enough to be with a woman who might overtake him on the career ladder. Fuck, you're already close."

"So that's your conclusion?"

"My conclusion is, my sister needs a cerrrr . . . tain type of man, and N-Nick ain't it." He holds up his glass, and I chink mine with his in toast.

"I don't need any man right now, but I hear you."

"Good." He leans forward. "Knock one on my cheek."

I plant a kiss where ordered, rolling my eyes to myself. My brother forgetting who's eldest is a regular problem. "Now, please, let that hair back down and have some fun. You can be driven and spon-spontaneous at the same time, you know?"

I laugh, but it dries up when I see Jude across the club heading this way, looking savagely angry. And I realise.

"Oh no."

"What?" Clark yells, coming closer again.

"Please, please, please." I slip off my stool and set my glass down, ready to block Jude's path to my brother, but I'm too slow. He's got Clark bent backwards over the bar in a heartbeat, and poor Clark looks more than stunned as Jude growls in his face. I can't believe this. "What are you doing?" I hiss, shoving Jude back, incensed, as he heaves before me and rakes a hand through his mussed hair.

"You think that's okay?" His yells blend with the loud music. "Flaunting yourself with any man to get a rise out of me?" Stepping into me, he leans over my shorter frame, his face up close to mine. "Well, here I fucking am, Amelia, giving you a fucking rise."

I stare at him, stunned, and without warning to me or Jude, my hand flies out and slaps him clean across the face. He thinks I'd play those games? I'm a fucking woman, not a drama-thriving little girl.

Jude blinks, shocked, and I retract my hand, the sting real. *Shit.*

I look back at an alarmed Clark. Does he think a man like this will suit me? "Doesn't seem like you need me to step in and be all brotherly," he yells, glancing at my burning hand.

"Clark," I say, my voice unstoppably wobbly, "meet Jude Harrison."

Jude's lips part as realization finds him. "Shit," he mouths. "Fuck, Amelia, I—"

I don't want his apology. I turn and give Clark a kiss. "I'll call you." And push past Jude, leaving. I don't know where I'm going or how the hell I'm going to get there, but I'm suffocating. I'll walk. Get some air.

"Amelia, wait," Jude yells.

I look back and see him straightening Clark out, patting down his suit as he keeps a frantic eye on me retreating. My pace increases.

And he comes after me. I'm not surprised.

I thrust the doors onto the terrace open and hurry through the crowd of smokers, finding the path, my heels crunching across the stones as I rush beneath the pergolas.

"Amelia!"

His shoes join the sounds of mine. He's running. *Fuck.* I stop and pull off my heels, and immediately regret it when sharp stones bite into my bare feet. "Shit, shit, shit." My plan to escape faster fails. I hiss and shout as I step across the gravel.

"Amelia, for fuck's sake."

Do *not* let him get to me. I look back, my heart sinking when I see him sprinting. Closer, closer, closer.

"Stop!" I yell, swinging around, the force making my hair tie fly out. God, how many people saw that happen in there? How will I explain this, especially to Clark?

Jude skids to a stop, breathless too, but at least his fucking feet won't be cut to shreds. Furious, I march back to him, enduring the pain, and slam my palm into his hard chest, thrusting him back. He has a whole foot over me as I look up at him.

"This has to stop now." I find my breath, or at least try to. Around Jude Harrison, that seems impossible. Calm. *Give me calm!* "No more, Jude." I walk away, gritting my teeth to endure the pain in my feet. And oddly, a pain somewhere unexpected.

In my fucking chest.

What the hell is that?

I make it to the door and wrench it open, and he catches it before it closes, doing the exact opposite of what I've asked, as per usual. He follows me through the glass tunnel, past reception, through the spa area, and into the changing rooms. I pretend he's not there. It's the only way. If fucking impossible. I pull my bag out of a locker, throw it onto my shoulder, and leave again, pushing past him, ignoring the surge of electricity that flies through my body each time I touch him. It's anger.

Not chemistry.

But I don't make it out the door. He pulls me back, puts me in front of him, takes my bag from my shoulder, and throws it to the floor.

"You think I'm playing a game?" he asks tightly.

I look up into his eyes.

And drown.

Everything inside tingles with want. With need. I've never known desire like this. I've never wanted something so badly. I'm trying so hard to push back these unanticipated feelings and failing at every turn.

His lips part, his eyes smoke.

My thighs clench. My breasts become achy.

"Why are you making this so fucking difficult?" he asks.

I inhale.

Swallow.

Shake my head.

"Amelia," he whispers, coming closer. "Give in to it."

I look down, searching my head for words to speak and instructions to follow. It scares me so much, my lack of sense around him. My powerlessness. My inability to do the sensible thing. How he consumes my head, how my body responds to him.

"No," I whisper.

"Why?"

"Because I don't want this."

"Bullshit."

"I don't want this," I repeat. "I don't want this, I don't want this."

"Bull-fucking-shit, Amelia!"

My lack of control fails me again. Fatal. I look up at him, our breathlessness loud. My mind is screaming conflicting things at me.

Kiss him.

Don't!

Walk away!

But again, I have never felt a craving so acute. Like if I don't kiss him, I'll die here and now.

Jude stares at me, waiting, his eyes on the greener side of teal, something swirling in their depths. "Just let it happen," he whispers.

Let it happen.

Because this chemistry and attraction is stronger than me.

"Let it happen," he breathes, his lips moving slowly.

I lose my internal battle and move into his body, pulling his mouth down to mine, our lips colliding on a whimper of pleasure and desperation. He catches me around the waist and staggers back, hitting the wall with force. "Fuck," he gasps, opening up to me instantly, his tongue meeting mine, soft and hot. My kiss is forceful, full of frustration, and at the same time, full of relief. Desire travels through me like wildfire, reaching between my legs. My body starts to throb. He tastes unbelievable. Feels incredible. His scent engulfs me—oud and musk, and my mind blanks. Nothing exists, only need. A need I'm terrified is so strong, my attraction so potent, I might not ever quench it. And this kiss is only affirming what I've been afraid of.

Perfection.

One hand on his cheek, the other on his neck, I pull him closer, and he moans, moving his hands from my hair, his shoulders hunching as he holds my face and kisses me like every woman should be kissed, with passion and purpose. Like they're owned.

Then he rolls us so it's me now pinned to the wall, the full length of his hard body pressing into mine, his mouth and tongue relentless.

Our first kiss. It's fuelled by anger. It's fucking electric. Everything I never allowed myself to believe it would be. Consuming. Mind-blanking.

Another step over the line into dangerous territory.

Proof that Jude Harrison fucks with my sensibility. Makes the intelligent part of me malfunction.

No!

I rip my lips away from his and push my palms into his chest, forcing him back. Heaving. "There," I gasp, scrambling for my sense. "You've got what you wanted."

His eyes widen in disbelief, and he steps back and laughs, roughly wiping his wet mouth. "Are you fucking with me?"

"I'm n—"

He comes back at me, kissing me hard, owning me, and I'm a puppet again, succumbing to the power. Strong, large hands reach for the backs of my thighs, and he hauls me up his tall body. A loud rip sounds—my dress, but it doesn't stop me. Not this time.

"You drive me fucking insane," he growls, sweeping his tongue through my mouth, biting my lip, before plunging deeply again. My arms naturally circle his shoulders, pulling him closer, my mouth accepting his.

I can't stop!

"Good?" he asks, moving his mouth onto my neck, sucking and biting.

My head drops back, my blurry vision on the ceiling as he hums across my skin, mixing licks with his bites, kisses with his sucks.

"Yes," I breathe. "So good."

His mouth suddenly stills. He takes a deep breath and slowly peels his body away, setting me on my feet. Confused, I look at him as he sweeps his hair back.

"Thank you for proving what I fucking knew." He slams his mouth on mine again, a fucked-up kind of encore, kissing me hard but chastely. "I dare you to say no when I ask you to have dinner with me again," he says quietly, his voice strong and deep. He holds my jaw, making sure he keeps my eyes. "I fucking dare you, Amelia." Then he releases me, turns, and walks out.

And I stand there in silent disbelief, watching the door close behind him, every nerve ending I have screaming for his touch. His mouth. The fire, the electricity.

The freedom from thinking.

Of being in control.

I face the mirror and stare at myself. Flushed cheeks. Wild eyes. My mind is racing, trying to wrap around what's just happened. I can still feel his lips on mine. "Shit." I wedge my hands into the sink and breathe. "Shit, shit, shit."

What was that?

Pulling my dress into place, I take a few moments to compose myself before hauling the door open and looking for him, wanting an explanation.

Not that I need one. I know what just happened.

Just like he said, he proved what we *both* know. What I'm fucking stumped about is why he didn't take it further when I was obviously so willing. After everything, the innuendos, the chance meetings, the chemistry, the chase.

Why didn't he take me?

I let out a little puff of laughter.

He's in control. Jude Harrison is a man who wants control.

But it's up to me if I give it to him.

I retrieve my phone, wincing at the missed calls from Clark, and stuff my bag into the locker again before walking back through to the lobby. There's no sign of Jude. The Library Bar. No Jude. I peek down at my dress, cursing at the split that's a few inches higher up my leg than it should be. "Shit."

I'm a mess as I walk back to Evelyn's, my eyes darting, looking for him. He's nowhere.

"Where the h-h-hell have you been?" Clark slurs when I find him on the terrace smoking, his phone in his hand. He looks me up and down.

"I was using the ladies'." I grab his drink off the tall bar table and swig it, exhaling. Shaking.

"What was that?" he asks, swaying. He's on his way to complete obliteration. "You and . . . what's his name?"

"Jude Harrison." I scratch through my mind, searching for any tale I can spin. "You parked in his parking space."

"What?" Clark rocks back on his heels, his drunken face a picture of confusion.

Jesus Christ. "You parked in the space reserved for him." I huff and cringe at the same time, my eyes darting still.

"A bit of an overreaction, wasn't it?" Giving up on standing, Clark drops his arse to a stool. "I parked where I was told to." He gets up again. "The lamppost in the green suit guided me to that specific space," he goes on, indignant. "We should make a complaint."

"Wait," I blurt as he starts to wobble off. "I already did." Fucking hell, this is painful. "Don't worry, enjoy your freedom." I put his drink back in his hand and smile, hoping it's convincing. "Big sister fixed it."

He grins, all boyish, and totally my baby brother. "That slap was a stinger." Then he stumbles off toward the dance floor.

And I drop to a chair and take a breath.

I walk through the door at just gone midnight after hanging around waiting for everyone to finish partying at Evelyn's. Jude was nowhere to be seen. It was a slow torture, and worse, I wanted him to come back to me. I wanted him to find me. If that was his whole point—to make me crave him more—he succeeded. Although I'm not sure how I could possibly crave him more. I can't stop thinking about him. About our kiss. The feelings, his scent, my irrepressible and unhealthy craving for him. It's all knocked me for six, and I'm at a loss for how to deal with it.

Abbie's on the couch in her robe, flicking through the channels on the TV. She looks up at me, smiling. "I didn't want to go to bed until I knew you were ho—" Her face falls, and she jumps up from the couch, tossing the remote control aside. "What's wrong?"

I don't know what's gotten into me. Tiredness? Stress? Pressure? All?

I let out a pathetic whimper and drop my bag to the floor, covering my face. She's with me in a heartbeat, her arms around me, and I need it.

"Amelia?" she says, so many questions in her voice.

"We kissed, and then he left. He just fucking left, like he'd proven his point." I look at Abbie, finding her eyes are even wider. "What kind of fucked-up bastard is he?"

"And did he prove his point?" she asks quietly.

"Yes. Yes, he proved it." I bury my face in my hands again. "He dared me to say no to him the next time he asks me to have dinner with him. Oh my God, Abbie, I gave him exactly what he wanted." I'm such a fucking idiot.

I feel her arm come around my shoulders. "Don't you think it was kind of inevitable?"

"Probably," I murmur. "I just . . . I don't know. I get the feeling there's more to him than I'm seeing."

"You mean a multimillion-pound estate in Oxfordshire?" she quips, and I laugh over a pathetic snivel as she leads me to the couch and sits us down.

"And the temper," I add. "After he kicked away a colleague's chair, he had Clark up against a bar." My brother seemed drunk enough to swallow my pile of bullshit. I hope. *For fuck's sake.*

"But you still let him kiss you."

I wilt, sheepish, wiping my eyes with the back of my hand. "Actually, *I* kissed *him*. The first time, anyway." I pout, pointing to the split in my dress that's now reaching my thigh. "He broke my dress."

"Shit, I love this dress."

"I know," I grumble, tugging at the material, hoping a seamstress will be able to fix it. "So how was your night? I'm sorry I didn't make it for our cheese coma."

Abbie chuckles, falling into my side, and cuddles me. "Utterly boring compared to yours, by the sounds of things." We both exhale collectively and collapse against the back of the couch together. "Go to bed. You'll be thinking more clearly in the morning."

"Okay," I say quietly, staring into space.

I dare you to say no when I ask you to have dinner with me again. I fucking dare you, Amelia.

Thinking clearly?

That's proved impossible around Jude Harrison.

Chapter 13

The rest of the week drags, and I limp my way into Friday. I've struggled to concentrate and have been checking my phone repeatedly. He's not been in touch. I hate that I'm constantly wondering why. Clark called me the morning after, throwing questions at me. I stuck to my bullshit story. And he didn't question it, although I sensed mild suspicion.

Tilda Spector was right, Mr. Neilson emailed me this morning with instructions to get the ball rolling on cashing in his investments, ending my week on a low. It's left a hole in my portfolio and made my target even bigger. I should be winning business, growing my portfolios, not losing investments and leaving a higher hill to climb for partner. On top of that, I had to listen to Leighton Steers spout off about his new connection with the Cartwright sisters, two wildly successful—but utterly dull—entrepreneurs from Liverpool, who he's buttering up. They're an overnight success story, their creator tech tools exploding. Fuck, that would be a good catch for him and undoubtedly earn him mega praise from the partners.

I tap my pen on the edge of my desk, in a daydream, half my mind devoted to whether Leighton is going to screw up my chances of making partner, the other half wondering why the hell Jude Harrison blew my mind with his mouth, finally got me where he wanted me, and then walked away, leaving me standing breathless and dizzy in the ladies'. My hand clenches around my pen, my knuckles turning white.

"Shit," I whisper, dropping it and pushing it across my desk, my eyes following it. "Why did you walk away?" I startle when my phone rings, and I scramble to pick it up, but drop it again when I see who's calling me. "Fuck." *Fuck, fuck, fuck.* My feet wedge into the floor and push my chair away from my desk. Distance.

But I want an answer.

So I swipe it up and take his call. "Yes?"

"So cold," he says softly.

I inhale slowly and quietly, trying to relax. "What can I do for you?"

"Come to dinner with me."

I dare you to say no. I fucking dare you, Amelia.

I purse my lips, flicking my *loose* hair over my shoulder. "Thanks, but no thanks." I hang up and yell at the ceiling. What the fuck am I doing? Getting up, I start pacing my office, cursing constantly. I'm being childish. Playing that game I insisted I wasn't playing. Proving my point? What the fuck is my point? I want to have dinner with him. I want to let him invade my mind and body.

I. Want. Him.

And now, after tasting him, I crave him so badly. "So what the fuck is your point, Amelia?" I shout, throwing my arms up.

"Alright?"

I whirl around and see Gary on the threshold of my office, looking at me with slight concern. I slap on a smile. "Just considering some minor plan shifts." I scoot over to my desk and lower calmly, collecting my pen and tapping it, my smile breaking my face. "Everything okay?"

"What happened with your brother and Jude Harrison?" he asks, settling in a chair opposite. I freeze, my smile faltering. Gary's been working from home since the conference, so I've not caught up with him. Not that he'll want to hear what I've got to share, and neither do I want to tell him.

"Nothing happened."

"Someone mentioned an altercation."

I shake my head, at a loss. "A misunderstanding."

"About?"

"A parking space, I think. Trivial." I wave a hand flippantly and pull a file over. "Bad news," I say, knowing my ploy will work. No financial adviser wants to hear *that* at work. It means losses. "Mr. Neilson will be cashing in all his ISAs."

Gary's eyes bug. "That's twenty years' worth of investments."

"I know." I deflate once more. "But I'll make it up. I have a ton of leads, and I had a really interesting conversation with Tilda Spector."

"Oh?" His interest is piqued. Gary won't care who Tilda passes her clients on to. So long as it's to someone in this company—like Leighton or me. Problem is, Tilda gave no indication as to who, or even which company, she's swaying toward.

"I'll keep you in the loop," I say, forcing another smile.

He nods and stands. "Have a great weekend, Amelia."

"You too," I call, chirpy but not feeling it. I'll spend my weekend carving out a plan, a backup plan, and a backup backup plan, because Mr. Neilson and his cash-in are proof that you can lose business as quickly as you can win it.

I read a message from Abbie in our WhatsApp group asking if I've heard anything. No comment. Charley wasn't all too impressed when Abbie fed her the latest. Abbie, however, seems to think some fun would do me good. Problem is, this doesn't feel like fun, waiting around to be called. And he just called. And I tried to claw back some control. Am I fighting a losing battle? Who even am I right now? I sigh loudly and drop my head back against the chair, exasperated by myself. The gym is calling. For the second time today.

But as I'm about to get up, my phone dings, and I hate that my heart leaps as a consequence. I drop my eyes but not my head, seeing a text message from his number. My heart rate accelerates. But can I reach out to get my phone and read the message?

I stare at it, just stare at it, while trying to make sure I don't go into cardiac arrest.

Get a fucking grip, Amelia.

I blow out my cheeks and gingerly drag my mobile towards me. It takes another whole minute for me to find the courage to open the message.

Check your emails. Jude.

I chew the inside of my cheek, my stomach fluttering as I turn to my computer and refresh the screen, inhaling when I see an email from Reservations at Arlington Hall. I click it open and read, and my ability to breathe becomes more difficult with each word.

Dear Miss Lazenby,

We look forward to welcoming you to Arlington Hall. Your Luxury Spa Day is confirmed, and one of our dedicated chauffeurs will arrive promptly at 11:00 tomorrow morning at 10 Green Street SE1 to collect you. Your package includes three luxury treatments, which you can choose from the treatment menu when you arrive, as well as a champagne dinner in our renowned Michelin-starred restaurant, the Orangery. I have attached our standard terms and conditions, along with a brochure with information you may find useful. We hope you leave Arlington Hall feeling recharged, refreshed, and bursting with clarity. If you have any questions, please do not hesitate to reply to this email. Otherwise, we look forward to seeing you tomorrow.

Best,
The Reservations Team

The Invitation

I sit back, staring at the screen, my skin prickling, wondering how he knows Abbie's address. But of course—he's checked the forms we completed on our spa day. *Bursting with clarity.* "Oh Jesus," I whisper, grabbing my phone and FaceTiming the girls. Abbie answers first, followed quickly by Charley, and it doesn't take me long to realise Abbie is in Charley's kitchen. "What are you doing there?" I ask Abbie as Charley bounces Ena on her hip.

"I stopped in on the way home from work. Because, you know, it's Elijah's birthday."

I try so hard to stop my eyes widening in horror. "Of course," I squeak. "I'm just leaving the office, will be there soon!" I hang up, deciding my dilemma must wait, and shoot up from my desk, grabbing my bag and rushing out. "Fuck!" I hiss as I hit the call button for the elevator.

I'm the worst friend.

◆ ◆ ◆

After an emergency stop off at Hamleys, I arrive at Charley's bearing gifts and a smile. "Where's the birthday boy?" I sing, pushing my way past Charley, the giant Hamleys bear in my arms hampering me as I hurry down the hall to the kitchen, practically getting wedged in the doorway. I can hear Abbie laughing. Can't see her.

"Aunty Ammy!" Elijah sings, delighted.

"Hey, baby," I coo, dropping the bear. He climbs straight on top of the gigantic thing, which cost me a small fortune and earned me many raised brows on the Tube. "Why didn't you remind me?" I hiss at Abbie.

She slows her chewing of an olive. "I did." Then pops another one into her mouth. "Last week *and* on Wednesday by text."

I scowl and check my phone. And there it is. Abbie's message. "Shit."

"What?" Charley asks.

I spin, grinning, and accept Ena when she off-loads her on me. "Nothing. How's your day been?"

Charley goes to the sink, giving me a tired look as she rinses a wineglass. "Don't try to fool me, Amelia Lazenby. You forgot his birthday."

"I temporarily misplaced the mental note I keep in my brain," I say, feeling terrible. I let my shoulders drop. "I'm sorry."

"Forget about it." Charley flicks me with water, her way of telling me we're fine. "What I'm more interested in is *why* you forgot."

"Yes, why, Amelia?" Abbie chimes, her voice an irritating tone of sarcastic. "Little Miss Organised, what made you forget our precious Elijah's birthday?"

I sigh and perch on a stool, dropping a kiss into Ena's hair and smelling her. I might not want a baby, but I do so love how they smell. "Why are you both insisting on wasting our time? We all know."

"Have you heard from him?" Charley asks, pouring me a wine.

I look between them as they wait with interest. I don't tell them but instead get my phone out and open the email, handing it to Charley across the island. Abbie shoots up and joins her, reading over her shoulder. And I wait, taking a sip of wine, watching their faces, as Ena plays with a coaster, bashing it on the marble.

"Oh my," Abbie breathes. "That's quite the invitation."

I flash her a look to suggest I was hoping for more than the obvious.

"I find it quite refreshing that you're thinking of something other than work," she adds.

"Ha. Ha," I drone.

"Do it."

"Wait," Charley pipes up. "Let's be sensible."

"Sensible about what?" Lloyd asks as he wanders into the kitchen, yanking his tie loose. He drops his briefcase to the kitchen floor, casting his eyes around the three of us.

"About Amelia accepting a spa day from the hunk who wants to get in her knickers," Abbie chirps.

"The hunk who owns the hotel where the spa is," Charley adds, making Lloyd's eyebrows shoot up. "The hunk who got all aggressive possessive when he saw Amelia chatting to another man."

"He was my brother," I say, exasperated. She makes it sound like I've got a harem of men on the go.

"The dickhead from work isn't." Charley passes my phone across the island.

Poor Lloyd looks overcome as he glances between us. Then he settles on his daughter on my lap and collects her up. "Ena and I are going to watch Clarkson's Farm," he says, dropping a kiss into my hair. "Be careful."

I smile. "I will."

"And love the new hair," he adds, grabbing Elijah up off the floor and running from the kitchen with a kid under each arm. "Come on, birthday boy."

"It's not new hair!" I call after him, slumping back on the stool.

"Go," Abbie says, resolute.

Charley swallows, as if she's struggling. I know she is. "I can't tell you what to do."

"Damn straight you can't," Abbie pipes up, earning herself an elbow in the ribs.

"Just . . . be sensible, okay?"

I nod.

Be sensible.

Simple.

Except Jude Harrison has proved he's anything but simple, and I'm not very good at being sensible around him.

Chapter 14

I lie in bed the next morning almost scared to get up. And that's unheard of. I'm always up early, whether it's a weekday or a weekend. In the gym by six on weekdays, showered by seven, and in the office by eight. On Saturdays, in the gym by eight and M&S by ten buying my weekend treats and healthier weekday meals.

It's Saturday. It's now nine thirty. I've not worked out, not showered, and not thought about what I need at M&S. I heard Abbie leave at six thirty to go to the wholesalers. Apparently, her newly acquired apprentice—a.k.a. my mother—is doing a second shift today. She didn't knock, even though she knew I'd be awake. But she did text telling me to let her know if I'm going.

Take his offer.

Or . . . don't.

I dare you to say no.

I dared. How ridiculous. I wonder if my subconscious is keeping me under the sheets, telling me the chauffeur will come and go if I remain in bed and don't answer the door. Probably. Wise subconscious. The problem is, Jude Harrison is far more powerful than my subconscious.

And my resistance.

I slide my mobile off the nightstand, calling Dad to see what he's up to—and how he's taking Mum's newfound ambition. She's always been steadfast in her role as wife, mother, and homemaker. I'm happy for her, but I'm certain it will have thrown my dad for a loop.

"Morning," I say when he answers, propping myself up against the pillows.

"Morning, darling," he chirps back, surprising me. I expected sulks.

"What are you up to today?"

"You mean because your mother is off gallivanting on the weekend when we should be spending time together?"

I smile and roll onto my side. "You're supposed to be retired, therefore have all week to spend time with Mum."

"Exactly," he says over a laugh. "I retired and your mum goes and gets herself a bloody job."

"She's helping out. And you're not retired if you still go into the office most days."

"I like to know what's happening."

"Right," I breathe, throwing the covers back and getting up. "So, what are you doing with yourself?" Let's steer the conversation away from working. I must look into those golf lessons.

"I've got a suit fitting."

"Oh, nice."

"And Clark and I are having lunch with his best man, what's his name?"

"Grant."

"That's the one. Grant. And the ushers."

I put the kettle on. "Lovely."

"Then your brother is taking me to some of those microbrewery places he always raves about."

"Don't get drunk."

"You know me, darling. I don't surrender to the weakness of alcohol."

"God forbid." I grab a cup down and stuff a tea bag in before going to the fridge to get the milk.

"And what are you doing today?" he asks.

I still, the fridge door open. What am I doing? Good question. "Looking for an apartment." *I must check in with the agents.*

"Oh?"

"Well, I can't stay with Abbie forever, and you drive me nuts . . ."

"The cheek!"

"I'm joking." I laugh, carrying my milk across the kitchen and finishing my tea. "I'll pop by tomorrow."

"Okay, darling. Have a good day."

"And you. Send me pictures." I hang up and slide my phone onto the counter, taking my tea and wandering around Abbie's apartment in my I Need a Hug That Leads to Sex hoodie. I'm hoping to also find my sense as I roam aimlessly, clutching my tea with both hands.

Three laps and a full cup of tea later, there's no sense to be found. And for the first time since it was bought for me, I agree with my hoodie.

I shower, shave, wash my hair, moisturise, blow-dry my hair—leaving it down—apply tinted moisturiser, dab some blush into my cheeks, a few strokes of mascara and some gloss, and pack my bag. *Dinner in one of the Michelin-starred restaurants.*

I pluck out my black satin slip dress and gold KG heels, then stand wrapped in my towel wondering . . . what should I wear? I flick through my hangers, passing my work suits and dresses, my gym kit, my loungewear, heading for the casual weekend section of my wardrobe. Jeans. Too casual. A dress? Not warm enough. I settle on some cream slouchy trousers by Reiss and a cropped satin shirt. I finish by twisting the straighteners through my hair, looking into my eyes the whole time, asking myself if I know what I'm doing.

No. The answer is no. And yet I continue going through the motions as if on the outside looking in on myself preparing for . . . what?

I know what. It won't be a hug. I know what's going to happen if I accept his invitation and go to Arlington Hall.

I'll be in even deeper.

I take a breath, wondering how deep this can go. It's obvious what kind of man Jude Harrison is. But what's the harm in taking what he's got to offer? No strings attached.

Because that kiss . . .

My body rolls just thinking about it. It was nothing short of extraordinary. It's as if he knew if he could just get our mouths to touch, I'd never say no again.

And I fear I won't.

When I hear a car pull up outside, I go to the window and move the curtain back. An old gent in a green suit and hat steps out and opens the back door. I swallow. "Here goes nothing," I say to myself, collecting my bag and cream dustcoat and taking one last breath of confidence before leaving. I pull the door closed and smile lightly when the driver tips his hat.

"Miss Lazenby," he says, adjusting his round specs as he motions to the car. "I'm Humphrey, your chauffeur for today."

"Nice to meet you, Humphrey." I approach, offering my bag when he reaches for it. "Thank you." I slip into the back of the plush Rolls-Royce and glance around at the incredible luxury. The softest leather I've ever felt, a bottle of San Pellegrino sparkling water in the seat rest, enough dials and switches to operate a spacecraft. He nods and shuts the door, and I hear the boot open and close.

I take a breath and look down at the screen of my phone when it dings.

I hope you enjoy your day. Jude.

Something tells me he's going to make sure of it. *Deeper.* I chew my lip, my thumbs hovering over the screen. I'm not sure what to say. So I say nothing and instead save his number. Jude Harrison. *Oh, please don't be the death of me.*

Humphrey slips into the driver's seat and looks up at me in the rearview mirror. "Do you have everything you need, Miss Lazenby?"

"Have you got any sense for me?"

"Pardon?"

"Never mind." I pick up the bottle of San Pellegrino, unscrewing the cap. "I have everything I need."

"Jolly good." He flashes a smile. "Just give the screen a tap if you need anything."

"What screen?" I ask, just as one starts to rise behind the front seats. "Oh."

"Some privacy for you, Miss Lazenby."

"I don't need privacy," I say, but the divider is in place before I finish, revealing two TV screens. Both start playing simultaneously, and I watch as I'm taken on a journey through some stunning gold gates, through an orchard ripe with big, red, juicy apples, before the camera sweeps down to the surface of a clear, sparkly stream. The drone hovers above the water for a few moments, allowing me to see the plump bright-orange fish weaving; then it starts travelling down the stream slowly, through rushes and water lilies, getting faster and faster and faster, until it eventually sweeps up into the air and reveals Arlington Hall in all its glittering, sunlit glory. I exhale at the sight, my skin prickling, my heart pounding. *Incredible.*

I get a tour of the grounds, the walled garden off the kitchen full of freshly grown produce, the maze, the golf course, the tennis courts, a glimpse of the outside section of the pool. I watch as guests are greeted, a helicopter lands, plates of art are served in the Orangery, and golf carts rumble across the hilly planes of the course. It's another world of luxury, and I smile when Clinton appears, showing off with a cocktail shaker, spinning it, tossing it, catching it, and then a close-up of the drink being poured into a glass with a palm leaf. *Hey Jude.*

I breathe in.

And then the suites. Lavish furniture, enormous beds, and white marble bathrooms, all with roll-top, clawfoot bathtubs. Showers big enough to fit an average-size family in comfortably, twin sinks, and vanity cabinets that could probably house the cosmetics department at Selfridges.

No expense spared.

Evelyn Harrison's dream.

And it's absolutely stunning.

I call Abbie and Charley, and their faces pop up on the screen. It's the fastest both of them have ever answered. "I'm in a Rolls-Royce," I say, turning the screen around so they can both appreciate the lavish interior of the car. "With a chauffeur. His name's Humphrey."

"Is that Amelia?" I hear my mum say. *Fuck.* I quickly get my face back in the phone, giving Abbie wide eyes.

"No, it's Charley," Abbie sings, her screen jumping as she removes herself from the vicinity of my mother. "Sorry." She shrugs. "I think she bought it."

"So you're going," Charley says, a mug at her lips.

"I'm going." I can't *not* go. And not because I dare not refuse, but because Jude Harrison is a drug, and my addiction is real.

"I want details later," Abbie says. "If you come home, that is."

I never thought about that. Will I be home later? My stomach flutters, and it's the oddest feeling. Anticipation. I hardly want to admit that, for the first time in my life, I'm excited about something that doesn't involve numbers. Excited *and* apprehensive. "Okay."

"Are you nervous?" Charley asks.

"I don't know what to expect."

"A good seeing to, I'd say." Abbie laughs.

"You're terrible." Charley scorns her, disgusted. "Besides, Amelia's number one rule is not putting out on a first date."

"Yes," I say, nodding in agreement. But this feels like more than a first date.

"So you're just going to have a massage, maybe a facial, and have dinner with him?"

I nod, unable to confirm it with words. "I'll call you both later. I just wanted to let you know I'm on my way." They both nod, blowing kisses at the screen before it goes blank.

I settle back and close my eyes.

Just have dinner with him, like a regular first date. That's what I should do. Problem is, Jude Harrison has proved all my rules are null and void where he's concerned. So I can't promise anything. And I won't commit. If I commit and fail, I'll feel like I've let myself down. So I will simply see how today plays out and take it one minute at a time.

Chapter 15

When the Rolls-Royce slows to a stop, Humphrey lets the screen down before getting out and opening the door for me. I step out and look up at the building as one of the staff invites me inside. I smile my thanks at Humphrey as he hands my bags over to Stan and tips his hat. The registration plate of the Rolls-Royce has me shaking my head in wonder at the never-ending attention to detail.

AH 1.

Anouska is in the lobby when I pass through the glass interior doors. "Miss Lazenby."

"Please, call me Amelia. Do you ever have time off?"

"A weekend here and there." She smiles, giving Stan instructions to deliver my bag to the Windsor Suite. A suite? Does that mean my luxury spa day includes an overnight stay?

"Should I check in?" I ask, motioning to the lady behind the white desk.

"I'm looking after you today," Anouska says. "Let's talk treatments. What shall I book you in for? A massage?"

"Definitely," I say, rolling my shoulders, feeling the tension there as she hands me a leather-bound folder. I flip it open and scan the list of treatments available, but the truth is, I'm not absorbing any of the information, my nerves accelerating.

Anouska must see my struggle. "Maybe a manicure and pedicure too?"

"Yes, that," I say, snapping the folder shut. I look around, wondering where Jude is. But I don't want to ask. Anouska must know why I'm here. Right?

"Well, it's lovely to welcome you back to Arlington Hall."

"Anouska, do you know why I'm here?"

"You're Mr. Harrison's guest."

I nod, assessing her disposition. "Does he have many *guests*?" The question falls out without warning, and she smiles.

"Let me show you to your room."

No answer.

And isn't that an answer in itself?

"Please, this way," she says, motioning to the stairs, but she barely makes it to the bottom step before she stops, turning at the sound of someone calling her name. I catch Anouska's profile, definitely seeing her lips purse in displeasure. "Katherine," she grates, smiling. It's forced. I follow Anouska's eyes and find a black-haired woman in workout clothes, her face damp. Even sweaty and red in the face, she's obviously very attractive, her legs long and willowy, her stomach taut, not a ripple or crease in sight.

"Where's Jude?" she asks.

"Otherwise engaged," Anouska replies, clipped. "Can I help?"

The woman, Katherine, spies me hovering nearby and smiles before returning her attention to Anouska. "Just tell him I'm looking for him. He's not answering his phone."

"Will do." Anouska starts to climb the stairs, and I follow, looking back over my shoulder as Katherine walks through the doors toward the spa. *Damn, who was that?*

I follow the curve of the rail to the top, and we cross a circular landing, my feet sinking into the sumptuous carpet, the pattern a swirl of creams and beiges. And still spotless. I have the urge to remove my shoes. We pass a dozen gloss-white ornate doors, until Anouska stops at some double doors. She taps the card on the reader on the wall and turns the gold knob. "Here we are," she says, smiling as she opens the way.

I wander in, gazing around, floored. It's bigger than Abbie's apartment. Probably even my parents' home. A lounge, a dining area, a workspace, all dressed beautifully in creams and matte gold.

"Am I moving in?" I ask on an uneasy laugh, following my feet to a door that leads to the bedroom. A dressing room, a bathroom.

"Mr. Harrison requested the best suite for you."

"But it's a bit wasted if I'm going to be in the spa all day."

Anouska smiles. "Make yourself comfortable, Amelia. Your first treatment is in half an hour. You know where to go, right?"

"I know," I say as she leaves me. I see my bag on the giant bed and go to it, pulling out my dress and hanging it on one of the gold hangers in the dressing room. My one dress has a whole room to itself. I fetch my shoes and set them on the cream carpet.

Chew my lip.

Glance around.

I open a wardrobe and find a supersoft white robe, the Arlington Hall crest embroidered on one breast. I pad to the drinks cabinet by the dining table and open the fridge. Endless bottles of Veuve Clicquot greet me. A champagne fridge. The next fridge holds an array of miniatures and mixers. The next is full of soft drinks and water. Various ornate glasses decorate the surface of the cabinet. I pluck the lid off the ice bucket. It's full. Even the ice is perfectly formed, the cubes sharp and clear.

I hear my phone ringing from my bag and walk across to the couch, finding it. It's the first time his name's appeared on my screen now I've saved his number. My nerves rocket as I answer and lower to the couch. "Hi."

"How are you settling in?" His voice glides across my skin, my back straightening as I look around.

"It's very extravagant for a spa day," I say quietly.

"And night."

I swallow, nodding. He's booked this room out for us. *Oh God.* "I don't sleep with a man on a first date." I usually don't kiss them either, but I've already broken that rule. *And* he was a whisper away from getting me off over the phone. I stand and start walking up and down, feeling a bit stifled and even more nervous than before.

"So you came all this way for . . . what?" he asks.

He's got me. "A massage, of course."

He laughs, low and throaty, and I stop my pacing, looking up at the ceiling for strength. I'm fooling myself. *Irresistible.* "You wore your hair down."

I still, my eyes automatically searching the corners of the ceilings. My God, they wouldn't have cameras in the guest rooms. What am I thinking? He's laughing lightly again. He needs to stop that. It makes me disintegrate.

"I'm not spying on you, Amelia. Go to the window."

I turn to the window by the drinks cabinet and slowly tread towards it, looking across the glass roof of the Orangery to another wing of the mansion. Five large windows stretch from one end of the wall to the other, all with pulled-back drapes at the windows. I breathe in when I see him emerge from the darkness of the room, putting himself in one of the windows.

A towel wrapped around his naked waist.

"Oh God," I whisper, the beads of wet on his smooth chest glistening. He rakes a hand through his hair and then rests it on the window frame, leaning into it. My eyes cross. His lazy eyes sparkle, his smile small.

"I'm glad you came."

"I'm still on the fence," I reply, not holding back, making sure he knows I'm all over the place.

"You think I'm bad for you."

"Aren't you?"

"Maybe," he muses, serious. "I have a feeling you could be bad for me too."

"Why?"

"Because you're on my mind. Constantly."

"I know how that feels," I admit.

"So are we done playing games?"

"It was never a game to me."

He nods mildly. "You look incredible."

"You look . . . naked."

"Nearly." His voice is quiet. Husky. So damn sexy. "There's something on the chair by the bed for you."

I narrow my eyes, glancing toward the bedroom. "What?"

"Go see."

I walk backwards as far as I can, only turning when I reach the door to the bedroom. I spot a gift-wrapped box that I completely missed before on the cream brocade, high-backed wing chair.

"Open it," he says gently.

I click him to speakerphone and set my mobile on the floor as I kneel and pull the bow free, dragging the ribbon away. On a deep breath, I lift the lid and find a mass of black tissue paper. I move it aside. "Lingerie," I whisper, reaching for the straps of the black lace balcony bra and lifting it out. The quality is sublime, the lace delicate, the detail exquisite. A gold disk hangs in the centre between each cup, a white pearl in the middle. I look at the tag and don't know whether to be delighted or insulted that he's got my size spot-on. "How did you know my size?"

"Do you like it?"

I drop my arse to my heels. "You didn't answer my question."

"And the knickers?"

I breathe out, resting the bra on my thighs and pulling out the knickers. They have a matching gold and pearl disk on the front.

"You struck me as a bikini-style kind of woman."

"You certainly know your female underwear."

"Did I get it right?"

He wants my approval? This is happening, and it's happening in the wrong order.

Or is this the right order?

"Something tells me you're a man who rarely gets things wrong, Jude Harrison." I pick up my phone, stand, and go back to the window, greedy for another look at him in his glorious semi-nakedness. Reaching the glass, I get as close as I can, my small smile unstoppable as I admire him. His hair looks darker wet, the damp waves flicking out adorably messily. His shoulders. His smooth chest. Those perfectly formed hips, his tight stomach.

My hands all over every bit of him.

"You're stunning, Amelia Lazenby, even more so when you smile."

And now I blush. This isn't me. And yet I'm completely in the moment. Drowning in Jude Harrison's world. "I have to get ready for my massage."

He nods slowly, pushing off the frame of the window, taking the towel and holding still for a moment as I brace myself. Then he pulls it off, dropping it to the floor, and I exhale so sharply, my upper body folds forward as I stare at his semi-erect cock. "Don't miss me too much." He hangs up and backs away, every glorious naked inch of him shimmering under the hazy glow of the moody lighting in his room.

"Missing you already," I whisper, my phone lowering, my mouth watering.

My knees weak.

I take myself to the nearest chair and sit, dazed, knowing beyond anything I've ever known that I'm being drawn into something huge.

The question is, can I handle it?

Handle *him*.

Chapter 16

When I make it to the spa in my robe, a lady wearing a green tunic and a friendly smile is waiting for me. "Miss Lazenby," she says, standing. "I'm Maria, one of the therapists here at Arlington Hall. I'll be looking after you today. Please, take a seat."

I lower into the chair beside hers as she joins me, my eyes naturally darting, the vision of Jude standing unapologetically naked in the window unshakably stuck in my mind. Confident. A man who knows he has a body to die for, wields it like a lethal weapon.

And I want to die by that body.

"I'm just checking over your information. Has anything changed since your last visit?"

"Nothing," I say, distracted, looking up when someone enters the spa. An elderly lady in a fifties swimsuit and swim hat.

"Good afternoon, Mrs. Hodges," Maria says as she passes.

"Morning, dear."

"She's here every day without fail for her swim," Maria tells me. "Now, are there any areas I should pay particular attention to?"

I roll my shoulder blades in, feeling the stiffness there. Feeling stiffness *every*where.

Maria smiles and makes a note. "I hear you," she says. "Let's get you settled. We're in treatment room four, at the very end." She leads me down the glass-walled corridor, the gym on one side, a workout studio on the other. Clean, calming air hits me when she opens a door, the dim lighting not achieving what it's intended to achieve. Calm. At least, not for me.

Maria goes to the massage bed, the widest I've ever seen, and pulls the top blanket back. "If you'd like to slip off your robe and bra and get comfortable front down. There's a hook on the wall by the bathroom. I'll give you a few minutes."

"Thank you." The soft sound of waves registers, the subtle scent of roses breaking through the lavender. God, I need this. I need someone to work the tension out of me and relax me, because I am strung, my heart thumping relentlessly. I slip off the robe and hang it up, shivering a little, despite the room being warm, as I remove my bra, leaving my knickers on. Lying on my front, I pull the blanket up my back as far as I can, resting my face in the padded hole, closing my eyes and exhaling.

Relax, relax, relax.

Breathe in, breathe out.

Someone please rub this stress and tension out of me.

The door opens and closes, and in the darkness, I hear Maria moving around, the clinking of glass bottles delicate. Her hands press into my back on top of the blanket a few times before she takes the edge by my shoulders and draws it down to the base of my spine, exposing my bare back.

And I wait for her warm touch to meet my skin. And wait.

For a moment, I wonder if she's left the room. But then I feel her palms rest on my lower back and gently press into me.

And an inferno instantly rages within.

My eyes fly open, staring at the carpet below, and air leaves my lungs in a rush, my body erupting with tingles. I would know his touch amid a million touches. My body already knows him. *What the hell?*

I start to turn, needing to check I'm not losing my fucking mind, but his touch slides up to my shoulders and presses down, encouraging me to stay. *Oh my God.* His breath is suddenly in my ear, my senses invaded by the musk and oud smell that's wholly Jude. He doesn't speak, just breathes.

But he doesn't need to speak.

I hear him.

The universe hears him.

The energy in the room is supercharged, electric.

What's happening?

His hands leave my back, and mine clench into balls. It takes all my resistance not to spin over. See him. Is he naked? "This is so wrong," I whisper, knowing he can't hear me. My body is screaming for him, my skin demanding his touch. The throb of my inside walls is carnal, sensing what it wants is close by.

The wave music dies and something else starts. And it does *not* help my condition. The sound of a woman breathing heavily fills the room, mixing with my own fitful breaths, and then a choir of men singing in French. It takes me only a few seconds to recognise the music.

Enigma. "Sadeness."

"Oh my God," I murmur, as the fire of his touch meets my back again, melding gently into my flesh, kneading, stroking, feathery touches mixed with firmer ones. I groan, unable to stop myself, surrendering to his masterful hands working my body, drifting away, the music filling my head, his hands taking me to new realms of pleasure. And that's all I can think about. How just a kiss and a touch can blindside me. How him massaging my hands with soap can render me useless. Have me imagining all the ways he can use those hands on me. How his voice over the phone built me up to an explosion.

It started with a look.

Then a touch.

Where is this leading?

I don't mean sex, I know that's going to happen. And I know it's going to be biblical. But where then?

I haven't the capacity to think about that while I'm at the mercy of this gift. I roll my head as he pushes his thumbs into the space between my shoulder blades, feeling like I'm spiralling into complete delirium. I can smell him, I can sense him, I can feel him, but I need to see him.

Taste him. I try to turn again, but he forces me back down. I growl my frustration but obey his silent order, and he continues to massage me all over, his soft, firm hands unreal, my mind lost.

Coolness meets my spine, and I jerk. Oil. He's dripping oil on me. The heel of his hand pushes into the base of my spine and glides firmly up to my neck, seeming to push every inch of doubt out of me. I'm taking this. Taking *him*. I couldn't say no if I wanted to, and in this moment, I don't.

His palms splay across each side of my back, drifting down onto my hips, spreading the oil, then back up again, brushing the edges of my breasts. My breath hitches, and for the first time, I hear his breathing too. Deep, long breaths. The blanket is pulled off my legs, leaving me completely bare except for my knickers. Exposed. Vulnerable.

Another brush of my breasts as he drags his hands back down, hooking his fingers into the top of my knickers when he reaches them. My eyes open. My hands ball and flex. My heart pounds. Harder and harder and harder.

The music goes on as I lift my hips and let him draw my knickers down my legs. His palms wrap around my ankles and hold me for a few seconds before he slides them up my calves. Onto my thighs. Stops. Works circles, kneading a little. Then up some more, stroking softly over my arse. I gasp when I feel his lips push into my left cheek. His mouth opens, he bites down gently, and my lips press together, but a smile breaks as he sinks his teeth into my butt, the pain tolerable.

And then he swats it before spinning me onto my back.

And I see him.

"Oh Jesus," I whisper, my thighs wet with my desire as I stare up at his naked physique, my eyes delighted. I prop myself up on my elbows. His hair is messy, falling forward, forcing him to rake it back. His mouth is lax, his chest undulating, and . . .

Shit.

I think I'm in fucking love.

I shake that crazy thought away, getting back to the matter at hand. The Adonis standing over me like a polished marble statue waiting to feed my every desire. He rests his hands on the end of the bed by my feet and leans forward, his eyes on mine. I definitely detect a hint of triumph in his dark gaze, which is particularly green today. I can't even be indignant about his obvious satisfaction. But he still doesn't speak, and I keep my mouth firmly shut too, at risk of blurting something wholly inappropriate.

Lock me up and inflict this pleasure on me every day for the rest of my life!

His eyes drop to the strip of hair at the apex of my thighs, his tongue tracing his bottom lip, wetting it. I fall to my back, covering my face with my bent arm, bracing myself for his assault as his hands slide under my knees and yank me farther down the bed.

Straight onto his mouth.

"Jude!" I scream, the instant pleasure lifting me off the bed.

"Shhhh," he hums across my wet, aching flesh, licking me straight up the centre. I hold my breath and grab fistfuls of his hair, very aware I could raise the dead and alert the whole of Arlington Hall about what's going down in here.

He nips at my inner thighs, sucks hard, bites harder, his forearm spread across my stomach to hold me down. I'm out of my mind, my loud breathing and the sound of him gorging on me blending with the provocative beats of the track. His tongue circles my clit, kisses the tip, lashes through my very centre, pushing inside me, fucking me. My head starts to shake, thrashing from side to side as I feel my pleasure climbing, the pressure building. I don't know what to do with myself, don't know how to deal with this level of wonderful torture. His working mouth gets firmer, faster, his hands sliding up my torso to my breasts and tweaking my nipples brutally, making my back snap into an arch. He forces me back down. I pant. He licks me. I whimper. He kisses me. I groan. He sucks me into his mouth.

I release my fierce grip of his hair and start hitting the bed by my sides, feeling beads of sweat trickling down my temples. My stomach muscles ache, my thighs scream.

It's coming.

And he knows it, his pace increasing, his working mouth ravenous. I'm burning up. My heart can't sustain this kind of strain.

Can it sustain him?

I come on a suppressed scream, my body bending to the point I'm sure it could snap my spine, and the rush of pleasure just keeps on coming, holding me in an arch, my head thrown back, my eyes clenched shut. His mouth has slowed down with its assault, but that doesn't curb the sensations hijacking me. Everything distorts. My entire world just shifted on its axis, starting to turn in another, unexpected direction.

A direction I'm not sure is the right one for me.

Because of one fucking orgasm.

I slump down on the bed, my lungs burning, trying to shake my vision clear, as Jude wipes his mouth and jerks his head, flicking his hair back as he gets on his knees at the end of the bed and crawls his way up to me. His dick is dripping with need, spotting my stomach as his face comes level with mine, his lazy eyes scanning mine. I need him inside me. The burn is quickly taking over again, my body not done with him.

Will it ever be?

Oh God, I am in so much trouble.

I blink, staring up at his stunning face, feeling something shift inside. Somewhere near my heart.

How?

No.

Impossible. I hardly know him.

Although he knows me *very* well now. *Keep it physical.* I reach for his arousal, but his hips lift and he shakes his head. I cock mine. Then he lowers and kisses me, keeping his hands where they are on the bed, no touching anywhere else. I open up and close my eyes, letting his wonderful mouth take me off to a place only Jude Harrison can take me, my hands on a feeling frenzy across his chest.

Euphoric.

Out of this world.

I hum my happiness, soak up the perfect pressure of his tongue, my internal muscles still rolling with the aftermath of my climax.

Then he suddenly pulls away, kisses the corner of my mouth, gets off the bed, tugs his jeans on and walks out.

What the ever-loving fuck?

A short, disbelieving puff of air passes my lips as I prop myself up on my elbows again, staring at the closed door. He left? I'm lying here, postclimax, ready and willing, and he left?

Falling to my back, I stare up at the ceiling, trying to unravel what kind of fucked-up game he's playing.

So no more games?

I'm still fighting to catch my breath.

I dare you to say no to me.

But he can say no to me?

Control.

He's guaranteeing by the end of this dance, I'll be begging for him. The hands, the phone sex, the kiss, and now this? Getting me off with his mouth and leaving?

He's taking control, and I'm letting him.

I crane my head up, silently cursing him to hell and back. The slow seduction. Giving me little bit by little bit to prolong my torture and his satisfaction. I huff, indignant, and quickly still when I hear the door handle.

"Oh my God." I sit up fast and grab the blankets, yanking them over my naked body, just managing to cover myself before Maria walks in. Heat explodes in my cheeks as she smiles mildly, awkwardly, and unhooks my robe from where it's hanging on the wall.

"Callie will be in treatment room two when you're ready for your manicure and pedicure."

I accept my robe but remain on the bed. "Thank you." I want the ground to open and swallow me whole. I'm still quivering from the aftershocks of Jude's sweet, long, merciless torture. Maria must know exactly what's just happened.

I'm mortified, fresh off the back of a Jude Harrison special. Kill me now.

Maria leaves, and I remain on the massage table cringing my arse off, but at the same time I feel light. The weight of my conundrum has lifted. I've accepted what needs to be accepted. I'm taking all he's got to give. And if Jude has his way, I'll be begging for it. No shame.

Groaning, I slip off the table, scanning the floor for my knickers. No knickers. He took my knickers? "God damn it." I feed my arms through the sleeves and tie the robe, grabbing my bra and stuffing it in my pocket as I go to the door. I peek up and down the corridor, certain my face must be a telling shade of postclimax, before I walk on fast feet to treatment room two and push my way in.

A curvy, young, red-haired beauty greets me, smiling brightly. "You must be Amelia."

"That's me." I close the door and put myself in the chair Callie points to, a huge cream leather piece with a foot bath in front of it and a low stool for Callie to perch on—the perfect height for her to reach my feet. "Nice to meet you, Callie."

"And you." Scanning my face, she tilts her head. "Steam room?"

I laugh out loud, rubbing at my cheeks. "Yes." Jesus Christ, how red and sweaty am I? "Lots of steam."

"It's so relaxing, don't you think?"

I hum, batting off flashbacks coming at me from all directions. All Jude. I'm still tingling between my legs. Still pulsating. Callie pats the stand on the bath, and I pull the robe in around my thighs and place my feet where indicated, making sure I keep my legs closed. What the bloody hell has he done with my knickers?

She inspects my toes and reaches for the tap on the mini bath, flipping on the water and holding her hand beneath the flow to check the temperature. "What colour are you feeling today, Amelia?" She holds up two bottles, and I look between them with a furrowed brow.

"Those are my options?" I ask, pointing to one. "Nude and . . ." I indicate the other. "Nude?"

"Both complement your skin tone wonderfully."

"What's my skin tone?"

"Ummm . . ." She scans what she can see of my skin. "Fleshy?"

My frown deepens, my mind going into overdrive. Oh my God, did he . . . ? "Callie, did someone choose a colour for me?"

"Oh no, I just thought that you looked like a nude kind of woman." She grins, all toothy.

"You've never seen me before I walked through that door."

Her eyes drop, her fluster growing rapidly as she flips the tap off.

"Callie," I say again, this time quiet. "Did someone pick this colour for me?"

"Yes, yes, okay, Mr. Harrison may have stopped by and influenced the choices."

He's dictating what nail polish I should wear? I huff and scan the row of polishes on the glass shelf behind Callie. "I think I'd like that one. Third in from the right."

"Seafoam?"

"Yes." I nod. I've never in my life chosen any shade of blue or green polish. "Perfect." It reminds me of Jude's eyes. I frown to myself.

"But . . ."

"It's perfect," I say again, thinking. I am *way* out of my depth. *So no more games?* Something tells me Jude Harrison is having a lot of fun. But what happens when the game ends? Who wins? I wince at the pang of pain that flares in my chest, automatically reaching up and rubbing into my robe. What the hell is that?

He chose nude polish. Isn't he the one who's gone on about being more . . . loose? As in adventurous. I laugh under my breath and close my eyes, letting Callie at me. Here I am. My God, what on earth am I doing? This isn't me, bending to a man's will, begging for him, dreaming of him, rendered useless by him. Jude Harrison has brought out a side of me I never knew existed. *Submissive*. I'm not sure how comfortable I am with it. Except . . . I sigh. I can appreciate the step out of my everyday life, escaping expectation and letting someone lead.

In my darkness, I think in circles, going over the same things again and again, as if something new might pop up and offer a different take. It doesn't. I keep coming back to the same conclusion.

I love how he so easily wipes my mind of everything except the moment I'm in with him—whether it be a moment of frustration, desire, or anger. I love how he consumes my thoughts. I love how he so easily distracts me from work, giving me momentary—and needed—freedom from the pressure I place on myself. It's like handing the reins of a part of my life over to someone else and letting them steer me for a while. Because when I surrender to him, I'm light. Free. Happy to go wherever he takes me.

That's not so bad, is it?

I open my eyes and see Callie has finished soaking my feet and massaging a foot scrub into them, and is now painting my toes. I smile at the lovely bluey-green shade as she places a UV lamp over my right foot to set the gel polish before starting on my left foot.

"Same for your fingers?" she asks, not looking up.

I look down at my perfectly neat coral nails. "I think so."

The door knocks, and Callie calls out for whoever it is to come in. I wilt in the chair when it opens, revealing Jude, his hair now perfectly back in place and tucked behind his ears. I breathe in, feeling the scratchiness of his facial hair on the inside of my thighs. *Where's my knickers?*

The corner of his mouth lifts in the semblance of a knowing smile as he steps into the room. He's still in those faded jeans he pulled on before walking out of treatment room four—*what a treatment*—but he's added a casual white linen button-down shirt, his sleeves rolled up. I mentally faint on the spot.

"Mr. Harrison," Callie says, abandoning my toes, looking a little panicked. It's the nude polish. I'll defend her to the end.

Jude frowns down at my toes and turns interested eyes my way. I don't shy away. "Green?"

"It's seafoam, actually," I say, inspecting my feet casually, thinking how it's a similar shade to Jude's eyes when he's about to send me delirious with pleasure. His accusing glare licks my skin. Over nail polish? I look out the corner of my eye. He doesn't seem impressed.

"Callie, would you give us a moment?" he says calmly.

What?

"Of course!" She's up and gone before I can protest, and Jude's soon sitting on the little stool she's just vacated in front of me.

Reaching for the leather arms of the chair, I hold tight, stiffening from head to toe as he takes my ankles and starts to pull my legs apart. I fight him with everything I have. No, we're not doing this again. I tense harder, resisting his force, but I'm no match for him. My legs spread, and I go lax in the chair, surrendering to him *again*, as he moves his stare to between my legs. On a long, deep breath, his chest expands, and he sighs, tilting his head, having a good study while I sit there and just let him, his large hands flexing around my ankles.

"How was your massage?" he finally asks, keeping me exposed to him.

"Overrated," I say quietly, making him smile a little, peeking up at me. I'm unable to stop myself from mirroring the glorious sight, my own small smile breaking. He's maddening. And fucking wonderful.

"Maybe you should leave a review on Tripadvisor."

A burst of laughter erupts from me. If I leave a review on Tripadvisor, he'd be fully booked for the rest of his life. And, weirdly, that makes me wonder about all the women who have come before me.

And those who will come after.

I flinch.

Using my feet as a prop, he rises and leans in, getting his face close to mine. Then he releases one ankle and walks his fingers up the inside of my leg and strokes through my recovering flesh. My lips part, air streaming past them, my body instantly convulsing.

"Overrated?" he whispers, bringing his finger to his lips and sucking it clean.

Fuck.

"You're going to a lot of effort to get a woman into bed," I say quietly, my eyes glued to his.

"Do you think I go to all this trouble for—"

"Every woman you want to fuck?"

He takes a moment, thinking. "I don't, to be clear."

Probably because he usually gets little resistance. "Lucky me," I breathe as his mouth moves closer. The heat of his fresh breath warms my face, his signature musky scent sending me dizzy. He rests his lips on mine but doesn't advance his move into a full-blown kiss. It doesn't stop my insides from furling, though, my hands twitching, ready to grab him and haul him into me as I look into his eyes, waiting, my impatience growing. I can't help but think that any kiss I experience in my future that isn't with Jude Harrison will be subpar. How depressing. I release my tongue, lightly slipping it into his mouth, meeting his, and he groans, pushing his mouth harder onto mine and devouring me for a few brief moments before pulling away, leaving me listless and breathless.

"Let's talk about your choice of polish," he says, lowering back to the stool before me and lifting my feet onto his thighs. "Blue." He pouts.

"I told you, it's seafoam."

"I chose nude."

"They're *my* nails."

"Tonight, Amelia, you're all mine, so I get to choose." He stands and moves onto a chair beside mine. *Just tonight?* "Callie," he calls, and she pops her head around the door. I close my legs and pull my robe in, making Jude smile mildly. "Amelia has changed her mind," he says, matter-of-fact.

"Have I?"

"She'd like nude."

"Would I?"

He looks at me with a dash of playful warning. "Just let me do all the thinking." He takes my hand as Callie resumes her position and picks up her small nail drill, starting to remove the seafoam polish. "Hand massage?" Jude asks.

"Oh no," I snatch my hand away, shaking my head. Definitely not.

"It's part of the service." He reaches for the hand cream on Callie's workstation. "Isn't that right, Callie?"

She giggles and blushes, keeping her attention on removing my polish as Jude pumps a few blobs of cream into his palm.

"And I know for a fact that you love a good hand massage," he says, claiming my hand. Callie chuckles again, peeking at me.

"I don't need a hand massage." I glare at Jude, silently begging him not to do this here as he starts working the cream into my hand. Of course, my plea goes unanswered. I grit my teeth, closing my eyes, digging deep for the strength to sustain the next phase of his seduction as his fingers slip through mine. I'm taken back to the bathroom at my office building, when he blindsided me, and my recovering flesh starts to throb greedily for him again. A million curses are let loose in my head. I'm trying so hard not to tense so Callie feels it. I know I'm failing when she repositions my foot to where she wants it.

Jude's soft, huge hands work slowly and effortlessly over mine, the fire inside me raging. "Jude," I whisper, flexing my fingers as he rubs between them.

"It's not nice?" he asks, pushing his bottom lip out, as if hurt.

My jaw tightens as I stare at him, tingles erupting, his magic hands crucifying me yet again.

He smiles. "I'm really fucking glad you accepted my invitation."

"Your invitation to send me wild?" I ask on a whisper, making his smile widen.

"If it makes you feel better, you send me wild too." He leans over and hovers his mouth close to mine, apparently unbothered by his staff in our sexually charged orbit. "If I kiss you, will you be able to control yourself?"

"Probably not," I admit. "Will you?"

"No." He moves closer. "And that's what I love about being around you."

"Your lack of control?"

"You're consuming," he whispers. "Can you imagine how incredible it's going to be when I'm finally inside you?" His lips skimming mine has me folding to his power, opening up to him, my head yelling at him to make that happen now.

But the door opens, and Jude pulls away, looking over his shoulder to who's entered. Anouska sighs. *I feel the same, Anouska. He's exasperating.* "You have a call," she says, holding up a mobile.

"I'm busy," he counters, continuing with his fun, back to rubbing my hand while I die on the chair with an audience.

Anouska turns her eyes onto me, her intrigue real. I shrug, at a loss. "It's Rhys," she says.

That soon wins Jude's attention. He drops my hand fast and stands, and I rest back in the chair, not for the first time wondering what's happening. And yet I don't feel like it's a question I can ask him. I hardly know him, and yet I've never felt this kind of intensity before. I'm not sure how to deal with it, except to succumb to its power.

Oh my God, I'm thinking in circles.

Jude strides toward Anouska and takes his phone as he passes. "Rhys," he says. "What's up?"

My curiosity rages as Anouska gets her surprise in check and Callie silently resumes removing my seafoam nail polish. And I don't stop her. There are so many questions swirling around in my head right now. Who's Rhys? Is that a man or a woman? Why did Jude react so urgently?

"So nude," Callie says, smiling up at me.

"Yes, nude," I reply, sinking farther into the chair.

Just let me do all the thinking.

I wholeheartedly wish I could do that, just surrender to the force of Jude Harrison with no doubts or hesitation. Problem is, I feel like a thousand red flags are being waved in my face.

Chapter 17

After Callie is finished pampering my fingers and toes, I go to the changing rooms.

With my nude nails.

Not that I'm paying much mind to the fact that Jude made his demand and I submitted. My thoughts are still chasing in circles. I lower to a bench, smiling at a lady as she passes in her workout kit, heading for the gym or a class. I need the girls' thoughts, so I get my phone from my locker, wincing at the missed calls from Mum. All five of them. I check the time. Three hours ago. A message from Abbie confirms my fears.

> Your mum's suspicious. She knew it was you on the phone and she wants to know whose Rolls-Royce you were in and where you were going. I'm avoiding her.

"Shit," I curse, going back to the seat and tapping my phone on my knee. What can I tell her? I don't have a chance to think about that, because she calls me again. My face bunches. "Mum," I say, standing and starting to pace.

Another lady wanders into the changing rooms in her swimsuit, soaked. She stops before me and indicates behind me. "Can I get to my locker?"

"Oh, I'm so sorry." I move out of her way.

"Locker?" Mum asks. "Who was that? Where are you?"

"At the gym," I say quietly, shrinking.

"Oh, and you got there in a Rolls-Royce, did you? What's going on, Amelia? And hurry up and explain because I have customers waiting."

I exhale and drop heavily to a bench. I don't know what I can tell her. That I'm on a date? That'll lead to all kinds of questions I don't want to answer, and I know she won't approve, no matter who I'm on a date with. It's been only weeks since I walked out on Nick. It would be insensitive to declare I'm dating so soon. It doesn't matter that this isn't actually a date. I don't really know what the fucking hell this is, and if I don't know, how on earth will I explain it to my mum? And then there's my father. He *definitely* can't know. Definitely won't approve.

"Mum," I say, not wanting to lie to her. "There are some things about my life you shouldn't know." What a stupid thing to say.

"Well, now I'm even more worried. Are you in some kind of trouble?"

"God, no. I promise, I'm not in any trouble." I glance around the luxury changing facilities. That's not true. I'm in so much trouble. "I'm just taking a bit of time out for myself. Trying to relax." Silence. That was probably an even stupider thing to say. Since when have I ever been good at relaxing? I'm too busy trying to succeed. On that thought, I roll my shoulders, and I don't feel one muscle pull. I'm . . . loose. "I'm okay, Mum," I breathe, exasperated by myself.

"Then where are you?"

"At a spa." Truth.

"Where?"

"In Oxfordshire." Truth.

"Oxfordshire? Isn't that where you went with the girls on your birthday? Why go all the way to Oxfordshire? We have endless lovely spas around here."

Because the sinfully handsome creature I've unexpectedly met brought me here. "Mum," I say softly, with only a little warning, reminding her that I'm a thirty-year-old woman and I do not need to explain myself to my parents. "You have proof of life. I'm fine, trust me."

She huffs, indignant. "Fine. I have to go. Are you still visiting tomorrow?"

"I'll be there at noon."

"Good." She hangs up without so much as a goodbye, which is a solid indication that I've upset her. I shouldn't have to hide anything. To my own point, I'm a grown woman. And yet, as per my previous thought, I don't know what this is. Feeling a little deflated and not so relaxed, I send Abbie a voice message giving her a condensed version of how that went. She might want to carry on avoiding my mother for the time being.

I get up to put my phone away, stalling when a picture message pops up from Dad. I smile and open it, smiling wider when an image of him in a fine suit appears, a tailor bent down beside him pinning the seam of his jacket. I swipe through a few more images of my brother in his suit too, a beer in his hand as adjustments are made to his trousers. When I reach the final picture, my smile drops. "Why, Dad?" I blurt, staring at an image of Nick giving the camera a thumbs-up. I quickly call Clark. "Why is Nick there?" I ask as soon as he answers.

"How do you know?"

"Because Dad just sent me a picture."

"Oh."

"I—" I still, thinking. "Oh my God," I breathe. "He's still an usher?"

"What did you want me to do?" Clark whispers. "You broke up with him, Amelia. I couldn't kick him in the stomach too."

I drop my head back, looking at the ceiling in despair. "Oh God, Clark," I cry, hearing myself. Whiny. "You said you'd tell him." I can't spend a whole day at my brother's wedding avoiding my ex. I want to celebrate, not hide.

"I will," he says. "In the meantime, he's getting fitted for a suit."

"Jesus Christ." I slap a hand on my forehead, wondering if I should man up and take the responsibility off Clark. After all, I split up with

Nick, not him. But Clark offered, and I gratefully accepted, keen not to be the one to hurt Nick again. I don't think my brother thought it through. You'd think Nick would step up and step back.

No, because he's still hoping.

"Where are you?" Clark asks.

"Trying to de-stress." What a joke. The door behind me opens and Anouska appears. "I've got to go. Try not to ask my ex to be godfather to your firstborn, please."

"Very funny."

"Steam room time," Anouska sings when I hang up.

"What?"

She looks down at her clipboard. "Four o'clock, steam room."

I don't know whether to dread it or fling my bikini on and race there. "Steam room," I say to myself, my loose muscles suddenly tightening again. "Okay, steam room." I throw my mobile into the locker and drag my bikini out. "Does he have a preference on which steam room he'd like me to pass out in?" Of pleasure, not of heat.

Anouska presses her lips together. "Last one on the right." Then leaves me to ready myself for the next stage of Jude's seduction. "I better get penetration after all this," I mumble to myself, irritated to high heaven. I need to erase the conversations with Mum and Clark and forget that my father is an insensitive old idiot sometimes.

Bring it on, Harrison.

I need this.

I slip into my black-and-gold bandeau top and bikini pants, swing on my robe, and walk with determination to the steam room. I'm not surprised to find it empty. I check the temperature and knock it down a few notches before lowering to the tile bench, my arse slipping across the wet surface.

And I wait for him.

And wait.

And wait.

But he doesn't come.

And I'm enraged.

Where the hell is he when I actually need him? *Calm down.* I close my eyes, working on doing exactly that, but all I can hear are my own damn questions chasing circles in my mind. What is this? What's happening? Why the big, elaborate effort to bend me to his will? And why does he walk away when I *do* bend?

I stand, so fucking angry, and take one step toward the door.

It opens.

I stop.

And everything inside me calms in an instant. Relief is within reach. I should read into it, but I don't. Not now.

He steps in and closes the door, and my breathing goes to shit. I can't wait for him to decide when I get to lose myself. I need this. So I go to him, circling his shoulders and taking his mouth with confidence and conviction.

And frown.

His shoulders feel . . . smaller.

His lips feel . . . different.

"Christ," someone says against my mouth. A man.

Not Jude.

I'm frozen, my brain trying to catch up with what's happening. Not fast enough. The door swings open again, and the steam escapes, allowing me to see whose lips are stuck to mine. My horror is instant, and I retreat, staring through the haze at an alarmed-looking man.

"Oh. My. God," I squeak. He appears as frozen as I feel, blinking rapidly.

"What the fuck?"

I startle at the sound of a furious voice and find Jude through the haze, standing on the threshold of the steam room, his face a picture of rage.

"It's not . . . I didn't . . ." I don't have a chance to plead my case. Jude grabs the man and drags him out of the steam room. "Jude!" I yell, going after him. My horror multiplies when I find he's got the poor, unexpecting guy pushed up against the nearest wall. "Jude!"

"What the fucking hell do you think you're playing at?" he yells in his face, as the guy fights Jude's hands away from his chest.

"Calm the fuck down." The guy pushes Jude away.

"You're fired!"

"What?"

What?

I stare at the man, noting, now that steam isn't hampering my vision, he's young, maybe mid-twenties, and he's in really good shape. Fired?

"You fucking heard me." Jude points a finger in his face. "Get your shit and get the fuck out of my hotel."

"She—"

"I don't want to hear it. Get out before I fuck you up, Jenson!"

"Fuck you, Jude. You're un-*fucking*-hinged. I'm done." Jenson stalks off, knocking a bale of towels off a shelf as he passes, cursing the entire way, and I stand like a useless idiot while Jude stalks in circles, constantly raking a hand through his hair.

Then he stops and all his anger is suddenly directed at me. "What the fuck was that?" he yells, throwing a deranged arm out toward the steam room door. "Are you purposely trying to send me over the edge?"

"What?" My shock is leaving, and coming fast up the back is anger. "Do you think I skulk around local steam rooms jumping men?"

He huffs and turns his back on me. "I know what I fucking saw, Amelia."

"I thought it was you!" I shout, outraged. "And don't turn your back on me."

He swings around, his jaw tense, his eyes dark, dark blue. "Well, it wasn't me!"

"I know!" I snap my mouth shut when Anouska walks into the spa, her heels skidding to a stop when she sees us.

"How dare you let another man taste you, Amelia. How dare you!"

I blink as Anouska slowly backs out, wary and shocked. Good, I'm glad, because his reaction to this is shocking. "How dare I?" I ask. Who the hell does he think he is? "You don't own me. I'm not yours."

"Wrong," he hisses, crowding me. "You are so fucking wrong."

What? God, my head feels like it could fall off. This is crazy. I sag where I stand. In my fucking bikini.

"It was an honest mistake," I say calmly, hoping he feeds off me because this is getting us nowhere, and my head is hurting now more than ever before. *Are you purposely trying to send me over the edge?*

I'm on the edge with him.

"And how many 'honest mistakes' can I expect you to make going forward?" he asks.

Going forward? Where the hell are we going? *Someone please tell me!* "Are you hearing yourself, Jude?"

"Yes, I'm fucking hearing myself." He slips an arm around my lower back and hauls me into his body. My palms find his shoulders, my bare front compressed to his. "I don't want anyone else touching what's mine." His face softens as he gazes at me. I don't bother telling him I'm not his again. It would be fucking pointless, because when he has his hands on me, his mouth on me, his eyes on me, God damn me, I am.

"I thought it was you."

"No, Amelia, this is me." He sweeps in and swallows me whole with a kiss, making it hard, passionate, and urgent. His tongue lashes through my mouth, and mine has no choice but to follow, accepting the force. I'm a slave to his demand. Once again, lost. Once again, at his mercy. Once again, consumed by him.

Jude gasps when he breaks our kiss, pushing his forehead into mine firmly; then he pulls away, not looking me in the eye. "I'm sorry," he whispers, taking a few deep breaths, looking troubled. Then he turns on his bare feet and walks away, leaving me in a riot of confusion.

"Jude," I call. "Jude, stop."

He doesn't.

My heart races, my lips sore from his forceful kiss. He's sorry? The door closes behind him, and I glance around the empty space, lost. What now? Does he want me to leave? Stay? And does it matter? What do *I* want to do?

I want to go after him and nail him down, press him to kill this curiosity inside, answer all my questions, tell me where this is going.

But that would be dumb. After all, we're nothing, just two people with an inexorable chemistry who are exploring it.

Right?

I don't know!

I snatch my robe down and cover myself, leaving the spa and making my way through the glass corridor, stopping when I pass the gym. I see him lying on a bench at the far end, away from everyone else, doing chest presses, his pace rapid and smooth. Exorcising his anger. *My God, Jude Harrison, what is going on in that head of yours?*

I carry on to the changing rooms and get my phone, calling Abbie and Charley. The moment they both see my face, they start firing questions, none of which I can or want to answer. Which begs the question of why I called them.

"It's been . . . intense," I say, feeling so pathetic. "I don't know what's happening. I don't know what he wants, what he expects." I laugh. "I don't even know what *I* want or expect."

"Oh dear," Charley breathes.

"Then talk to him," Abbie blurts.

Sounds easy, doesn't it? But, I admit, I'm scared about what he might say. And what I might confess.

I met this guy a couple of weeks ago, and it's been a roller coaster since. And frighteningly, I fear this is just the start of the ride. A thrilling but scary ride.

I should get off the roller coaster. I don't need or want this kind of complication in my life. The aftermath, this uncertainty, isn't why I came to Arlington Hall today.

So why am I still here?

Chapter 18

I question whether I should go to dinner. Whether—after what happened in the steam room—he'll even be there. But then a card is pushed under my door confirming my reservation. For two. So it looks like I'm staying on the roller coaster. I'm trying not to forget that I just walked away from a man for wanting what I couldn't give him. And now I'm getting involved with a man who wants something I can't give him. Control. But isn't that okay to an extent? To allow him *some* control? Take freedom from the pressure when I want it? Is that how this could work? And is that realistic?

Fuck, I don't even know.

Talk to him. Just talk. That's my plan for dinner. Lay my cards on the table and see what he says. I can take the fling. Want to, actually. What I can't take are the interludes of drama and conflict spiked by his mood swings and extreme reactions. *Possessive.*

Except I'm not his to possess.

So why the fuck am I slipping into the underwear he's bought me?

I close my eyes, hiding from myself in the floor-length mirror, as if avoiding explaining myself to myself, as I shimmy into my satin slip dress, pulling the straps into place. The material, cut on the cross, skims my hips, falling just below my knee, the low-scoop neckline sitting only a fraction above the balcony cups of the bra he chose. I sit on one of the armchairs and slide my feet into my slingback gold stilettos and stand, taking my hands over my shoulders and lifting my hair, pushing it away so it tumbles down my back.

Ready.

But not.

I leave the suite and make my way down to the restaurant, smiling mildly at Anouska as I pass her in the lobby. "Enjoy dinner," she says, a touch of knowing in her tone.

"Thank you." The moment I reach the doors to the restaurant, I see him. He's at the far back of the Orangery, at a table for two, looking out across the rose garden. As if he's sensed I'm here, he cranes his neck and looks over his shoulder. And the moment our eyes meet, my heart turns. I'm winded. He literally takes my breath away. His face. It kills me, the raw, rugged beauty. His eyes sparkle as he gets up, revealing himself in his full, devastating glory. He's in a light-grey suit, his shirt stark white, his darker grey tie perfectly knotted.

I'm fucked. So completely fucked. It defies reason. It defies *me*. This guy, in all his visual perfection, has some serious issues—I should run in the opposite direction, end this slow creep into the unknown. And yet . . .

I'm here begging for more. Begging for *him*. He's definitely struggling with something, and I have an unshakable desperation to know what. I have to know him. What makes him tick, who he is, where he's been, and where he's going.

The maître d' approaches, and I point to Jude. "I'm with Mr. Harrison," I say quietly.

"Oh yes, of course, please." He sweeps an arm out, and I start walking on shaky legs through the tables to Jude, admiring his faint smile as he slips his hands into his pockets, getting comfortable in his stance, and watches me.

I slow to a stop before him, my heart going crazy. "I'm glad you came," he says, his voice deep but soft. Did he think I wouldn't?

"I wondered whether I should," I admit, keeping his gaze. His eyes are a muted grey this evening, a hint of green around the edges of his irises. He's calm. It's insane that I can tell that from the shade of his eyes.

Nodding very slightly and removing just one hand from a pocket, he leans in, almost cautious, and slips it around my lower back, kissing my cheek. "You definitely should."

That's yet to be determined.

Releasing me, he pulls out my chair, and as I lower, I glance around the restaurant, feeling eyes on me. I'm not wrong. My presence has attracted interest from various guests, including the woman I saw in the lobby this morning. Katherine. She's at a table with a man on the other side of the restaurant. She smiles, and I return it, smiling at another three people all looking this way before getting back to the man opposite me. The man who, obviously, doesn't dine with women here often.

That settles something in me.

"Wine?" Jude asks, passing me the menu.

I don't take it. *Let me do all the thinking.* "What do you recommend?"

He falters, retracting the menu, a wave of satisfaction travelling across his perfect face. He likes me handing the reins to him. It's just wine. "I recommend Krug."

"Champagne? Are we celebrating?"

He waves the waiter over and orders a bottle before looking at me across the table, resting back in his chair. "Why do people think they can only drink champagne when they're celebrating?" he asks, his face straight but light. "Every day we get to live is cause for celebration."

I sense a deeper meaning to his statement and think about his mother. The sadness I detected when he talked about her on the stage. But he didn't talk about his dad. "So I should drink champagne every day?" I ask.

He shrugs. "Why not?"

"Because I'd be bankrupt," I reply on a light laugh, and he smiles, his sparkly eyes squinting a little as he thinks, studying me. The intensity of his gaze constantly on me will have me sliding off this chair soon.

"Well, luckily for you"—his voice is quiet—"I have an endless supply in the wine cellar." The waiter returns and pours, and Jude leans over the table and picks up my flute, offering it to me. "Tell me what you think."

Accepting, I take a small sip and nod. "It's lovely."

"Agree."

"Where's the wine cellar?" I ask, wondering how many hidden nooks this place must have. It's extensive, the gift that keeps on giving. Like its owner?

"Under Evelyn's."

"I love how you named the club after your mum."

He smiles. "I don't usually frequent Evelyn's. I prefer the Library Bar." He glances around the restaurant, prompting me to as well. We're definitely tonight's stars of the show. I hear him laugh a little as he returns his eyes to me. Then he stands suddenly and picks up his chair, moving it around the table, sitting next to me rather than opposite me. My eyes follow him back down to the seat, my frown mild as he collects his glass and holds it up.

"What are we drinking to?" I ask, lightly tapping my glass on the side of his.

"Today."

He sips, turning his body more toward me, and leans forward, sliding his palm onto my nape and encouraging me closer until our lips brush. And he kisses me gently. So gently, but the impact hits me as hard as when he's owned me with a kiss. I taste the bubbles on his lips, feel endless eyes on us. Is he making a point? I don't know, and I don't care, because in this moment I'm oblivious to the world around me. And isn't that the beauty of Jude Harrison when he's in my orbit?

My eyes closed, I absorb the light pressure of his lips on mine, floating, tingling.

Lost.

"Shall we order?" he asks, pulling back and dragging his hand onto my cheek. "The lamb is something else. It comes from the farm a few miles away."

I nod my agreement and let Jude order.

"Any allergies?" the waiter asks, looking at me.

"Nuts," Jude says. "Amelia's allergic to nuts."

The waiter nods and makes a note before leaving, and Jude pours more champagne. "Tell me about your family."

"Oh, are we going deep?" I shift in my chair when his hand slips under my dress and rests on my bare knee. I know Jude Harrison has a habit of inappropriate behaviour in inappropriate places, so I'm bracing myself for a slow torture at this table.

"Deep," he muses. "As deep as my tongue was in your pussy earlier." His face is deadpan, watching me as I cough under my breath.

"Do you get a kick out of shock tactics?"

"No, I get a kick out of how badly you want me."

I laugh, quite loudly, but he squeezes my knee, silencing me quickly. "You must be used to women wanting you."

"Not the right ones," he replies quietly, making me tilt my head in curiosity. "Your family," he prompts again. "Come on, Amelia, let's go deep."

"I'm one of two children," I say, his hand burning my skin on my knee. "I have a younger brother, you've met him."

He pulls a pained face. "Clark."

"Yes, he's getting married soon."

"Oh, the younger sibling is getting married?"

"Yes," I confirm, almost tiredly, rolling my eyes at his not-so-subtle sarcasm. "Dad says he's retired, but he isn't really."

"What did/does he do?"

"Finance."

"Like you," he says. "Runs in the family?"

"My grandfather set up the family company in 1959, Dad joined when he was twenty-two, Grandpa retired in 2007, my brother joined the firm after he'd finished university, and Dad retired two years ago and handed the reins to Clark. Or he claims he retired."

Jude's head cocks. "And you?"

"I joined the company fresh out of university and left when my dad bypassed me in favour of my younger brother."

"Ouch."

"It's fine, I'm over it."

Jude nods, clearly not believing me. "The stiffness makes total sense now."

"I am not stiff, Jude Harrison," I breathe, going for bold and slipping my hand under the tablecloth, sliding it into his lap. His eyes widen—they're definitely greener now—his smile delighted as I stroke over his growing erection. I tilt my head as he sits up straight, the electric energy bouncing between us climbing a few more notches. "I left the family business to carve out my own career," I say, squeezing lightly over his bulge. "It was the best decision I've ever made."

He flexes his hips upwards, his lips parting a little. "Go on."

"I started at LB&B Finance Group as a junior adviser and got my head down." I flex my hand, and Jude strokes up the inside of my thigh some more. "My goal is to make partner."

"Yes," he breathes. Up he flexes again.

"I just have to smash my targets and irradicate the competition." I'm beginning to throb.

"Who's the competition?"

"Leighton Steers." A breath. "He's the man whose chair you kicked out from under him."

"He's no threat," Jude says, his hand hovering at the seam of my knickers. "Crush him."

"Me or you?" I ask, breathing in sharply when his finger slips into my wetness.

"You," he confirms. "Be careful of him."

"Why?"

"Because he obviously wants you." His finger enters me, and he leans forward, his gaze falling to my slightly open mouth. "But he can't have you. Can he?"

I shake my head, whimpering as his finger withdraws and slips around my clit. "Jude," I whisper, feeling my blood heat. He only smiles, continuing with his torment, working me under the table. I'm forced to release my hand from his lap and return it to the table, my fingers clawing the tablecloth.

"What about your mum?" he asks, cool and collected. Good for him.

So much for only talking. "She's the consummate wife and mother." *Fuck, I'm going to come.*

"Traditional?"

"Just how Dad likes it." My widening eyes dart around the restaurant, my panic growing with my building pleasure. I can't promise my control when I hit my climax. "Jude, please." I could stop him, push his hand away. And yet . . . I can't.

"Look at me," he breathes.

I do, pushing my back into the chair, shaking my head mildly, silently begging him to spare me. "You're wicked."

He pouts, taking my champagne and placing it in my hand. I can't believe he's doing this. I've no doubt some of the guests are watching us. And he's giving them a show. "Drink champagne while you come, Amelia."

My whole body hardens as I fight to keep myself in my chair, and I drink some champagne as Jude sips his, so fucking casual.

"Now," I breathe, making him push into me deeply, my walls hugging his fingers as I jolt in my chair and my flute hits the table a little harder than it should. My face burns, my release rippling through me gently, my thighs clamping down around his hand, my fucking toes curling in my heels.

"Oh, baby," he groans, sinking his teeth into his lip as he watches me fall apart. "You look fucking stunning."

I breathe out, my body sinking into the chair, as Jude slowly pulls his fingers out of me and squeezes my thigh before taking a napkin and wiping his hand, his smile full of satisfaction. I swallow and drink some more Krug, hoping the icy liquid will cool the relentless heat inside.

Relaxed.

I laugh on the inside in disbelief. What has come of me? Letting a man get me off in a Michelin-starred restaurant? I gaze around and die a thousand deaths when I find Katherine, as well as the man she's with, looking this way. *Oh God.*

Jude sees me looking and reaches for my hand. "Ignore them."

"They'll put in a complaint."

"And what will happen?" he asks. "I'll be asked to leave my own restaurant?"

I laugh. True.

"They don't know that I just fucked you with my fingers, Amelia. They're just curious."

"About me?"

"Yes, about you."

"Why?"

"Because you're here with me." He flicks his eyes to mine briefly, looking hesitant, as if he's not sure he should have said that.

I smile, and he rolls his eyes. It's adorable. I was right. He's never brought a woman here.

"So tell me about your previous relationships," he says, a definite edge of hesitance lingering.

"Is that wise?" I ask, coy. He looks at me out the corner of his eye. He's wondering if it's wise too.

"You mentioned you were on a breakup diet of wine and work."

I hum to myself. Now it's wine, work, and Jude Harrison. I take a breath and take the plunge. "I recently ended a long-term relationship." His head tilts. "His name was Nick."

"*You* ended it?"

I nod, chewing at the corner of my lip, uncomfortable. "We wanted different things."

Jude sits back, interested. "Care to elaborate?"

"He wanted commitment, I wanted a career."

"Commitment . . ."

"Marriage and babies."

"Sounds disgusting." He smirks, and I laugh, feeling the tension leave the table. "So he's out of the picture?"

Nick's out of *my* picture, yes. I'm not sure I'm out of his. But I say yes anyway, because Jude's short history with men around me isn't pleasant. The poor man in the steam room, case in point. I don't love Nick, but I wouldn't wish Jude's temper on him. "And what about you?" I ask.

"Previous relationships?"

"Yes." Do I want to know?

"Nothing significant," he says quietly, smiling. But it doesn't quite reach his eyes. I question whether to push him. Do I want to know?

The waiter appears before I can answer my own question, placing two plates down and turning each one meticulously so the Arlington Hall crest is precisely at the top. Then he proceeds to give a description of everything on the plate, how it's cooked, the ingredients, and where it's all sourced. "Thank you, it looks delicious."

"Thanks, Ken," Jude murmurs, sitting back. "Dig in."

I collect my silverware. "I'm not sure one should *dig* into a plate that looks this good." It's a masterpiece. I slice off a piece of lamb from the cutlet and hum, the meat literally melting in my mouth, the mint strong but not overpowering. "This is really good."

"It is," he agrees, starting to eat too. And now he's got me off while listening to me pant an answer to every question he had, it's his turn to go deep.

"Do you have any siblings?" I ask.

"Two brothers," he answers. "I'm the eldest. Rhys is twenty-eight, Casey is thirty-one."

The Invitation

Rhys. It was his brother who called him. "And you're . . . ?"

He tips a small smile my way. "Thirty-five. And you've just turned thirty."

"Did you memorise *all* the private information you hold on me when you abused your position of power?"

"Yes," he says, reaching for his napkin and wiping the corner of his mouth. "I've been abusing my position of power since I met you." He frowns a little, lost in thought for a moment. God, I'd give anything to know what those thoughts are.

"Can I ask about your parents?" I say tentatively, focusing on my cauliflower puree, mixing the rich gravy with it. When I see him pushing a carrot around his plate out the corner of my eye, I know I've hit a raw nerve. He's staring at his dinner.

"Dad died when I was twenty-four." He smiles to himself, but it's such a sad smile. "Mum was lost without him. When she found Arlington Hall, it lifted her. Gave her something to focus on. Obviously, it didn't look like this then."

I instinctively reach for his hand. He was too young to lose his dad. I won't ask how he died, that would be insensitive. And his mother too?

Jude looks at my hand in his and squeezes it. "I don't know what she saw in the place, or how she even came to be out here. It was off the beaten track; she had no business being in the area." I can see his mind travelling back in time. "She called me, told me she'd stumbled upon a beautiful building in the middle of nowhere and she wanted to buy it." He huffs. "I was worried. It was so spontaneous, but I couldn't bring myself to shit all over her excitement, so I let her drag me out here, and, Jesus, it was a fucking wreck."

I smile. "Not anymore."

"Not anymore," he says, giving up on his dinner and placing his fork down, keeping hold of my hand on the table. "Mum died three years into the restoration." He smiles at me, seeing my slight recoil. He lost them so close together? "She didn't get to see Arlington Hall as you see it, and isn't that a fucking tragedy?"

It really is. God, he looks so beaten all of a sudden. "I'm sure she would have been very proud of what you've done."

"I know she would." Abandoning my hand, he tops up our glasses. "Now, if you don't mind, I didn't plan on such a sombre mood during dinner with you."

Lighten things up. "But you planned on sending me wild and bringing me to climax over conversation?"

"Of course," he replies, simple as that. "But as you know, Amelia, you send me wild too."

Speaking of which . . . "Shall we talk about earlier?"

His face falls a little. "I'd rather forget it ever happened."

"I'd rather understand why it did."

He flicks his eyes up from the glass he's fiddling with. "Is it wrong to want you to myself?"

"It is if we're not on the same page."

His eyes darken. He didn't appreciate that. "What page are you on?"

"I don't know," I admit quietly.

"I'm not sure how much clearer I can be about what page I'm on. I want you."

My next question should be for how long. But I'm reasonable enough to know that's a stupid question to ask someone I've known a couple of weeks and *not* slept with. That alone seems crazy. I've not slept with him. Done many things, but not actually slept with him. "The possessiveness, the gifts. I feel like I'm in a relationship and we've not even had sex. Or is that all part of your seduction?"

"Seduction?"

"Isn't that what this is? To get me into bed?"

"Amelia, I could have had you in bed the first time we met."

"Are you saying I'm easy?"

"No." He sighs, his body language screaming uncomfortable. "I'm saying I'm really—"

"Good at seducing women?"

The Invitation

"Stop putting words in my mouth," he snaps, and I withdraw, stung. He breathes out, rubbing his forehead with the tips of his fingers. "I'm saying I'm really into you."

"I don't understand, Jude. You worked your arse off to make me surrender, and yet all the opportunities you've had to sleep with me you've passed up."

He falls back in his chair, exasperated. "I don't want you to think I'm nothing but a fuckboy."

I inhale. Shit. Isn't that exactly what I need him to be? A one-track-mind man. A man I can depend on not wanting more than I want to give? And there's my problem. Jude feels . . . different. This is all new. And he seems to want a lot of me.

"Why me?" I ask quietly.

"Aside from the fact I fancy the knickers off you?"

I hold back my grin. Just. "Aside from that."

"You're smart, obviously very ambitious." He hitches an amused brow. "Determined."

I laugh a little. "My determination has been squashed since I met you."

"Determination to avoid me?"

"Exactly."

"Why do you want to avoid me?"

I press my lips together. I don't want to talk about my ex. I also don't want to tell Jude that I'm scared of going too deep with him. "This is . . . intense."

"You're scared."

"Wary," I counter, and he nods thoughtfully as he plays with the stem of his glass. "So aside from the attraction, how smart I am, and the fact I was a very determined woman before I met Jude Harrison, what else is there?"

"Are you fishing for compliments?"

"Just trying to understand what I'm getting myself into."

His eyes squint, and for a moment I think he's flinched. Then he smiles. "I sense my wealth is of no consequence to you, given you didn't know who I actually was until recently."

Was that a ploy on his part? He said earlier he doesn't get attention from the right women. *Gold diggers.* And has that been a past problem for him? "You don't know that for sure," I say casually, taking my champagne and sipping. "I might marry you, stake a claim on your fortune, then file for divorce."

He laughs lightly, and the sound has me a quivering wreck, the light fans at the corners of each eye making them twinkle madly. "You'd marry me?"

Whoa. "Hold your horses, champ."

"Champ?"

"Casanova?"

"How about Jude. Plain and simple Jude."

"Jude," I say quietly, taking a breath of confidence. "And the possessiveness?"

He pouts, giving me a boyish grin. "It's new to me."

New to him? Interesting. "What about the anger?"

This time, I definitely know it's a flinch, which tells me anger is an issue for him. He has a temper. My only reassurance right now is that he's aware of it.

"I can work on that," he says, putting his hand on the table, palm up. If I give him my hand, I'll be accepting him. Giving him my patience and understanding. Is he angry about his parents' deaths? About how he naturally reacts to me?

It's rare, in my experience, that people recognise their own faults, so I truly appreciate his admission and sincerity. He doesn't want to be angry.

"Who was that guy?" I ask, giving him my hand. He lifts it to his mouth and kisses my knuckles before setting it gently back on the table.

"The one I found you eating alive in the steam room?" My fork hits the plate, my lips straight, and Jude peeks at me with only mild wariness. "Jenson," he says. "A PT from the gym. I think I need to call him and apologise."

That's comforting too. He's got self-awareness. Owns his mistakes. "And maybe offer him his job back," I say. "I've been thinking about getting a PT for a while."

"Stop it, Amelia." Jude smiles down at his champagne. "If a man has something he wants, shouldn't he guard it with his life?"

"Only if the other person wants to be wanted."

"Do you want me to want you?"

My silence speaks volumes, but he wants more.

"Well?" Turning toward me, he leans forward, his elbow on the table. "Tell me, Amelia." His spare hand slides up my dress again. "Do you want me to want you?" I go stiff in my seat as his finger slips past my knickers and reacquaints itself with the slickness. "I'd say you do," he whispers, pushing deep and high, his moist lips parting as he watches me swallow and tremble. "I think we're done debating this." He pulls out of me and returns his body forward, sucking his finger and taking more champagne.

I shake my head in wonder, my attention caught by that woman, Katherine, again. She quickly looks away when our eyes meet. It's beginning to get awkward. Everyone else seems to have lost interest, the novelty of Jude Harrison dining with a woman wearing off, but not for her.

"That woman," I say, discreetly indicating with my glass. "With the blond guy."

Jude doesn't look, just hums.

"Who is she?"

"Nobody."

My eyebrows raise in surprise at his quick, definitive answer. "You don't even know who I'm pointing to."

His jaw pulses a little, and he makes a meal of showing the inconvenience I'm causing him, turning slowly in his chair to look behind him. Then he turns back. "That's Katherine Jenkins and her husband, Rob. They're members of the golf club and health club and often dine and drink in one of the bars or restaurants here."

"Oh," I say quietly.

"And on that note." Jude stands, and my gaze rises with him. He pulls the champagne out of the bucket and rests it on the table, letting the cloth soak up the melted ice on the bottom of the bottle. His eyes smoke, the green shining through, and my insides burst into flames. "I believe your pussy has a date with my cock."

I stare up at his tall body looming over me, not as shocked as I should be.

Here he is. Jude Harrison.

Dragging the champagne across the tablecloth, he blinks lazily, his eyes making a thousand promises, before he turns and walks away. My stare is nailed to his back as he goes, his gait smooth, his strides long, the champagne swinging by his thigh.

"Fuck," I whisper. This is about to go to another level. I gaze across the table, at our unfinished meals, my head and my heart at war.

Help.

I call the girls.

"How's it going?" Abbie is first in, as always.

"Do I need to come knock some sense into you?" Charley asks.

"Probably."

"Why?" they say in unison.

"Because I'm about to follow him into the unknown."

I don't wait around to see if they try to talk sense into me. Maybe because I'm worried they'll succeed. I hang up and stand, knocking back the last inch of my fizz. I don't know who I was trying to fool, convincing myself I was having dinner with him to talk. He proved that plan null and void the moment he put his hand on my knee. But we did talk, and damn him, damn *me*, I enjoyed getting to know him more. I liked what I heard, saw something more vulnerable and genuine beneath the confident facade and boldness.

But I like his boldness. I like that he overpowers the inherent, constant focus I have on achieving. I like the reprieve he offers me. The calmness I find in emptying my mind and being in the moment with him. Red flags be damned.

I follow Jude, mildly unsettled by the pull leading me. Only mildly. Everything inside is screaming at me to explore this. I'm laser focused as I walk through the tables, my eyes forward, my mind at peace. I can't say no. Won't say no.

When I make it into the lobby, I look up at the sweeping staircase as I move, seeing Jude halfway up, his suit jacket now off, the material of his crisp white shirt stretched across his broad back. I take the handrail and the first step, my heels steady, my heart steady, the beats sharp but consistent, my neck craned to keep my eyes on him as I ascend. He stops at the top and looks back at me following, reaching for his tie and tugging it loose.

I'm not in control. I'm owned, my moves manipulated by the pure intent in his eyes. When I'm only a few steps behind him, he continues, walking casually down a corridor and through some doors, stopping to hold it open for me before carrying on. We're in a private lobby, another set of white-gloss doors ahead of us, console tables lining each side, all with a vase of roses set upon the top. Reaching the double doors, he taps his phone on a keypad and opens the doors, stepping inside. I stop on the threshold, looking up and around, searching for the source of the music everywhere. Jan Blomqvist. "Dancing People Are Never Wrong."

I take a breath, my flesh pulsing harder as he places the champagne on the round table immediately inside the suite before turning and closing the door. Then he faces me, his eyes on mine, and he swallows, holding his hand out. I watch as mine lifts and our fingers brush, sparks firing. I inhale. Jude curses.

And he hauls me into him, his mouth on mine in a heartbeat, hungry but soft, his body swathing me, his hands in my hair, his tongue plunging into my mouth.

And I'm his.

Crippled by the instant rush of blood to my head, dazed by the intoxicating chemistry.

I grab his tie, returning his kiss hard, pulling it off and tossing it aside as he walks backwards, taking me with him. My dress is scrunched at the sides, lifted over my head, and dropped to the floor, and his hands are soon back in my hair as I work his buttons, my impatience off the charts. Abandoning the final one, I rip it open, shoving it down his arms as a supressed grunt hits my ears. I throw it down with force, getting my hands back on him, feeling his chest, his pecs, his stomach, before I grab fistfuls of his hair and force him harder onto my mouth, moaning. My bra is discarded and tossed to the floor, and his palms cover my breasts, making my torso concave, my nipples stinging with the pleasure of his hands brushing across them.

"Jude." I'm so fucking frantic for him.

"Amelia," he pants, ripping his mouth off mine and holding my face, his jaw so tight beneath his stubble. He stares into my eyes as I grasp his wrists, our faces so close, our loud breaths colliding. He looks almost angry as he gazes at me. I must look so dazed. But I am far from confused. Him. He's like a hit of life to a part of me I never knew was dead. This feeling is consuming. The connection is bending my head. Is this what happens when you meet the one? Explosions, fireworks, a burning heat inside that might make you disintegrate? As I look into his eyes, I know I could drown in them.

And I am.

Sinking, struggling to breathe. "What's happening?" I whisper, my mouth out of control, something taking over me.

His eyes dart across my face, his palms increasing their pressure on my cheeks as my hands grip his wrists tightly. "I don't fucking know," he breathes, tackling my mouth again, kissing me hard and purposefully, walking me to the nearest wall and pushing me up against it. "Let's talk about that in the morning."

I'm not going to argue. If he doesn't sate this fire inside soon, I'm going to lose my mind. I yank his belt loose, push his trousers over his arse, and dig my fingernails into the solid globes of flesh. He hisses, kissing his way over my cheek, onto my shoulder, across my décolletage, onto my boob. I smack my head against the wall and look up at the ceiling, my lungs burning. His warm mouth covers my nipple and sucks as my hands drag up his back and grip his shoulders.

"Trousers," he demands hoarsely, placing his hands on the wall on either side of my head, his eyes heavy. I slide down the wall, exhaling at the outline of his erection as I pass. Urgency has me lifting one foot in turn and pulling his shoes off, then his socks, before I reach for the waist of his trousers and fight them down his legs. He kicks his way out of them and hauls me back up his body, my legs wrapping around his waist. "Fuck, fuck, fuck," he breathes, turning and carrying me across the room blindly, his lips back with me, our chests splattered together, his neck craned back to accommodate my mouth. Soft sheets meet my back, his front splayed on mine. Our kiss is chaotic and loud. He moans, I moan. He fists my hair, I fist his. Then he rolls us so I'm straddling him.

Biting his lip, I drag it through my teeth, and he groans, squeezing his eyes shut briefly before opening them and watching me kiss my way down his chest, onto his stomach, over his boxers.

"Shit, Amelia," he barks, reaching down and yanking me back up, rolling us again and returning the favour, licking and biting his way across my breasts. I whimper, my back arching violently, desire overwhelming me. Air is hard to find, my panting loud as his mouth crosses my stomach, his thumbs slipping up the sides of my knickers. Sweat starts to bead on my forehead as he inches the lace material down my legs, kissing his way onto the inside of my thighs.

Then he licks through my slickness and I cry out, my stomach muscles tightening, the stabs of pleasure sharp. Discarding my knickers, Jude gets to his knees and pulls me to mine, taking fistfuls of hair, holding me in place, his eyes wild, his hair in disarray. I breathe in his face, reaching for his boxers, and slip my palms inside onto his arse, stroking, feeling, watching him bracing himself as I edge them down and drag the tips of my fingers over his tight hips to his lower stomach. I brush lightly through the hair, down, down, down, as my tongue leaves my mouth and licks across his parted lips. A low, supressed grunt vibrates at the back of his throat, and he waits, his body rolling with mine as I move my touch to the very root of his arousal, delivering teasing, feathery strokes with the tips of my fingers across the length of him. I reach the weeping head and wrap my fist around him, rubbing my thumb through his precum, fascinated by the darkening of his hooded eyes, starting to work him, slow and steady. His grip of my hair increases. His face strains beautifully, his head dropping back, giving me access to his neck. Moving in, I worship his throat with my mouth, his dark-blond scruff rough against my lips and tongue.

His Adam's apple bulges from his swallow, and his hand is suddenly over mine on his dick. "Stop." He strains the word, his breathing becoming rapid. "Just give me . . . I need . . . Fuck, give me a second."

I wait while he gathers himself, feel him throbbing in my unmoving hand, returning to his neck and inhaling his manly scent, tasting the salty sweat on his skin. He suppresses a low, deep growl, pulling me away by my hair.

Looking down at me, he scans my damp face, moving his hands onto my cheeks, stroking softly. "I didn't expect this, Amelia." He pushes me down to my back and crawls up my body, blanketing me. "There's no going back after this." He shifts his hips and slides into me, inhaling sharply, and his eyes clench shut, the strain on his face just fucking beautiful.

"Yes," I breathe, as he fills me inch by inch until I'm full to the brim with him, my walls throbbing, gripping. The fullness, the rightness. It makes my head spin. I feel so incredibly free trapped beneath his hard body.

"Breathe," he whispers, remaining still, allowing me to meld around him.

I didn't realise I was holding my breath. I exhale, bending my legs, opening them wider. "God, you feel good." I can feel every pulse of him inside me.

"Yeah?" he replies, gruff, wedging his fists into the mattress to hold up his torso. He grinds, withdrawing, advancing, and every move makes the muscles in his arms and chest swell and ripple.

The heels of my feet wedge into the backs of his thighs. "Yeah." I roll up, meeting his next drive, and his chin drops to his chest, his teeth clenched. Taking another moment. And I'm happy to let him, happy to watch him dealing with the sensations. He looks so stunning, his face pained with pleasure. Tilting his hips, he starts moving again, driving in and out methodically, the friction perfect, each thrust hitting me satisfyingly deep.

My head is empty except for my appreciation and the pleasure being inflicted on me. I could stay here forever. Watch him forever. Feel like this forever.

I reach for his face, smooth over the creases as he looks up through his lashes, his hair falling onto his forehead. I would walk off the edge of a cliff if he told me to right now. That's the level of impact. That's the deepness of this moment.

Balancing on one hand, Jude moves one of mine to above my head, then lowers to a forearm, stroking his other hand up the inside of my arm and lacing our fingers, gripping hard.

"Kiss me," he whispers against my lips, and I obey, tackling his mouth fiercely, my urgency upping the pace of his drives. I hum, moan, flex my hand in his, claw my nails into his shoulder. The pressure is building, the heat travelling through my body to my head. His dick expands within me, and he squeezes my hand tight, pushing it into the mattress.

Then he's suddenly moving, rolling onto his back and taking me with him, still buried inside me as I come to rest on his hips. I cry out at the deeper invasion, splaying my palms on his stomach as I breathe through the mild stab of pain, and Jude pants, his hands falling to my thighs. I gather myself, filling my lungs.

"Okay?" he gasps, waiting. I can only nod, rolling my hips a little.

His fingers dig into my flesh, a rough groan rumbling deep in his throat, and once I know I've got a handle on things, I start to move, rocking back and forth, dragging my heavy head and heavier eyes up.

He holds up his hands to me, fingers splayed. "Hold on to me," he says softly, prompting me to place my palms against his and watch as he slowly folds his fingers over mine, our hands entwined tightly. My anchor as I ride him. His gaze constantly moves from my thighs to my bouncing boobs to my eyes, his face straight, his jaw tense. He starts to flex his hips, and I whimper, blood rushing to my head. Jude nods, seeing I'm close, holding my hands tighter as I ride him harder. "Fuck, Amelia," he barks, using my hands to pull me down, kissing me with force before pushing me back up. My hair falls all over my face, and I toss it back, focused on the building pleasure and grabbing it until I'm smashing down onto his hips and he's pounding up. "Fuck!" I'm pulled back down, flipped onto my back, and he's inside me again, his arms cradling my head, my nails scratching at his back. He hisses, kissing me hard and chastely, biting my lip, moving his mouth to my ear, breathing into it. "I want to come with you," he whispers, sending tingles from my ear to my pussy. "I want your pussy sucking every last drop of my cum out of me."

His words serve as a catalyst, and the creeping pleasure starts to steam forward.

"I feel it coming," he growls, thrusting on, his hips meeting mine every time I lift them into him, his mouth kissing across my face to my other ear. "Do you feel out of control, baby?"

Black dots start to hamper my vision, my head feeling like it's going to burst with my body. "Jude," I say, begging.

He licks the shell of my ear. My hands grapple at his back. "It's coming," he whispers.

"Jude."

"Coming."

"Jude!"

He stills and I yell, slipping my hands into the hair on his nape as he lifts his head and gazes down at me. The look that passes between us is charged. Understanding. This is . . . something.

"Coming," he breathes, gritting his teeth as he retreats and rolls, recapturing my climax and nudging me over the edge, in total control of my pleasure.

The intensity paralyses me, and Jude barks his release, starting to shake, to the point he's forced to drop his head into my neck. The heat of his breath on my skin, his hot body engulfing me, it's stifling.

And yet natural.

"Jesus," he gasps, shuddering.

Our bodies roll, the music melding with our loud, chaotic breathing, the beats sinking into my recovering body.

What just happened?

I stare at the ceiling, overcome, exhausted, hot, sweaty.

And fucking terrified.

"Okay?" he eventually whispers, remaining where he is. I can't help but think he doesn't want to see my face or he doesn't want me to see his.

"Are you?" I throw it back at him.

"I think I'm in more trouble now than I was an hour ago."

"Me too," I reply quietly, an unexpected lump forming in my throat. What the fuck? I fight it with all I have, trying to make sense of this, as my body recovers from my orgasm and my heart tries to find its normal rhythm. I question if it ever will again. *Marked.* Oh God, what's happening? I am *not* going to cry after sex. How pathetic. And proof if ever anyone needs it that people do not think clearly during the throes of passion.

I blink back the building tears, praying Jude stays exactly where he is until I have this strange bout of emotion under control. But then he moves. *Fuck.*

As he slips out of me, I wince, the soreness instant. He rests on his forearms and takes some hair from my face, pushing it over my ear. "You look as fucked as I feel."

I have no idea how I should take that. Physically fucked, or has he noticed the sheen in my eyes? "And you look beautifully fucked." I scrunch my nose, as I admire Jude Harrison postclimax. It's a sight to behold.

He smiles, kissing the corner of my mouth before getting up and walking away.

"Lord have mercy," I whisper, propping myself up on my elbows to get the best view of his back. His arse.

"Mercy granted."

I gasp quietly. "You heard that?" I'm thrown back to our spa day when Charley and Abbie caught sight of Jude in the Library Bar and joined me, a puddle on the floor.

"I heard that," he calls as he disappears through the door.

I drop to my back, grabbing a pillow and covering my mortified face. I should be smiling, on a postclimactic high.

I think I'm in more trouble now than I was an hour ago.

What have I let myself in for? It's a ridiculous question. I knew what would happen if I came here. But I honestly never expected that. The most powerful experience of my fucking life. "Oh, Amelia," I whisper, throwing the pillow aside and, for the first time, taking in my surroundings. A bedroom. A very large bedroom, decorated in an array of neutral tones, the soft furnishings various textures—velvet, chenille, suede. I get up and go to the window, biting my lip as I look across the glass roof of the Orangery to another window. My suite. He stood here, naked, enticing me.

And here I am.

Backing up, I follow my feet to a door across the bedroom, entering a dressing room, each side lined with sliding doors. I push one open and peek inside. Suits. Many suits. Another reveals an array of ties in endless colours. I close it and open the next. It's empty. Except for a pair of beautiful green mules perfectly positioned on the middle shelf. I reach for one on a frown, feeling the expensive silk material, and the questions multiply. Whose shoes are these? And will the knickers he took of mine join them? Pouting, I replace them and close the door, carrying on through to a bathroom that's drenched in cream granite and gold fittings. The shower spans the entire wall on the far end, a glass screen stretching most of the width, leaving a gap at the end to walk in. An egg-shaped tub sits in the middle with a gold floor-standing tap curling over the lip. A sink wide enough to bathe in is on the wall adjacent to the shower, and another door leads to an enclosed toilet. I go to the sink, scanning the male products scattered across the surface, smiling to myself as I pick up a bottle of cologne, popping the lid off and smelling. My eyes close in bliss. It's Jude in a bottle. I check the label. Creed.

"Do I smell good?"

Turning, I find him comfortably resting his shoulder on the doorframe, his arms folded. Still beautifully naked. As am I. I flash a guilty look and place the bottle down. "Do you live here?"

"It's my apartment, yes."

"Apartment?"

He holds his hand out to me. "Come, I'll show you round."

I look down my front. "Can I get dressed?"

"No." He claims my hand and pulls me out of the bathroom. "Dressing room," he says as we pass back through it. Looking over his shoulder, he gives me a mild grin. "But you already found that on your snoop."

I roll my eyes, desperate to ask him who owns those beautiful green mules. "Like you snooped through my spa questionnaire?"

"It was an essential part of my investigative work," he says, and I laugh as we emerge into his bedroom. "Where I sleep." He doesn't slow, making his way out into an open-plan living space. "Lounge, dining." He walks on, tugging me behind him, and we enter a huge separate kitchen.

"Wow." I release his hand and wander around the oak island, taking in the white cabinetry, handmade for sure, the intricate woodwork and detailed edges stunning. A huge fridge with mirrored doors is a focal point, making the space feel even bigger. Baskets line some chunky oak shelves on the far wall, a few plants are scattered around, and a round basket full of oranges, lemons, and limes is positioned dead centre of the wooden island. It's spotless, hardly looks used.

I go to the sink and find the dishwasher, tugging it open, surprised to find it half-full of dirty dishes and cups. "So you cook."

"All the time," he says, resting his naked arse on a stool. "Did you think I wouldn't?"

"Just for yourself?" I ask as I close the door and circle the island slowly, dragging my fingers across the oiled wooden surface. I peek at him. He's smiling a little. It's still knicker melting, though. If I had knickers on.

"Just for one," he confirms. "I was tempted to cook for you tonight, but I thought you might have resisted being with me in private."

"What, in case you tried to finger fuck me under the table?" I ask seriously, eyebrows high.

"You're so crass."

"Says the man who finger fucked me under the table."

Reaching for my arm, he drags me close and puts me between his spread thighs, and God help me, I'm immediately short of breath. His hands slide onto my arse and mine slip onto his shoulders. "Would you have let me cook for you?"

I shake my head. "Too personal too soon."

"But this isn't?" One hand slips around my hip to my front, moving down into my throbbing flesh. *Fuck.* I push myself closer and kiss him gently, moaning into his mouth as he starts to work me. "Greedy." His whisper vibrates against my lips as he finds my hand and guides it to his lap, forcing me back a little. I take him in my grip, relishing his low growl. I *am* greedy for him. It's unapologetic, unquenchable greed.

His fingers slide through my desire in time to my fist thrusting up his shaft, our mouths becoming firmer, our breathing louder as we both climb to another high. It hits me unexpectedly, and my torso folds in, pushing me closer to him, my hand losing its rhythm, becoming clumsy and erratic, forcing Jude to knock me away and finish himself. He tears his lips from mine as his fingers slow and soften, watching me ride my release. It goes on and on, relentless, holding me prisoner to the pleasure he's inflicting as he works himself to meet me at the peak. His eyes darken, his face straining more, and as gorgeous as it is, I have to see him pleasuring himself.

I pull back, dropping my eyes to his groin, and just the mere sight revives my fading orgasm. My God, he is something else, his big fist clawed loosely around his raging hard-on, thrusting, the beautiful, swollen head glistening. I don't know what compels me, but I bend, replacing his hand with mine around the base and wrapping my lips around the pulsing length. I advance and retreat slowly.

"Fuck, Amelia!" he chokes, his hands moving to my hair.

I suck, lick, advance again, feeling him hit the back of my throat.

"Fuck, fuck, fuck."

My head bobs as I gorge on his cock. I swear, I've never tasted anything so delicious.

"Baby, I'm coming."

It doesn't stop me. Nothing would stop me, an overwhelming animalistic urge overcoming me. The vein on the underside throbs against my tongue, Jude solidifies beneath me, yelling, and then he jerks, and I feel the hot, salty essence of him hit the back of my throat.

I close my eyes and swallow, sucking my way to the tip and exhaling, circling my tongue around the head before kissing my way up his stomach, his chest, and onto his neck, climbing onto his lap, straddling him, and working my way to his lips. He hums, cupping my arse, indulging me for a few moments before taking my jaw and pulling me off his mouth. He holds my face as he gazes at me. He's not smiling.

In fact, his expression is unreadable. Almost questioning. But I don't shy away, my arms looped loosely around his neck, my eyes on his.

"What?" I eventually ask, waiting.

His lip tips a little at the corner. "Nothing." His hand moves from my jaw and strokes through my long tresses as I play with the hair that flicks out at his nape. "Thirsty?"

I nod, and he stands with me hanging from his front, placing me on the stool and going to the fridge. The sound of my mobile ringing in the distance pulls my attention over my shoulder.

"I should get that." I get down off the stool. "It'll be one of my friends making sure I haven't been savaged by the mysterious rich man who's been stalking me."

"Savaging can be arranged," he calls.

I smile and find my bag, pulling my mobile out, but it rings off before I can answer. My eyes widen at the screen. Ten missed calls? "Dramatic, Abbie," I mumble, going to the couch and calling her back.

"Thank God," she breathes in answer.

"What's up?"

"Just checking you're alive."

"I'm alive," I confirm. Died of pleasure a few times, but I've come back to life. Silence falls, and it stretches for a while. "And . . . ?"

"Oh fuck off," Abbie hisses. "Have you . . . ?"

I press my lips together and glance at the doorway to the kitchen. "I'm in his apartment."

"Apartment?"

"He has a private apartment in the hotel."

"And . . . ?"

"And I'm naked," I whisper, clenching my eyes closed, trying to stop the stupid girlie grin stretching across my face as butterflies explode in my belly.

Abbie gasps. "Your voice."

"What about it?"

"Oh my God, you're catching feelings."

The Invitation

"No." I grimace. "People don't catch feelings after one date."

I think I'm in more trouble now than I was an hour ago.

Me too.

"Fuck," I whisper, getting up, walking back to the bedroom, through the dressing room, and into the bathroom. I close the door behind me. "I really like him, Abbie," I say, admitting it out loud, resting my arse on the edge of the bath, my face in my palm.

"Oh shit," she breathes. "I guess that means he's as good as he looks like he'd be in bed."

"Better," I say quietly into my hand. "But it's not just that."

"Oh, you mean the dirty great big luxury hotel and the fact he was clearly first in line when God gave out good looks is swaying you?"

"He's charming." I fill my lungs and come out of my hiding place. "We talk, he sounds genuinely interested in what I say, he's funny in a dry, serious way, seems to have his head screwed on, says all the right things. And I've seen vulnerability. He told me he lost both his parents. His dad when he was just twenty-four, and his mum during the renovation of Arlington Hall. She never got to see her dream completed."

"Wow, that's tough."

"I know."

"Are there *any* cons?"

"Apart from the fact I've just stepped out of a relationship and need to concentrate on my career?"

"Yes, apart from that."

"I think he could be a little possessive." A little? No, a lot. And there's no *thinking* about it. "And he maybe has a bit of a temper." Maybe?

Abbie hums. I'm not sure I like that hum.

"What are you thinking?" I ask, desperate for her thoughts.

"I'm thinking you're at risk of being in my boat."

"What?"

"But at least you know who blew your world apart."

It clicks. "The man in France," I say quietly. She's never got over that brief, explosive encounter with the nameless guy she met in a backstreet café. Compares every man she's dated since to him. "Do you still daydream about him?"

She laughs. "Every fucking day, and it's been two years, Amelia. The universe was definitely being plain fucking cruel giving me that gift."

I chuckle, looking up when Jude appears with two glasses of champagne. "Hey, listen, I have to go."

"Call me," she demands.

I hang up and stand. "Abbie."

"She's a good friend."

"She is." I go to him and take a glass. "Now she'll be reporting back to Charley."

Jude nods, taking my hand and walking us back to his bedroom.

"I should probably get out of your hair." I look around for the speakers when I hear music again. Moby. "Porcelain." Christ, he has the ultimate playlist for seduction.

"No, you shouldn't."

"No?"

"No." He sits me on the end of the bed and pushes between my boobs, sending me to my back. I yelp when the champagne splashes out of the glass all over my chest. "Oops," he whispers, setting his glass down and wedging a fist in the mattress by my head, his eyes sparkling as he claims the flute in my hand and sips. And I'm utterly rapt again. *Standard.* Dipping, Jude hovers his mouth over mine and releases, trickling the cold bubbly liquid over my lips.

Here we go again.

And I'm here for it.

My tongue dashes out and gets one sweep before he sucks my bottom lip into his mouth, releasing it on a pop, kissing down my neck and licking across my chest. My body bows, my arms reaching above my head, looking for something to hold on to. I'm too far away from the headboard. So I find his thick waves and grip.

Hard.

"Jude," I groan, my head turning from side to side as he works his way across my body. "Jude."

My pleas go unanswered.

Standing, he reaches for a candle that's burning on the bedside table, and I inhale as he gets on his knees on the bed, straddling my stomach. He takes one arm and puts it by my side, holding it there with his bent leg. Then he switches the candle to his other hand and repeats, immobilising me. Watching me as he makes his moves. And I let him. My breathing turns into pants, my chest rising and falling violently, anticipation swirling.

Resting on his forearm, he brings his face close to mine. Smiles mildly. Dips and bites at my cheek. Even that sends shock waves through me, my body trying to buck and failing.

"Keep still," he says, sitting up, his cock lying across my stomach.

He holds the candle up, scanning my torso, settling on my boob.

"Oh, God, please," I murmur, throwing my head back and clenching my eyes closed.

"Come on, Amelia." His hand wraps around my jaw, shaking. "Watch."

I gather some resistance and open, meeting his eyes. Dark, dark green. "Do it," I whisper, clenching my fists where they're held. His smile of satisfaction is blinding and beautiful, every muscle in his stomach rippling as he sits back up and tips the candle a fraction. I hold my breath and gasp when the wax hits my boob just to the right of my nipple. "Fuck." The burn is instant and intense but brief, the heat fading quickly, the clear, perfect round drop of liquid turning opaque. I exhale, taking a moment, because I know he's not done.

The approval in his eyes is incredibly motivating. "Again?"

Swallowing, I relax into the mattress, bracing myself for the next drop as the candle hovers over my nipple and tips. Two drops this time, and I grunt under my breath, gritting my teeth, my back arching. This man will be the death of me.

No.

I blank my mind, not letting it go to places that could ruin this. "More," I whisper, tensing everywhere as Jude tips the candle again. "Fuck!" Three drops this time, the burn more intense, more prolonged. I throw my head back, my body bending into a rigid arch.

"Too much?" he asks, definitely short of breath himself.

"No," I snap, adamant, returning my eyes to his. "Never too much."

His head tilts, his moves faltering. "Never too much," he murmurs, lowering and kissing me gently. "You're going to be my ruin, Amelia Lazenby."

"Not if you ruin me first," I breathe, plunging my tongue into his mouth, hungry, determined to get everything I can. It's like my subconscious is telling me to make the most of this. That I won't have this feeling again.

Jude accommodates my demand.

Before he suddenly pulls back, breathless.

My head slams against the mattress. I scowl hard, and it clearly delights him. I don't know how much more of this I can take. The suspense, his godly chest in my face, rippling and swelling, his hair all ruffled and damp, his lips wet and ready.

"Jude," I whisper, flexing my arms pointlessly.

"What do you want, baby?" he asks, his gaze moving slowly and seductively across my skin.

"You," I grate.

He looks up. "Oh, you've got me." Then he tips the candle and moves it slowly from side to side, dripping the hot wax continuously. "The question is, can you handle me?"

I cry out, jolting, hissing my way through the prolonged pain until it starts to subside. "I'm asking myself that question all the time." I gasp, my endurance waning.

"You can handle anything."

"That's enough." I find his eyes and see he hears me. Releasing my arms, he crowds me, rewarding me with a deep, long, worshipful kiss.

"One more," he says quietly, unbending his body. "Give me one more."

I see his intention in a second and hold my breath as he levels the candle.

And tips.

The heat hits my nipple, and fuck, it's intense. I cover my face, battling through, and then jolt, but not because of the pain. No. The pain's gone and sparks of pleasure have just shot like bullets down to my pussy. *Jesus.* He pulls my hands away from my face, and the moment I have his eyes, I just *have* to ravish him. I shoot up and climb into his lap, devouring him.

"Fuck," Jude blurts. "Amelia, the candle!"

I rip my mouth away, my breathing laboured, as Jude grabs the glass container off the bed and blows out the flame, tossing the candle aside before tackling me back down to the sheets, smothering me, our kiss loud and frenzied, hard but soft, hands everywhere.

"Hot?" he asks.

"Really fucking hot," I confirm.

"Let me fix that." He rolls us, getting me on top of him, then pushes me up so I'm standing by the bed, him sitting on the edge before me. He reaches for the ice bucket, and his intention clicks. My God, he's hell-bent on breaking me. Taking a cube, he works it in his hand for a few moments, and I'm quickly calling on my strength again, holding my breath.

He places the cube on my breast and rolls it around my nipple. My head drops back.

Then it's gliding down my stomach.

Between my legs.

And he pushes it into me.

I gulp at the shock invasion, my muscles naturally clenching around the ice, the cold almost unbearable. "I don't know if I can hold it."

Jude drops to his back. "Sit on my face."

Oh God.

"Get on my fucking face, Amelia." Taking my hand, he pulls me forward, my knees hitting the bed on either side of his legs. He helps me into place, my thighs framing his face, and I look down at him as my pussy comes to rest on his lips.

Air leaves my lungs on a long, loud gust when the heat of his mouth mixes with the ice, the pleasure instant and out of this fucking world. "Oh my God," I gasp as he licks, sucks, laps, and swirls, his eyes glistening up at me. Reaching back, I lean on his stomach with one hand, looking up at the ceiling, concentrating. Focusing.

Coming.

So hard.

I start to rock on his mouth, the pressure building.

I rock harder.

Building.

"Fuck!" I yell, a lightning bolt hitting me straight between my thighs. I crumple, folding forward over his head, completely covering him, gasping and panting, squeezing my eyes closed. The power of my release is incapacitating. I can't move. Can't speak. Jude's probably suffocating beneath me, smothered in my pussy.

So I force some strength into my arms and push myself up, and he helps me shuffle down his body so I'm sitting on his stomach. He smiles at my torso and reaches for the dots of wax, peeling them off one by one and flicking them away.

"How was it for you?" he asks.

"One star."

His brows pinch, and he shoots up, tackling me to my back. And what do I do? I squeal like a little girl, my head thrown back. I laugh so fucking hard as he ravishes my throat.

"You're staying the night," he says, matter-of-fact.

"Okay." I feel his hair, smiling at the ceiling. His face is suddenly in my field of vision. His perfect face, sexed-up hair, his twinkly eyes, his dark-blond scruff. Adorable.

Something shifts in my chest as his mouth lowers slowly to mine and he kisses me softly. With a gentle purpose. Like I mean something to him.

And I match it.

Fuck.

Way, way, *way* more trouble.

Chapter 19

I frown in my darkness. What is that? Whale music? Opening my eyes, staying still on my back, I scan my surroundings. Before I can even begin to piece together where I am, the soreness between my thighs tells me. I drop my head to the side, smelling he's close, and the moment I set eyes on him, I'm fully awake. Fully alert.

My heart thrums its presence. "Oh shit," I whisper. He's on his front, his mouth open, his breathing quiet. Stunning, beautiful man. "Oh shit, oh shit, oh shit." A replay of yesterday and last night parades through my mind. *Amazing.*

Worrying.

"Oh shit." I grab a pillow and pull it over my face, grimacing. Aching. In the best possible way.

"What are you hiding from?"

I lift the pillow and peek out. Jude's not moved but his eyes are open.

"Morning," I say with a touch of awkwardness, which is crazy after yesterday. There can't be an inch of my body he doesn't know, hasn't kissed or felt. And I'm confident I know every inch of the masterpiece that is Jude Harrison. At least, every inch of his body. What about his mind?

"Morning." He props himself up on his forearms, his dazzling, sleepy eyes scanning my face. They're lighter this morning. A greeny grey. Calm.

How can he look so fucking perfect with bedhead? *Morning.* That's all he's groggily said. And I'm giddy. *Ridiculous.*

He continues to study me, thoughtful.

"What?" I ask. "What are you looking at?"

"You." Slipping a hand over my stomach, he drags me closer by my hip, getting on top of me. I'm cocooned, his arms framing my head. "Is that a problem?" He drops his mouth close to mine, subtly flexing his hips into me, and my rousing brain and body answer to his call. It's true. Never enough. It's like someone's swept in and swept away my senses.

"No problem." I lift and catch his mouth, and he hums happily as we kiss, my arms circling his shoulders, my legs his waist. No problem at all. He throbs against me. Something needy and greedy inside me begs for him all over again. Never, *ever* enough. I groan into his mouth, flexing my hips up, and he slips into me quietly and slowly, breaking our kiss to retreat into my neck.

"God." He stills, buried deep, absorbing my throbbing walls, and I wait patiently for him to move, stroking softly across his warm skin, feeling so calm. And when he does move, the world lights up in tiny but powerful explosions of light.

It's serene, the pace easy, the build gradual. The need inside hasn't dulled after a marathon of Jude Harrison yesterday. Scarily, I'm only left more insatiable.

I float away, absorbing his every drive, arching and relaxing, feeling and stroking his back. "This is the best wake up," I murmur, nudging his face from my neck, needing his lips on mine, kissing me to release.

"Agree," he says on a whisper, turning his head one way, swirling his tongue, biting my lip, before tilting, taking another angle, moaning. I move my hands to his bare arse and apply pressure, stroking over the solid rocks of flesh, sinking my nails in. He grunts, I swallow it, he moans, I reply with my own.

Bliss.

Breaking away, Jude gazes down at me, still rocking into me, a sheen of sweat peppering his brow, strands of his hair falling onto it and sticking. My hands stroke up to his shoulders, into his hair, and push it back, giving me all of his divine face.

His jaw tightens. "Amelia," he whispers, my name sounding strained and urgent. "Fuck, Amelia." He lowers his face back into my neck, his pace rising to another level. My blood pumps harder, faster, and hotter, and I know when he's on the cusp because he sinks his teeth into my flesh, biting down lightly.

"Are you coming?" I ask, and he nods, grinding, pushing deep. It's easy to go with him. Natural.

Sucking in air and holding it, I lock down every muscle around his shaft and roll over the edge, pulsating around him as he curses, his body rigid but shaking all over me. And peace floats down over us, the tingles strong but bearable.

Perfect.

Jude gasps lightly, licking the spot where his teeth held on, dotting kisses across my throat. And we rest, holding each other. Recovering. I might need a week to get over this.

Or a lifetime.

My lids become heavy, the weight of Jude unfamiliar but natural as he hums across my neck, and I lie beneath him, relaxed, content, his softening dick still submerged.

"You smell yummy." He moves slowly and with effort, and kisses the end of my nose. I hum sleepily. He chuckles. That sound alone gives me the energy to open my eyes. I'm immediately hypnotised at the sight of him, and my resting heart picks up its pace again. He must surely feel it against him. *Fuck.* A lock of hair falls onto his forehead, and I instinctively push it back over his ear. I feel nothing but wonder as he looks down at me, unabashed. "What's happening?" he whispers, revisiting last night.

I shake my head mildly, unsure if I have the energy or headspace to go there right now. I've loved every moment I've spent with him. The small blip in the steam room aside. Jude Harrison seems too good to be true. He frightened me the second I saw him and my body reacted

The Invitation

in a way I've never experienced. Uninhibited attraction. But with each encounter, that fear grew. Now?

I hardly want to admit how I'm feeling. Overwhelmed. Blindsided. And so much more.

Jude sighs and kisses me chastely, rolling off and reaching for the machine on the bedside. The sound of whale calls stops. "I should be in the gym," he says, falling to his back.

"Me too."

Cocking me a sideways smirk, he stretches out, every limb lengthening, every muscle enhanced. *Christ alive.* "Do you want to work out together?"

Interested, I prop myself up on my elbow, unable to resist tracing over the ripples on his stomach. "And what would you have me do?"

He pouts and matches my position, facing me. "I'd get you sweaty and wet." He reaches forward and tweaks my nipple. I yelp. "Among other things."

"I'd like a full, comprehensive training plan before I commit."

"You want details?"

I nod, biting at my lip. Listen to me. I may as well be on my knees for him. "How will you make me sweaty and *wet*?"

He shoots up and pins me to the bed, biting at my cheek, and I laugh, squirming, getting rubbed in all the right places. "With little effort, it seems." Pulling back, he cups my face and scrunches his nose to match mine. "You're insatiable." Shifting, he sits on the edge of the bed and picks up his phone, raking a hand through his hair to pull it off his face.

I'm giddy as I sit up, ready to go in search of my own phone to check my emails, but I catch sight of the time on the nature machine, and it stops me in my tracks. "Oh no."

Jude looks over his shoulder at me. "What?"

I groan and fall to my back again. How the hell did I sleep in until ten thirty? *Dumb question.* "I've got to be at my parents' for lunch at noon." And I'm in Oxfordshire. *Fuck it.* "Are any of your chauffeurs available to take me back to London?"

"I'll check." Jude rises and wanders off, and I'm momentarily distracted from my lateness. I would so rather stay. Can't.

Grabbing the sheets, I groan and haul them over my head, wincing when the soreness between my legs screams. I'm aching, I'm tired.

And I've never felt so good.

What's happening?

"They're all out driving guests."

I push the sheets back and find Jude pulling on some boxers. "Shit."

"I'll take you."

I wince some more. "All the way back into London?"

"Sure."

"You could just drop me off at the nearest train station."

"Amelia, it's not a problem."

"It'll be a big chunk of your day gone going there and back."

Jude comes to the bed and hauls me out of it, standing me up and clenching my cheeks. "It's not a problem," he repeats. "Okay?"

"But—"

"Are you arguing with me?" His face is suddenly stern, his head tilted.

I scowl. "And if I am?"

A wicked glint in his eyes blinds me as he reaches around to my bare arse and digs his fingertips in. I yelp, grabbing his arms, shooting up to my tippy-toes. My lips press together.

"Are you arguing with me, Amelia?"

I shake my head, leaning back when his face comes closer. "Never," I whisper.

"Good." He swoops in and sends me dizzy with a deep, hot kiss, and I'm putty in his hands again. I'm not going to think too deeply about this. He's my only chance of making it to my parents' on time. I'm never late, and I really don't want to explain to my parents why I am.

"I need to get my stuff from the fancy suite you booked out for me not to sleep in," I say around his mouth.

"I'll go get your stuff, you take a shower." He swats my arse and leaves to fetch my things, and I watch him go, something new and alive inside screaming for more. Not sex, although I'll happily take it. But this feeling of utter contentment.

Chapter 20

"This is your car?" I gaze across the bodywork of the classic Jaguar that Clark had a hard-on for as Jude opens the door for me.

"One of them, yes." He helps me down to the seat, and the smell of old leather hits me. One of them? How many does he have? Jude falls into the driver's seat and slips on some tortoise and gold-rimmed Ray-Bans, raking a hand through his hair. His hand on the wheel, one on the gearstick, he looks across at me. I cry on the inside. In his cream chinos and white Ralph Lauren shirt, he looks as classic as the car. Classically handsome. Classically gorgeous. "What?" he asks.

"You."

"What about me?"

You're derailing me. "Nothing." I settle, Jude turns the radio on, and "Waterfall" by the Stone Roses starts.

"Nothing, my arse," he murmurs, giving me an accusing, playful look. *What's happening?* "What's your parents' address?"

"Call yourself a stalker?"

His hand is squeezing my knee instantly, and I jolt in my seat on a laugh. "Pack it in." He passes me his phone. "Google Maps."

"You mean this thing doesn't have satnav?"

His eyebrows rise with his shades as he lifts them, and I pucker my lips, making him lose all warning from his face. He leans over and steals a kiss, and it's all so very easy. Natural. He's calm. Easygoing. It's

The Invitation

not only his persona telling me so, but his eyes, which are a beautiful muted greeny grey.

Jude lowers his glasses and pulls off slowly, while I tap in the address for my parents'. ETA: 12:08. I cringe. Still late. "Fuck."

"What?"

"I'm going to be late."

"By a couple of minutes," he replies. "Stop stressing."

"Easy for you to say, you've not got a melodramatic mother ready to file a missing person's report." The moment the words leave my mouth, I know I've fucked up. Jude's hands tighten around the steering wheel, his bottom lip disappearing between his teeth, his entire seated posture changing. *Fuck.* "Shit, Jude, I'm sorry."

"It's fine."

"No, it's not," I counter, kicking myself repeatedly. "It was stupid and insensitive. I wasn't thinking."

"Amelia, it's fine."

I scold myself and reach for his hand on the gearstick. "Tell me about 'Hey Jude.'"

He smiles mildly, looking away briefly, taking in air. Or taking in strength to talk about it. "It was my parents' favourite song."

"So they named you after the Beatles song?" How romantic.

"Yeah." He smiles across at me. "Are we going deep again?"

I laugh under my breath. I'm not sure if we can go much deeper. I'm about to set his phone in the holder attached to the blower by the steering wheel but falter when a WhatsApp notification drops down from the top of the screen.

Katherine? The woman in the restaurant? There's only a small preview of the message, and I know I should slam my eyes closed, not read it, but it's right there in front of me.

How can you . . .

The message slides back up. *God damn it.* How can he . . . what? I quickly put the phone in the holder and rest back, my mind reeling. Why would she message Jude? According to him, she and her husband are members of the spa and golf club and eat occasionally at Arlington Hall.

"Okay?" Jude asks.

"Sure." I turn a smile his way, but it's an effort, suddenly endless doubts creeping in. His phone dings again, another message sliding down. Jude's quick to clear the screen. Then another comes in. Then another. And another. "Someone has a lot to say." I look at him and seriously don't like the awkward vibes he's giving off.

"It's no one," he says shortly, irritated.

No one.

Okay.

And suddenly things aren't so natural and easy. Am I overthinking? Is he being off? What did she want? Why didn't he just tell me who it is if it's nothing?

Oh my God.

Am I obsessing?

I sink farther into the seat and scrape through my mind for something to say. Something to break the growing, unbearable silence. I have nothing, and judging by Jude's lack of conversation, I'm guessing he's feeling the sudden tension too.

It remains the entire way to my parents' house, only the music breaking the screaming quiet in the car.

When Jude turns into the cul-de-sac, I see my brother's car and cringe. "You can pull in here," I say, knowing my dad's radar ears will hear a car pulling up outside.

Jude doesn't question me, slowing at the kerb a few houses down from my parents'. I take the handle to let myself out, keen to escape the

The Invitation

horrible atmosphere. I'm pissed off, my contentment crushed. He could clear this up with a quick explanation, and yet he hasn't. But does he owe me an explanation? No. And he obviously doesn't think so either. So last night was . . . what? Fuck, I don't like this version of myself. I thought this thing would be easy and uncomplicated, but this horrible apprehensive feeling inside doesn't feel very easy, and I'm suddenly revisiting all the signs that Jude is anything but uncomplicated.

"Amelia, wait," he says when I have one foot on the road, my arse still in the seat. I still but don't look at him. "This isn't how I want our first date to end."

First date? *Jesus Christ.* Yesterday wasn't a first date. It felt like we bypassed all the usual stages of dating and hopped straight to full-blown. At least, it feels like that to me. And is that the problem? I feel like this is something and he doesn't? *I'm in more trouble now than I was an hour ago.* My God, my head could pop.

I pull a smile from nowhere and turn to him. "We're good," I say, leaning over and kissing him. "Thank you for the ride back."

The frown that passes over his face is deep but fleeting. "Welcome. I'll call you?" It sounds like more of a question than a statement. Not very Jude at all.

"Okay." Another chaste kiss before I get out. As I walk away, my heart sinks with every stride. I'm very quickly falling from my high. *Falling.* My heart clenches. *No no no.*

I push my way through the front door and meet Clark in the hallway. He looks me up and down as I make a pointless effort of smoothing the creases on the clothes I wore yesterday. "There you are," he says. "Mum was about to report you missing."

I roll my eyes and drop my bag. "I'm ten minutes late."

"In the history of Amelia Lazenby, you have never, and I mean *never*, been even *one* minute late. Ten minutes is practically another day in your world."

"You're being ridiculous." I drop a kiss on his cheek and pass him. "Are Grandpa and Grandma here?"

"In the lounge," he calls after me. "Um, Amelia, dear sister?"

"What?" I turn and find my brother with his face pushed up against the window by the front door.

"Why's that fancy car from Arlington Hall driving off down the road?"

I freeze, my mind emptying. "Um . . ." *Think.* "What car?" *Idiot.*

Clark turns, his lips straight. "My dream car. The rare one. Only two of its kind in the country. And one happens to have been at Arlington Hall, and now is driving out of the close where our parents live."

My whole face twists. I've got nothing.

"Oh my fucking God, you're seeing that bloke from Arlington Hall."

Seeing? Fucking? Falling for? "Not exactly."

"I knew there was something going on after he had me by the throat! A parking space? I knew you were acting weird."

"You're so dramatic."

"You're seeing him, aren't you?"

"What qualifies as 'seeing'?" I ask weakly.

"Fucking."

"Clark!"

"I thought you were focusing on your career? That's why you ended things with Nick."

"I ended things with Nick because he wanted more than I'm comfortable with right now." I pace toward Clark, looking over my shoulder to make sure we're still alone. "Don't you remember telling me you thought Nick ruined me?"

"That wasn't code for *fuck the next man you find.*"

"It's nothing. I had a date and—"

"He dropped you off here the next morning? Just a date?"

Indignant, I huff. "My private life isn't any of your business. And I'd appreciate it if you keep your big, fat trap shut."

Clark recoils, injured. "And is that code for *don't tell Mum and Dad*?"

The Invitation

"Scout's promise," I grate, throwing our childhood tradition in his face.

"You weren't in the Scouts," he grumbles.

"If you include all the nights I camped in the garden with you because you were too chickenshit to do it on your own, I count as a Scout."

"Low blow."

"Deal with it." I pivot and head for the lounge to see Grandpa and Grandma.

"Here she is!" Grandpa sets his broadsheet aside, and Grandma drops her knitting needles. "You're late."

"It's fashionable, Grandpa," I say, bending and dropping a kiss on his old, wrinkly face before going to Grandma.

She squeezes my cheeks, scrunching her nose and pushing it to mine. Then she stills. Sniffs. "You smell like a man, Grand Girl," she whispers. "A very lovely-smelling man."

Fucking hell. "You're imagining things, Grandma."

She hums, suspicious, releasing me, as Mum and Dad bowl in. "Ah, finally," Dad says, looking at his watch. "Can we eat now?"

"Amelia, darling." Mum rushes to me, her oven gloves on her hands, and checks me over. Checks there is no evidence of where I might have been. "Are you okay?"

Good heavens. "I'm fine, stop fussing." I go to the couch and drop to the seat, dragging Dad's copy of the *Financial Times* onto my lap. "What's for lunch?"

"Your mum's famous roast." Grandpa smacks his lips and rubs his belly before sheepishly glancing at his wife of nearly sixty years. "Not as good as yours, dear."

I smile and open the paper, burying my face in the first article. *War. Trading ceased. Shares to drop.* They're all trigger words that would have me devouring the information with interest and worry, except my mind is elsewhere. And isn't that evidence enough that I'm stepping out of the frying pan with Nick and into the fire with Jude Harrison? I huff and slam the paper shut.

There's a knock at the front door.

"Who's missing?" I ask, looking through to the kitchen. "Where's Rachel?"

"Emptying the dishwasher."

"Oh, sister," Clark calls in an annoying singsong voice.

I look toward the door that leads into the hallway, getting up from the couch.

"Who is it?" Grandpa calls as I leave the room.

I find Clark at the open front door. "What's up?"

He looks back at me with raised, accusing brows. "Someone for you." Then he moves.

Revealing Jude.

My mouth goes lax, all bodily functions abandoning me. "Jude," I breathe, stock-still on the spot. Fuck, what the hell is he playing at?

He holds something up. "You left your phone in my car when you were rushing to escape me."

Clark looks between us, interested. "We've met," he says to Jude, holding out a hand. "Although not formally."

Jude smiles through straight lips, accepting and shaking. "Apologies again."

"No sweat." My brother narrows one eye my way. "It's all beginning to make sense."

I pass Clark, panicked, and step outside, pulling the door closed behind me. "Thank you," I say, taking my phone and faffing with it in my hand, unlocking the screen, locking it again.

"Welcome," Jude murmurs, stuffing his hands into his pockets. "Amelia, for the sake of clarity and for the avoidance of doubt, I don't date more than one woman at a time."

There's that word again. *Dating.* I peek up at him.

"In fact," he goes on, his rolling jaw indicating his mood, along with his darkening eyes. "I don't usually date at all."

So he just fucks women? Seduces them and gets them into bed? One at a time. I close my eyes and breathe out. I feel like I'm going mad. Yesterday wasn't a date. Dates aren't that amazing.

"I'm not looking for anything serious," I say quietly. It's the truth, and I need reminding of that. Especially after last night.

"Are you for real?" Jude nearly chokes over his words. "Because last night felt pretty fucking serious."

And isn't that my point? "Jude, this is all happening very fast."

"Deal with it," he snaps. "I am."

I shrink, my head a mess of conflicting thoughts. I don't know what's happening with Jude, but I do know how I felt when I saw that message appear on his screen. Jealous. Injured. Vulnerable. I'm not ready for this.

I look over my shoulder to the closed door. "I have to go."

"You don't want them to know you've met someone?" he asks.

Met someone? It's inadequate. *Blindsided, derailed, smitten.* "I don't want them thinking that it's more than it is."

"What is it, Amelia?" he asks, his voice softening.

"I'm not sure."

"Do you think you might figure it out soon and let me know?"

I brave facing him and wish I hadn't. He does *not* look happy. "There's no need to be like that."

"Yes, there is," he barks, and I flinch. "Remember last night? This morning?" He moves in closer, and I retreat, scared for him to touch me. Scared I'll get a waft of his lovely cologne. Scared he'll saturate every sense I have. I need to think. I need space. "Right," he says. Then he laughs under his breath, the sound far from amused. Anger. I see it brewing in him, his dark eyes darkening further. "You win." He turns and stalks off, and I wilt, folding on the inside. My brain is asking me what the hell I'm playing at, sabotaging something amazing. My heart? That's cheering me on, backing me up. Protecting itself.

It's an all-out war going on inside me.

I back into the hallway and take a moment to compose myself, giving Clark a warning look.

"So who was it?" Grandma calls.

"Just a salesman," I say, heading to the kitchen at the back of the house, my heart sinking. My head a mess.

I win?

So why do I feel like I've just lost?

Chapter 21

"So you had the best time of your life and then ended it?" Abbie asks from the treadmill beside me. "I don't get it. Well, I do; you're falling for him. You're scared. You should have just asked him about the message. What it said. Who she is. We're all adults."

"I don't want him to think I'm some crazed, possessive, dramatic woman."

"Well, that's very gallant of you, considering his reaction when he saw you talking to another man."

"And kissing another man," I grumble.

Abbie chuckles. "I still can't believe you did that. Look, we all know you're not crazed, dramatic, and jealous."

I *felt* jealous. God, I don't want to be that woman. Of course a man like Jude Harrison has a history. We all do. But history doesn't text you repeatedly. I grimace. "Can we talk about something else?"

"Like what? What's more interesting than your current mindfuck over a disgustingly handsome millionaire?"

"How's Mum getting on at the shop?"

"Oh, yay," Abbie drones. "So interesting."

I scowl and increase the pace on the machine. Hopefully I'll soon be so out of breath, I physically won't be able to talk.

"Charming," Abbie grumbles, knowing my game. "Whatever. I have to get to the wholesalers." Slamming her fist on the slow button, she works her way down as I work my way up. "Charley wants to go out this weekend. She has some I Owe Yous she wants to spend."

I nod, unable to talk, already out of breath.

"I'll call you later to see if you've pulled your head out of your arse."

Another nod and another slight increase of the machine. I run fast, until my legs are numb, my heart is thrashing, and the sweat is pouring off me.

How will you make me sweaty and wet?

"Fuck!" I yell, wedging my hands into the bars and lifting my feet off the runner, setting them on the sides. I stare down at the belt spinning beneath me, Jude's voice haunting me.

I'm in a lot more trouble now than I was an hour ago.

Last night felt pretty fucking serious.

I growl to myself and slam the stop button on the machine, giving up and going for a cold shower. Hopefully that will shock me back to real life.

"Morning," Shelley calls as I pass her desk. "Good weekend?"

"Not bad." I smile—it's strained—and push my way into my office. Dumping my bag on the floor, I drop into my seat and stare at the computer screen, as if I've forgotten what it is. I haven't worked all weekend. It's unheard of. I tried last night and got precisely nowhere, the information I was reading not sinking in. *God damn you, Jude Harrison.*

I reach for my phone and check the screen. There are a ton of unopened emails, endless news bulletins notifying me of movements on the market, acquisitions, breaking news from floating companies. I sigh and push my phone away, standing and going to the kitchen. I need coffee.

I shove a cup under the machine and hit the button for a flat white, resting my hands on the counter as I watch it drip out.

"How's my favourite colleague this morning?" Leighton's voice has my skin instantly crawling.

"Raring to go."

"Good weekend?"

"Not bad."

"But not good?"

I cast him a blank sideways look, pulling my cup off the stand. "It was fine."

"But could have been better?" He smiles, leaning back against the counter next to the machine.

"Always room for improvement."

Nodding, he drags his leering gaze down my dress. "You look nice in black."

"Thanks." I pivot on my heels, shuddering.

"Amelia," he calls, stopping me by the door. I look back. "We never got to finish our chat last week."

"What chat?"

"The one at the conference."

Oh, he means the one when he was laying it on thick? Offering to get a room? I face him. "Do you want to finish it now?"

The smile that stretches across his face makes me want to slap it off. He wanders over, all casual. "Free for lunch?"

"Yes, I'm free," I say, moving toward him, watching as anticipation crawls through his body and has him standing up straight. I lean in. "Are you asking me to lunch?"

"Sure."

"Why?"

The look on his face tells me he's taken aback by my question, but he soon gets his surprise in check. "I love how you play hard to get."

His arrogance is exhausting, and I do not have the energy for him today. "I'm busy." Turning, I walk out, wondering if my Monday is going to improve anytime soon. I get behind my desk, push every thought of Jude Harrison out of my mind, and start working through the structure plans and clearing down my inbox.

Chapter 22

By Wednesday, I'm back in my work groove and have caught up with all my emails and updated my portfolios. No contact from Jude. And I can't lie, it hurts. I have no right to feel this way, I know that. But I do.

At four thirty, I've achieved far more than I thought I would, preparing for my calls tomorrow too. I click out of my email to catch the closing stocks, make a few notes, and email Gary my latest figures and projections. I can't get away from it—my end-of-year forecast is optimistic and massively dependent on some big hitters throwing me their cash to invest. Tilda Spector would be the answer to my prayers. But I'm not a vulture. And, damn it, I know Leighton has some tasty potential clients lined up. Like those twins from Liverpool. God, I hope they see the slick slimeball I do and think better of handing over their financial interests to him.

It's gone six by the time I'm done. I tidy my desk and grab my bag, leaving the office. As I'm walking to the elevators, I see Gary and Leighton in the conference room through the glass, both perched on the table rather than sitting in chairs, telling me it's a casual chat. It doesn't stop me wondering, though. Gary sees me and holds up a hand in goodbye. Leighton flat-out ignores me. It's no hardship. Damn it, what are they talking about?

I get in the elevator, texting Abbie to see if she wants me to pick her up anything from M&S, shifting farther toward the back of the cart when more people board as the elevator stops through the floors on its way to the lobby. When the doors open, I move with the crowd as everyone steps off, making my way to the glass doors and out onto the street. I look up from my phone, and my heels falter when I see someone I recognise.

Katherine.

She's standing by a pillar on the pavement, her expensive handbag in the crook of her arm. I slow my pace the second her shoulders straighten and conclude just from her body language that she's here because of me.

I damn myself for becoming jittery as she flicks her dark hair over her shoulder and starts toward me, confident. I was right. There's . . . something. Skintight black jeans hug her thighs, and her knee-high stiletto boots click on the concrete.

"Amelia," she says, offering a hand. Weird. "I'm Katherine."

Thinking I should keep this civil, whatever *this* is, I accept her offering. "Yes, I've seen you at Arlington Hall."

Her smile is definitely tight. "Yes."

"What can I do for you, Katherine?" I ask, releasing her hand. *Tell me what your texts said!*

"You can stay away from Jude."

I withdraw, and I don't know why. I think I expected that—I just suppose I never expected her to shoot so straight. The best thing I could do right now is walk away. Not ask questions. Not get drawn into the drama. After all, Jude and I are obviously done.

"You're married," I say like a fool.

"And . . . ?"

"And?" I laugh. "Do married women usually go around warning other women away from men who aren't their husbands?"

"He's my best friend."

I blink, surprised. *What?* I can distinctly remember Jude brushing off my question, which, in effect, told me Katherine was of no importance. There was no mention of best friend status. Then she texted him, things got weird between us, and I finished it. Or did he? *Jesus.* "He's not talked about you."

"Well, I don't suppose you did much talking when you *ate* at Arlington Hall."

I feel my face begin to flame. Humiliated. And I'm suddenly stuck for words. My God, does she think I'm the kind of woman who opens her legs for a man with money? Is she being protective, assuming I'm just another gold digger? Jude said himself he's a magnet for them. Or, at least, he alluded to it. For God's sake, it's not like he's got nothing else to offer. He's a stunning man.

Has she voiced this to Jude? Is that why I haven't heard from him? Because the Jude I met is persistent. Won't take no for an answer.

Not that any of this matters.

"It's been lovely chatting," I say, trying my hardest to erase the edge of cynicism. And failing. I pass Katherine, feeling my blood beginning to boil. A gold digger. A slut. She thinks I'm both, and the thought of her being in Jude's ear convincing him I'm disingenuous pisses me off. I can't help it.

"Wait," she calls, but I keep moving. But then she's suddenly in front of me, and I have no idea how she managed that in those boots. "He's more than my best friend."

I hate the prickling of my skin. Hate the thumping of my heart. "I'm not interested in what Jude is to you." A barefaced lie. I'm so fucking curious, and yet I know I'm going to hate the answer.

"He's my lover."

My stomach knots, my mind bends. "Excuse me?" *Lover?* And not *was* but *is. Don't rise to it.* Wasn't my reaction to her declaration of best friend status enough for her? Fucking hell, were they her green mules in his closet? A sick kind of calling card, left to mark her territory? "But you're married."

She shrugs. "It's an arrangement that works."

"Your husband knows?" I splutter.

"Yes, he knows."

I stare at her, flummoxed, my thoughts swirling so fast I'm struggling to unravel them. And I have nothing else for her, so she'll be disappointed if she was expecting a standoff or a deranged hissy fit from the latest gold digger her best friend / lover is fucking.

"Are we done?" I ask, feeling everything inside wilting, unable to find the stony facade I want her to see.

"We're done," she chimes, smiling. "Lovely chatting." Slipping her shades on, Katherine twirls and struts away, and I start toward the Tube in a daze. With each step I take, my disbelief fades and anger rises. I knew it. I fucking knew there was more to him.

Don't do it, Amelia.

Don't do it.

Keep it classy.

"Fuck it." I don't owe Katherine a thing, and I certainly don't owe Jude. I stop just shy of the Tube station and hammer out a message.

> Katherine just paid a visit to my workplace and enlightened me about your little "arrangement." Don't contact me again.

I stamp my foot on a yell, feeling so fucking stupid. He hasn't been in touch anyway, so Katherine's had a wasted journey and squandered her breath warning me off. Her little fuckboy is still at her disposal. And suddenly I remember what Jude said to me. *I don't want you to think I'm nothing but a fuckboy.* He said that. While the woman he fucks regularly was sitting at a nearby table with her *husband*. All the lovely words Jude said, the playfulness, the amazing sex, the looks, the kisses, the intensity.

It was all a fucking joke.

And I'm the clown.

The Invitation

I hate him. I hate him for making me believe instant chemistry is a thing. I hate him for being relentless in his pursuit, for giving me endless orgasms, for being the best night of my fucking life. I hate him for momentarily making me wonder if he was the one I wasn't waiting for *or* expecting.

I hate him.

Chapter 23

I can't let go of the anger. And to make it worse, I've heard nothing from him in response to my scathing message.

That I sent an hour ago.

He's probably digesting it. Drafting a pathetic excuse. If he even cares. Maybe he's gone to Katherine to make himself feel better.

Still obsessing.

Fuck.

Abbie and Charley sit silently with wide eyes as I spew my anger out on them over a bottle of wine, necking my drink in between my tirade. "How could I have been so stupid?" I cry, slapping a hand on my forehead. "What's happening? That's what he asked." I look at the girls as I swig some more. "As he gazed into my eyes, his cock still inside me postclimax, he asked me, on a fucking whisper, I'll add, 'What's happening?' And me, stupid, idiotic, foolish me, lay there and wondered if I was falling in love with a man I'd known for a heartbeat." I laugh. More wine. "Why the hell didn't you stop me from going?"

Both of them blink as Lloyd walks into the kitchen after putting the kids in bed. He looks between all three of us. "What's up?"

"Men are fucking wankers," I bark, finishing the last of my wine and pouring more. "That's what's up."

Poor Lloyd steps back, wary, out of the firing line, and Charley reaches for his arm and pats it lovingly. "Bad breakup."

"Nick?" he asks, confused. "I thought that was done and dusted."

The Invitation

I slump forward and hit my head on the marble, the alcohol starting to take effect, my head swirling a little. It feels good. I've not succumbed to the relief of total drunkenness since I walked out on Nick and me and the girls got so obliterated at Amazonico, we forgot to pay our bill, albeit obliterated for totally different reasons. With Nick, I was trying to drown my guilt. With Jude, I'm trying to drown my hurt. I've just granted myself the freedom to get totally shitfaced. I surrender the glass and take the bottle, swigging.

"Not Nick," Charley says.

"Oh, the rich hotelier?"

"Bastard," I grumble.

"I thought that was casual."

I slam the bottle down, and poor Lloyd jumps.

"I think I'll leave you girls to it." He drops a kiss in Charley's hair and retreats to the lounge to watch rugby.

I feel my throat start to close up. My lip begins to wobble.

"Oh shit," Abbie breathes, hopping down off her stool and rounding the island, taking me in a hug.

"I don't even know why I'm crying," I sob, my eyes streaming. "It was nothing. A fleeting fling. One night! I'd already pulled away before his bit on the side accosted me and delivered the blow." Wait. No, that's wrong. Jude's *her* bit on the side. I snivel, wiping my face into Abbie's shirt. "I just feel so fucking stupid. What kind of husband lets his wife shag another man?"

"Stranger things have happened," Charley says as Abbie wipes under my eyes with her thumbs. "Lloyd and I went to the tennis club the other night. Thought we might join, maybe get the kids into tennis when they're a bit older."

I frown and knock Abbie away, facing Charley. "The tennis club?"

"Yeah, you know the one off the high street?"

I look at Abbie as Abbie looks at me. She's desperately trying not to laugh. "You mean Swingers HQ?"

Charley gasps. "You knew?"

"Everyone this side of London knows," Abbie says, giving in and falling apart. I join her, in hysterics.

"I didn't!" Charley blurts. "And neither did Lloyd." She sits up straight. "Wait." Then she's off her stool, marching to the lounge. "Lloyd, did you know that place is swingers central?"

"I may have heard the rumours," Lloyd says, sheepish.

"Oh my God, Lloyd! Are you saying you want to swing?"

"Oh, shut up, Charley. I was curious, that's all. I didn't expect to feel like a steak being dangled over a lion's den."

I lose all control of my bodily functions, including my ability to swallow, my wine dribbling out.

"I was a steak too!" Charley says, outraged.

"A filet mignon, babe."

She huffs and comes back to the kitchen, reclaiming the wine from my hand. "He's right. We were steaks."

I pull myself together, my amusement fading. I think I was a steak too. And Jude was definitely a lion.

And now I'm just a fucking mug.

Chapter 24

By Friday, my hangover has just about left the building. I'm disappointed. Focusing on the raging headache was a hell of a lot more appealing than this sense of loss.

What the fuck is wrong with me?

I wanted this. Work, no distractions.

I place the phone down on my final call of the day and rest back in my chair. On the plus side, it's been a productive two-day hangover. I've secured two new clients and inched that little bit closer to my projections.

I stand and gather the few portfolios I plan on working on this weekend and head for the elevators, seeing Gary and a few of the other senior partners around the table as I pass the conference room. I hold my hand up in goodbye but slow when Gary stands and waves me back. I reverse my steps and push my way in. "Hey."

"Good job this week," he says.

"Thanks." I smile as the other senior partners mumble their agreement and praise.

Bob, who's been at the firm longer than I've been alive, stands. "We've got our monthly meet this evening. Nothing too formal, just a few drinks and obligatory casual catch-up. It would be good if you could join us."

My heart speeds up, my interest piqued. They're inviting me to one of their infamous out-of-office meets? "Sure," I say, smiling, my optimism soaring. "I'd love to."

Gary winks at me. Saying something without saying it? "We're heading a bit further afield this evening. You can expense your transport."

"Yes." Sue stands and smooths down her power suit. She's a force to be reckoned with, and the only woman on the board. I hope she'll be rooting for me to join her and start evening out the numbers. "It would be lovely to have some female company for once," she says, her eyebrows arching harshly as she flashes all the men a coy smile.

There's a collection of gruff grunts as everyone stands and starts filtering out of the room until there's only me and Gary left. "They're very impressed with your continued growth, Amelia," he says, his smile almost proud.

I laugh, starting to walk with him to the elevator. Given I've had a hangover these past few days, I feel like this is an even bigger achievement. "What does this mean, Gary?" I ask. No one gets invited to partner drinks. Ever.

"It means what you think it means, Amelia." He hits the call button for me. "We meet at eight." The doors open, and I step inside. Gary looks down at his watch. "I'll be heading straight from here once I've sent a few emails and freshened up. You'd better get moving if you want to change into something more casual." He looks down at my pencil dress. "And comfortable."

The doors start to close. "Where am I heading?"

"Evelyn's." The doors meet in the middle, and I stare at the metal, frozen.

"What?" I must have misheard him. Or at the very least there's another bar, club, restaurant by that name. *Please be another venue by that name.* I pull out my mobile, my pulse quickening, and dial Gary. No network. "Shit." The lift stops at every floor on the way down, the space becoming more and more crowded, until it finally arrives at the lobby and everyone spills out. I dial him again. "You said Evelyn's, right?"

"Yes, do you remember it?"

"Arlington Hall," I say quietly. "That Evelyn's?"

"That's right."

"In Oxfordshire?"

"I did say you'd better get moving if you're going to make the eight o'clock meet."

He did, but why on earth would they travel to another county for their monthly meet when we have hundreds of bars and clubs on our doorstep here in London?

"We've got a golf day tomorrow," he goes on. "I recommended it after the conference, and Bob just so happens to know a member who got us on the course with guest passes for the day tomorrow."

"Convenient," I murmur, staring ahead at the busy lobby, my stomach dropping into my heels.

"I'd tell you to get a room, but the company's budget doesn't stretch to a grand a night for accommodation." He laughs, and so do I. The irony.

"See you there." I hang up and send a million mental prayers to God. I also ask him . . . why? Why would he do this to me?

Chapter 25

"You're not seriously going?" Abbie says as she follows me from the bathroom to my makeshift bedroom.

"Of course I'm going. No one gets invited to the partners' monthly meetup." I rub myself dry and shake out my hair from the towel. "Besides, I remember him saying very clearly that he hardly ever goes to Evelyn's." He prefers the Library Bar.

"He went there the night you were there for the conference. Don't you remember? He had Clark up against the bar by his throat."

I give her a tired look. "He won't know I'm there." There's an entrance to the club around the side of Arlington Hall. I'll use that one. I'll crawl combat-style if I have to.

"You're mad."

I sit down on the floor in front of the mirror. Maybe. But I don't have much choice. "It'll be fine," I assure her, and she shakes her head, picking up a basket of washing and dropping it on the end of my bed. "Thanks." I smile mildly.

"Wearing this?" She plucks something off the top of the pile. The bra Jude bought me.

"Throw it away." I pick up my blow-dryer and drown out her sigh.

◆ ◆ ◆

The Invitation

After clearing the gateman, my Uber drives painfully slowly toward the splendid old building, the driver releasing constant sounds of awe. I fidget in my seat, faffing with my hair. When he rolls around the fountain, I see the army of staff waiting to greet me, help me, escort me.

"Just keep going to the end," I say, leaning forward, wanting to minimise interaction with anyone. "To the car park around the side." Would they recognise me? "I can walk through the grounds, it'll only take a few minutes."

"I'm being signalled to stop," he says, slowing down.

"Damn," I murmur. My door is open before I can put a bag over my head, and I smile my thanks to Stan as I reluctantly step out. "I'm meeting colleagues at Evelyn's," I say. "I'll just make my own way round."

"Oh, I would highly advise against it."

"Why?" I flinch when something hits my head, just as Stan produces a golf umbrella and the heavens open. "Oh my God," I gasp, as heavy, fat drops of rain start pounding down. "Jesus." I lift my clutch bag and hold it over my head as Stan fights to get the umbrella open.

"Here we go, miss," he says, covering me as we run to the doors. I make it and shake my bag, looking down at my white wide-leg trousers and gold silk camisole. "Shit." Patches of wet everywhere, the material the worst for showing water marks.

"The ladies' are just through there, if you'd like to use the facilities."

I look up and find Anouska before me. *Double shit.* "Thanks." I give her a tight smile. "Could you do me a favour?"

"A towel?"

"Don't tell him I'm here."

She cocks her head. "So you're not here to see him?"

"No, we're not . . . I'm not . . ." For fuck's sake. "It's over." I frown. "Not that there was anything . . ." *Someone kill me now.* I sigh. "I wouldn't be here, but my bosses chose this of all places for their monthly meeting, and I couldn't not come."

"I see." Anouska nods. "Well, in that case you'll probably be pleased to hear he's not here."

I feel everything in me deflate. *Thank God.* Now I just need to put him out of my head and focus. I look down my body. And dry off. "Thanks, Anouska." I leave her and go to the ladies', dropping my purse by the sink as I thank the hand dryer gods for the super powerful Dyson hanging on the wall. I pull my top out from my trousers and slip it off, dropping it between the drying blades, flapping it as it roars to life. It's dry in no time at all. Happy, I slip it back on and shimmy out of my trousers, dipping them in and out too, smiling awkwardly at an elderly lady who enters and does a double take at me in a camisole and gold strappy heels. "Rain," I explain, getting back to the task of drying my trousers.

By the time I'm done, it's bang on eight o'clock. Which means I'm going to be late. I hurry out of the ladies', answering my phone to Abbie as I make my way to Evelyn's. "He's not here," I say in answer, knowing she'll be worried.

"I know, because he was just here."

I skid to a stop, my blood cooling. "What?"

"He just showed up demanding to see you."

"Are you joking?"

"No, I'm not fucking joking. I had to prove you were out."

"How did you do that?"

"I let him stalk round my flat checking all the rooms."

"Jesus Christ."

"Fucking hell, Amelia, he was *not* in a good mood."

Just as she says that, my phone starts beeping. "I told you he has a temper." I pull my mobile away from my ear and wince. "He's calling me." I reject the incoming call and get back to Abbie. "Please tell me you didn't say where I was."

"Of course I didn't! I told him you were on a date."

My jaw hits the floor. "You did what?"

"I'm joking. I didn't disclose your location."

"What did he say?" Jesus, what did *Abbie* say?

"Before or after I gave him a piece of my mind?"

The Invitation

"Before."

"Not much. I asked him if it was true about Katherine."

"Oh God," I breathe, as my phone starts beeping again. I reject his call.

"He didn't confirm it, but he didn't deny it either."

"I really don't have time for this right now." I get moving, reeling. It's been two days since I texted him. Why now? "I need to concentrate."

"I just wanted you to know."

"Well, if he's there, he's not here," I say. "I'll call you when I'm leaving. Don't wait up."

"Don't forget tomorrow night," Abbie blurts before I can hang up. "Charley's looking forward to it."

"I've not forgotten." I hang up and silence my phone when Jude tries to call yet again. "Not now," I say, wondering if I would answer if I weren't here. I shake my head, unwilling to let my mind go there.

I find everyone on the far side of the club, all comfortable in velvet club chairs, various shaped glasses decorating the small gold table in the middle of the circle of chairs. Gary spots me and stands, welcoming me.

"I'm sorry, I got caught in the downpour," I say, accepting his kiss on my cheek before everyone rises in turn to welcome me.

"What are you drinking, Amelia?" Bob asks, waving a server over.

I lower to the chair Gary's pulled over and slide the cocktail menu from beneath a glass.

"This is divine." Sue moans her pleasure as she wraps her pink lips around the straw. "What's it called, Gary?"

"Hey Jude." He confirms what I knew, and I smile tightly.

"I think I'll have a dirty martini." Something short that I can sip slowly. I have to remain switched on. *Always stay a few drinks behind the rest.* Thank you, Tilda.

"Did anyone see the news?" Uptight Uriel asks, looking as relaxed as I've ever known him, his foot resting on his knee.

"The base rate?" Spencer says. "Unmoving."

"Well, that's faded all hope of the FTSE making a miraculous recovery," Ted grumbles.

"It was a slow start to the week," Gary says. "But I'm comfortable on where we closed today."

"And the news of HighTac's bumper profits was welcome," Sue adds around her straw. "The question is, are we going to see any shift in the right direction soon?"

They all hum, and Gary looks at me, smiling over the rim of his glass. "What are your thoughts, Amelia?"

"Me?" I blurt, accepting my martini, all attention suddenly pointing my way. "Well." I take a small sip, buying myself some time. *Pressure.* "It's been a topsy-turvy month for sure, but I don't think it's a sign of a broader market panic. I'm definitely looking more towards the longer-term plans. I've had a few clients' plans mature this week. One of my recommendations has been to reinvest in one of the six-year Global Defence plans. High risk, yes, but if things go as I predict—and hope—they could top a twelve percent return."

"Twelve?" Bob asks. "You're lucky to get eight these days."

"I know, but when they guarantee the return of your initial capital, provided all underlying indices are at or above sixty-five percent of the initial strike level, it's worth paying attention. You know they're not playing when their minimum investment sits at fifty grand."

"Oh, I do love a ballsy adviser," Sue says, placing her glass on the table. "Where's the fun in low-value, safe investments?" She looks at Gary, who smiles wide. And a deep, warm feeling floods me.

I've got this.

A few hours later, talk of the Dow Jones and FTSE 100 is a distant memory, the music is chilled and not too loud, and I've loosened up some more with the thanks of a few more dirty martinis. Although I have ensured I remain two drinks behind. And I'm all the more grateful for that when Sue comes close, her eyes definitely a little heavy with drunkenness.

"You know," she says quietly, "I have to tell you, Amelia, I think I might quit if that Leighton makes partner."

I snort. "Stop," I whisper.

"No, I mean it. He's a fucking snake. When you've been in this world as long as I have, you know one when you see one."

"The guys like him," I say, trying not to fish but unable to help myself. Opportunities like this do not present themselves often.

"Of course they like him. He's a dick-swinging prick. They all are, truth be told. Some just know how to control their urges. Leighton's young. Got something to prove to these dinosaurs."

"And you?"

"What about me?"

"Has he tried to prove himself to you?"

She huffs. "He's a boy. I think I intimidate him."

I laugh to myself. "I know the feeling."

"Oh?"

I wave her interest off. "He just needs putting in his place every now and then." I stand. "Another drink?" I should *not* get into a slagging match with a senior partner, no matter how tipsy she is.

Sue flings her arm in the air with her empty. "Fill me up."

"I'll order, then pop to the ladies'." I head off, smiling, happy with how the evening has panned out, and very grateful for the insight and inside information.

I leave my order with the barman and use the loo before washing my hands, reapplying my lipstick, and checking my phone. "Fucking hell," I whisper, scrolling through the endless texts and missed calls.

> You're out, apparently. Where?
> Answer me, Amelia.
> We're not done.
> For fuck's sake, we need to talk.

Delete.

Delete, delete, delete.

I head back out, willing my heart to calm. It's making me shake. I take a few controlled breaths at the bar as the barman loads the glasses onto a tray, digging deep. It's been a great evening. I need to keep it together a little while longer. I take the tray and head back to the partners, laughing when I see Bob and Sue on the dance floor swaying to Jan Blomqvist's "More," their eyes closed.

"Old ravers," Gary says, chuckling.

"I fear some very dodgy shots on the golf course tomorrow." I lower to the chair next to him.

"Oh, the hangovers will be rotten. Always are. I don't think we've played a game of golf sober in our entire working relationships."

"Does Sue play?"

"She's the best."

"Oh, I love it."

"Perhaps you should get yourself some lessons, Amelia," he says, giving me a telling look.

"You think?" His words remind me that I still need to get my father sorted. I put it on my mental list of things to do, along with calling some agents to see if there's anything new on the rental market.

"Oh, I definitely think. And I know Sue would love a bit of backup on the course." His eyebrows waggle.

Is that code for backup in the boardroom too? "Maybe I will." I smile around the rim of my glass, settling back in my chair, watching Sue and Bob on the dance floor.

"Can I offer some inside information?" Gary asks, sitting forward. I definitely detect a little slur. Not too much, but enough to tell me the drink is about to talk.

"Sure."

"When . . . *if* you make partner, there's a whole new world of rumours waiting for you."

The Invitation

"Okay," I say, trying not to get ahead of myself. The decision on *if* I make partner isn't entirely Gary's.

"There's whispers," he goes on, "of a merge between two of the big investment banks."

"Oh?" I ask, interested, moving in closer. "Two that may feature heavily in some of my recommendations?"

"Indeed. I'm just throwing it out there, and they are just whispers at the moment, but you know there's no smoke without fire."

"Do I need to be reserved?"

"It could propel things, depending on how the banks' boards handle PR. Or it could sink." Which means one of the banks is struggling. "Just keep your ear to the ground and be ready to make some changes."

"Got it." I nod, my increasingly fuzzy mind wondering if Gary's shared this information with anyone else. Like my adversary. "I appreciate your . . ." My words fade, my mouth dries, and I slowly rest back in my seat. *Shit.* Jude's sitting at the end of the bar, his hand wrapped around a short glass, and he's looking this way like he wants to kill someone. *Fuck.* His eyes pass over to Gary. *Oh God, oh God, oh God.*

I return my attention to my boss, who's now chatting with some of the others. What the hell should I do? I can't let Jude come over here. He doesn't have a very good track record when it comes to dealing with me talking to other men. He could completely fuck up my entire night. And career.

"Excuse me," I say, standing and collecting my clutch bag, breathing in deep and heading over to Jude before he can go all caveman on my boss. His fiery eyes follow me the entire way, and I don't shy away, crying on the inside at the unholy perfection of him in some jeans and a black slim-fitted T-shirt, the material clinging to his toned torso and biceps. His thick hair is its usual beautiful mess. His face its usual gorgeous ruggedness.

I shake away my awe and get back to the matter at hand. *Remember why you're here, Amelia. Remember that he lied to you.* I've had too much to drink to take on Jude Harrison, but just you try to stop me. "You said you hardly ever come here," I say, my voice strong.

"I don't."

"So who told you I'm here?"

"It's irrelevant."

"Like you sleeping with Katherine is irrelevant?" God damn me, I did not want to fire that bullet, but as I stand here looking at him, struggling for reason and strength while also fighting off the inevitable effect of Jude on my senses, I'm getting worked up. Angry. He should have fucking told me, and, actually, he owed me that. I *did* deserve that information, so I could have at least been prepared when she inevitably warned me off.

His jaw rolls as he lifts his drink and takes a casual sip. He's having his own battle, clearly working hard to keep himself in place rather than spinning off the handle. He looks stressed past his stony facade, his pissy glare constantly moving to the group I'm with. Did he just come here to be all passive aggressive? Stand there and make me feel awkward and uncomfortable? Anxious of what he might do? The least he could do is fucking apologise to me.

"Fucking talk!" I snap, my blood beginning to boil. He remains silent, unresponsive. I want to bash into his chest with my fists. Scream at him for giving me the time of my life, making me believe in something that isn't real, and then shitting all over it.

"What does it matter?" he asks, his face straight. "You're not looking for anything serious anyway."

I recoil, injured. But he's right. I said that. And this, my reaction, is revealing. Feeling my control slipping, my anger rising, tears forming, I throw back my drink. "Fuck you, Jude." I slam down my glass and escape before my emotions get the better of me, shoving my way into the ladies', yelling my frustration, startling a poor, unexpecting woman who's applying some blusher. "Sorry," I murmur, throwing my purse on the sink and bracing my arms against it, my head hanging, my eyes low.

I think I'm in more trouble now than I was an hour ago.

The Invitation

Last night felt pretty fucking serious.

Flashbacks assault my woozy head, images of his face as he blew my mind in bed, our limbs entwined, his smoky eyes as he maintained eye contact throughout the most intimate and explosive experience I've ever had with a man.

A man I hate to admit I'm mad for.

Was mad for. Now he's just a good-looking guy who is guaranteed to play me. A man to be avoided. *Dangerous.* Just as I initially thought.

I'm so fucking stupid. Just seeing him, I'm trembling. Hot. My body's reacting in ways I'm not comfortable with, even though I'm mad with him. I need to remember the aftermath, the turning of my stomach when Katherine messaged him. The panic that hit me when I considered what the uncomfortable sinking of my heart could be. The friendly visit she paid me at work.

The information she shared.

It could be easy, no strings, a bit of fun. No commitment, no distraction.

But that changes the moment feelings happen, and after just one night together—fucking hell, even *before* our night together—I felt those feelings creeping in.

My reaction to Katherine is prime proof. I can't do this. I can't risk free-falling into a mess.

I breathe in deep and exhale, looking at my reflection. I'm alone now.

Then . . . not.

Jude pushes his way into the ladies' and lets the door close, standing with his back against it. Our eyes meet. The universe shifts. My whole world tilts.

Did I think he would come? Yes. Did I want him to?

My throat thickens, my swallow lumpy as I look away from him. *Do not fall.* I hear him approach, and he's suddenly behind me, his gaze still steely.

"Do not touch me," I warn.

He plain ignores me, his hand lifting, his lips straight.

"No, Jude."

His touch closes in.

"I said no."

"And yet you're not moving away," he replies, his voice grainy. "Why's that?"

I don't want to answer. His hand meets my elbow, and delicate eruptions pitter-patter across my skin, aiming right for my heart.

"No!" I cry, turning and physically shoving him away. He fucks a married woman. He said she was no one. He let me walk into a fucking lion's den.

Jude steadies himself and comes right back at me. *No!* Desperate, I swipe a hand out and slap him clean across the face. He blinks, inhales, and comes at me again, taking the tops of my arms and holding me, his face tense. He's in better control than me. It makes a change. As he eases me up against the nearest wall, his eyes drop to my mouth, his intention clear. The heaviness that falls between my thighs forces them to clench. I will my body to behave, *beg* it, as he slowly drops his lips to mine, kissing me gently. The rush of blood that coasts through me nearly puts me on my arse.

Jude pulls back, his wet lips glistening. "Are you going to argue with that?"

I wrench my arms free, push him away, and deliver another stinger of a slap. He clenches his eyes closed briefly, his nostrils flaring, as I pant before him, half-furious, half-turned on. *God damn me.*

After a deep inhale of perseverance, he's coming at me again, our lips crashing together, his kiss more forceful this time, stealing my breath. His body compresses mine to the wall, my boobs start to ache, my head gets messier. I growl to myself and force him back, slapping his face *again. Do not fall.*

"I'm losing my patience, Amelia," he grates, shaking his daze away and slamming his mouth onto mine.

The Invitation

"Fuck off." I bite at his lip, shoving him back, my stinging hand on autopilot, swiping at him again. *Slap*. His head jerks to the side, and he holds it there, breathing through his rising anger as I breathe through my rising craving for him. I'm in fight-or-flight mode, and the anger is ruling which option to take.

Fight. Fight him with everything I have. Hurt him. Protect myself.

Jude licks his lip as he slowly lifts his eyes to mine. They're so dark. So full of rage, but I see his desperation past the sheen of anger. I don't think straight around this man. I lose all reason, shift from stable and sensible to senseless and irrational.

I heave against the wall, my brow dampening, my body calling for him. And as I drop my eyes to the fly of his jeans, I see he's turned on past his anger too, the bulge prominent. I want it. I want *him*.

Praying for help in maintaining my diminishing resistance, I look up as Jude snarls, moving slowly in, bracing himself for my out-of-control hand to come at him again. But I'm out of fight. I'm done. He slips a hand onto my waist, tugging my hips into his, his eyes hooded, his breath spreading all over my face. My palms find his hips, my cheek rubbing against the harshness of his bristle when he nuzzles me.

His cock pulses against my lower tummy.

My nose is invaded by his scent, calming me further, his hands working at my strung muscles across my back until I'm boneless against him. Settled.

His mouth moves to my ear. "I want you, Amelia," he whispers, stamping all over my willpower with his words as well as his touch. "I want you so fucking much." He kisses the sensitive spot beneath my earlobe, and my knees wobble. "We've got to figure this out together." Taking my chin, he directs my face to his. "We can have angry sex now, you can take everything out on me, or you can come with me and let me try to fix this." His eyes pour with sincerity that I can't ignore. I just can't. "But walking away isn't an option."

I bite at my lip, scared to say the words bubbling in my throat. Scared to seal my fate.

"It's not an option," he whispers, reinforcing it as he holds my face. "Come with me."

"I have work people out there," I say, remembering where I am. Why I'm here. "The partners. I can't just leave." My phone starts ringing, and I look across to my purse by the sink.

"Don't answer it," Jude says. "Please."

"I have to." It could be Abbie or Charley. They'll be worried. Jude reluctantly breaks away, letting me get to my phone. It's my boss. Oh God, did he see me with Jude? "Gary?"

"Just checking you're okay," he says. "We're heading back to the hotel."

I wince. Am I okay? I look at Jude in the reflection past me. He's waiting patiently, but I detect his wariness.

"I'm okay," I say quietly. "You go. I have an Uber coming."

Jude starts mildly shaking his head, refuting that.

"You sure?" Gary asks.

"Yes, I bumped into someone I know in the ladies' and got talking." I visibly wince. "Sorry."

"Hey, don't worry. Like I said, just checking you're okay."

"Have a great day on the course tomorrow, and thanks for tonight."

"My pleasure, Amelia. See you Monday."

I hang up and inhale when Jude's front is quickly pushed up against my back. He reaches past me, takes my purse off the counter, and slips his hand around mine, leading me out of the bathroom and through Evelyn's. I can feel my heart beating in my throat, my mind racing. Where's my resolve gone? Where's the disgust, the anger, the determination to avoid him?

The pull is too strong. I keep going back for more, and I'm terrified I always will.

We leave Evelyn's, Jude leading me, his hold of my hand tight, and pass through the glass corridor back to the main hotel. I see Gary up ahead with the others.

"Jude," I breathe, slowing, making our arms stretch between us. He looks back at me in question. "My bosses," I say, and he checks, quickly diverting us down another corridor and up a different staircase.

When we make it to his apartment, he drops my phone on the couch, picks me up, and walks me to the kitchen space, sitting me on the counter and getting between my thighs.

Cupping my face, he pulls it down to his, but he doesn't kiss me. I wrap my palms around his wrists. Wait for his words to make everything better. "I should have told you about Katherine."

That doesn't make everything better, but at least he's owning his mistake. "Why didn't you?"

"Because I was afraid it would put you off."

"It does," I say frankly. "I'm not interested in becoming part of a love triangle."

"Well, on Sunday you weren't interested in anything serious," he says over a laugh. "So tell me, Amelia, what the fuck do you actually want?"

I blink at him, surprised, outraged. And now he's being an arsehole? "You're doing a stellar job of trying to fix this," I snap, yanking my face from his hold and getting down from the counter. "Fuck you, Jude." I can't deal with these seesaw emotions. Mine *or* his. Lust one second, rage the next, despair, calm, joy, anguish. This isn't healthy, and it's not what I want.

"Amelia," he barks, making a grab for my arm. I dodge his lunge and retrieve my bag. "Oh, great, so now you walk away again. Brilliant. Very fucking reasonable of you."

"Reasonable?" I cry, my voice high-pitched. "You're fucking a married woman! Is it all a fucking game to you? Bending women to your will, brandishing your charm left and right. What's wrong with you?"

I see it coming. The explosion. "Everything is fucking wrong with me!" he bellows, completely losing his shit. He swings around and smashes his fist into the wall, and I jump back, alarmed, as plaster crumbles around his balled hand. "Fuck!" He yanks it free and curses his way to the sink, shoving his scuffed knuckles under the cold tap.

He takes a few deep breaths. Clenches his eyes closed. "I'm a fuckup, Amelia," he says calmly. "A total fuckup, so, yes, the best thing you could do is leave and crack on with your life."

I baulk at him. "That's exactly what I was trying to do until you turned up tonight."

"You were in my club," he grates.

"And you were hammering on my best friend's front door before that, so don't you dare throw the blame for this shitshow my way." I fling my arm toward the door, pointing. "You just led me up to your apartment with the promise of fixing it, and all you've done is make this fucking worse." I underestimated his anger issues. His temper. He looks absolutely crazed as he shakes his hand and grabs a tea towel, drying it, his lip curling in contempt. *I'm a fuckup, Amelia.*

He's not wrong, and he's fucking me up too. My anger, the frustration. I feel out of control.

"You let me lead you up here, Amelia, because you wanted me to fuck you like you love me fucking you."

"Go to hell."

"I'm already fucking there!" he yells as I storm out, slamming the door behind me, my face certainly every shade of furious. Stomping to the next set of doors that lead back into the hotel, the pressure in my head growing, I haul the door open.

And come face-to-face with Katherine.

"Oh," I laugh, as she looks me up and down. "Well, this is fucking perfect."

"Excuse me?" Indignant, she glances past me, and I turn to see Jude jogging this way, his face a picture of horror, fury, anxiousness.

Fuck.

Him.

I smile, sweeping a hand out to Katherine. "Look who's here," I sing, delighted.

Deranged.

"Have fun, you two." I leave, damning the pinch at the back of my eyes, pushing my way through the various double doors until I'm at the top of the stairs. *Bastard.* I'm a fucking idiot.

"Amelia," Jude yells after me.

"Fuck off," I hiss, wondering if I've ever cursed so much in my life.

"Amelia, for fuck's sake."

I take the stairs but make it only three down before I'm dragged back up. "I said fuck off!" I scream.

"Not on your fucking life," he seethes, his face up in mine. "We've got things we need to discuss."

I laugh. "What, like how much of a fuckhead you are?"

"If it makes you happy." He grabs the top of my arm and starts guiding me back toward his apartment, but just when I'm about to fight back, Katherine appears, and the expression of shock on her face tells me I look as wild as I feel.

His fault.

This . . . because of a man.

What has become of me?

Jude wrestles me past her, and the filthy look I give her should turn her to stone. "You're welcome to him," I seethe, getting a warning squeeze from Jude for my trouble.

"You say that like the choice is yours," Katherine replies, deadpan. She truly means it.

"Enough, Katherine," Jude warns calmly, marching me on.

"Tell that to your bit of stuff," she retorts.

I cough over my indignation, breaking free of Jude's hold. *Slap her. Claw her eyes out. Fucking strangle her.* "Bit of stuff?" I parrot, gunning for her, my mind and sense completely gone. "Correct me if I'm wrong, but I believe *he* is *your* bit of stuff, since you're the one who's fucking married in this situation."

She hums, pouting, her head tilting as if considering that notion. "Correct." She smiles, and it's smug. She's enjoying this. My upset, my loss of control. "Mine," she adds.

What the hell is this madness? What the hell have I got myself into?

Katherine sighs, feigning impatience. "Jude, if you're going to sleep around, could you at least find someone with a bit of class *and* who knows her place?"

"Oh my God," I breathe.

"Katherine!" Jude barks. "Shut your damn mouth."

Locking down every muscle so I don't launch myself at her, I have a stern word with myself. I'm better than this. *Keep it classy.* Too late.

Leave.

Go.

I need to get out of here before I embarrass myself even more. I pick one foot up and yelp when I'm hauled upwards. "What the fucking hell? Jude!"

"Shut up," he snaps, throwing me over his shoulder and marching back to his apartment. The door crashes closed, and he dumps me on my feet. "I'm not fucking done."

"I am!" I scream. "I'm so fucking done. I wish I'd never laid eyes on you. I wish you didn't exist. I wish I could forget you! I wish I could go back to before I met you and make some better fucking choices."

Jude blinks. Recoils. He's hurt? Give me a break. "You could forget me if you wanted to."

"No, I can't." And that fucking sucks. He's scratched into my mind. I'm fucking doomed, destined to live with regret because of the stupid decisions I've made. I was right all along. He's dangerous.

I need to go.

I have to leave.

I search for my purse, realising quickly that I must have dropped it outside. I point to the door. "My purse is out there," I say, my shortness of breath indicative of my exhaustion, physical and emotional.

"Why can't you forget about me?"

My arm lowers and my brain empties. The expressive eyes staring back at me could break me.

"Tell me, Amelia. Why?"

"I'm leaving."

"You're not leaving. You're going to stay and help me figure out what the fuck is going on here."

I bite down on my lip, so fucking torn. I can't be with a man who pimps himself out, no matter how serious or insignificant. This, what we're experiencing, isn't insignificant. *Fuck, I know this isn't insignificant.*

Approaching cautiously, Jude watches me carefully for any signs that I'm about to bolt. I feel like my feet are stuck to the carpet. My resolve is cracking. I'm a slave to this man, and there is nothing I can do about that. Do I just have to accept the inevitable?

"My eyes are on you and you alone, Amelia," he says quietly, closing in on me. He reaches out, offering himself up. "So fucking take me. Devastate me. Do what the fucking hell you want with me, because this begins and ends with you."

His declaration crushes me as I look at him before me, his hands held out, offering them to me. "Stop it."

"Only you. Do you want me?"

My teeth clamp down on my lip, trying to stop it wobbling.

"Answer me," he demands.

The dam holding back my need and desire collapses as I reach for his hands. It's my answer. I'm tugged into his body, and neither of us holds back, our lips finding each other's, our frustrations and desperation getting the better of us. Our kiss is all wild tongues, clashing teeth, our hands are everywhere, feeling each other.

Untameable.

Unquenchable.

Inevitable.

I wrench his T-shirt up his torso, practically ripping it over his head and throwing it down, my hands going to his belt and yanking it open. Jude groans into my mouth as I unbutton his fly, keeping his lips on mine, his tongue lapping, as he wriggles out of his jeans, kicking off his shoes, reaching to pull his socks off, before he starts on me. He tears my camisole off, pushes my trousers down my thighs. I moan, biting at his lip as he circles my waist and lifts, letting me shake my heels and trousers off. My back is soon against the wooden island counter, Jude bent over me, my legs wrapped around his hips as he yanks the cups of my bra down. I cry out, throwing my head back as he kisses his way over my breastbone and bites at one boob, massaging the other.

"Fuck, I've missed this body," he mumbles around a mouthful of my flesh. "Fuck, these tits, your mouth, your begging pussy." A finger slips past my knickers and into my desire, and I grab his hair, pulling and tugging, squeezing my thighs tighter around his hips. He gasps, drives deep, and withdraws, coming back to my mouth, slipping his palm under the back of my head and encouraging me up, making our kiss forceful. "You feel so good." His tongue laps at mine rapidly, any control fading fast, his dick fighting for freedom. I reach down to his boxers and slip my hand inside, holding him, gasping at the heat and throb. "Shit," he grunts, momentarily losing the pace of his kiss. "God, I need you so badly." He rises, dragging his palm down my front to my stomach, watching his moving hand. My body rolls, anticipation ruining me. The sight of him towering over me, adoring me, worshipping my body.

Irresistible.

Mouthwatering.

Heartthrob.

Jude peeks up at me through his lashes, his eyes hooded. The way he's looking at me? It's crushing. Need. So much need. "Why are you a fuckup?" I ask quietly.

He strokes back up my body, forcing my spine to bow, my chest pushing up. I can't take my eyes off him. "I don't want to ruin this," he whispers, scanning my eyes.

"Then don't." My breathing is loud. My pulse throbs in my ears.

He nods and turns me onto my front, effectively bending me over the counter, and draws my knickers down my legs.

"Oh shit," I whisper, my palms flattening against the wooden surface, my boobs squished. I look over my shoulder to Jude looming over me, both of his hands smoothing across my arse cheeks. The hunger in him is something else. I can't possibly be misreading the utter desperation on his face. His eyes flick to mine as he pushes his boxers down, his dick springing free, jutting out, long and hard. I blow out my cheeks and brace myself.

"Watch me fuck you over the kitchen counter, baby." He nods past me, and I swallow and look forward. To the mirrored doors of the fridge. A small, awed wisp of breath leaves me as I push up onto my forearms. The sight. "Quite the vision, huh?" He reaches for my hair and pulls my head back, and then he enters me slowly on a long exhale, his eyes on my boobs in the mirror, mine on his face, the strain taking his beauty to new heights. His abs bulge, his pecs swell, his hair falls onto his face. I close my eyes and absorb the fullness, humming when he bends over me and presses his lips to my back, kissing from one side to the other. "Are you ready?" he whispers.

I nod, dizzy with pleasure, and he starts moving, driving in and out, grinding firmly, working us both up, finding his pace, maintaining it for a few mind-bending minutes, before upping the ante, no longer driving, but hitting deep in short, fast bursts.

"Jude," I groan, my head lolling. "So good." I watch him in the mirror, owning my body, strong and powerful.

Sliding his hands onto my shoulders, he pulls me back onto his advances, his jaw taut. I'm forced to my tippy-toes, his hips thrusting, increasing gradually until they're going like pistons.

I cry out constantly, but my eyes remain nailed to him in the mirror. The veins in his neck bulge, and I am helpless, at the mercy of his command, his fingers clawing into my hips. I can't describe the pleasure. The sight of him, of us, his face, the gratification plastered all over it. The sounds of our bodies crashing together, the smell of sweat, Jude, and me, all mingling. The telltale heat rises from my toes, my stomach furls, my muscles tense. I hold my breath, try to seize the teasing orgasm creeping forward, his dick banging into me relentlessly. His eyes smoke out, and his head drops back, his lips parting.

Balling my fists, I press them into the wood, trying to anchor myself. This is going to be powerful. "Yes," I breathe, chasing the release, willing it forward. "Yes, yes, yes."

Jude sucks air through his teeth, powering on, merciless, unstoppable. "Come on, come on."

"Yes!" I shout, the pleasure sizzling on the edge, waiting to spill over and engulf me.

"Fucking hell, Amelia!" he yells, fucking me hard, banging all the tension and doubts away.

I'm fixated, enthralled, his slick chest swelling, his neck bulging. "Yes!"

"Fuck."

"Yes!"

"Amelia!"

"Yes!"

"Fuck, I adore you."

Bang, bang, bang.

"Talk to me, baby," he bellows. "Tell me."

"Now!" It grabs me and tosses me into a euphoric state, my vision blurring, my hearing fogging, Jude's yells and shouts becoming fuzzy and distant. Every inch of me is hypersensitive, my body reacting violently, twitching. "Oh God," I gasp, dizzy, fighting back the fog as Jude comes with me, his upper body folding over my back, his shuddering fierce. We're both rendered useless as we deal with the pleasure, and it's never-ending, me splattered against the wood, Jude splattered against my back.

"Fucking hell," he gasps, sniffing, rubbing his wet forehead across my skin, his hair tickling my back.

Tremors are still slithering through me. I'm paralysed, unable to move, hardly able to catch my breath, panting across the countertop. I can't talk, and I wouldn't know what to say if I could. My head is all over the place. Sex does not make things better.

The Invitation

Fucking take me. Devastate me. Do what the fucking hell you want with me.

Dazed, my clit still pulsing, my walls still throbbing, I close my eyes and try to imagine the best outcome here. My heart intact would be the best outcome, along with my dignity. I never anticipated this. I never anticipated *him*.

And now I feel royally fucked, because Jude is right. Walking away isn't an option.

It's also impossible.

Unnatural.

I'm a fuckup. A total fuckup, so, yes, the best thing you could do is leave and crack on with your life.

Except I can't seem to leave, and when I stupidly tried, he stopped me.

I don't want to ruin this.

God, is that what he's scared of?

His touch drifts over my shoulders and up my arms to my hands, holding them. Squeezing. "You're quiet," he says softly, dotting kisses across my shoulder blades. "Talk to me."

"I don't want you to ruin this," I whisper, surprising myself with my honesty. "And I don't want to ruin it either."

"I should have told you about Katherine," he says quietly.

"I'm scared," I admit. "I didn't expect you either."

Jude shifts, and he slides out of me, the slickness he leaves behind hot and coating my thighs. Turning me, he hooks an arm around my neck and pulls me into his chest, resting his chin on my head. "I've got you."

He's got me.

But do I trust him to keep hold of me?

I don't have the headspace to think about that in my postclimax state. I'm wrecked, drained. "Okay," I say, accepting his comfort. Hugging him.

Kissing my hair on a sigh, Jude dips and pulls me up to his body by the backs of my thighs, encouraging me to hold on to his shoulders. "You're staying the night," he says as he carries me to the bed. I'm lowered onto the silky-soft covers, and he climbs in beside me, pulling me into his side. My hand on his chest, I stare across the planes as he places his hand on mine where it rests.

"I don't want you to sleep with her again," I say quietly.

"Okay" is his simple reply.

Chapter 26

The whales wake me again, calling to me. I note the empty space in the bed and roll onto my back, breathing out. How did I end up here again? It's a stupid question. Memories of last night dance through my mind, giving me a full, comprehensive recap of where we're at.

Fucked is the answer. In many senses. Jesus, I have never behaved so erratically. Never lashed out so spectacularly. I'm horrified. Mortified.

I shuffle to the edge of the bed and pull the sheet with me, wrapping myself up in it. I find Jude at the island in the kitchen, sitting exactly where he had me bent over last night. He has one hand in his wet hair, holding his head, the other on the trackpad of his computer. He's showered and dressed. Casual in beige chinos and a white T-shirt. Barefoot.

"Morning," I say, sheepish.

He looks up, pushing his computer away and turning on the stool. "Good morning." He gets up and approaches me, taking the sides of the sheet around me and reversing his steps back to the stool, pulling me with him. He lowers to the seat and puts me where he wants me, between his thighs, looking at me with interest.

God, I feel so ashamed of myself. "I'm sorry about how I reacted last night."

His lip quirks a little. He's amused? I laugh on the inside. He wasn't last night when I was on the rampage. "I'm hardly a poster boy for control when it comes to sharing *you*, am I?"

Very true. "What about Katherine?"

"What about her?"

"Was she here last night to . . ." I can't say it.

"Probably."

"She just shows up, and you accommodate that?"

"If I'm in the mood."

I nod, my brain aching. It's too early for this kind of hard-hitting conversation. Does he remember the last thing I said last night? That, I don't regret. And, more importantly, does he remember his reply?

"And now?" I ask. I want no ambiguity whatsoever. Last night was hideous.

"I'm only in the mood for one woman," he says, dropping a kiss on my cheek. "And she isn't married." He hitches a brow. It's adorable. "Is she?"

"She's not."

"Then I'm happy. Are you?"

"Are you going to make that clear to Katherine?"

"I don't want you to think about Katherine." Reaching for my cheek, he traces his finger down the bone. "So, I will ask you again. Are you happy?"

I'm almost scared to admit it. But not thinking about Katherine? I don't feel like that was an answer. "I'm happy," I say, but it's half-hearted, and I know he senses that when his eyes narrow just a little and he sighs.

"Answer me honestly."

"I'll be happy if you tell me you won't be sleeping with Katherine again."

His lip quirks. "I thought I did last night."

So he does remember. I scrunch my nose, and Jude mirrors it, biting the end of mine and opening the sheet. He drags his gaze down my naked front. "And in case you're interested, I'm *very* happy." My body lights up. Unstoppable. He uses the edges of the sheet to pull me closer, guiding my boob onto his mouth, and I sigh, letting him feast on me. "Time to get ready for work." He slaps my arse and moves me out of his space.

"What?"

"I have work to do," he says. "And you're going to help me."

"But it's the weekend."

"Don't tell me you abstain from the pull of an email or two during a Saturday or Sunday."

More than an email or two. "What am I helping you with?"

He kisses my cheek and snaps the lid of his laptop down before sliding it off the counter. "Meet me in the Library Bar in half an hour." He heads towards the door. "Your purse and phone are on the island."

"Where are you going?"

"I have a few calls to make."

"Oh." I fetch my phone, bracing myself for the barrage of missed calls and messages. I'm not wrong. "Shit." I call Abbie first, and the moment she answers, I get a request to switch to FaceTime. Fuck it. I cringe and accept, lowering to a stool.

Abbie takes me in, the sheet, my hair, probably my swollen lips, then looks past me. "You fucking idiot," she breathes.

"You'd call me something harsher if you saw me last night."

"Wait. I'm getting Charley on the call. You will face both of us."

I sink farther onto the stool, making myself small, as Charley joins, Ena on her hip. She scans me, the background. "You fucking idiot," she breathes.

"She is," Abbie grunts. "What happened?"

"He showed up at the club." I still don't know who told him I was there. Does it matter? "It was . . . heated."

"And what's his excuse for being a deceitful fucktart?"

"He has no excuse. He has an arrangement with Katherine, and her husband knows."

"I don't get it," Charley breathes.

"Me either," I admit. "But it's over and—"

"You're under." Abbie raises her brows. "Amelia!"

"I can't help it," I cry. "I look at him and disintegrate. I get this funny feeling inside of me, and it feels so good. He touches me, I melt. He talks, I shiver. I smell him and could faint."

"Jesus." Charley passes Ena to Lloyd and gets closer to the camera. Yes. This is serious.

"So what now?" Abbie asks.

"I don't know," I admit, getting up and following my feet to the dressing room. I open the end door and swallow when I see the green mules. "He's said he's only interested in me." Closing the door, I go into the bathroom.

"And you believe him?"

Are they right? Am I being a complete, foolish dickhead? *Again.* But then, it's easy for them to draw unattractive conclusions. They're not the ones feeling what I'm feeling. "I believe him." If they'd seen the way he looked at me last night, they would too. "Look, I don't know what to tell you guys." I flip on the shower. "But I do know that I can't walk away, so here I am waiting to find out where this goes."

"Marriage?" Charley asks.

"What? No!"

"Babies?"

"Don't be ridiculous."

"So this is purely sex, is it?"

"What's your point?" My irritation is real. Because I know what her fucking point is.

"My point is that you just walked out on Nick after five years because he wanted to get very serious, and all I'm hearing right now are clues that you might think this thing you've got going on with Jude Fuckboy Harrison could be very serious."

"And you don't want serious," Abbie chimes in, shoving a marshmallow in her mouth and smiling sarcastically around the giant lump of pure sugar.

I stare at my best friends, at a loss. "What's the plan for tonight?"

Both of their heads drop back, and both of them groan their exasperation.

"Look, let me figure this out as I go along," I say, dumping the sheet in the wicker wash basket. "Why do I even have to put a name on it?"

"Because I feel like both parties in a situationship like this should know what each other's expectations are." Charley, ever the sensible one, starts bobbing on the screen, walking somewhere in her house. "I've got to go. We have a poonami happening. Meet here at six?"

"Six," I confirm, giving my attention to Abbie when Charley leaves the call. "I'll be back soon. We can get ready together."

"Be careful, Amelia."

"You've changed your tune," I say, laughing.

"Yes, well, now I have opinion-changing information. Don't be a mug, okay?"

I smile before I hang up, lowering to the edge of the tub, spinning my mobile in my hand. Trying not to overthink. What are my expectations? What are Jude's? And after last night, the tension, the anger, the yelling, shouldn't we have discussed that?

Or did we?

I groan, dragging myself up from the side of the tub, wincing when my phone starts ringing. Nick. "Oh God," I whisper, flipping the shower on to drown out the sound of my ex trying to call me *again*.

Chapter 27

The lobby is buzzing with weekend guests arriving as I pass through, luggage and golf bags being carried in by the staff, and glasses of welcome drinks being handed out. I dip and weave my way to the Library Bar, halting on the threshold when I see him at the end of the bar on his mobile. The exact spot Jude Harrison was in the first time I laid eyes on him. He's slightly to the left of the smoky-blue, ribbed glass shade, giving me clear sight to him. And I'm as shook as I was on that day, my stomach fluttering.

"Oh, you beautiful, confusing man," I whisper, as he looks up and spots me. He places his phone down, sitting back on the stool, arms crossing, studying me studying him. *Doomed.*

"Get your arse over here," he says seriously, jerking his head in order. "Now."

"And if I don't?"

"Are you arguing with me?"

I chew my lip, uncharacteristically coquettish. "Maybe."

Revealing a hint of a smirk, he leans forward and rests his forearms on the bar. "Then I look forward to punishing you later."

"Can't wait."

A beautiful, wide smile breaks, and he sighs, holding his hand out. "Come to me, baby."

Melting.

I walk to him and take his hand, letting him hold it as I slip onto the stool next to him. Clinton raises an interested brow as he heads our way. "Good to see you again," he says, turning his interest onto Jude.

I just catch Jude's tired look before he shuts the lid of his laptop and pulls a file closer, flipping it open. I wince at the sight of his scuffed knuckles. "Let's do this," he says.

I crane my neck to try and see what he's looking at. "What are we doing?"

"Cocktail tasting."

"You said I'm helping you with work."

"You are." He reaches for my lips and drags his thumb across the bottom one, watching me come over all hot and bothered. "Clinton's been working on some new recipes for the cocktail menu, and we have to try them."

"It's ten a.m."

Jude smiles mildly, and another whoosh of tingles bursts inside me. "We're tasting, Amelia, not getting out-of-our-skull drunk."

"First up is the Arlington," Clinton says, drying his hands on a cloth before pinching the stem of a coupe glass and setting it in front of us.

Jude folds his arms and nods for me to go ahead, so I do, taking the glass as Clinton leans on the bar, studying me.

"Can I just check something?" I admire the huge decorative cube of ice that's encasing a cherry. "There's no nuts in any of these, is there?"

"No nuts."

"Shit," Jude breathes, his face falling. "I should've checked that."

"I checked myself."

"But *I* should have."

I frown at the irritation growing before me. "It's not your responsibility to investigate everything I put past my lips, Jude."

The irritation seems to escalate before my eyes, and I lower the glass, stumped. Why is he getting so worked up over nothing?

"I should have checked," he mutters, using the foot stand on his stool to push himself up and peek over the bar. "Those there," he says, pointing to a few glass jars. "Do any contain nuts?"

Poor Clinton is as bemused as I am as he picks up a jar. "Almonds."

"Why the hell do we have almonds?"

"To top the Celeste."

"The sweet martini cocktail?"

"Yeah."

Jude swings his gaze to me. "Never try that one." Then he scans the bar as I watch, slightly concerned. "And those there, what are they?"

"Chili nuts," Clinton replies. "And those are pistachios, and those are walnuts, and those are dry-roasted cashews."

Jude looks like he's about to have a hernia. "Why the fuck do we have so many nuts?"

"It's a bar, Jude," Clinton says. "People like a bowl of nuts with their drinks."

"Okay, we need to get rid of them."

"Jude," I whisper, exasperated. "The nuts are fine where they are."

"What happens if you eat nuts?"

"I don't eat nuts," I point out. "Because I'm allergic."

"What if Clinton touched one and then handled the glass you're drinking from?"

I drop my gaze to the glass. "Have you touched any nuts today, Clinton?"

"Only my own, but I washed my hands."

I burst out laughing, placing the glass back down.

"This isn't fucking funny," Jude snaps.

"Will you chill out?" I chuckle, patting his knee. "I've survived thirty years managing my allergy. I'm still here." What on earth has gotten into him? I pick up the glass and take a sip, widening my eyes over the rim, humming. "Oh, that's good."

Jude pouts. "I can't believe how laid-back you are about it."

"I can't believe how uptight *you* are." I hand the glass over. "Try it."

He curls a lip playfully and accepts, nodding his approval. "Very good."

"Like sweet and salty."

"And no nuts," Clinton adds, slamming the lid on his mixer and shaking it vigorously. "Is it a yes?"

"It's a yes from me," I chirp. "What's next? I like this game." But I will have to mind my pace or I'll be pissed out of my mind before we make it to lunchtime and useless for our girls' night out tonight.

I peek at Jude, feeling him looking at me. "What?"

"Nothing." He reaches for my knee and squeezes over my trousers. "You dirty stop-out." His eyes fall down my clothes from last night.

"I'm a dirty stop-out because *you* demanded I stay the night."

"You're staying tonight too."

I shake my head. "I have plans with the girls."

"Oh," he grunts, disappointed, but his disappointment soon disappears when he glances past me, and of course, I look to see what's caught his eye and distracted him from the fact I'm not staying tonight.

Katherine.

She glances between us and lifts her chin, heading to a table in the window and lowering to the chair, facing this way. What is she doing? I return my body forward, my eyes on the wooden bar, feeling her glare burning into my back. Jude's hand is suddenly in mine, his stool moving closer.

"Next up," he says, pointing to the martini glass Clinton's put down.

"What is she doing?" I ask, the atmosphere shifting from easy to extremely *un*easy.

"Ignore her." He picks up the glass. "Drink."

I try to ignore her. I try so hard, sipping the cocktail. "Nice," I say, forcing a smile and passing Jude the glass.

He doesn't take it, but instead leans in, getting his face close to mine. I look into his eyes as he licks from one side of my mouth to the other. "Delicious," he whispers, and all my woes are forgotten. There is only him.

Until I hear a dramatic huff, a chair scraping the wooden floor, and the stamping of heels.

I bite my lip, seeing Katherine storming out. "That was bold of you," I say to Jude, not looking at him. Not until he pulls me back around.

"It's a yes from me," he says quietly, stroking my thigh.

"And me," I reply, pushing Katherine out of my mind.

"Two down, eight to go," Clinton sings, getting back to work. Eight? *Jesus.* "The next one's yet to be named. It's a fast invasion of your senses and packs a punch."

"Let's call it the Amelia," Jude says drily, squeezing my thigh. Clinton lets out a bark of laughter, while I turn a narrowed eye onto Jude. His nose wrinkles as he bends forward and offers me his lips. "I bet it's got a fiery aftertaste too."

"Let's find out," I murmur, edging closer, his gaze burning into mine. *Drowning.*

A cough snaps me out of my mesmerised state. "The Amelia," Clinton declares, presenting me with a flute. "Enjoy."

I take a sip and moan my appreciation. It could be the best thing I've ever tasted.

With the exception of Jude Harrison.

"Here," I say, passing it to Jude. "I think that's my favourite so far."

He nods mildly, taking a little sip, humming. Holding the glass up, he observes it as he tastes, thoughtful. Then he turns his calm eyes onto me. "*Definitely* my favourite," he says quietly.

I feel a little foggy by the time we're done, despite strictly only having a sip of each. Admittedly, I could have finished most of them. Especially the temporarily titled *Amelia*. That was a gift in a glass.

Clinton thanks us and disappears through the door behind the bar.

The Invitation

"You're staying the night," Jude says again, this time more surely, swivelling my stool to face him and leaning close. I can see he's about to deploy the big guns.

I shake my head, and he pouts—it's quite cute, even if there's an edge of seriousness to his expression—laying his hands on my thighs. "Are you sure?"

No. "Very sure." I lift his hands and return them to him, and he narrows an eye, obviously running over in his mind how he might convince me.

"Tomorrow?" he asks, surprising me.

I should say no. Should. "Tomorrow."

Nodding, Jude stacks his file and laptop. "Tell me about the meeting you had with the partners last night."

And again, I'm surprised. He's interested? I cross one leg over the other, charmed. "It wasn't a meeting, more an insight."

He tilts his head as he reaches over the bar and helps himself to a jar of crisps, opening it and dipping in. "Tell me more." Slipping one past his lips, he crunches, and my eyes root on his mouth as he slowly eats it.

"I don't know what to tell you." He's eating a fucking crisp, and I've come over all unnecessary. "Or think, really." *Someone cool me down.* "I know I'm on their radar. Me and the nice fellow you attacked."

He rolls his eyes, taking another crisp. "I caught my foot on the leg of his chair. Total accident."

"Sure."

"I didn't appreciate his body language. Or the way he was looking at you."

"Me either," I agree. Jude smirks. It's dirty. "All the signs point to them offering me partnership, but I don't want to assume." I take a crisp and bite into it, semi-scowling at his amusement. "And numbers play a big part."

"Are you on track?"

"I am."

"And the nice fellow whose chair I accidently kicked from under him?"

"Leighton's a prick, but he's successful. He's also ruthless. He has a certain type of client, if you know what I mean."

"Women."

"Yes."

"Then you need to watch your back."

I smile. "There's an adviser, Tilda Spector. She's independent and starting to ease herself into retirement, so she'll be dispersing some of her clients."

Jude nods, thoughtful, offering me the jar. "And she's got her eye on you?"

"I think so." I take another crisp. "These are really good."

"I know."

"We talked at the conference," I go on between chews. "She's super knowledgeable. Recommended I get a mentor to help me with my journey."

He hitches a brow. "I'll happily mentor you."

"In the bedroom?"

"Everywhere." He purposely crunches another crisp, his eyes smoking, and I clear my throat, giving him a warning look. "Why don't you just let me exterminate this Leighton prick and clear the path for you?"

"You'd do that for me?" I ask, my hand on my heart, serious.

His gorgeous smirk breaks at the corner and slowly spreads across his face, and I laugh when he grabs me and hauls me onto his lap, giving me a teasing dig in my ribs. I squeal, buck, but I get nowhere, trapped in his arms, at his mercy. It's apt. He eases up on the torture and kisses my neck, working his way up onto my face.

I sigh happily as he pushes my hair back, looking into my eyes. "I think you're incredible, Amelia."

I puddle on the spot. This whole feeling is new to me, is amazing me more every minute, and his sincere interest in my career and ambitions is intensifying this unfamiliar but incredible sense of contentment. "Thank you," I whisper, looping my arms over his neck.

"You've got this."

He'll never appreciate what it means to hear that. Unable to stop myself, I lower my mouth to his and savour his hum of pleasure as he opens up to me and circles his tongue slowly with mine.

Last night's drama feels like a world ago.

"Come with me, I want to show you something." Jude stands and pockets his phone, putting his laptop behind the bar before leading me by my hand through Arlington Hall. And I follow, no objections. We take the outside route to Evelyn's, which is closed, but the lights are on and the staff are cleaning or restocking. Jude leads me through a barn-style door and down some brick stairs, and some lights pop on, not bright, but just enough to see where we're going. Which is where? "Watch your step," he says, looking back to check I am, in fact, watching my step. He smiles mildly at my heels as I negotiate the bricks.

"What?" I ask, taking the rail for extra support.

"Bad shoe choice," he muses.

"Well, they're my *only* choice, so here we are." We reach the bottom, and I stop dead in my tracks. "Oh my God," I breathe, taking in the brick tunnel.

"It was an air raid shelter before it was a wine and champagne cellar," he says, giving me a moment to take it all in. "Are you cold?" He comes in behind me and starts rubbing my bare, chilly arms.

"Not too much." I break away, gazing around as I wander slowly down the long passageway. Racks of wine line each side, and brick arches stretch the width every ten metres or so. "This is incredible."

"I know," he says quietly behind me. The chink of my heels on the cobbles echoes around the vast tunnel. I see a few big wooden barrels dotted around. "We offer wine tasting days."

"Of course you do," I muse, smiling to myself as I drag my fingertips across one of the wooden racks, taking in the corks of the hundreds and hundreds of bottles. "How many are there?"

"Two thousand."

I look back at him in astonishment. "You do nothing by halves, do you, Jude Harrison?"

A wicked glint in his eye blinds me. "Keep walking," he orders, picking up his feet and slowly following me, his hands buried in his pockets.

"Yes, sir." I do as I'm bid, venturing farther into the tunnel, my cool skin heating as he pursues me. Up ahead, there's what looks like a glass screen, and it's not until I'm closer I see it's a glass box.

"The champagne store," he says, his voice getting closer. I stop and take in the end of the tunnel that's closed off by a huge pane of glass, seemingly endless bottles of champagne stored from floor to ceiling beyond, the wooden grid built in the recess of the brick arch. A ladder on wheels rests at one end. An oval wooden table is in the middle, flutes lined up precisely.

It's incredible.

His hand comes over my shoulder, his finger pushing a button that makes a hissing sound as the glass slides open. Cool air coats my skin. I look back at Jude, and he nods his instruction to enter.

Stepping over the threshold, I walk the length of the room, totally enchanted. "Why is it kept separately from the wine?" I ask.

"Temperature variations." Jude pulls a bottle out and checks the label. "Bollinger La Côte aux Enfants 2013." He peeks up at me with hooded eyes, and that's all it takes for the thrum to start between my legs. Peeling the foil off, he walks over to a button inside the glass room and hits it, making the door slide across.

I don't know much about champagne, but I know the year counts, and that's over ten years old. "Jude, I've really had enough alcohol for one lunchtime." I'll be fit for nothing come this evening when I'm out with the girls.

"You're not drinking it," he says, watching his working hands as he pulls the foil off. "Take your trousers off."

The Invitation

I stare at him, not that he would know. He's quite engrossed in what he's doing. I take in the glass wall. The wine cellar stretching as far as the eye can see. "Jude, I—"

"Take your trousers off," he says again, this time looking at me. "Or they're going to get wet, Amelia."

Oh my fuck.

I pull down the zip on the side and let them drop to the floor, stepping out of them.

"And your camisole." His smirk is dark but oddly playful. "And your bra."

God help me.

"And your knickers," he adds, resting the bottle on the table, casual, waiting. He tilts his head expectantly.

He will. He'll be the death of me.

Compliant, I do as he's bid and strip until I'm naked, heels on, my skin an arousing mix of cool and flaming hot.

"Come here."

I pace to him, anticipation swirling, and he pushes his palm in between my breasts, forcing me back to the table. I lower my arse, my eyes on his, my hands wedged into the wood behind me, and wait for what comes next. Jude steps back, twisting the metal on the side of the bottle until the caging comes off. Then he pops the cork, and I jump at the sound, just before champagne bursts from the lip. All over my chest. I inhale sharply, stiffening from head to toe as a river of bubbly, insanely expensive liquid streams down my torso and straight between my thighs. My mouth opens on a gasp, I fall to my back, and Jude wastes no time taking my ankles. I don't have a moment to brace myself.

His mouth meets my pulsing, begging, wet flesh, and the heat mixed with the chilliness of the liquid sends me through the roof. "Fuck!" I yell, my body snapping violently into an arch. My hands fall to his head, tug at his hair, as he feasts on me hungrily, sucking on my clit, biting at my lips, plunging his tongue into me. "Jude." The pressure is building already, my body rolling, the scratch of his scruff on my tender flesh sore but wonderful. I look down at his head between my legs, out of my damn mind on him and his devilish ways. My heart beating erratically, I close my eyes and rest my head back on the table, my toes pointing in my heels, my legs squirming around him. "Oh God," I pant, pushing into the back of his head. "Jude," I say again, warning him. "Jude, I'm coming." My words seem to egg him on, the sounds he's making pure indulgence. "Jesus, Jude." He bites my clit, then sucks it hard, and blood rushes to my head, my body goes up in flames, and my climax bursts out of me on a scream of his name. "Jude!" I come undone, pleasure racking me, having me jerking on the table under his mouth. The room starts to spin, my lungs shrink, the spasms so strong they're lifting me off the wood. I can't see straight. My poor heart is screaming for relief as I'm held prisoner to the pleasure of his mouth sucking my orgasm out of me. "Oh, fucking hell." I exhale the words, loosening my hold of his hair, certain I've pulled tufts out.

Jude slows his assault, dragging his tongue up my centre to my stomach. Finding the strength to lift my head, I peek down at him lapping up the sparkly liquid from my stomach, humming his pleasure. I drop back down to the table on a sigh, letting my arms fall over my head. The brick ceiling stretched above blurs as my eyes close and Jude takes his time licking me clean.

"Recovered?" he whispers in my ear when he makes it there. I only have the energy to shake my head. My jaw is taken in his grip, directing my face to his. His eyes are the darkest green. "On your front." He takes my hips and encourages me over. "You'd better hold on." He guides my hands to the edge of the table, and the sound of his trousers hitting the floor has me tensing again. He takes a fistful of my hair, pulling my head back, the crown of his weeping cock pushing at my entrance. "Ready?"

For Jude Harrison? Never.

I grip the edge of the table hard and stare forward, down the dimly lit tunnel. "Ready," I whisper, crying out when he pounds into me and holds himself deep, letting me mould around him. He's done with foreplay. He's got me soaked. It's his turn.

I catch the reflection of him in the glass, his chest bare, and though the sight of him looming behind me isn't perfectly distinguishable, I still see the strain on his face. His jaw is pulsing. He slides out slowly, pauses, and slams back in on a grunt from him, a moan from me. Out slowly again. My clawed fingers flex where they're gripping. *Bang!* I grunt, feeling every inch of him sliding back out calmly and painfully slowly. *Bang!* My scalp tingles with the pressure of him holding my hair, my eyes drowsy. *Bang!* I zone out, my legs jelly when he grinds deeply before retreating. *Bang!* I give in to my heavy lids and let my eyes close. *Bang!* The darkness swallows me, the heaviness between my legs revived. *Bang!* His pace is increasing. *Bang!* I'm climbing again. *Bang!* The pressure of his taut shaft against my walls stimulates more pleasure. *Bang!*

Faster.

Bang!

Faster.

Bang!

He bellows my name, and it bounces around the glass room as I drag my eyes open and look over my shoulder, needing to see him when he comes, about to tumble over the edge again. His heavy eyes, his damp brow, his jaw pulsing, his straight, serious face. *Stunning.* Jude releases my hair and flips me onto my back, getting my legs over his shoulders and slamming back into me on a yell.

And my view is suddenly unmatchable. My God. His face tight, he drives into me on constant grunts, his fingers digging into my thighs, the slaps of our bodies meeting ringing around the room.

Sparks ignite between my legs, my stomach aching from tensing. I'm going to come again.

"Shit!" It takes me out completely, and I free-fall, the orgasm ripping through my body viciously. Jude's head drops back, the veins in his neck bulging as he roars his release, slamming into me wickedly one last time, holding himself deep. The ripples of his own orgasm mix with the pulsing of mine.

My body heaving with my laboured breathing, I drag air into my burning lungs, my chest pumping as he folds down onto me, crushing me to the wood, his breathing in my ear loud and fast. "Jesus," he wheezes, his wet chest slipping across mine.

And we lie there, recovering, getting our breathing back to a safe rate. "That's definitely worth a five-star review," he whispers.

I'm fucked, knackered, beat. But I still manage a wide smile as he slips out of me and helps me to my feet. He pulls his jeans up, and I take the time while he's buttoning his fly to feel across his chest. When he's done, he slides his hand into my hair, massages a little, as if sensing my scalp has suffered. "Sore?" he asks, his eyes sincere.

"Everywhere," I confirm, knowing I'll be feeling him between my thighs until the next time.

"Good." He pushes his lips to my forehead before fetching my clothes and slowly dressing me. I watch him, fascinated, loving the mess of his waves. His eyes flick to mine as he fixes the straps of my camisole. His lip lifts a little. "What?"

"Nothing."

"Have I convinced you to stay the night?"

God, I wish I could. But I reluctantly shake my head, and he sighs, claiming the half-empty bottle of champagne and my hand, hitting the button with the neck of the bottle to open the doors.

"How much is that bottle worth?" I ask as he walks us out, my legs on the rickety side of stable. "Or *was* worth."

"Fifteen hundred," he says, casual, unaffected, as I baulk behind him. He looks back, serious. "Best fifteen hundred I've ever spent."

I scrunch my nose, content. "You need to take me home."

"If I must," he murmurs, unhappy.

We're back on track.

And I'm feeling the most content I ever have.

Chapter 28

When Abbie and I arrived at Charley's house, she was ready but obviously frazzled. Lloyd got home an hour later than he promised, so she was rushing getting ready, and quite pissed off. In the taxi to the restaurant, she declared any talk about men was banned for the entire evening. I assumed that included talk about Jude, so I was happy. I have no idea what to tell them. I've gone from hating him to adoring him again in a heartbeat.

"Are you guys sure we should go to Amazonico?" I say as we turn the corner onto Berkeley Square.

"It's my favourite," Charley says. "We have to go."

"Yes, but the last time we were there, we made a spectacle of ourselves and didn't pay."

"They said we *did* pay."

"Except none of us have proof of payment," I remind them.

"It'll be fine." Abbie links arms with me, looking down at my cream silky slip dress. "I love this dress."

"Thanks." I scrunch my nose. It's loose and light, which means it's not rubbing against the tender flesh of my inner thighs.

We reach the doors, and the doorman lets us pass with the confirmation of our reservation. I watch his face for any recollection of us. There's none.

"See, it's fine," Charley says, giving her name to the maître d'. She too smiles and lets us pass, handing us over to a waiter. Charley gives me a nod of reassurance, and my nerves settle. "Nothing to worry about."

We're seated, Abbie grabs the menu, and I start to relax. I recognise our server when he approaches, an Asian guy with both nostrils pierced. He's who served us last time. And when he falters on his way to the table, I fear the worst.

His disapproval is obvious. "Do I need to get security to guard your table so you can't leave without paying again?" he asks.

"Oh my God," I whisper, shrinking into the plush velvet fabric chair. *Kill me now.* I throw Charley and Abbie a death stare. *I told them!* But . . . wait. I sit up straight. "I called the next day, and your colleague said the bill was settled."

"By a couple sitting a few tables away," he says, waggling a condemning—slightly playful—finger at us.

"Wait." Charley frowns. "Someone paid our bill?"

"Yes, after you'd staggered out, and I realised you'd gone." He pouts as he pours our water. "I think they took pity on me."

I look between the girls. They're thinking what I'm thinking. It isn't cheap here. Who on earth would pay the bill of three drunken women? "Did they leave their details?"

"Nope." He smiles. "I'm Fendy—in case you forgot my name—and I'm your server this evening. Please don't leave without paying again."

"It was an honest mistake." I'm mortified. "We had one too many and assumed each other had paid. Like I said, as soon as we realised the next morning, I called." With a raging headache.

"I know." He whips out his pad. "Cocktails?"

"Yes, but if we ask for shots, please, please, please refuse us," Abbie says, and Charley laughs. "I'll have a Porn Star." Fendy's plucked eyebrows hitch. "The martini variety," she confirms on a coy grin.

We all put in our order and Fendy disappears. "A couple paid for us?" I glance around the restaurant. "So weird."

"What's everyone having?" Charley chimes, uninterested.

Me, though? I'm stumped by that.

An hour later, we've picked our way through some sharing plates, and none of us have dared have more than two cocktails. Fendy has watched us like a hawk. *So* embarrassing. I drag my clutch purse off the table and stand. "I need the ladies'," I declare, leaving the girls.

I use the toilet and stand at the sink washing my hands, my mind naturally wandering. What's he doing tonight? Damn it, I miss him. I bite at the corner of my lip, feeling the tenderness between my legs, and top up my lipstick, smacking my lips and leaving the ladies'.

I'm halfway across the restaurant when I spot someone I really don't want to see. "Oh shit." I pick up my feet and divert around the other way, hoping she doesn't see me. I dump my arse on the chair. "Get the bill," I order, making Abbie and Charley recoil. "Katherine is here." Both their jaws go lax, and they automatically start scanning the restaurant. "Don't look!" I wave Fendy over. "The bill, please," I say, smiling, trying to make myself small.

"Who's she with?" Abbie asks.

I keep my body blocked by Charley's and peek around her. "I don't know." She's with another woman. "Where's the bloody bill?"

"She's pretty," Abbie muses, and I gape at her. "Sorry. Total troll."

I shove my phone at Fendy when he holds out the machine, and as soon as it pings the payment has been authorised, I'm up. "Let's go." But the moment I stand, the universe fucks me over, and Katherine looks this way. "Oh God," I whisper as she sits up straight in her chair, interested.

"Does she have an Amelia radar?" Charley stands too, as if showing a united front. "We'll fight her to the death."

"Where's my war paint?" Abbie adds, joining us. "Fuck, she's coming over." She lowers back to her chair, but I remain standing, bracing myself for whatever venom she's going to spit my way.

Kind of.

"Amelia," she purrs. "How lovely to see you."

Is it? The last time I was near this woman, Jude nearly had to drag me off her. It takes every effort to smile, and I try so hard to make it genuine, but I know it's tight.

Katherine's friend joins her. "Chardonnay, this is Amelia," she says, eyes still on me.

"Oohh, Amelia?"

"Yes, Jude's latest plaything."

"Okay, we're leaving." I give wide eyes to the girls.

"Plaything?" Charley laughs, moving in front of me protectively.

"Charley, leave it."

"Absolutely no fucking way. You're married. What kind of man is he to be cool with you fucking another guy?"

"Time to go!" Abbie sings, all high-pitched, taking Charley's elbow. "Before She-Ra lets loose."

I hate the smug smile on both the women's faces as we leave. Hate it. "Oohh, Amelia?" I mumble as we all hurry out of the restaurant. "What the hell did she mean by that?"

"She's obviously been saying lovely things about you to *Chardonnay*." Abbie smirks back at me.

"I need a drink."

Plaything?

"You know, some women just project *bitch*, don't they?" Charley links arms with me and smiles. "I'm sorry, but Jude's got a lot to prove to me, babe."

My heart sinks. I don't want my friends to dislike him, but I can hardly blame them. "I know," I say grudgingly. Will he prove himself?

"But just because I'm wary of him doesn't mean I'll stand by and watch some ex-lover of his try to humiliate you."

"God, I miss this Charley," Abbie sings, linking my other arm.

"It's the kids," Charley declares. "They ignite the inner lioness."

"Inner?" I ask. "I thought I was going to have to pry your claws out of her eyes."

"Roarrrrrr," Charley yells, and we laugh.

After a vow mid-irritated-march to the nearest wine bar to *not* mention Katherine again, we settle and get our night back on track, being a bit more liberal with our alcohol quota now we're not being watched as potential drink-and-runs.

We're on our fifth cocktail, we're all a little tipsy, have discussed every girlie holiday we've ever had, laughed, reminisced, and planned another for next year. We're going to Barcelona. Abbie's already scrolling through Airbnb options. It's long overdue.

"Hey, did either of you two see that reunion invitation?" Charley asks, picking up her phone. "On Facebook."

"I don't go on Facebook." I wave to the waiter for our sixth cocktail. "Same again?" They both toast thin air. "Same again," I call.

"Reunion?" Abbie opens Facebook on her phone. "I didn't see any invitation."

"Here, look." Charley thrusts her mobile under Abbie's nose as I open the app on my phone and wince at the endless notifications. "It's a group," she goes on. "You'll have an invite to join. I haven't accepted yet because I wanted to see if you two will go."

"Here it is." I find the invite and click on it.

"I don't have an invite," Abbie says. "Who's organising it?"

I scan the page. "Fiona Fuller." I press my lips together and notice Charley is pulling the exact same face as me. It's an *oh fuck* face.

Abbie gasps. "The fucking bitch," she blurts, taking my phone and checking the page. Another gasp as she scrolls. "She has literally invited every single person from our year except me."

"I guess she's still not over you snogging her boyfriend behind the bike sheds." I titter on my stool, tipsiness moving aside for drunkenness. "What was his name?"

"Ben Hunter," Abbie grumbles. "We were sixteen!"

Charley cracks up, and I snort, trying to supress my amusement. Abbie slams the phone down. "I don't suppose it would be so bad if she hadn't married him." Then she necks the rest of her cocktail and practically tackles the waiter for her next when he reaches the table.

An hour later, I'm not even sure what my name is, but I do know we're all going to Barcelona next spring. I've also signed up for golf lessons, Charley's booked a consultation for a boob job, and Abbie's applied for the London Marathon. Basically, we're wankered, and it feels so good. So freeing. No talk of men, no stressing about what this means, what that means. It's just us being our old selves before jobs, careers, responsibilities, and babies changed everything. As Abbie wobbles her way back to the table with yet another round, my phone lights up on the table. I squint and smile when I see who's messaging me.

Abbie gets her face up close and personal with my mobile. "Oh, it's Jude Fuckboy Harrison," she slurs.

"Or Jude Fuckboy *Millionaire* Harrison," Charley sings, swiping up her drink. "A filthy-rich man who does dirty, filthy things to you." She cheers the air, her drink spilling over the edge. "Here's to filthy!"

"Filthy!" we all sing.

I'm not so drunk I can't remember the filthy things he's done to me. I grin to myself. Then frown. Did I tell the girls about the champagne cellar? Abbie reaches for my phone and taps the message, then puts in my passcode. "I hope you had a lovely evening with your girls," she reads, in a shockingly bad and very slurry male's voice. "What time shall I pick you up tomorrow?" She frowns. Looks at me. "You're seeing him tomorrow?"

"I thought we weren't talking about men tonight?"

"No men!" Charley yells.

"He's fucked up." I scowl to myself, wondering where that came from.

"What?"

"That's what he said," I go on. "He's fucked up." The best thing I could do was leave, except he didn't let me when I tried. Not that I really wanted to.

"Have you asked him about that?" Abbie says, her serious face contradicting the slur of her voice.

"He said he doesn't want to ruin this. That he should have told me about Katherine." *I'm a fuckup.* The anger he was projecting when he bellowed those words makes me feel like there's more to it. Why would he tell me to leave and crack on with my life? Jesus, I'm too drunk to give this the headspace it deserves.

"That is quite sweet, though." Charley smiles to herself. "Jude texting her."

"Is he allowed to be sweet if he's filthy?" Abbie asks.

"I don't know." Charley pouts. "Let's call him and ask." She lunges for my phone and hits the contact icon on the top. It's ringing before my drunken brain can register what's happening.

"Amelia?" Jude's voice is low and thick with sleepiness.

Abbie and Charley put the backs of their hands on their foreheads, fainting over the table. Then they spring up. "Filthy!" they yell in unison, before they fall apart laughing. I must be drunker than I thought. I have no idea what's going on.

"Amelia?" Jude says, louder this time. "Are you okay?"

"Jude?" I pick up my phone and put it to my ear.

"I'm here."

"Fuck!" I cry, feeling like a megaphone's held by my head.

"It's on speaker, you dick." Abbie chuckles.

"Amelia, what's going on?" Jude asks. "Where are you?"

I look around, picking up my fresh cocktail and slurping. "In a wine bar." I close one eye, trying to read the neon sign on one of the shelves behind the bar. "Gropes Cock."

"What?"

Charley's cheeks balloon and burst, spraying us. "Shit!" I blurt. "Furry cocks ache." I stand to wipe myself down. I shouldn't have. "Oh fear." I sway, seeing three of Charley and four of Abbie. "We need to book more flights if we're all going." I fall back to the stool, the bar spinning, Abbie's and Charley's laughing faces blurring in and out of focus. "I think I've had too many winetails."

And that's the end of my night.

Chapter 29

I already know before I open my eyes that this hangover is going to overstay its welcome. *Jesus fucking Christ.* I squeeze my closed eyes tight, groaning, bracing myself to face the world. And light.

I open one eye.

Frown.

"I'm seriously pissed off," Jude says, his face a twisted mess of disapproving lines as he leans over my horizontal form. "Do you always drink until you're legless and incoherent?"

"No." My voice is quiet. Sheepish. "Hardly ever, actually." Just a few times in as many weeks. Ironically, more since I met Jude Harrison. I grimace and ease myself up to sitting, groaning as I do. "What are you doing here?" I ask, rubbing at my eyes, my head banging so hard. Then I register where I am. "Wait, what am *I* doing here?"

"I've never seen a woman so drunk in my life." He stands, making the bed move. The ripple sends a shock wave through my body into my skull.

"Shit."

"Seriously, Amelia, you were absolutely battered."

"Alright, Dad," I grumble. Jude raises surprised brows at me, and I roll my eyes. Mistake. "Ouch."

"Here," he mutters, holding out a bottle of Evian.

"Thanks." I try to unscrew the cap, try with all my might, but the strain sends stabbing pains through my temple and into my skull. "I can't do it," I mutter. "It's too tight."

Jude huffs and removes the lid, handing it back. I chug down the ice-cold, heavenly liquid as he towers over me, waiting for me to finish so he can resume scolding me. I gasp and drop to my back, pulling the sheets over my head. Jude whips them straight back off. "Did you tell your friends I have anger issues?"

I freeze. Did I say that? Oh my God, I have absolutely no recollection of last night. Regardless . . . "How do you know what I've said to my friends?"

"Because they told me."

"When?"

"When I was carrying you all one by one to my car." Accusing eyes drill into me.

"Oh." I wince. "You were at the bar?"

"No, I came to the bar when I finally got some sense out of one of you."

"Oh."

"And took your friends home."

"Oh."

"Filthy?"

"What?"

"Jude Fuckboy Harrison?"

I press my lips together, cringing. "Sorry."

"You will be." He lays himself over me, pressing me to the bed, his lovely, clear complexion annoyingly fresh. "You stink."

"Get away from me then," I retort.

"Never." He swoops in and kisses me hard and long, probably tasting the copious amount of alcohol I allowed past my lips last night. But still. This is nice. And an unexpected wake-up.

I hum, my hangover forgotten, my libido raging as I circle his bare shoulders and trap him in my thighs. "I'm blaming the cocktail-tasting session you forced on me."

He huffs. "Sure. You'd better check in with your friends."

"Soon."

He breaks away, and I grumble. "Your phone's been ringing. I would have answered, but I'm not sure I want to talk to your ex." Another hard kiss before he breaks away and walks off.

I shoot up to my elbows and pay for it. Fuck, the pain. I clutch my head. "Why's Nick calling me?"

"I was wondering the same thing."

I cringe and throw the sheets back, going in search of my phone. "I haven't got the energy to deal with sarcasm." I zigzag all the way to the lounge and find my mobile on the coffee table, cool air spreading across my front. My naked front. Just knickers. Groaning at the three missed calls, I clear them and go to the kitchen, perching on a stool. "Would you mind filling in the blanks?" I ask Jude's back as he stands in front of his open fridge. My eyes drop down to his boxers. His arse. His thighs.

The door closes and he turns with some oranges in his hand. "I received a call at four minutes past midnight." He dumps them on a chopping board. "It didn't take long to figure out you were out-of-your-mind drunk. So when I finally got some sense out of you, I broke all speed limits from here to London and found you and your two silly mates performing dance moves that I'm pretty sure are illegal."

Oh God, what were we doing?

Jude pulls a juicer out of a cupboard and plugs it in. "After being groped and given an ear-bashing about my apparent anger issues and life choices"—his head cocks accusingly—"I got you all in the car and was forced to call Charley's husband to find out where they live because none of you could remember."

"Oh."

"He looked about as happy as I felt." He starts feeding oranges into the juicer, his reproachful eyes on my wilting form. "He was even more thrilled when Abbie threw up all over the hallway and woke the baby up with her singing."

"Oh dear."

"And Charley fell up the stairs and woke the other one."

"Sounds chaotic."

Jude flicks the button for the juicer, and it roars to life. The sound is torture on my delicate being. And he knows it. I close my eyes and cover my ears, waiting for him to turn the damn thing off. "Abbie stayed at their place, and I brought you here. I didn't want you choking on your own vomit or anything." He pours some juice and slides it across to me. "You don't deserve it."

"I'm sorry," I say, genuinely feeling it. It sounds like he had quite a night, and I'm certainly paying for it. "I don't know what happened. Forgive me?"

"Maybe." He leans on the counter. "How will you make it up to me?"

"However you want. Name it." I drink some of the juice, purring my appreciation.

"You might regret that." Pouring himself some, he downs it and swills the glass under the tap.

"I don't regret anything."

His small smile is knowing as he puts the glass in the dishwasher. "That's reassuring. Get dressed. My biggest little brother's turned up. I want you to meet him."

I cough over my glass. Meet one of his brothers? "Jude, I'm nursing a pretty horrific hangover. I must look atrocious." What will he think? And isn't that in the realms of *very* serious? Is this very serious? *Idiot.*

"You look perfect." He reaches for my hair and pushes it back over my shoulder. "But you smell gross."

"Thanks."

"Go get a shower. I'll meet you in the Piano Bar. It's on the right past reception." He wanders off, raking a hand through his waves as he goes, making every muscle on his back undulate. Is he punishing me?

"No sex?" I call.

He looks over his shoulder. "Oh, baby, you're getting it so hard later."

"Don't tease me."

He shakes his head and disappears, and I grab my phone, calling Abbie. She doesn't answer, so I try Charley. The call connects. But it isn't Charley.

"Hi, Lloyd," I chirp, folding over the counter, without the energy to hold myself upright.

He grunts, unhappy, and the next minute Charley's on the line. "I need to remember that hangovers are no fun when you've got kids."

"Are they ever fun?"

"When you can lie in bed feeling sorry for yourself all day, they're way more fun than the hell I'm in now."

"How's Abbie?"

"Green."

"And Lloyd?"

"Not talking to us. He just asked me why I've an appointment confirmation for a breast augmentation in our shared inbox."

I snort. "Oh my God."

"And you're starting golf lessons next Monday."

"What?"

"It's all slowly coming back to me. I'll update you as and when the information lands. Fuck!" she gasps. "You're with him."

"He's not happy either."

"God, we're such disappointments. Elijah! No, don't eat Aunty Abbie's lipstick. I've got to go. I think I might throw up again, and I need to clean the hallway carpet."

"Wait!"

"What?"

"We didn't see Nick last night, did we?"

"I don't think so. Why?"

"He's been calling me."

"Maybe he heard you're shacked up with the richest, fittest man in England." She hangs up, and I shudder. Fuck, I hope not. My phone rings a second later.

"Oh my God, I think I'm dying," Abbie groans.

"How the hell did we get so drunk?" I'm blaming my lunchtime tasting session, which means this is all Jude's fault.

"Copious amounts of cocktails. You needed it after an encounter with that prickly thing."

"Katherine," I gasp. "Shit, I forgot about her."

"You see, there are some benefits to complete obliteration."

I rub at my pounding head. "I'm not drinking again."

"Me either. I want to dislike Jude Fuckboy Harrison, but it feels wrong, given we'd probably still be trying to remember where we live if it wasn't for him."

"He wants me to meet his brother."

"Ohh, that sounds serious. Do fuckboys usually introduce their fuck buddies to their brothers?"

"Stop it."

"I've got to go. I think I'm going to throw up, and Lloyd will never talk to me again if I don't make it to a toilet this time." The line goes dead, and I place my mobile down on the counter, wondering why the hell Nick's called me. Is it just Nick being Nick, still hoping? Or has he found out I'm seeing someone? I could message and ask. But I really don't want to.

So I go take a shower instead and get dressed in last night's clothes, using my lip and cheek stick to try and make myself look less dead. I inspect myself in the mirror, roughing up my waves and blinking rapidly to try and moisten my dry eyes. Eye drops. I need eye drops. Would Jude have eye drops? I pout and open one of the cupboards under the sink, recoiling at the amount of man products in there.

Crouching, I scan the masses of shower gels, lotions, and potions, sending a mental thanks to the eye drop gods when I spot a bottle. I pluck it out, faltering when something catches my eye.

A box of pills. I reach for it and read the label. "Antidepressants?" I quickly put the box back, shut the door, and stand up straight, staring forward, my delicate head spinning. He suffers with depression? *I'm a fuckup.* Biting my lip, I come over so guilty, but also empathy steams forward. He lost both his parents so close together. It's no wonder. Does he still take them? Need them?

I can't ask. But . . .

Full of shame and unable to stop my curiosity, I crouch and open the cupboard again, checking inside the box. There are four strips of pills, and only two have been taken from one strip. I scan the label on the box that details Jude's name, his address. The date. My gut twists, my worry and uncertainty unstoppable. He was prescribed these last month?

I jump when my phone dings, stuffing the strips in the box and putting them back, closing the cupboard.

Did you fall back into bed?

I quickly reply, before getting up close and personal with my reflection, putting in the eye drops and wiping away the trails down my cheeks. Then I take a deep breath and head downstairs.

In my cream slip evening dress.

I roll my eyes to myself as I follow the signs to the Piano Bar, nervous as shit, and enter the stark white space. Even the grand piano is a glossy white wood. Jude's sitting on the far side of the bar in a huge midnight-blue velvet chair, laughing. I momentarily forget where I am and what I'm doing here, captured by the head-spinning magnificence of him. Right now, he doesn't look like a man who suffers with anything except being irresistible. But flashes of his anger, the pills, and his apish reactions say otherwise. Beautiful. Complicated. A work of art that you need to look closer at to see that, actually, it's quite messy up close.

Eventually gathering my thoughts, I make my way over, taking in the man opposite him. He's a looker too, his hair as thick as Jude's but shorter and darker. He clocks me, his smile knowing, and his sudden diversion of attention has Jude craning his neck to find me.

"I guess this is her." Jude's brother stands and steps around the white table between them, as Jude stands too.

"This is her." He smiles mildly. "Amelia, this is my biggest little brother, Casey."

"Amelia." Casey kisses both my cheeks. "You're quite a surprise."

What am I supposed to say to that? I look at Jude, and he shrugs. "It's lovely to meet you." Casey looks down my front. "Nice dress."

I die a thousand deaths. "I didn't expect to be here this morning."

"Sit," Jude says, lowering. I join them and accept the coffee Jude pours me, smiling my thanks.

"Yeah, I heard you had a heavy night last night."

I throw Jude a disbelieving stare. He shrugs again. "Your brother's embellishing."

Jude snorts into his cup, and Casey laughs. "What do you do for a living, Amelia?" he asks.

"I'm a financial adviser," I tell him, trying to keep my frown at bay. "It's utterly boring."

"And how did you two meet?"

So we're skipping foreplay, are we? No gentle ease into conversation. I look at Jude, curious. He hasn't shared that key piece of information, or what I do for a living? Because surely they're among the first things a loved one would ask if you've declared you've met someone. *How did you meet? Where did you meet? What does she do?* Jude peeks up at me, remaining silent, relaxed in his chair as he cocks an elbow on the arm and an ankle on his knee.

"I was here with friends for a spa day," I reply.

"Nice."

"It was a birthday gift from my friend."

"Generous friend."

I laugh. "She got it for a bargain in the promotion."

He frowns. "Promotion?"

Jude shifts in his chair, clearing his throat. "For the five-year anniversary," he says. "We did a special offer on a limited number of spa days."

"I see," Casey muses, interested. "Since when do you run special offers?"

"Since now." Jude's tone is flat, a certain warning look in his eyes. I study him, curious. Tetchy. Why?

Casey backs off, his face thoughtful. "Sounds like you got more than a spa day for your money."

"Casey," Jude breathes, his look definitely darkening. Am I missing something? I feel like there's a conversation going on that I'm not a part of.

"So you met on your bargain spa day and . . . ?"

"We met again when Arlington hosted an annual finance conference." I'll skip over the bits in between.

"And you host business conferences now too?" Casey says, amused. "Bargain spa days, boring business functions. Mother would turn in her grave."

I sit back in my chair, wary when Jude's jaw rolls. "Don't go there," he cautions, and suddenly the box of pills I just found in his cupboard are front and centre of my mind.

Casey gives Jude a cocked brow. "It sounds like the stars were aligned and you were destined to meet." The atmosphere is swiftly frosty, the brothers glaring at each other. "I hope it works out for you, brother."

Jude leans forward and takes his coffee. My phone ringing couldn't have come at a better time.

"Excuse me." I stand, and the men rise too. "I need to take this." I wander off, looking back to see Jude glaring at *me* now. He thinks it's

Nick. *God, please don't be Nick.* I rummage through my bag and breathe in when I see Mum's calling. "Hi, Mum."

"Amelia, you sound dreadful."

"I only said hello," I say over a laugh.

"Are you hungover?"

"I'm fine. What's up?"

"What time are you coming over?"

"I didn't say I was."

"But you always visit on Sundays. Grandma and Grandpa are here."

"I'll come by after work tomorrow."

"Oh. Well, what are you doing?"

"Working," I breathe, exasperated. "What's with the Spanish Inquisition?"

"You've not been yourself lately."

I look back at the entrance of the Piano Bar. "I promise I'm fine."

She hums, obviously unsure. As am I at this moment in time. "Then I'll see you tomorrow. I'm sure Grandma and Grandpa can make it then too."

"Make it? They live around the corner. They're at your house most days."

"Don't be smart, it doesn't suit you."

"I know, Dad tells me all the time."

"Goodbye." Mum cuts the call so she doesn't hear my exasperated deep breath, and I head back to Jude and Casey, not sure if I want to put myself between the two brothers again. There's definitely something going on between them.

"A pussy is just a pussy," Jude says, and I stop just shy of the pillar that's between me and them, hiding me. "It's the connection that makes it explosive. She's fucking brilliant, Casey. I just didn't expect it, and now I'm . . . well." He sighs. "I feel fucked, to be honest."

"Jesus, Jude, what the hell have you got yourself into?"

I flinch, staring at my feet, bypassing all the lovely things he just said and homing in on his tired, beaten, final words. He feels fucked. Why?

"You're the eldest," Casey says. "You're supposed to be the most stable."

Antidepressants. Do his brothers know? And why the hell does Jude being involved with me deem him unstable?

"Just let me figure this out." Jude's voice is quiet. Thoughtful.

"I hope you do."

"I will," he grates. "She's worth it."

What the hell is he figuring out? Does Casey know about Katherine? The questions circle as I walk back a few paces, making sure the clicks of my heels are loud enough, before making myself known. Jude stands, as does Casey. It's an effort to wipe the unease from my expression. "Sorry, it was my mother."

Casey nods, putting his hand out to Jude and hauling him in for a hug when he takes it. "I'm back for a few weeks until my next charter."

"Have you heard from our brother?"

"No," Casey says, his face telling me he's wary. "You?"

"I told him to call you." Jude reaches for me and pulls me close, and I don't miss Casey's interested eyes. "He's got himself in a spot of bother."

Casey laughs. "Standard Rhys. What's he done now?"

"Got himself a sex tape situation." Jude shakes his head.

I baulk, and Casey laughs. "Fucking hell. Are you surprised?"

"He was in Dublin, so I flew over on Monday for a few days. Tried to figure it out with his PR team."

His PR team? What does he do? "And did you?" Casey asks.

"They're slapping injunctions left and right. Rhys is rebelling. I stuck around for a few days, but I can't deal with his dramas right now." He casts me a sideways look that I read into and don't like. He can't deal with his brother's drama because he has his own to deal with. Brilliant. So that's where Jude was? In Dublin trying to sort out his brother? "He'll call me when he's thinking straight. Always does."

"Well." Casey faces me and bows. "It was a pleasure to meet you, Amelia."

"You too."

He comes at me and kisses my cheeks. "Don't let my big brother ruin you."

"Fuck off, Casey," Jude breathes, reclaiming me and pulling me into his side protectively.

I don't want to ruin this.

I have so many questions. But topping the pile: Does Casey know about Katherine?

Casey leaves, having one last look over his shoulder before rounding the corner out of the bar.

"I'm sorry you're having to deal with your brother." I have more questions on that, naturally, but my head is kind of busy trying to figure out what's going on with Jude.

"Don't be. I'm always dealing with his shit." He turns me into him. "How are you feeling?"

She's brilliant.

I'm fucked.

What have you got yourself into, Jude?

"Good," I say, smiling. It's a lie. I'm feeling apprehensive, my questions returning and multiplying.

Jude hunkers down to get to eye level with me, frowning. "You sure?"

I nod, smile wider. I don't know if he's buying it, and the small tilt of his head in question confirms it. "Feeling a little jaded."

"Can I interest you in a Hey Jude?"

My cheeks balloon, bile rising, mixing with the other sickly feeling I've got going on in my tummy. Something just feels . . . off.

"Maybe some fresh air," he suggests, holding his hand out to me. Taking it is natural. "Come on."

Jude walks us out the back of Arlington Hall past the Kitchen Garden, quiet, as I try to fight back the unease. He constantly smiles down at my heels on the uneven ground. "Did you have a nice evening before you lost all memory of it?" he asks.

The Invitation

Now's my opportunity to tell him about Katherine. Except I bail. What good will come of it? "It was lovely." *Until your ex-lover showed up.*

"Where did you go?"

"Amazonico. It's our favourite." I will the atmosphere to fuck off, the small talk just not cutting it.

"Okay," he says on an exasperated sigh, stopping at the entrance to the maze and facing me. "There's something up. What's going on?"

Tell him you heard him! "Nothing." I smile, making sure this one is convincing as I reach for his lips, kissing him. "Like I said, just jaded." My phone starts ringing, and Nick couldn't have made his timing any worse. His name glows on the screen, and the atmosphere drops from cold to icy.

"Want to get that?" Jude asks, a certain edge of impatience to his tone.

I look at him tiredly. "Do you think I do?"

"You tell me."

"Oh my God, are we about to have another disagreement, because I don't think I've got the energy for you at the moment." I hit reject with a forceful thumb, watching as Jude's chest begins to pulse from where he's trying in vain to maintain steady breathing.

"What the fuck is that supposed to mean?"

"It means you need to fix your passive-aggressive possessiveness," I snap, turning on my heels and walking away across the lawn, my stupid damn heels sinking in, forcing me to stop and remove them.

"Did you see him last night?" Jude grates.

"No, Jude, I did not see him last night." I start to walk on, but stop, whirling around and pointing one of my shoes at him. "I saw Katherine, actually," I declare. He recoils. "I saw her at the restaurant, and she made a point of saying hello, if you know what I mean." The sarcasm in my smile is potent. "And I didn't tell you because I didn't want us to argue *again*. What the hell was she doing in London?"

He exhales tiredly, rubbing his temples. "She lives closer to London than Oxford."

I would ask why on earth she travels to Arlington Hall to work out, dine, and drink, but that would be a really stupid question. My phone starts ringing again. "Fuck off!" I yell at it, trudging off in no particular direction. "Don't follow me," I snap back at him, reaching for my head and rubbing. I'm too hungover for this bullshit.

His huff of disbelief smacks me in the back only a second before his body. A strong arm circles my waist from behind, he lifts me from my feet, and I sag in his hold, exhausted by us. Fight. Make up. Over and over.

Jude walks into the maze and follows the sea of green, turning corners, seeming to be heading into the unknown. How apt. "Why don't you ever listen to me?" I mutter, held tight against his chest, his strides long and purposeful.

"Because you talk shit."

I baulk at the trees.

"Why don't you ever listen to me, Amelia?"

"I do listen." I start to wriggle in his arms, peeling his forearm away from my stomach. "And that's how I heard you tell your brother you feel fucked."

He stops dead in his tracks, and, surprisingly, he releases me. I don't give him a chance to explain. Like I said, I'm too hungover to deal with Jude Harrison today, so I turn around and push past him, walking back the way we came. I think. It all looks the same. I turn left and meet a wall. Back up.

Into his chest.

I'm spun around, the backs of my thighs are grabbed, and I'm hauled up his body. His mouth is quickly on mine, and I'm instantly swept away from my frustrations to that unbelievable place where my head empties and my body fills with lust. I return his force, kissing him hard, pushing my body into his. My outlet.

And I need an outlet right now.

I scramble to tear his T-shirt off, forcing him to put me down. My dress is ripped up my body and thrown aside. I yank open the fly of his jeans. He turns me and pushes me down to my hands and knees, coming in behind me.

Angry foreplay over.

He moves my knickers aside and slams into me on a yell, and my hands clench fistfuls of grass, my head dropping back as the feeling of him filling me to the hilt dominates my mind.

"Move," I demand. *Smash this uncertainty out of me. Show me why we're good together.*

"Beg," he rasps, taking my hips. "Beg me."

"Please," I whisper, my walls pulsing, greedy, desperate for friction. "Please, please, please."

"Oh, baby." He strokes down the centre of my spine. "And again."

"Please!"

"Are we good together, Amelia?"

"Yes!"

He slides out slowly. "Do you trust me?"

"Yes!"

Back in hard. "Beg again."

"I beg you," I grate, my vision clouding.

"Yes," he breathes, slamming his palm down hard on my arse before he lets loose, pounding into me, constantly shushing me when I cry out. My God, he's powerful. So deep. The pain and pleasure are bending my head. My release steaming forward. His slick cock glides in and out easily. The perfect fit.

"I'm coming, Amelia," he warns, his pace increasing more. "Fuck, I'm coming."

I yell, feeling him swell, and it hits me between my legs like a lightning bolt, making my knees give. I collapse to the grass, Jude coming down with me, and gasp for air as he grinds into my arse, soaking up every last bit of pleasure.

"Shit," I whisper. That wasn't supposed to happen. I'm mad at him.

But isn't that the beauty of us? Even hopping mad with each other, we still create magic.

"I feel fucked because you've caught me by surprise, Amelia," he pants in my ear. "I feel fucked because you literally take up every bit of my mind. Constantly. I'm fucked because I can't focus on anything but you." He turns his mouth into my ear as I continue to pant across the grass, making the blades quiver along with my body in the aftermath of my high. "Do you hear what I'm saying to you?"

I nod, even if I'm not entirely sure. Why does that make him fucked? Jude lifts his hips, sliding out of me, and rolls me onto my back. His body settles over mine, and he holds my face with both palms. "I like whatever this is," he says reverently, watching me struggling for breath beneath him. "What we have. Us. I really like it."

Ask about the pills.

"Me too," I whisper, bottling it. *What do we have?*

It's a stupid question. I'm falling in love with him.

"Good." Jude drops his mouth closer to mine in silent demand, and of course, I obey, circling his shoulders and kissing him. "You're staying the night," he says around my mouth, rolling to his back and taking me with him.

"Stop it." I push myself up so I'm sitting on his lap. "I can't stay every night."

"Why not?"

"Because I live in London. Work in London."

"But I miss you so badly when you're gone, baby." He juts his bottom lip out, and I smile. "Would you ever consider moving out of the city?"

I still, my brief contentment disappearing. "What?" Like, give up my job to move closer to him?

Jude's eyes widen. "Whoa, wait," he says, locking his hands down on my thighs to stop me running. "Do not read too much into that question. I'm not asking you to give up anything, especially not your career."

My God, he will never know how much I needed to hear that. "Well, that's a relief."

He rolls his eyes. "I want to be close to you."

"You're pretty close now."

"All the time, Amelia."

"That's sweet."

"Don't mock me."

I lower and kiss him gently. "We'll figure it out," I say, truly meaning it. And we have plenty of time to.

Jude hauls me down and hugs me. "I'm so glad I met you."

It seems ridiculous to ask why. But . . . it's an odd statement to make. "Are you okay?"

"I . . ." He clears his throat. "I think I'm . . ."

I still, wondering . . .

"Fuck, I don't know how to say it." He growls to himself. "I think I'm—"

"I'm lost!" Someone yells, the kid's voice close by, coming from over the top of the hedge running down the side of us.

"Fuck," Jude gasps, diving up, taking me with him. I'm in a flat-out panic, wondering what the hell I should be doing as I stand naked, waiting for someone to appear. "Get dressed, Amelia," he hisses, kicking my dress toward me as he yanks his jeans up his lovely long, strong legs.

Right, yes, get dressed. I snatch my dress up and fight my way into it, getting my arms all tangled in the straps. "Shit, I'm stuck," I mumble, turning in circles, trying to get my dress down my body. The sound of a knicker-melting laugh suddenly has me forgetting what I'm panicking about, and I stop, listening to Jude chuckling.

"Come here," he says, helping me unravel my dress and get it on properly. "There."

I blow my hair out of my face and press my lips together, restraining my amusement, as Jude cups my cheek with a hand, his smile adorable. Looking at me closely, like . . .

I shake my head, not letting my thoughts go there. "Oops," I whisper, and he laughs, moving in and kissing me softly.

"Ewww!"

With Jude still holding my face, we peek to the left and see a boy, perhaps ten years old, his cheeks ballooned like he's about to vomit.

I laugh, the kid dashes off, and Jude sweeps me off my feet, carrying me out of the maze across his arms. I cling around his shoulders, studying his profile.

"You're staying the night," he says again, matter-of-fact.

"No, I—"

"Are you arguing with me?"

I grin and let my head rest on his shoulder, absorbing him in his entirety, and when he turns his lips to me, kissing me gently, something happens in my chest. It's a beautiful warm feeling, and I know I'm not mistaking what it means.

Oh . . . dear.

Chapter 30

I still feel jaded come Monday, but my head isn't only foggy after I abused my liver on Saturday night. It's also spinning because of Jude Harrison. I spent the rest of yesterday with him. We ate in the Piano Bar, where the dining is more casual, and then went back to Jude's apartment and ate each other before I reluctantly told him I needed to get back to London, and he reluctantly brought me. In a lovely black Ferrari. And then I lay in bed all night wishing I'd let him win the argument and keep me at Arlington Hall, while coming to terms with the fact that I've fallen in love with him. It's impossible *not* to love him. His quirks, his vulnerability, which I'm quite sure he hasn't revealed to many. If anyone. I'm in love. Well, shit.

Every single one of the senior partners has stopped by my office at some point throughout the morning to say hello and tell me about their golf day. Sue thrashed them all. She was gracious in her victory, but I detected the smug smile she was hiding. I grab a coffee late morning and call the golf club where I booked lessons, asking to transfer it to my father's name. That's one thing taken care of. I send the email confirmation to Clark and then call the estate agents to see if anything has come up that fits my brief. Nothing.

And all the while, I miss him, constantly having to have a stern word with myself to keep my working day on track.

The ding of my computer has me looking up from the file I'm working on. And there it is, just his name. My smile is instant. My heart bursts.

I reach for my mouse and open his email.

> To: amelialazenby@lbandbfg.co.uk
> From: JH@arlingtonhall.co.uk
> Re: Business
>
> Miss Lazenby, I need some advice.
>
> Sincerely,
> Jude Harrison
>
> Arlington Hall Luxury Hotel & Spa

> To: JH@arlingtonhall.co.uk
> From: amelialazenby@lbandbfg.co.uk
> Re: Business
>
> What will I get in return for this advice you seek?
>
> Amelia Lazenby
> Chartered Financial Planner
> LB&B Finance Group
> www.lbandbfinancegroup.co.uk

> To: amelialazenby@lbandbfg.co.uk
> From: JH@arlingtonhall.co.uk
> Re: Business
>
> What do you want?

Sincerely,
Jude Harrison
Arlington Hall Luxury Hotel & Spa

To: JH@arlingtonhall.co.uk
From: amelialazenby@lbandbfg.co.uk
Re: Business

Sweaty and wet.

Amelia Lazenby
Chartered Financial Planner
LB&B Finance Group
www.lbandbfinancegroup.co.uk

My phone rings immediately, and I rest back, answering. "Hey."

"I'm calling to arrange the fulfilment of your request."

I smile, and it's wide. "What advice do you need?"

"I need to know what time I'm picking you up from work. You're staying tonight."

I wince. "I have to go see my parents after work." And after doing absolutely no work this weekend, I'm unusually behind. I can't take my eye off the ball; I've come too far.

"Oh," Jude grumbles. "Does that mean I'm not seeing you tonight?"

"It's a lot, going back and forth to Oxfordshire during the week," I say, getting up to stretch my legs.

"I'll come to you then."

I look at the stack of files I've yet to draft my recommendation letters for. If Jude comes to me, I still won't get any work done. He's a wonderful distraction from work, but I have to control it.

"Can we do tomorrow?" I ask, feeling the disappointment myself. I miss him. So, *so* much. "I have to catch up, and after Friday with the partners, it's important I keep myself a step ahead."

There's a slight, uncomfortable pause before he sighs. "I get it," he says, and I deflate, relieved he's not going to give me a hard time about it. Jude can be quite convincing when he wants to be.

"I'm sorry."

"Don't ever apologise for having to work, okay? I'll get over it. I know how important your job is to you."

I lower to my chair slowly, my heart swelling. "You're important to me too," I reply quietly, almost unsure if I should voice it.

"And you are to me," he says softly. "Hence, I want to hog all your time."

I laugh, reaching for my pen and tapping it on the desk. Damn, I want to see him. "Can you do lunch?" I ask, checking the time. I could steal an hour.

"Wish I could. I've got a few meetings Anouska needs me to sit in on. Wait a minute." He falls silent, and then a request comes through to FaceTime. I quickly jump up and close my office door, accepting. And the moment his face appears, I sigh. "There she is," he muses, his phone at arm's length as he walks. He's suited and booted. His scruff is on the perfect side of not too neat. Delicious.

"Where are you?" I return to my desk and sit, propping my phone up against my computer screen.

"On my way to meet the sommelier in the wine cellar to review the wine list."

"So you'll be drinking on the job again?" I ask, making him smile and rake a hand through his hair. He's so fucking handsome I could cry.

"I just wanted to see your face." He slows to a stop and leans against a wall, staring at me. "To get me through the next twenty-four hours."

"You're cute when you're romantic." I bite at my lip, and Jude smirks.

"Have you heard from any of the partners today?"

"They've all stopped by to say hi."

"You've obviously made an impact," he says. "I can relate."

I laugh. Oh, the scale of impact Jude Harrison has had on me has left me in pieces. But my heart is still intact.

He looks past the camera and nods, holding a hand up to someone. "Shit, I've got to dash."

"Okay."

"Amelia?"

"What?"

There's a long, stretched silence. "I miss you."

My nose scrunches, my lips pressed together to stop my beam from breaking. "I miss you too."

Jude laughs under his breath, almost embarrassed. "I better go before you turn me into a full-on lump of cheddar."

I let out a laugh, falling back in my chair. "I like cheesy Jude."

He rolls his eyes. "Make sure you do your stretches."

"What? Stretches? Why do I need to stretch?"

"So you don't break when I bend you to my will tomorrow."

"I *really* like dominant Jude."

"And I *love* submissive Amelia." He hangs up, and I sit at my desk, spinning my pen, falling into a daydream. My body's still achy from yesterday, the skin on my thighs still sore. He *loves* submissive Amelia. I chomp down on my lip, reaching for my chest and rubbing.

I jump when my office door flies open. "Someone's popular today," Leighton muses, casually wandering over to one of my shelving units and perusing the spines of my files. I slowly look up through my lashes, my hand falling to my mouse and closing down various screens. So he's noticed my flurry of visitors today, huh?

"Good day?" I ask, ignoring his observation. Not feeding it.

"Very." He faces me and smiles. It's as sincere as I know him to be.

"Is there anything I can help with?"

"I've heard through the grapevine that you were out with some of the partners on Friday evening."

I turn off my computer and grab my bag. "Oh, it's lunchtime," I say, passing him and leaving, scorning myself for my secret, smug smile.

He's worried.

◆ ◆ ◆

I call out my hello as I let myself into Mum and Dad's, dropping my bags and files in the hallway before I poke my head around the lounge door. "Hey, you two."

Grandma and Grandpa look up from their usual spots and beam at me. "Here she is," Grandpa says, dropping his paper and beckoning me to him. Old, squishy lips press into my cheek.

"Where's Mum and Dad?" I ask, going to Grandma.

"Your mother's in the kitchen and your father's at the office."

"He's supposed to be retired."

"Hello!" Clark yells from the hallway, the door slamming soon after. He appears in his suit.

"Look how dapper he is," Grandma sings as Grandpa pats the arm of his chair.

"Come, Clark, tell me about your day."

I roll my eyes and leave Clark to talk business with Grandpa, passing him as I head to the kitchen. "Have you told my ex he can't come to the wedding yet?" I hiss, scowling playfully.

"I'm working on it," he grumbles.

"You'd better hurry up, it's next week," I remind him, entering the kitchen. "Whoa," I say, coming face-to-face with a giant bouquet of peonies.

Mum turns from the stove, a wooden spoon in her hand. "They're for you."

I can't hold back my exasperated sigh. Here's me hoping Nick will give up, but instead he's upped the ante. This bunch is double the size of all the other bunches.

Mum's lips are a little pursed as she waves the spoon at the mass of blooms. "Maybe you should read the card."

Guilt flares as I approach the bouquet, searching for the card amid the spray. "Mum, I take no pleasure from this." I pluck the card out and open it. "I've tried to be considerate, but I think I'm just increasing his hopes."

Mum turns and folds her arms over her chest, her body language saying everything I expect she wants me to hear. It's not fair that they're making me feel guilty too. I pull the card out.

Missing you.

"Shit," I breathe, sighing and staring at the beautiful flowers. "Mum, I don't love him."

"They're not from Nick."

My head retracts on my neck.

"I helped at the shop again today." She comes to the table, looking past me, checking for listening ears. "A man came in. Tall, extremely handsome, dark-blond hair to here." She indicates her nape as dread finds me. "Fine suit, fancy black sports car parked outside. Imagine my surprise when he ordered the most expensive bouquet"—she points at the spray in the middle of the kitchen table—"and writes down *your* name and Abbie's address for the delivery."

Oh fuck. "Imagine that," I whisper. "So instead of having them delivered, you brought them home?"

"Amelia," she hisses quietly. "You've just dumped Nick to concentrate on your career!"

"What's going on?" Clark asks.

"A man bought Amelia these. A man called Jude Harrison."

"Oh," Clark says, casual.

"You know his name too?" I blurt.

"Of course! I needed it for the order form."

My arse hits the chair, my head going into my hands. "I'm a grown woman, Mum."

"Is he why you finished things with Nick? Were you two-timing?"

"What?" I look at her, outraged. "No!"

Clark moves in and gives my back a supportive rub. "Leave her alone, Mum," he warns gently. "There was no crossover."

She gasps. "You knew about this?"

"Why are you talking like I've committed a mass crime?" I snap. "A man bought me flowers. That's it."

"That's where you were, wasn't it? When you didn't come yesterday. And when you were in a Rolls-Royce, that's his car." She comes closer, her intrigue overflowing. "Or one of his cars. Who is he, Amelia?" she whispers.

"Mum, please," I beg, looking at my brother for help.

His lips press into a straight line. "I'd get rid of these before Dad gets home," he says, trying to exercise damage control.

"Yes, oh God." Mum's quickly in a dither. "He'll know these aren't from Nick. They're too . . ." She looks at the huge bouquet, overcome. "Expensive."

Clark snorts, and I slap his arm. "Shut up and help Mum hide the flowers." I haven't the energy to face my father's interrogation.

"Yes, I don't want to listen to your father's grievances." Mum starts flapping around the kitchen.

"Wish you'd say that to him," I grumble.

"Oh, Amelia, you know what he's like. Do you think I can change him now, after nearly forty years? He just wants what's best for you." She pushes out her bottom lip. "Why didn't you tell me? I'm your mother."

Best for me? I'm so tired of listening to it. "Because then I'm making you keep secrets from Dad, and I know you don't like keeping secrets from Dad."

Her shoulders drop. "Well, it's not ideal, is it? Right off the back of your breakup with Nick. How did you meet him?" she asks, and I inwardly snort. "What does he do for a living? I mean, a Rolls-Royce, a fancy sports car!"

"Mum," I breathe.

"Oh God, I don't know what your father will say."

The Invitation

"We're not telling him," I retort, sure. Not that I'm ashamed, I just can't be bothered with a lecture and guilt trip right now. And besides, I don't even know what there is to tell. *You're in love with him, idiot!*

"I don't know what the issue is." Clark sounds as exasperated as I feel. "You both want her to settle down, get married, make babies and stews and soups. Maybe this is the guy she'll do that with."

I look up at my brother in surprise. "I'm sleeping with him, not marrying him."

"Amelia!" Mum snaps.

"Well, I am." I laugh, flinching at my own words, quite sure Jude would have something to say about my claim. But I must play this down for a while. Give them time to get over Nick, and for Nick to get over me. And who knows where this is going with Jude?

Am I being delusional?

"I'm sleeping with him," I repeat, stronger. "And I—"

The front door opens, and I still, hearing Dad coming in. "Shit," Clark mutters, grabbing the flowers.

"Oh dear," Mum whispers.

"Fuck," I hiss.

"Amelia!" Mum scolds me as I get up, ready to assist Clark hiding the flowers, taking them from his arms, just as Dad wanders in. We both freeze.

"Nice flowers," Dad says.

"I got them for Rachel," Clark blurts, grabbing them back and grinning. I sigh, rubbing my forehead. This is ridiculous.

"They're mine." I claim them back off Clark, smiling my appreciation for him trying to cover for me. But I'm thirty years old and single. I do not need to sneak around.

"Yours?" Dad asks.

"I'm seeing someone."

Dad recoils, just as somebody appears behind him.

My mouth turns lax. "Nick," I breathe.

"Oh shit," Clark curses.

"Oh," Mum whispers. "Oh, this is unfortunate."

I stare at Nick, as he stares at the over-the-top flowers in my arms. "I invited Nick for dinner," Dad declares, unashamed, as I glare at him, so fucking angry.

"What's going on?" Grandpa hobbles into the kitchen on his stick. "Oh, Nick, how lovely to see you."

"You're seeing someone?" Nick's voice is so quiet, hurt splashed all over his face.

"It's nothing serious." Mum starts flapping around the kitchen again. "She's just sleeping with him."

"Mum!" Clark and I yell in unison.

"Who?" Nick asks as Dad places a hand on his shoulder and rubs, his unimpressed eyes nailed to me. The villain.

"Nick, it's—"

"Who?" he repeats, his eyes definitely clouding. *Oh God.*

"It's no one you'd know."

"Who?" he snaps, getting himself worked up. "Who is it?" He gasps. "Were you having an affair? Is that why you left me?"

"No, Nick, of course I wasn't."

"Well, you met someone pretty damn quickly, didn't you? I thought you didn't want a relationship? I thought your precious career was more important than me and our future."

"Okay, I think everyone needs to calm down," Clark says, taking my elbow. "They're just flowers."

Just flowers.

I feel my throat closing as I look at Dad, feeling the disapproval and disappointment. "I wasn't having an affair." I need to make that clear. "I met someone unexpectedly and he's sent me flowers."

"And you're sleeping with him," Nick adds. "Is it serious?"

I can't answer that, and not because I don't know how serious it is. I'm honestly so uncertain about everything. I know how I feel about Jude, but I'm terrified about admitting it out loud, to Jude especially. And besides, it's early, it's intense, and it's really fucking fiery.

"I have to go." I walk out with my flowers and snatch up my bag and files.

"Amelia," Nick calls as I pull the door open. "Wait."

I march on, being sure to hold back my tears of frustration. Nick grabs my arm and pulls me to a stop when I reach the road. "No, Nick."

"I love you, Amelia," he says, pleading. "Please, let's try again. I'll forget the kids, no marriage, whatever you want."

I shake my head. "It's too late."

"But I love you," he croaks. "And I know you love me too."

I don't think I ever loved Nick. I admired him, respected him, but I don't think I truly loved him, or even saw a future with him, and I don't feel good admitting that. But feeling what I've been feeling since I met Jude? It's made me realise what love feels like. And the fact there's so many question marks over what's happening with me and Jude, and yet I still feel like this? It's unstoppable, untameable love. Being vulnerable. Putting your heart at risk and hoping the person you're handing it to will be careful with it.

"I don't love you." My reluctance to say the words is clear. I don't want to hurt him. "Please, Nick, you've got to let go." I turn and walk away.

"Never," he yells. "I'll never stop trying! I'll make you realise!"

All he's made me realise is how deep I'm in with Jude, because my feelings toward him feel like they're on a whole different level.

Love.

I stop when I hear Nick get in his car, and he drives off fast, taking the corner out of the close practically on two wheels. He's angry.

"Fuck," I hiss to myself. That was *not* how I wanted him to find out about Jude.

"Amelia, darling!"

Grandma hobbles down the driveway. "Grandma, what are you doing?" I hurry back, taking her arm to help her.

She swats me away. "I knew I smelt a man on you," she whispers, pulling her knitted cardigan in before reaching for my cheeks, cupping them with both hands. "Does he make your tummy flutter?" she asks, surprising me. I take a breath and nod, and Grandma smiles mildly. Knowingly. "Does your heart beat harder?"

"Yes." So bloody hard. Always.

"Do your insides tingle when you think about him?" She smiles, impish. "Fanny flutters?"

"Grandma!"

She rolls her old eyes. "Well?"

"Yes," I whisper, mortified.

"Then you have him, Grand Girl. And don't let anyone try to tell you that you can't." She squishes my face and kisses me, before turning on her slippers and going back to the house.

I could cry.

Looking to the sky, I wish with everything I have that I'd just let Jude pick me up from work. Followed his lead.

"Shit," I breathe, picking up my feet and heading for the Tube. A bombardment of messages from Nick keep me company on the way.

> Who is it?
> I at least deserve to know who he is.
> How could you do this? You've made a fool of me.
> I hope you're happy.

I ignore them all on constant winces, my heart feeling heavy. I don't want to hurt Nick any more than I already have.

Chapter 31

After letting myself in the front door, I set my flowers on the table and give them the admiration they deserve before getting a bottle of wine from the fridge. I smile when Jude calls. "Hey," I say, holding my mobile to my ear with my shoulder as I pull the cork out of the bottle.

"Hey," he replies, simple as that, stretching my smile.

"Thank you for the flowers."

"Welcome."

"Did you know the florist you got them from was Abbie's?" I ask.

"I did. But she wasn't there, so I was served by an older lady with silver hair."

"My mother." I collect a glass from the cabinet.

"What?"

"That was my mother."

"I ordered flowers with your mother, and she didn't think to mention that the woman I asked them to be delivered to was her daughter?"

"Apparently not." I can only imagine Mum's face when she was confronted with Jude Harrison. "She also didn't have them delivered. She took them home and gave them to me when I popped in earlier. I thought . . ." I just catch myself before I tell Jude who I thought they were from.

"You thought they were from your ex," he says, and I nibble my lip as I pour. "Wait. Has he been sending you flowers?" My lack of an answer gives him my answer. "Do I need to step in?"

"Let's not argue anymore," I plead quietly, lowering to a chair at the table. I've had a bellyful today.

He sighs. "Tell me about the rest of your day."

"The end of the financial year is approaching, so I've been lost in my end-of-year recommendation and reinvestment proposals. Am I boring you yet?"

"Never."

I smile, taking a sip of wine. "How was your meeting in the wine cellar?"

"I couldn't take my eyes off the table where I fucked you. It was quite distracting, made me miss you more, but on the plus side I've found the next bottle I plan on pouring all over you and licking off."

I subtly inhale, pressing my lips together. "What are you doing now?"

"I'm about to get you to climax with my voice," he murmurs. My body instantly responds. "Put the wine down." I swallow and look at the glass. How did he know? "Put it down, Amelia."

Placing it on the table, I wait with bated breath for his next instruction. "Lift the skirt of your dress."

"How do you know I'm wearing a dress?"

"Lift the skirt of your dress."

I purse my lips and wriggle it up my thighs with my spare hand.

"Lick your fingers."

I take a deep breath and slip my fingers into my mouth, wetting them. "I prefer you doing this," I say quietly.

"Then you should have seen me tonight," he retorts, making me scowl. "How wet are you?"

"Drenched." I suck in air as I slide my fingers past my knickers, slipping across my flesh.

"Fuck," Jude breathes quietly. "Feel good?"

I hum, sinking further into my chair. "Are you touching yourself?"

"It would cause a bit of a scandal, baby," he says, serious. "I'm in the Library Bar."

A sharp burst of laughter leaves me, making me lose my rhythm.

"Concentrate," he orders quietly.

"I'm concentrating."

"Slide your fingers—"

The door behind me flings open and Abbie bursts in with arms full of flowers. "Shit," I hiss, covering myself as she stops and takes me in, her face just visible through the mass of blooms. She's frowning. "Abbie's home," I sing, and Jude groans. "I'd better go."

"Fine." He sounds bereft. "Fuck, I miss you."

And I'm pooling on the kitchen floor. "You too," I say, my chest swelling with happiness.

"Call me back when you're alone again, okay?"

"Okay."

"And, Amelia?"

"What?"

"I lo—" He catches himself, and a long pause ensues. I wait . . . wondering. Hoping. He . . . what? "Nothing," he murmurs. "I'll speak to you in a bit." He hangs up, and I swallow, resting my phone down, staring at it. Does he . . . ? My heart starts to gallop as Abbie passes me, her eyes accusing.

I shy away guiltily. "Did you know Jude got these from your florist today?" I ask, pointing to the bouquet.

Abbie checks it out. "Looks like Corey's work."

"Mum served him."

"No way. Did he know? Did *she* know?" Abbie lowers to the chair and puts a call in to Charley, propping her mobile against the place mats on the table so she can see us both. "Jude Fuckboy Harrison went into Flora Flora today and ordered flowers for Amelia with Jenn," Abbie tells her.

"No way," Charley gasps. "Did he know who she was? Wait. Did your mum know who *he* was?"

I sag into my chair and take my wine, grimacing at the tingles still lingering between my legs. "Jude filled out the card to me and gave Abbie's address to deliver. So Mum knew. Jude didn't until I told him. Mum took the flowers home for me. I thought they were from Nick. Then Dad walked in just as Clark was trying to hide them. *With* Nick. So now Nick knows I'm sleeping with someone. He accused me of cheating. And that's all the drama for today." I swig my wine and smile.

"Fuck," they say in unison.

"It sucks to be you right now," Charley adds.

I huff, sigh, swig. "In other news, I think I'm in love."

"That's old news." Abbie rolls her eyes, and I stare down into my glass, thinking about our call. How he went to say something but didn't. How he did the same yesterday.

What was that?

"I've got to go," Charley says. "We have date night."

"Tennis club?" Abbie asks on a cheeky smirk, making Charley curse her before hanging up. "So," she goes on, arranging the flowers. "You've finally admitted it to yourself."

"He drives me nuts." I sigh. "But . . . I don't know. Something's holding me back from embracing it fully."

"Like?"

"I found some antidepressants in his bathroom cupboard." I cringe to myself. "I was looking for eye drops."

Abbie fetches herself a glass and joins me back at the table, filling it with wine. "So he's taking antidepressants. Is it any wonder after what you told me about his parents?"

"That's just it. I don't think he's taking them. They were tucked at the back, and the date on them was only last month, so he's been to see a doctor recently about it."

"You should ask."

I nod mildly to myself, falling into thought for a few moments. "I've never experienced grief, but I guess it's common to need help after, right?" Even years later?

"Different people handle it in different ways."

"He's volatile," I say, almost reluctantly. "It's like there's a beast inside him that he's constantly trying to keep contained." His temper makes me wary. As does his possessive streak.

"But you're still in love with him," Abbie muses, resting back in her chair. I don't answer. I don't need to. "We all have our faults. If Jude's is a short fuse, then—"

"He fucked a married woman," I point out. "Who's hanging around like a bad smell." What the hell does Katherine's husband make of it? How can any man be cool with that? She's a lovely-looking woman, of course, but being an A-rated bitch makes her ugly. Is there something more I don't know? I groan at the pace of my thoughts, holding my head as I drink.

My phone dings on the table, and both our eyes fall to the screen.

> I've booked a table for tomorrow night somewhere special. Let's get deeper.

My heart flutters in my chest. My damn heart flutters. And then he does things like that, and all doubt is momentarily lost. But . . . let's get deeper? Why does that make me nervous?

"It sounds like he feels the same as you," Abbie says softly.

"Unsure?"

"He's sure. What more can you ask for?"

I nod and hit reply.

Look forward to it

> And I'm taking you away. Just us, your body, my body, and champagne

I smile down at the screen, my body responding to the reminder, and Abbie chuckles, getting up and tending to her flowers. "Shall I cook?" she asks as she fills a vase with water. "There's a new series started on Netflix that's getting a lot of hype."

I bite at my lip. "Do you mind if I pass?"

She looks over her shoulder. "Are you dumping me?"

I smile, getting up. "I miss him," I admit, the flutters inside real, just at the thought of him. I don't know why I didn't just see him tonight. Going to my parents' turned out to be a shitshow, and I feel wholly dispirited. Jude can fix that.

Abbie turns and leans back against the counter, her smile knowing. "Are you going to tell him how you feel?"

"That I'm in love with him?"

"Yes, that."

"Maybe." I shoot over to her and drop a kiss on her cheek. "Thanks for being you."

"Tell him," she calls to my back as I hurry to my room and collect a few things, including clean work clothes for tomorrow. I smile as I pack my gym bag, stuffing in my hoodie. I definitely need a hug. A Jude hug. And I know it'll lead to sex.

To heaven.

I don't bother changing, calling an Uber and walking to the main road, tracking it on my phone to the corner. I jump in.

"Oxfordshire?" the driver asks in question.

"I'll tip if you get me there within an hour."

A smile creeps across my face, the anticipation unstoppable.

I love him.

I didn't plan for it to happen, but here I am.

In love.

And I need to tell him.

Chapter 32

Stan is in his usual spot when my driver pulls around the fountain. "Miss Lazenby," he says as he opens the door for me. "Looks like you made it just on time—we have rain coming in. Do you have any bags?"

"On the seat," I say, getting out and letting him lean in to retrieve it as I look up at the black sky. "I can take it."

"Not at all. I'll have it delivered to Mr. Harrison's apartment."

I smile my thanks and hurry up the path to Arlington Hall. The glass doors slide open, letting me in, and I find the lobby is quiet, all guests probably in the bar or at dinner. I pass the empty reception desk, looking into the Library Bar, my steps faltering when I see Katherine's husband in one of the chairs by the fireplace, a beer in his hand, a smile on his face. I can't see Katherine opposite him, but I can see her black-booted stiletto heel by Rob's knee swinging a little where her leg's crossed.

On a mild scowl, I take the stairs two at a time, my anticipation growing.

I can smell him.

Pushing my way through various doors, I arrive at Jude's apartment and knock, my impatience getting the better of me. So I knock again, listening, waiting. Bursting with desperation to see him.

The door finally swings open, and there he is in all his wonderful, stunning glory. And I know in this moment, without doubt, I'm head over heels. My stomach is doing cartwheels. I move forward and put myself in his chest, getting my lips on his. *I love you!*

"Amelia," he says around my mouth, holding on to me. But he doesn't return my kiss. In fact, he feels tense.

I pull my face away from his but not my body, looking at him. All the wonderful feelings fall away. I don't like what I see. He's nervous.

"I thought I'd surprise you," I say, a horrible chill tickling its way down my spine.

"Well, you've certainly done that."

I retreat, putting him at arm's length. "Is everything okay?"

"Yeah, I'm just . . . I wasn't expecting you. You said you'd call me back."

This isn't the welcome I was hoping for. "I decided to come inst—" The chink of a glass from inside his apartment stops me from finishing, and I look past him, the chill down my spine turning icy. "You're not alone," I say quietly.

"I . . ." He rakes a hand through his hair. "Shit."

I swallow, pushing past him, marching into his apartment, my legs on autopilot.

"Amelia!" he yells, pursuing me.

The lounge is empty.

"Amelia, wait."

I stop by the dining table, just as another sound comes from the kitchen.

"Amelia," Jude breathes, blocking my path. He takes the tops of my arms, holding me in place, hunkering down to see me. "Before you—"

I wrench myself out of his grip and storm past him.

"Amelia," he shouts, sounding panicked as he follows me. "Listen to me."

I screech to a stop on the threshold of the kitchen when I find a woman at the oak island, a wineglass at her lips.

"Katherine," I breathe, as she turns on her stool, crossing one leg over the other.

"Fuck." Jude meets my back, taking my elbow. I shrug him off, noting Katherine's shoes. Red stilettos.

"I thought . . ." My head spins. "I thought you were in the bar with Rob."

"Oh," she says, her voice sickeningly low. Smug. Her red lips stretch wide. "Is he having drinks with his plaything?"

Plaything.

"Oh my God." I step back, meeting Jude's chest.

"Amelia, I—"

"Do not tell me to listen to you," I warn, the pain in my chest unbearable, but my anger is keeping me from folding to the floor in despair.

"Please, listen to me," Jude pleads, trying to turn me to face him.

"I said don't!" I push him away. I don't want him anywhere near me. The island is set for two to eat. Two plates half-eaten. Two wineglasses. There's a pan on the stove, some spices in jars by a chopping board. He's cooked for her? My eyes find Katherine. "Are you still sleeping with him?" I ask.

"Amelia." Jude appears in front of me again, bending to get my eyes.

I look at him with a cool, fixed expression. "I'm not talking to you," I say, equally as cool as I move aside, getting Katherine back in my sights. "Are you still sleeping with him?"

She slowly places her glass down and looks at Jude next to me. And for the first time, I ask myself why he hasn't refuted it, whether I asked him or not. "Well?"

"No," Jude answers. It's too little too late.

"No?" I ask. "Then what's this?" I motion to the island, where they've been enjoying dinner.

"Tell her, Jude." Katherine sounds almost bored, sipping her wine casually.

"Tell me what?"

Jude's jaw pulses as he fires Katherine a death glare. "Shut up, Katherine."

"Tell me what?" I yell, feeling my control slipping.

"You were a bet, sweetheart," she coos.

"Katherine!"

"We saw you out with friends. You're welcome, by the way."

"For fuck's sake," Jude curses, physically lifting me from my feet to get me away from the poisonous tongue of his lover. His lover. His married lover, whose husband is downstairs playing footsie with his plaything. What the hell kind of nightmare am I in? My brain spasms, and what she's just said drops in my brain like a bomb. They saw me out with friends.

Jude puts me down, and I look up at him, scared to ask. "You paid our bill," I whisper, remembering the waiter telling us. "It was you and her?"

His eyes close, his head dropping back, and my heart cracks that little bit more. "You have to let me explain."

"Was I a bet?" I scream, sending myself back a few paces with the force, the anger making way for devastation. "Tell me the truth for once in your fucking life!"

He swallows, and maddening anguish contorts his face. "You were a bet," he says quietly. Reluctantly.

My heart splits straight down the centre as I instinctively move away from him. He looks beaten. Broken. He has no fucking idea. "Why?" I breathe.

"Because he loves the thrill." Katherine laughs. It's like nails down a chalkboard. "The chase, the win, the buildup before he finally gives the woman what she's begging for and then walks away from her."

Jude flies around, savage. "Shut the fuck up, Katherine," he hisses. "You're fucking poison."

"But great in bed, clearly," she retorts, raising her glass.

I notice a smudge on Jude's jawline. Red. It matches Katherine's lipstick. I reach for it, and he flinches when I touch him, looking at me. "No," he says, his eyes panicked.

"I'm so done." I turn and walk out, trembling with the restraint I'm calling on not to fall apart. Cry. Scream. Hit myself for being so fucking stupid.

"Amelia!" Jude shouts, the pounding of his feet on the floor causing vibrations to travel up my legs. "Amelia, please, don't leave." I carry on, wobbly on my heels. "Let's talk."

"I have nothing to say." I wrench open door after door, stalking through the corridors of Arlington Hall, Jude one step behind as he chases me.

"You've got to let me explain," he pleads.

I take the stairs, holding the handle, very aware that he's not physically stopping me from leaving. Because he knows he can't.

I reach the bottom of the stairs and look into the Library Bar as I pass. I can see Rob's plaything now. She's blonde. Younger. The sick fucks.

Anouska walks in from outside, her face falling when she sees me doggedly marching toward her, a stressed Jude in pursuit.

"Did you know?" I ask her as I pass. Her face tells me everything. It's all been a fucking lie.

I make it outside, finding the skies have opened, the rain coming down in sheets. I keep walking, enduring the pellets hitting me.

"Amelia, I'm begging you, hear me out," Jude yells over the pounding rain, landing in front of me. I walk round him, my eyes set forward, refusing to look at him. "I was going to tell you."

Every word he speaks shoves the knife into my heart that little bit more.

"I didn't expect to like you so much."

Like?

"It was a stupid bet that escalated."

Keep walking. Close your ears.

"Come on, Amelia, where the hell are you going? It's dark."

Just keep walking. Get away.

"For fuck's sake, Amelia, stop."

I do, but not because he's told me to. I swing around, raindrops flying off me with the force, and find Jude equally as soaked, his white shirt sticking to his chest.

"I came here to tell you I'd . . ." I snap my mouth closed and try to think straight.

"What?"

Don't tell him! "That I was falling for you!" I scream, letting loose, releasing my emotions. Jude retreats, his face dropping. My tears come, mixing with the rain pouring down my face. "Was that part of your fucked-up game?"

He says nothing, a pathetic excuse of a man standing before me, mute.

"Don't ever come near me again," I say over an infuriating sob, backing up, making sure he doesn't come after me. "I fucking hate you."

I turn and walk, my tears pouring as hard as the rain, the pain in my chest unbearable. My sobs are racking my body. I can't breathe properly. Everything hurts. I look to the heavens and yell my anger as I walk on, feeling deranged, like I want to smash things apart, destroy everything in my path.

"Why?" I yell, reaching for my hair and pulling, punishing myself for being so fucking dumb.

I make it to the gates, soaked to the bone, holding my phone to the air to try and catch some service. I can hardly see through my tears, my screen slippery and wet. "Please," I whisper, walking up and down. Nothing. "Shit." I stumble down the road on the verge, praying for that one magical bar to give me the power to get the hell out of here. A sharp pain flares on my leg, and I look down to see a scratch from a nearby thornbush. I ignore the trickle of blood mixing with the rain soaking my leg, concentrating on finding some service. The verge becomes more overgrown, the weeds and brambles reaching my knees, my heels sinking into the soft ground. "Fuck." I lose a shoe and turn to retrieve it, searching the mess of branches and leaves in the darkness. Impossible. "God damn it." I abandon my lost heel, my need to get out of here more important. I remove the other, throwing it into a bush in a temper before trudging up the country road on bare feet, eventually finding the service I need.

I call an Uber, sobbing at my screen when I see it's going to be two hours. "No," I whisper, dropping to my arse on the verge, crying.

I cry so hard.

But he will never hear me. No one will hear me.

Because the pounding rain drowns me out.

RETURN TO ARLINGTON HALL IN

THE SURRENDER

A pawn in a man's callous game, Amelia Lazenby is trying to heal after being betrayed by the wealthy and scorchingly sexy Jude Harrison. Now he's saying all the right things, whispering apologies as sincere as his kisses, and refusing to let her walk away. It's hard for Amelia to resist a force as strong as Jude. Before long, he's making her pulse pound, her head spin, and giving her the rapture she craves.

But once she surrenders, Amelia can't help but fear she's risking her heart all over again. This time, maybe even more. Jude is every bit as mysterious and possessive as she remembers. His ex-lover is back to wreak havoc on their lives. And Amelia's own ex has returned from the past, knowing more about Jude than Amelia can imagine. As the secrets and shocking revelations keep coming, Amelia must decide what she's willing to sacrifice to stay with the man she loves and above all else . . . can't resist.

ACKNOWLEDGMENTS

It hardly seems possible that I've been knocking around this romance world for more than twelve years. It feels like five minutes. Back when it all started, I never imagined I'd still be here now, still writing and still dreaming up stories to tell. But more amazing is that you're still here too, eagerly waiting for my next tale (or alpha). Thank you. Nothing encourages an author more than the love and support of their readers.

A special thank-you to Georgie for telling me to get my JEM groove on! I did, and Jude and Amelia are here. This couple have kept me sane. I just know you're going to love them. And to Sasha and Lauren, thank you for loving this story as much as I do, and for giving it a home at Amazon Publishing.

Enjoy your time at Arlington Hall.

JEM x

ABOUT THE AUTHOR

Photo © 2019 Abby Cohen Photography

Jodi Ellen Malpas is the #1 *New York Times* and *Sunday Times* bestselling author of numerous series, including This Man, This Woman, One Night, and Unlawful Men, as well as the stand-alone novels *For You*, *Perfect Chaos*, and *Leave Me Breathless*, among many others. She is a self-professed daydreamer with a weak spot for alpha males. Her captivating storytelling and complex characters have earned her a dedicated following, and her ability to weave intense emotions with sizzling romance and heart-pounding drama ensures her stories resonate with readers globally. Jodi was born and raised in England, where she lives with her husband, boys, and Theo the Doberman. For more information, visit www.jodiellenmalpas.co.uk.